Killing by the Book

Ryan Stark

ISBN: 1519326637

ISBN-13: 978-1519326638

For Val, Emma and Laura.
My inspiration and my life.

ACKNOWLEDGMENTS

For me, this is a difficult section to write as, to be honest there are few acknowledgements to make over this work of fiction. However, I would like to thank Adrian Grogan, one of my oldest friends, for his help with some of the more technical matters herein. I hope I didn't cause too many problems with the emails to your work account. Enough said!

Additionally, I would like to thank the friends, family and work colleagues who have provided a little piece of their soul to my characters, mostly unknowingly whether they like it or not. Shelley and Alice, you know who you are.

Thanks also to Tracy Tonkinson for her apposite words of wisdom regarding publishing; advice she may notice I have followed.

Finally, my huge thanks go out to my family, whom I have bored witless with the idea of writing a novel. You have all perfected the humouring smile and good grace not to tell me to shut up.

Chapter 1

Chapel Rise, Hanwell, London

Why is it that men have to be such bastards?

The eyes staring back at Dawn Silverton in the rear view mirror were still angry and challenging. What had possessed her to meet Drew anyway? When had it ever been *just a quick chat?*

Wiping away a tear, streaking her mascara, the expletive sounded misplaced, unlike the ones earlier, all appropriate, all utterly deserved. The bruises on her arm aches, as if Drew was still holding her, railing and defiant.

The coffee shop was quiet. Though she was early, she knew he would be there first. That was Drew's thing. The upper hand. As she sat, she felt his eyes gravitate to the cavern of thigh as her skirt rode up; she ineffectually yanked it down, smoothing the creases as she crossed her knees. He knew she always drank a tall, skinny Mocha. On the table, her coffee was already cooling. The conversation began sub-zero.

"So you spoke to Thornton anyway, despite me telling you not to." His voice, hard-edged, low to avoid being overheard.

"Yes, Drew. We spoke on Friday. I needed get things moving. You know how important this sale is to me."

The sale of 53 Chapel Rise was taking an age but had finally completed, a millstone lifting. Once she had dealt with the extra money Drew had demanded. So she had spoken to Drew's boss.

"Look, it was just business."

Today though, like it or not, it had become personal.

"Nothing else?"

She sighed and rolled her eyes, and immediately gave the hornet's nest a firm jab. "No. Why? Should there be?"

"What do you think? You brought a whole bloody world of shit down on me last time."

"Oh, give it a rest, Drew. I didn't need to say anything. I assumed that a world of shit was sufficient for you to stop your stupid games without me telling tales. How should I know he would call in the auditor?"

Unconsciously, she had become apologetic. As she lifted her coffee, his eyes momentarily darted to the vee of her blouse and she felt how she had felt the last time they were together - unclean.

"All you have to do is keep quiet. I know it's a stretch for a female, but that's all. From now on, if you have anything to discuss with Barraclough and Leavis, it goes through me. OK?"

Incandescent, she warmed her hands on her coffee, refusing to rise to the bait. She needed to throw him off guard; to steal back the advantage. Perhaps now was the time to tell him.

"Drew. I'm pregnant. Twelve weeks." Delivered flat, emotionless.

Briefly put off-guard, his eyes flicked out to the street. Then he regrouped. "What do you want me to do about it?"

She had not thought that far ahead.

"I don't know. I do know we can't go on playing these stupid games of yours."

"We? What has this to do with me? You got yourself into this mess, you can get yourself out of it."

"I am having your baby, Drew. Surely that must mean something to you?"

"My baby? Says who? You? As far as I know, it could be anyone's. You're just like the rest of them. Every opportunity you can get to stick your noses deeper in the trough."

"This is not about money, Drew. This is about responsibilities."

"Don't you lecture me about responsibilities! Speaking to Thornton, undermining everything I'm trying to achieve. If you had any common bloody decency, you'd get a knitting needle and do away with the damn thing."

Drew was an expert at manipulating the emotions of others. She knew there was no talking to him. She reached for her coffee, searing her tongue, bearing the pain, expressionless.

"Pleasure, as always, Drew."

Grabbing her handbag, she made her way out into the wide, noisy, brightness of Ealing Broadway, following the alley to the rear car park. But Drew was a dog with a bone. He grabbed her arm and pinned her to the wall. She could smell his acidic breath in her nostrils.

She had narrowed her eyes and focussed directly into his. Gone were the days when this arrogant, self-opinionated boor could dominate her as he had when she was young and over-trustful.

"I knew this was a mistake. You always were a prick. You take your bloody finger nails out of my arm or I'll knee you in the bollocks and scream at the top of my voice."

Releasing his grip, Drew felt the pressure of her leg raised against his groin. He smiled as he knew she had felt him harden. He sneered at her.

"You haven't got the balls. And anyway, Dawn, with our history, no-one will take you seriously. "Anyone - anyone there? Woman in trouble!" And then, as the echoes faded, he had grinned at her helplessness.

"Listen to me, Dawn. If this goes to shit, we're all in trouble. Me, you and the rest of the Monday Club. You just remember that." His finger jabbed so close to her face that she had instinctively grabbed his wrist a little too hard.

"Look Drew. I've had enough. I want nothing more to do with you from now on. And don't expect any more business from Parkin-Wrights."

Now, a million miles away, she stared across at St. Saviour's, sat squat in its tiny grounds, craning her neck to check the clock on the tower. She had a quarter of an hour. She needed to pull up the shutters and focus on her next task, get her lines straight.

Four years she had been free from him, and now, one night when she thought she was over him. How could she have been so foolish after everything he had put her through? One sordid night of insanity and the rest of her life to regret it.

Leaving the car, basking a moment in the mid afternoon sunshine, Dawn pushed her shoulders back and smoothed her jacket. Before her, the road was a lazy meandering corridor of verdant hedges and billiard baize verges. On this Monday afternoon, a cacophony of birdsong filled the air, the rain had subsided and hollows of blue glowed through the trees. But Dawn was oblivious to it all, her mind conflicted.

Obviously she could turn her back on Drew, on them all,

perhaps even move back home. Mom and Dad were desperate for a grandchild. But she would be sacrificing her career, her independence, everything.

Then there was the unthinkable, which Drew had been so quick to suggest, but could she live with herself afterwards?

So she had to talk Drew round. They had been in and out of each other's lives so much; perhaps commitment was all that was needed to change him?

But commitment was not Drew's style.

As the church clock struck the half hour, she pushed Drew from her mind and turned to the new problem – No. 57. Selling 53 Chapel Rise had brought renewed interest in other properties in the street.

No. 57 was totally unlike No. 53. Some carefully aimed Luftwaffe ordnance had seen to that. In its place was a more modern house. Detached, secluded, surrounded by privet giving it an altogether more rural feel. With large windows and a long drive, it enjoyed the ultimate prize - a garage.

The viewer was already waiting. Dawn adjusted her smile and waved a greeting, practicing the part, making it real. Fumbled in her handbag, she found the key and eased open the door. Inside, there was an appearance of American Antebellum, a spacious lobby and sweeping staircase. Light filled every corner. Quickly she placed down her bag and tapped in the 4 digit code. As the high-pitch warble subsided, she turned back to her visitor.

"I just love this hou..." The sentence continued on inside her head but her voice stopped. She felt an enormous force on the side of her head and saw the brightest light she had ever experienced. And then her eyes were looking up at a blurry figure and she mouthed words that had no sound as the room faded to a red haze. And then nothing.

Chapter 2

Detective Sergeant Deborah Whetstone lurched across the car, as it cornered more sharply than was necessary. She had lost count of the number of such trips she had made since joining the North West London Homicide Unit two years ago. Beside her, Detective Inspector Scott Daley drove in silence. Counting each second of the ten minute trip to the crime scene, she checked her bag again. A reflex action.

Outside her bubble, streets slid by, shoppers gossiped, children yelled and played, drivers made deliveries, people ran errands in their lunch break. Normal life continued. Tomorrow, like today, somewhere, a mother, sister or child would be waiting for their car to arrive.

And then they were in Chapel Rise.

A tangled green canopy made the road claustrophobic, zebra striped in the sunlight. Behind Whetstone, Detective Constable Mike Corby, the new boy sat ashen faced. This was his first murder since joining the team, She knew the front desk would be running a book on her keeping her breakfast down too.

Parking up, Daley turned to address them both.

"OK. Guys. Unidentified female, early thirties. House has been empty for weeks. The postman noticed a smell, so he lifted the flap and gawped inside. After he had stopped puking, he gave us a call. Apparently, it's a bit gruesome, so Michael, remember today next time you opt for the full English in the canteen."

"Our guest pathologist is Professor Gascoigne and he will seriously kick ass if we corrupt the scene, so watch where you step. Also there will be lots of forensic robots around. They also get tetchy if you shit with their OCD."

To Whetstone, any crime scene was a paradox. To the killer, the victim, or an observer, it is as real situation as it gets. A catalogue of facts chronicling events from before the act until the crime is over. But it tells only part of the story.

To an investigator it is history; everything that had happened has already happened. It says little of the hours and days enjoyed or suffered by the victim beforehand. Windows break, not necessarily a burglary. Wrists get slashed, not always a suicide.

Daley concluded, "Remember, open mind, lots of notes and keep your eyes peeled."

Chapel Rise was a melee of high-vis radio chatter. A line of chequer plate led from the gate and disappeared under a portable tent erected over the front step of No 57. The team donned white romper suits before following Daley into the gloom of the tent. As her eyes adjusted, Whetstone noticed a thin stream of blood that had run through a drain hole in the threshold strip. She caught her breath. She watched Corby as they traversed the duckboard across the threshold, his neck and face almost indistinguishable from the white of his overall.

The hallway was bright, too well-lit under the circumstances. Beige and featureless, an exercise in modernist understatement or maybe architectural vandalism. Featureless apart from a staircase, the mottled oak parquet floor, the lake of blood and high arc of arterial spray that traversed the one remaining internal wall.

Whetstone's bile rose and she swallowed it down. Dragging her left wrist under her nose, she drew a deep breath. Menthol burnt cold and masked the metallic smell of death. Beside her, Corby's shoulders spasmed. He wheeled round and threw up into a paper bag that an enterprising forensic bod had sensed he might need.

Daley eyed her inquiringly.

"Fiver?"

"Tenner!"

"Bastard Harrison. Had me down for a fiver. Sod!"

Whetstone took in the scene. A *For Sale* sign in the front garden, the lobby pristine, prepared for viewings and shut up for some time. Dirt marks instead of pictures. At the rear, a sitting room and large kitchen diner looked over a compact back garden. She decided to check upstairs, but found similar bland, beige emptiness.

"Well?" Daley prompted her as she trotted off the last step.

"Nothing. The place is empty apart from a few dead flies, and I think even they wiped their feet before coming in."

6

The body of the woman lay in the lake of blood. The head rested in its own small separate pool, the auburn ponytail matted and wet, the mouth frozen part way through an unheard word. Below the mouth, a grotesque maroon hole gaped. Whetstone shuddered. Maybe this woman recognised her killer as her cheek felt the coldness of the floor.

Turning away, she looked back to the body. A handbag had spilled as it fell, a numbered marker next to it, photos being taken. Whetstone crouched and her heart became heavy as she saw a thin band of gold across the back of the ring finger. Somewhere a husband or fiancé, maybe children, parents, siblings, work colleagues, all aware that this woman walked the earth, unaware that she was gone. Subconsciously, she ran a thumb across her own unadorned third finger.

She turned her attention to the wall. The arterial arc sprayed towards the rear of the lobby, it's perfect curve marred as rivulets ran like crimson tears.

"Sir, over here." The SOCO indicated a smear near an under-stairs cupboard and a small red puddle by the skirting.

"Something has been leant against the wall here." said Whetstone

"Can we get that open?" asked Daley. The photographer burned a little more digital celluloid as the SOCO gently eased the door open, mindful of the fingerprints they knew would probably not be there. Wincing from an overpowering reek of surgical spirit and bleach, Whetstone's eyes slowly adjusted. In the dimness, there was a vacuum called Henry, a plastic bin bag and a three foot long samurai sword.

Chapter 3

Barraclough and Leavis, The Broadway, Ealing

"Carol, no distractions now. I need bit of peace and quiet."

"OK, Mr Carmichael. I'll bring your tea through."

As he released the intercom button, the wields on the back of Drew Carmichael's wrist stung. *Bitch!* He rubbed hard but that made them worse. Hopefully, he had sorted the problem. He drew down the cuff of his shirt. A few scratches would be a small price to pay.

He closed the folder and consigned Mr and Mrs Cartwright to *Filing*. Why do they need a house worth three quarters of a million, anyway? Still, there was a banker's draft for six hundred thousand. Every cloud...

Clicking the mouse, his computer screen filled with numbers in a gaudy arrangement of colours, some flashing, some stationary and all absolutely irrelevant. Except one. The fourth number across in the eighth row down was the one that mattered.

Pulling his feet up, crossing his ankles on the desk, Carmichael tried to put Dawn Silverton out of his mind. He hated this pokey, malodorous little broom closet, spending six chargeable hours with the great unwashed, and another couple sorting out the admin. *Clock in, clock out, clock in, clock out, pension, die.* What a pointless existence.

If only Gerald Thornton would get the message and retire. In Carmichael's view, he was the only natural successor. One day, he would have the large, airy, prestigious office. But could he wait that long? It could be ten more bloody years. Mind you, at the rate his fund was growing, he might not need to. Once it hit five million, Carmichael would be off...assuming no-one cottoned on to what he was doing.

Chapter 4

53 Chapel Rise, Hanwell, London

As a portable light flooded the under stairs cupboard, Scott Daley carefully prised open the mouth of the bag, instantly gagging as the fumes tumbled out. Inside, gently fermenting, was a pair of sodden navy overalls. Daley turned to the SOCO. "Photographed, bagged and tagged, please." Even in the gloom of the cupboard the sword's blade shone keenly.

Whetstone turned over a couple of transparent bags in her hands. A blood-stained driving licence showed the victim, smiling awkwardly, younger, the hair shorter with a notion of curl. Her name had been Dawn Marie Silverton, thirty-seven years old. Her business card showed she was an estate agent.

"Do we know when, Sir?" she asked.

"You know Gascoigne. Non-committal at the best of times."

"I heard that, Scott." The voice was gruff, the bark of a bulldog echoing across the lobby. "Ah, Deborah. Good Morning." Whetstone was always warmed when Professor Patrick Gascoigne used her first name. Always quick to point out he was not a policeman, he had a warm, avuncular style as long as one kept on his good side. Today, behind the mask, there was a tiredness in the eyes.

"Death was instantaneous. The edges of the wound are clean suggesting a single blow from a smooth sharp blade just below the left ear. Probably the one in the cupboard but I will know for certain later. Body temperature and the shrinkage at the edge of the blood pool suggests yesterday, maybe the day before. There is some lividity despite the exsanguination. Rigor has set in and relaxed so that suggests between twenty-four and forty-eight hours, but I'll know more later."

"Did you notice the this?" Daley pointed towards the severed head Above the glazed eyes, beneath wisps of auburn hair, the forehead was constricted in a frown of wonderment. Whetstone could see a black number '2' about an inch tall inscribed in black.

"What do you think it means?" she asked.

Daley glanced at Gascoigne. "Rachel Jones?"

"Yes. Same occurred to me." Gascoigne scratched his chin.

"Rachel Jones?" This was a new name to Whetstone.

"Three or four years ago, now. Before your time."

Daley had been told that the image of your first dead body never leaves you. For him, that was Rachel Jones. Her murder was strikingly similar and remained unsolved.

"Rachel Jones, an estate agent in Wembley. Found decapitated. No weapon, no clues. She had no enemies, very few friends, who either knew nothing or clammed up tighter than a nudist's ball sack in December. She had a number '1' on her forehead. The pens were from a specific to a range made that year and we didn't want to spook the killer into throwing away any spares he had. For weeks we expected to find another body with a '2' but nothing. The case went cold."

"Same killer?" asked Whetstone.

"Maybe." Daley sighed "No assumptions, right? At the time we withheld the number in case it sent out a message. The first of many. A serial killer. We didn't need the press putting the fear of God into the general public, giving the killer a nickname. Numeric Norman or Digit-Alex, stalking the streets."

"Are those the best nicknames you could come up with?"

"So what do you suggest, Sergeant Smart-arse?"

"Probably, something like 'One-trick Tony' because another one never did turn up, did it?"

Daley smiled wryly.

"Until now."

Chapter 5

Barraclough and Leavis

Carol Hughes reversed through the door carrying a tray dragging Drew Carmichael from his reverie. He dragged his feet of the desk and feigned busy. However, the look in her deep brown eyes told him she wasn't fooled. She hovered long enough to hear the sonorous *clink* from the latch.

"Here you go, Mr Carmichael." The Tyneside lilt was never more than a soft, lyrical purr.

"Drew," pleaded Carmichael. "Call me *Drew*. Just once, eh?"

"*Drew*." Delivered as a statement.

The nape of his neck prickled with a familiar anticipation. The cheetah weighing up the chase.

Carol had been a welcome change. Not the usual runt-of-the-litter dogs or pubescent adolescents the agency supplied. Carmichael's taste was eclectic, prowling the trendy neon and chrome wine bars that Guy Higson dragged him to for fresh meat. Like Guy, his attention span was short, but his pockets were reasonably deep. Unlike Guy, his tastes were exclusively heterosexual. Which was convenient, as all of the most beautiful women seemed to hang out with gays.

As a rule, Carmichael never mixed work with pleasure. Well, almost never. However, Carol Hughes was a conundrum. She had not warranted much of Carmichael's attention until the whole audit storm had blown in. A sudden deluge of guano falling from a great height. The board had got the jitters and each of the associates set about ensuring that their respective books were in order.

Which, for Drew had been an incredibly tall order.

He took up the tea and smiled. "Thanks. Now bugger off."

She met his eyes and smiled. "Charming! And I brought you Digestives from Mr Thornton's tin." She caught sight of his left hand. "Those look nasty."

He pulled down is cuff. "Just some vicious cat yesterday."

In the month they had spent on the accounts, he had gotten to know her well. How she leaned forward in her chair, crossing her ankles underneath. How her shoes came free as she arched her feet. How she brushed her hair behind her ear with her middle finger, drafting a zephyr of perfume which could drive every thought from his mind.

And she had discovered his secret.

Carol latched onto the pattern of postings and what it meant. The client accounts, the cross postings to the Fund, the delayed transfer to their chosen investments. How one of those clients, through Dawn Silverton, had sparked the spot audit. Then she had been instrumental in keeping them from the auditor's report.

For a price.

She had demanded a cut. Ten per cent but it could have been more. She had joined the select few who knew of the Fund, sizing up the pot, dipping their grasping paws into his cash.

Carol Hughes had become a pre-occupation, a distraction from what really mattered - the Fund. He had decided he needed to change the dynamics of their relationship. Late nights working together, more small talk, more familiarity. Soon he would coax their relationship closer still. Such was his unfailing belief in his abilities with the opposite sex.

He just hoped that, unlike Dawn Silverton, he would not have to resort to more extreme solutions.

Chapter 6

Chapel Rise

By four o'clock, the crime scene had been more or less tidied up. It reminded Whetstone of a town centre the morning after a concert, forlorn and desolate with scattered detritus and forgotten memories. Whilst the town centre could be cleaned, this house would forever bear the stain of death.

Following Daley into the comparative brightness of early evening, she squinted as her eyes adjusted, gulping in a lungful of the cooling air. Mike Corby stood on the step, his notebook open.

"Next of Kin, Doreen and John Silverton, sir. They live in Nottingham. We have a uniform going around to speak to them now."

More innocent bystanders about to be subsumed by this train wreck, thought Daley.

"We have an address for her. 12 Caernarfon Court, Copley Close. She lived alone."

Whetstone thought of the engagement ring, and looked down at her own finger, unadorned, not even a white band of untanned skin, and suddenly she felt absolutely abandoned.

"Alone? You sure? She had a ring on her ring finger." She needlessly raised her own hand and pointed.

"Well, that's what I've been told. Maybe there was someone but they hadn't made it public?"

Daley turned to Whetstone. "Deb, get over to Parkin-Wright's before they shut. See what you can find out. Mike and I will go around to her house."

Daley open Dawn Silverton's diary to the previous day. Flicking forwards, the entries petered out at the end of June – two months ahead, the extent of Dawn Silverton's professional future. Now, only one mattered. Her 2:30pm appointment at number 57, and the name 'Watkins' written beside it.

"Mike Today is the 23rd April. Exactly four years since

Rachel Jones was killed. To the day. How likely is that?

Corby shrugged. "Maybe the CSIs will find us something new to work on."

Daley threw the car keys to Corby and called Sergeant Dave Monaghan back at Lambourne Road. He needed everything they had on Dawn Silverton, her friends, her colleagues, even the guy that delivered her milk. Dave was the nearest the Met had to a super-computer and he didn't need a load of sandal wearing geeks to keep his database up to date. Just tea and DC Steve Taylor, who only seldom wore sandals.

Chapter 7

As the angry grey afternoon gave way to a frustrated tired evening, it had taken Whetstone thirty minutes to reach Parkin-Wright in Ealing. The uniform had indulged himself and waited on double yellows. Now, as she left the smart estate agents behind, he drew up to the kerb beside her.

Arriving unannounced, she had cast her eyes around the light, airy shop, her eyes alighting on a desk near the front and the small pile of business cards bearing the name Dawn Silverton FNAEA. Moments later, she had been ushered into the office of Norman Parkin, also an FNAEA.

Norman Parkin and his wife and co-director Jane Wright sang Dawn's praises. A stereotypically hard-working employee, Dawn Silverton was an associate of the firm. She managed her own diary. The name Watkins did not mean anything significant.

When asked if anything was troubling Dawn, they thought she had been pre-occupied by her relationship with her boyfriend. Whilst Norman Parkin had been non-committal on the matter, his wife had athletically leapt from the fence.

"I suppose the best way to describe their relationship was stormy. They had been together, off and on, forever. More off than on.

"Trouble was she was never so unhappy as when she was with him, sergeant. Some people are drawn to each other but should never be together. Poor Dawn. I think she and Andrew Carmichael were like that. After a time we just let it wash over us."

Jane Wright's eyes had drifted away to middle distance. Whetstone smiled. She envied Norman and Jane. Comfortable, successful, maybe just a little boring but safe.

"They were engaged?" Whetstone thought back to the band of gold across the finger.

Jane Wright chuckled at an in-joke. "Oh, no, sergeant. We had an incident a few years ago. So Norman and I bought all the single girls engagement rings to wear on viewings. They seem a lot happier."

"I think she and Drew Carmichael were on an off patch." Jane Wright interjected. "They had fallen out over something, again!"

"Do you know what they had fallen out over?"

"Well, Sergeant, I am sure you don't need my advice but never mix business with pleasure. Drew Carmichael is a tied financial adviser with Barraclough and Leavis, just down the Broadway. He and Dawn were in the habit of sharing customers; she would arrange the sale and he would make the finances work. All above board and legal, I assure you. It's just they never seemed to agree about anything. And Dawnie, well she never could leave work at the office door, so it always bled over into their private lives."

"Anything specific, that you were aware of?"

"Not really, sales are down at the moment. The market is slow. We have to wield the whip a little and I think she was finding it hard going. I know she had had some problems with a couple of properties. She had spent inordinate amounts of time in Chapel Rise, on No. 53. By any stretch of the imagination that was a slow sale, but it had moved and by all accounts has completed now."

"And that was one of the properties that Mr Carmichael looked after for her?"

"Yes, but they all were. It's a slow market, Sergeant. Buyers are dragging their heels. No. 53 is no different to a dozen others on Dawn's books."

"So this, er, Andrew Carmichael. What do you know of him?"

"He's very good at his job, very reliable, very thorough." Norman Parkin towed the company line. "We have very few problems with his work and the customer seemed genuinely happy."

"...But he's not a particularly nice man. I think Dawn could do... could have done.... a lot better. In my opinion, he didn't treat her very well."

"Was he ever violent towards her?"

"Not that I am aware of. Every relationship has its ups and

downs." She turned and cast cow eyes at Norman, who smiled uncomfortably back. "No, it's just that we all felt she spent her life running after him, chasing him, and he never really let her catch him up."

As the car pulled adjacent to her, she grabbed the door handle and piled herself into the relative silence of the passenger seat. The uniform, whose name was Keith, smiled warmly.

"How'd it go, Sarge?"

How had it gone? She had established at least one line of enquiry in Andrew Carmichael. She had established that Dawn and this Carmichael were the best of friends and the worst of enemies. At least that would give Daley something to get his teeth into. Bugger it. The Golf could stay in Lambourne Road, and that could wait until tomorrow. She had just bulldozed through the lives of another four people and the night was still young. She needed to get hammered and Detective Inspector Daley was not her partner of choice.

"Fancy a drink, Keith. It's been a bastard of a day and I need one."

***

Copley Close, where Dawn Silverton had lived, was a stark contrast to Chapel Rise, where she had died. The road ran a gauntlet of terraced tenements and ugly Eighties apartment blocks, peering over dumpsters, elbowing each other for a better view of the railway lines and Castle Bar Park station. As they drove northwards towards the 'better end', Daley smiled wryly. He ducked his head to look past Corby through the passenger side window.

"Just here, there used to be a pub called The Old Bill. Closed down a year or two back. Story goes that the landlord went bust 'cos every time he asked a customer what they wanted to drink they just folded their arms and replied 'I ain't tellin' you nothin' until I seen my brief'. Can't run a business like that." Corby chuckled politely. The space was now occupied by a forlorn, empty car park. There was no need for anyone to park there now. Further on, Copley Close changed its character. To the right, austere iron railings had been completely subsumed by a monstrous buddleia, claiming the pavement as it's own. To the left, the ranks of tenements had ceded to smart four storey apartment blocks with raised walkways, like lowered drawer bridges to the second floor level.

"How does an Estate Agent spend all day flogging properties that she could never hope to own and come home to a place like this?"

"Buggered if I know, Sir. Supposed you get used to it."

Corby took his eyes off a ginger cat prowling the footpath and turned to ponder the anonymous few yards of road ahead. Four monolithic blocks stood, peering through the equidistant lime trees, and over the hedge to the railway. Who needs an alarm clock with the 07:32?

During the daytime, the estate was a commuter wasteland. Unlike Chapel Rise, there were no mothers chatting, no prams, no balls lying forlornly under hedges. There were few children; living here, one couldn't afford kids. The place was sterile, devoid of life.

"All those upper class city types, with enough money to buy a street like this, smarming around looking at houses she could only dream of. And then they will probably moan about carpets and curtains not being thrown in or missing light bulbs. I don't think I could do a job like that. It would just piss me off and I'd end up hitting someone."

Corby squirmed. Small talk was not in his job description. "In a way though we do, Sir."

"Uh?" Daley's face contorted into what approximated confusion, turned to Corby for a short moment and then turned robotically back to the road as he crawled the Insignia along.

"We *do* do a job like that. We chase the villains, get into their heads, and understand how they work. In another world, we could be them." He lapsed into silence, not fully convinced by his argument, and decided to take a second or two to work on it. Twisting sideways, he peered at Daley, whose mind was in a different place. Shrugging, he nodded his head in the general direction of somewhere, just past the Health Centre.

"Take that apartment with the boxy olive coloured bay window. I bet we could break in and find enough stuff to steal someone's identity and they wouldn't even know we'd been in."

"No, I'd take one of the ones at the back. Less likely to be seen. Or get a van and climb in through a skylight."

18

"Same applies though, Sir. We've spent so long catching criminals, we could easily become one. Perhaps it was the same for her, er, Dawn Silverton...? Perhaps she 'became' one of those rich middle-class clients, perhaps, just like us, she researched her customers, thought like them, even pretended to be one of them. Every morning she went to work, put on her mask and played the part."

"Anything for a sale." Daley considered it. Anything for a collar. All good coppers knew exactly where the line was drawn, how far it would bend, how far they could stray over it. And much of that knowledge came from the criminals they chased, understanding how they had bent and broken the law. So Dawn Silverton would imitate her customers to schmooze them, as if they were buying from a friend, someone who understood their problems, their needs, and their world.

Daley glanced over at the building - Caernarfon Court - reading the apartment numbers and seeing the block that Dawn had chosen for her home. He parked perpendicular to the entrance under the shade of a towering Rowan tree.

At around 4:00pm, the gaggle of schoolchildren being herded home by their mothers had all but petered out, to be replaced by sullen, dawdling teens in grubby, ill-fitting blazers, gobbing and punching and squawking at each other. Daley peered down the street, waited for them to pass before he and Corby decamped and trotted up to the front entrance of Caernarfon Court. Beside the door, a small security panel bore the names of each of the residents; the third one down, no. 15, was Silverton, and Daley pushed them all, whilst Corby grabbed the door handle, listening for the minuscule clunk that would afford them entry. Immediately they were rewarded. So much for security. No. 15 was on the second floor to the rear of the block, insulated from the noise of the railway and the road. They donned latex gloves and Daley opened the door with keys recovered from Dawn's handbag. He slapped about at the wall beyond until he located the light switch, and then he blinked in the freeze frame world of Dawn Silverton.

Inside was a boxy entrance hall where a coat rack burgeoned with garments and hats. A set of gloves rested next to the phone and the red answerphone light winked to tell her that her dry cleaning was ready for collection. To the left, the living room hung in suspended animation, washing draped on an airer, tights dangled from the arm of an easy chair, the TV waited on stand-by. In the kitchen, the microwave door stood ajar and a bowl in a sink full of crocks bore a crust of dried porridge. All around hung a faint air of expensive perfume.

Nobody had told this apartment that she wouldn't be coming home.

Daley ushered Corby through to the living room, giving him instructions. He headed through a door into the bedroom, half expecting her to be lying in the bed, starting as he entered, grabbing the sheets to her breast and demanding he leave. Instead the room lay silent, the bed unmade and a pair of pale blue pyjamas folded on the pillow. He walked to the window and drew the curtains - the less obvious the better - and then he clicked on the bedside lamp and watched the room glow warm and comfortable.

At the foot of the bed, a tiny dressing table nestled against the opposite wall, strewn with all manner of potions and creams, most of which were a dark art to Daley. A pair of hair straighteners, now cool, lay on a small kickstand, the lead trailing over the edge of the surface. He eased open the drawers one by one, searching amongst the chaotic paraphernalia for something that he had yet to realise could be significant. Finding nothing, he moved to the small bedside table beneath the lamp. Opening it, he felt unclean as he rifled through the most intimate of Dawn's things; a butterfly vibrator, a pack of condoms and lubricating jelly. Immediately he became aware of the dichotomy. Items that would be equally at home to a single woman as to one in a relationship. Reaching in to the drawer his fingertips fell onto something pushed to the back, lying flat on the base of the drawer. Dragging it out, he scanned the face in the photo. It was the face of a man, beaming an impossibly winning smile as Dawn clung around his waist, her head on his chest, both squinting from bright sunshine, behind them an azure blue pool and ranks of white loungers. And again the dichotomy. The man stood straight holding himself in a self-assured, almost arrogant pose, upright, business-like, whilst Dawn looked like she was clinging to a horse that was threatening to bolt. Behind the smile lay an almost imperceptible hint of insecurity. Pocketing the picture and closing the drawer,

20

Daley made his way back to the living room, where Corby was busy examining the disgorged contents of a box-file from the bookcase.

"Anything?"

Corby half-turned, then returned to the pile. "Not a lot. TV licence is due for renewal. I found a couple of bank statements. She has £300 in her current account, no spectacular amounts in or out, and a passbook for the Nationwide with £6000 on deposit and into which she has been making regular payments of £100 a month, but she hasn't withdrawn anything in six months. Then there's the normal bills, the documentation for her car, her passport and birth certificate."

"Any evidence of a boyfriend?"

"There's this." Corby picked up a folder of photos from a processing lab. The inscription in biro on the flap read 'Carcassonne - 2011'. Inside there were more pictures of the man, and of Dawn, again the self-assured indifference counterpointed by an air of apprehension, his easy posture and her rather desperate expression. The two featured, either jointly or severally, in a number of the pictures. Daley counted seven different people, possibly eight if they had not shared photographic duties. He studied the faces, seemingly familiar, memories yet to crystallise. How many of these would he get to know better in the weeks to come?

"Is there an address book anywhere?" Mike reached into the box-file and handed Daley a small tall book festooned with daisies, crammed with small pieces of paper and business cards. Along with the photos, he stuffed it into his overcoat. "Come on, Mike. Not sure there's any more to find here. I'll send someone round to have another look when we know what we're after."

***

"Higson." The voice was flat and unconcerned, answering after four rings.

"Guy, it's Drew. You alone?"

"As per usual, until Brad Pitt sees the error of his ways. What's up, buddy?"

"About the audit..."

There was an exasperated sigh at the end of the line. It was becoming a daily occurrence for Carmichael to ring and each day the answer was the same. Guy had worked minor miracles before, during and after the recent audit at Barraclough and Leavis to ensure Carmichael's scam did not come to light. After a few moments Guy continued. "Look Drew, I'm not going through that again. It's sorted, OK? Everything's fine."

"Might look fine from where you're sitting. Dawn's been telling tales to Thornton again. I need to know that he won't find anything that will trace back to me."

"Ad nauseam, Drew, ad nauseam. I don't know what to tell you. Women are not my department, you know that." The line dulled to static, then after a pause, Guy continued, laboured and bored. "What exactly has she been telling tales about now?"

"Same as before. I saw her yesterday and she told me that she has seen Thornton. She wants me to stop. She says that if she goes down so will I."

"So what's the problem? Let her shout her mouth off to anyone that will listen, rancorous bitch. Look, I have covered your tracks. Thornton would have to bring in some real heavy guns to unravel the rat's nest of accounts I have put in place. She's just pissed because she is the one that gets the grief and she wants to take it out on you. So she cries to Thornton again and this time he takes her more seriously. When she starts bleating it will just sound like sour grapes because you won't make an honest women of her. I mean she has reason to. You two blow more hot and cold than a cheap hair dryer."

"Look, Guy, forget Dawn. What about the audit trail? Thornton may not be that clever but even he can put two and two together."

"And make what? There really is nothing for him to find. Jeez, Drew. I spent days with that PA of yours, covering your ass. If anything, it's her you should be worried about, not Dawn. For God's sake, Dawn must know it's in her best interests to keep her trap shut, surely? She's got as much riding on this as the rest of us."

"Even so."

"Even so nothing. The money is safe and we will all have a tidy nest egg in the very near future. Just keep your head down, brazen it out and sort that woman of yours before she hangs us all out to dry."

"Don't worry. Dawn's been sorted. I saw her yesterday. She will keep her mouth shut from now on. I am just worried she has queered my pitch with Thornton."

"There's only one queer around here, Drew, and I claim that dubious honour. I am telling you. The money is safe. It's well hidden. Thornton can blow up his own arse all he likes. As for Dawn, she's all talk. You know that. She always has been when she doesn't get her own way. As I say women are not my department but if you want my advice..."

"You're going to give it anyway."

"...if you want my advice. Marry the woman. Propose. Make the grand gesture. Take one for the team. Once she's got a ring on her finger, she will see the pound signs floating before her eyes and fall into line. Then in a few years time, she'll get bored with you and find some other schmuck to torment."

"I see what you're saying, Guy, but I am sure that won't be necessary."

***

So descends the silence on Dawn Silverton.

I had almost forgotten the rush of adrenaline, the rising crescendo and the final burst of exhilaration as the life is separated from the body, so long had it been since the Rachel Jones. Yet, as I swung the blade and felt the resistance, the edge seeking a path through flesh and bone and cartilage, there was an air of familiarity lost in the intervening years. Perhaps not the feeling of coming home but certainly one of purpose. The feeling that, however grisly, however morally repugnant the physical act, the end was justified by the means.

The killing had to start again. The canker had regrown and once more must be excised before the infection spreads further. Our secret must stay hidden. That is paramount. Not until the last one has paid the price will it see the light of day. And then only you will see it. What is hiding in plain sight will be revealed only to you.

And you will see that your shame is the reason for their blood.

23

Afterwards, I had stood shrouded in the silence that had descended on the house. I watched as her legs buckled and she kneeled before falling forwards onto the polished wood floor. I heard the pattering raindrops of blood. My head ached with adrenaline as I surveyed the perfect arc of crimson, blurring and running into the spreading pool on the floor. I saw the lips gaping, mouthing, subsiding into a half word fixed for eternity. I looked into her disconnected, mystified eyes and suppressed the years of hatred as I watched the life leave them, just as I had Rachel Jones.

Now that it was all over, the street returned to a sombre wasteland fluttering blue and white, it is as if yesterday was a scene from some semi-conscious half-dream. As well as time, I have lost all sense of place and purpose, the event drawing in a vacuum behind it. I had been on auto-pilot, well rehearsed and mechanical, following the plan to the letter - *fail to prepare and you prepare to fail*. The plan was flawless; the deed was done and lain undiscovered until I had sunk back behind you, the remora on the shark, the wraith in the darkness. Ever-present but just beyond your view. The other side of you.

And today, I was back there. I saw the cars flashing blue. I watched as they erected their tapes and their screens and their tents. However closely connected, I remained isolated and distant.

The killing had to start. Our secret has languished safe, almost forgotten for years. *You* had all but forgotten it, all but washed away the guilt that spawned me to guard it. But guard it I will, from just beyond your sight, behind your consciousness. I kept a watching brief as Rachel Jones had fixed her filthy, libidinous eyes on you and your weakness had consumed you. I watched as she pulled you to the abyss. I felt the awakening of the secret in her, the common memories surfacing and I heard her conniving in her blackmail.

I knew I had to act then to protect you from yourself, as I knew I had to act now. Dawn Silverton, not content that she could take you back at a heartbeat. I had to stop her wrapping her insidious tendrils about you and squeezing you into submission, into giving up the secret. You are weak and I am strong.

And the others? In turn each will follow Dawn and Rachel.

Each will come knocking on your door, hands outstretched, a look of betrayal in their eye. Each of them *will* follow Rachel and Dawn.

Their remorse is no longer sufficient for the damage they have done. Remorse is no longer required and forgiveness is not an option. The secret is a wheel, for one brief moment spinning wildly but then still for so long. Now by degrees it has started to turn again. No longer can they be allowed to continue their lives uninterrupted, as if that moment meant nothing. Simple Newtonian physics - *For every action there is an equal and opposite reaction* - I will rent apart their little group, make them cower in the corner like sheep in the abattoir, fully aware of their fate but utterly powerless to prevent it. And you will see it all, for the rear of the herd, you will see each one of them yield until finally you will succumb and at last we can both be free.

They still owe us a lot more of their blood.

Yes, the killing had to start and, apart from the intensity of the moment, I felt nothing. I wanted to feel euphoria, vindication, elation, even to some degree guilt and repugnance. But there was nothing.

How could there be nothing?

Chapter 8

Drawing his hands across his face, Daley wearily peered over his monitor at the Team Room. For as long as anyone could remember, bearing in mind most here drank to forget, the West London Homicide Unit, itself a backwater of the Met's Homicide and Serious Crime Department, had been squatting at Lambourne Road, as the Met awaited the Home Secretary's ruling on the Commissioner's consolidation plans. Housed in an open plan office about the size of half a tennis court and about half as appealing at 6:30am on a Wednesday, the whole floor exuded 1960's shabby chic or, as Daley preferred, was a right shit-hole. Needless to say neither the Home Secretary nor the Commissioner had ever visited. Luckier than most, Daley could see almost everyone from his desk and they could see him, whilst a boxy concrete pillar hid him from the insidious gaze of D/Supt Allenby sitting in his glass goldfish bowl - which of course he wasn't. No idiot gets into work this early in the morning. Except of course Monaghan, and Taylor...and Daley himself. At least the dubious company of *The Dispossessed*, as the team had dubbed themselves since being shunted out of Headquarters, was preferable to the echoing silence of his flat in Alperton. Another temporary arrangement, but this one was awaiting a divorce court ruling on the dismantling of his life.

Watching the screen flicker as the antiquated PC fired up, he blinked his eyes, straining to make sense of the myriad facts in countless files that he had read until collapsing comatose in the early hours of this morning. The five manilla folders chronicling the investigation into Rachel Jones' death contained surprisingly little of any substance, aside from a million blind alleys and even more contradictory witness statements.

He started as his phone buzzed in his pocket and a text message asked "wer the fck r u sr?" Slugging a quarter of his scalding tea, he muttered meagre excuses to no-one. Whetstone was waiting for him a quarter of a mile away at Loughton Street.

He had gleaned three important pieces of information from the files. Firstly, Rachel Jones had undergone an abortion shortly before her death and, whilst they suspected she was in a relationship, no boyfriend had ever been identified. Secondly, there were a few monochrome photographs of her friends, amongst them one of Dawn Silverton. It was clear that Dawn and Rachel had known each other. Indeed a couple of creased statements buried in the paperwork described Rachel's circle of friends and a link to Dawn Silverton dating back to university in the Nineties. Once the Post Mortem was out of the way, he and Deb Whetstone would get down to the nitty gritty of matching names to the faces.

Thirdly, he had resolved he would need to tread carefully. Allenby had made that abundantly clear in their regular session the previous evening. Four years ago, when Rachel Jones had been found, Allenby had been the DI on the case and Daley the Sergeant. Weeks had been spent investigating and interviewing, collecting evidence, finding witnesses. But there was nothing beyond the circumstantial. A lot of water had flowed under the bridge since then, but Allenby had wasted no time in dredging up the name of Andrew Carmichael. Part of the original investigation into Rachel's death, they had both suspected him as the boyfriend and followed that line of enquiry to it's final demise at the hands of one Edgar Sampson, a particularly highly paid, and very smart, lawyer. Now that the circus was in town again, Daley would need to be careful how he poked the tigers, and Allenby had told him as much.

He glanced at his watch, cursed under his breath and grabbed his coat from the back of his chair.

***

Heaving through the swing doors into the Post Mortem room, Daley was assaulted by the lingering smell of death and dissection. Fortunately it was empty; a male orderly in surgical greens was preparing for the morning's influx of carrion.

In the adjoining office, Gascoigne had been keeping Whetstone amused with his grim anecdotes, but had failed dismally, although bless her sweetness, she had humoured him so graciously. Professor Patrick Gascoigne was a stout academic man with a thinning wire-wool mop of grey hair atop a round bulldog face. A pair of wire rimmed spectacles perched on the end of his nose, as he surveyed the world over them, and a maroon bowtie sat askew under his chin. Allenby had once described to him as a curmudgeonly old buffoon but Daley had a soft spot for the man. The professor, wise to Daley's abhorrence of the pathologist's grisly art, had restricted any show and tell to photographs taken the evening before.

"Ah, Monsieur Daley. At last. What's the matter, watch broken?" Whetstone smirked. She had missed breakfast to reach the lab early. Daley smiled weakly and shrugged.

"Let's get started shall we?" Gascoigne laced his fingers and pushed out against an invisible wall, stretching the muscles, cracking the ligaments, starting the day.

"You can read the official report at your leisure. I am still awaiting toxicology but I don't think it's relevant. So, some highlights." Gascoigne leaned across the desk and clicked the button of his monitor. Navigating quickly to a folder, he brought up the image of a severed neck. He turned to Daley and, peering over his microscopic spectacles, he grasped a pen and ran it along the cut.

"With the unfortunate Ms Silverton, what you see is what you get. Decapitation. Apart from that, she has an extremely healthy head and a healthy, robust body with little to trouble her medically, aside that they are separate." Gascoigne adjusted the white laboratory coat, which had creased around his paunch. "A few things to point out. Firstly, the neck wound. It's a uniform slice, little in the way of bruising and no secondary indentations or marking. If we consider the alternative to an effing great sword, such as an axe, the wound would be much more ragged. Potentially, there would be a secondary indentation where the axe had been driven in deep enough to fully sever the head. Another alternative may be a saw or knife with a cutting or slicing action. Again, the wound is too clean. No tearing at the edges. Secondly, she was alive when decapitated. Note the haemorrhaging around the lesser vessels on this side - the torso side - caused by pressure from the still beating heart forcing blood from the vessels. There are a few other indicators, which I have added in my report. Thirdly, I can see no ligature marks around wrists or neck. It's unlikely that the bruising and discolouration around the very narrow slice, possibly five to ten millimetres across, would have completely concealed them. So sword it is. Based on liver temperature, degree of rigor and other factors, time of death was around 13:00 to 15:00 on Monday afternoon. The body was indoors on warm day for the time of year, say around 19 degrees Celsius, cooling would have taken place fairly uniformly so 14:30; her appointment at that house sounds like a reasonable time.

"So my report says that cause of death was exactly as we suspected. A bloody great sword hewed her head from her shoulders in one blow. Minimal bruising, no hesitation marks, a single powerful movement. Apart from that, she was very healthy. In fact, she was about eight to twelve weeks pregnant." Daley and Whetstone exchanged a puzzled glance.

"Well, there's a turn up for the books. Maybe the ring is genuine after all." Daley needed to find the boyfriend, if only to fend off Allenby. Whilst the parentage of the baby was probably immaterial, the boyfriend may have taken it badly whether or not it was his. "Do we know who the father is?"

"Give me a break, Scott. She's hardly cold and there is a backlog. I have asked them to rush it through, but still it takes a few days... Anyway, Simon," Gascoigne nodded at the lab rat next door, "examined her for puncture marks or other wounds. Apart from a navel piercing that had healed up and some reckless ear piercings probably done when she was a student, there was nothing. There were several post mortem abrasions to the face, and she had rather a fatty liver which, alas, is fairly common these days but not likely to cause her any harm until her late forties. Stomach contents – a bagel, some lettuce and tomato, relish, all eaten about an hour before death, and about a gallon of coffee. Oh, and a quantity of over-the-counter antacids to counteract the effects of the coffee. And she had taken a small dose of paracetamol.

"But, aside from the neck wound, what interests me the most are these marks..." Gascoigne selected a different image. It showed a forearm somewhat mottled through lividity. "We may well have missed them, but Simon is very, very good...just don't tell him."

With the end of the pen, Gascoigne indicated a number of deeper blotches amongst the mottling."

"Those are finger marks. If I may, Sergeant?" Gascoigne grabbed Deb's right arm above the elbow, his thumb on the inside and fingers closed around the outside. "Someone grabbed her like that, about an hour or two before her death. The bruising is light and can take twenty four hours to come out, and often is hidden by the lividity, so it's lucky we spotted it."

Who had inflicted the bruising? Was it a lover's tiff over breakfast? Maybe an argument about the baby, how they would manage. Maybe she fought with her killer?

"Can we extract fingerprints?" But even as he said it his head had begun to shake in unison with the professor's whose expression was disparaging.

"You watch far too much American TV. It is possible to get fingerprints from the skin, but the pressure that was exerted will invariably have smudged any sample and, of course, poor Dawn has been refrigerated overnight which will have destroyed them anyway. The bruises were only apparent this morning, I'm afraid. However, we did find some skin under her finger nails, so someone has some scratches to account for. DNA has been sent for matching but no results for a day or two."

Whetstone stuffed the report in her bag and made to leave, but it was very apparent that Daley had a few loose ends to tie up and wouldn't take the hint, so she sat herself back in the chair.

"So, apart from the bagel, and the apparent struggle some time before, that sounds exactly like the Rachel Jones murder." Daley set his eyes squarely on Gascoigne. He would need pathology on his side to convince Allenby.

Gascoigne turned his head towards Daley and eyed the young policemen over the rim of his glasses. "Scott, you know my role in this is to dispassionately collect and collate the facts, and to give my highly objective opinion. I cannot categorically connect two cases which happened four odd years apart..."

"But, they are the same, aren't they?" There was a dangerous glimmer in Daley's eye. "Both beheaded. Dawn was ten weeks pregnant and Rachel had recently had an abortion. Dawn's appointment was at 2:30pm, Rachel's at 3:00pm. Dawn's death was on the fourth anniversary of the Rachel's - *to the day*. It has to be the same killer, surely? What about the sword? Was it the same weapon?"

Gascoigne sighed and turned his chair to face Daley. He didn't want to be pressed on matters outside the evidence.

"I found minute fragments of the blade in the wound, small pieces of rust mainly. I sent them upstairs for spectral-analysis and asked them to compare them with scrapings from the actual blade of the sword. It's highly probable that that's where they came from. But I also asked them to fish out the evidence from the Rachel Jones case and the fragments I had removed from her neck. Back then, there was no spectral-analysis carried out because you never found a weapon."

"And?"

"They match – now I am not saying the same killer. All I am saying is that the same sword was used in each case."

"Yes! Thanks Doc. Let me know as soon as you have DNA and toxicology." Daley rose, the spring returned to his step, not listening, as Gascoigne called after him. "...It doesn't mean the same killer, Scott."

Chapter 9

Twisting his wrist, Carmichael peered at his watch. Then, with a tut, he glanced up at the clock above the door opposite. As usual the useless piece of crap was a minute and a half out. The only reason he tolerated the chirping, Eighties relic was to keep time on all of the pathetic self-righteous clients and simpering colleagues he endured during his working day. The watch said 9:00 and clock said 8:58. Bearing in mind the clock was made by some slanty-eyed chink in an Asian sweatshop, and the watch, his *Rolex Presidential*, was crafted by the most skilled, and most expensive, watchmakers in Switzerland, he knew which one he trusted. But he had to admit the irony. The same people who had made that shitty clock had netted him twenty-three thousand pounds overnight. Thanks a lot, Ho, or Hoo, or Hee, or whatever your name is. Thanks a lot.

The magic phrase had appeared at the bottom of the screen - 'HSI CLOSED' - and the number in red stayed at '23186'. He imagined the lines of code running on nameless computers across the world, shifting countless heads on countless disk drives, sending messages at light speed across thousands of miles of copper and glass, and writing new numbers into a myriad accounts of which only two interested him. Leaning forward he flipped to a different window and hit the refresh page button. When the hourglass disappeared and the account was refreshed, he couldn't help but congratulate himself as the balance read exactly the same as it had at 01:59 that morning when the entire balance of the Fund had been traded in Hong Kong before being returned as if nothing had happened...and twenty-three thousand one hundred and eighty six pounds had mysteriously appeared in an offshore account in the Cayman Islands administered by a guy wearing ridiculously garish shorts. Dismissing the stock tracker, he exhaled deeply, psyching himself up for the tedious banality of his day job and the awful truth of another eight hours in this godforsaken cell.

9:01am. Carmichael listened for a moment. The fan on his computer made a low pitched pulsing whirr and the wall clock chirruped, like some low tech dubstep. Was that a creak of a floorboard as someone crouched with their ear to the door? He had to remain vigilant, more so than usual, especially since the spot audit, which threatened to uncover his little scheme. Especially since she had once again been an interfering cow and sneaked on him to Thornton. And also since Monday. Perhaps that had been a little rash, inviting more trouble.

It was an unwritten law at Barraclough and Leavis that he was not to be disturbed between eight o'clock and nine. Of late however, he had noticed more people arriving early, each one of them, like him, scheming, inquisitive, planning their next move. Maybe planning their next move on him. Officially, his day started at 9:00am, but living on the outskirts of Richmond meant an hours drive in the morning rush, so he always started out early. Of course, there was the tube, but what is the point of a company Merc if it sits all day rotting on the drive? Added to that the expense account was limitless and he was going to milk it. Since last Monday, however, he needed to be here early. He needed to keep an eye on business, so that nobody else did.

Once more, it was Carol Hughes who brought him his morning coffee. Maybe the tall gangly YTS was off sick again?

"Good Morning, Mr Carmichael. I'm sorry it's a bit late but the girl has only just arrived with the milk."

"Good Morning, Carol. How's tricks?"

"I don't know anyone called *Trix*, but I'm OK. Thanks for asking."

He straightened his tie and fixed onto his face what he believed to be a welcoming smile, keeping his eyes on her as she crossed the six feet of space and flourished the newspapers across the desk before walking around to place the cup on the coaster next to his keyboard.

She was not stunningly beautiful, but attractive in that ordinary of way which sneaks up on men. She was slightly shorter than Carmichael, even in her heels, but today she wore flat shoes, which gave her an elfin, juvenile quality that always turned Carmichael on. Her hair, deep brown, so deep it was almost black, curved in a bob about her pale round face and the deep soft eyes offered an unwavering kindness. One may pass her a hundred times and not notice how attractive she was and then one day it would be there. Her beauty was in her smile, the asymmetric tilt of her mouth, the inviting fullness of her lips and the way the curve of hair fell away from her cheek revealing an expanse of cream coloured neck which teased the hand to caress. But the way she looked at him; a benevolent, caring look was harder to define. Professional detachment? This was the nearest that Carmichael came to an adequate description.

Still, she was a beacon of light in his tawdry life. He gained pleasure from casting his eyes over her body, hoping she didn't notice but knowing that she did. The way her blouse folded affording a glimpse of her translucent white bra and the fulsome bosom that only older women could boast, as she stooped to lower the saucer. Today was a cream blouse with a black skirt that ended just above the knee but had a deep vent at the back, parting to expose the crook of her knee and a welcoming expanse of leg above. He imagined his hand delving inside and forming around her thigh, the slightly abrasive nylon of her charcoal tights against his palms and the crease where her legs met her buttocks. Her wedding ring flashed in the light from his computer screen, her lips smiled and her eyes glistened. He often wondered if women could read the lubricious thoughts of men whose eyes stayed neutral but whose minds scoured the depths. Her voice was reciting the day's appointments but he didn't listen. They were always the same. He imagined his hand pulling her onto his lap, grasping beneath her skirt and tearing through the nylon as she panted for him to stop, and he felt himself react, that special quickening, the unconscious anticipation stimulating him physically. He reached for the cup, diverting his mind, forestalling the bulge, which she might see.

One day, maybe, but not today.

"She glanced at the computer screen, which displayed a random document opened by Carmichael as a cover for the stock tracker, and then back at Drew. "First cup of the morning and you've been here an hour already, Mr Carmichael. Do you ever think you work too hard?"

'Carmichael' not 'Drew'. His bubble was burst like a week old spot. For now, the chase was off. The cheetah settled back into the savannah grass.

"Tell me, how hard is too hard for you, Carol?" He smiled lecherously. "No, I just like to check the figures first thing in the morning." He purposefully eyed the curve of her backside and winked lasciviously.

"Down, boy! Back to business. I have moved Mr and Mrs Snelling to 10:30am with. But now, to add a bit of variety, you have some early visitors. The police." Her eyes twinkled with mischievous delight. "Have you been a naughty boy?"

The police?

A cold sweat engulfed him, as he juggled a myriad scenarios. Maybe the audit had not been as squeaky clean as he had thought? Having Guy Higson, an old University friend, as accountant, had certainly helped and invariably Carol had influenced it, but had there been a slip somewhere?

Tentatively, he asked, "Did they say what it's about?"

Carol lifted *The Observer* and unfurled it over the desk, the front page photograph and the smiling eyes, sparking a deep feeling of recognition. He sipped at the acrid instant coffee and nodded anxiously at Carol as she turned to leave. His mind recalled smells and sounds, as the eyes looked at him and synapses fired seeking a connection, but the recognition did not fully crystallise until he turned over the paper to take in the full picture. The eyes of Dawn Silverton, smiling and carefree, gazed back at him and it was all he could do to stop himself from smiling, remembering the day the picture was taken, the gentle warmth of the Languedoc summer they had all spent together two years ago. Then in an instant Carmichael's mouth dried and his heart leapt as the image, juxtaposed with the word 'murdered' consumed his attention.

***

Daley followed Whetstone along a gloomy corridor to the door bearing the name of *A. Carmichael*. It took a few mental adjustments to convert the *A* to *Andrew* from the *Drew*, which Dawn had consistently penned in her diary. Rounding the edge of the door, he wondered if the abbreviation indicated a level of pretension - *Alexander* shortened to *Xander* rather than *Alex*, *Charles* to *Chas* rather than *Charlie*. And the most pretentious of all - *Ralph* pronounced *Rafe* despite being spelt the same. Why had *Andrew* chosen *Drew* rather than *Andy*? Did the person choose the name, or did the name shape the person? Daley suspected the latter, and that he would know for certain within five minutes.

Carmichael stood as they entered and proffered two chairs near the large teak veneered desk. He was a tall man, slightly shorter than Daley, slightly broader, more masculine. Unlike Daley he stood upright, his shoulders back with an air of self-assurance that made him look much taller. A square jawed face and greying blond hair, sculptured and close cropped, framed a winning smile that flashed off and on like a Belisha beacon. Piercing brown eyes were scanning the pair, assessing them, attempting to define their purpose. He was dressed much as Daley had expected, a crisp white shirt and a neutral blue tie with a perfect knot. Silver cufflinks glistened from the extended arm and the faintest glimpse of what Daley assumed would be an expensive watch. He was instantly recognisable from the photos found at Dawns apartment, but a tiny flash of recognition told Daley that Carmichael had also recalled the last time they had met, four years ago almost to the day, when Daley had been the junior officer.

The office was small and tired, and strewn with piles of bound folders lining the skirting of one of the walls, and a few more open ones masking the surface of the desk. The secretary followed them through, retrieved the tray on Carmichael's desk and asked if they needed refreshment, which Daley politely declined. He doubted that they would be there for long.

Daley always enjoyed the first meeting with a person who may be instrumental to a case. He likened it to fly fishing, due to the meandering nature of the questioning. Not that he had ever actually picked up a rod in his life, except in some game with bits of plastic and magnets as a six year old in a caravan at Porthcawl. He just imagined they were similar. The process starts with the environment, comfortable on both sides, but not so comfortable as to instil apathy. So a foldaway seat perched on the greasy grass edging a murky river on drizzly day created just the correct degree of discomfort. For the fish, Daley supposed, the situation was the slightly different. Apart from the strange shimmering silhouette, broken and distorted above the surface, life was pretty safe, a momentary distraction. Carmichael was the fish, maybe a salmon, perhaps a pike, mean and predatory, Daley still wasn't too sure.

His hand extended, Daley felt the vice-like grip of a man used to a position of authority, but the palms were sweaty and there was a hesitation in the returned greeting. Whetstone set about her role of sizing him up. In the police force, a lot of store was set by instinct. That indefinable quality which allowed them to turn their line of questioning on a sixpence.

Carmichael peered at Daley inquisitively. "Have we met before Inspector?"

"Yes, Sir. I was a sergeant in a different enquiry a few years back."

The jaw wrenching smile returned, as if turned on by a switch. "Ah. OK. What can I do for you?" The room too was different; the office larger, the ego still more so.

Whetstone opened the conversation. "We're investigating the death of Dawn Silverton on Monday. I believe you knew her?"

"Yes, yes. Quite well. I just read it in the paper." Carmichael frowned; a pallor had come to his features. "We went out together at University in the Nineties. We broke up at the time but we stay in touch, er, *stayed* in touch." Carmichael glanced away.

Deb's pen paused for a moment and she gave an infinitesimal shrug. 'Stormy' and 'on-off' sounded like far more than simply staying in touch.

"And when *did* you last see Dawn?"

"About four, five weeks ago. She came into the offices here, and spoke to Gerald Thornton, one of the directors. I just saw her in passing, you know, said 'hello'." Carmichael shifted once more in his seat and his eyes darted left towards the window, as if trying to recall the event. Breaking eye contact. "I didn't really get to speak to her. That's quite sad considering..."

"And can you tell us your whereabouts last Monday the twenty-third? That's the day before yesterday."

"Oh, er, well, yes. I was here, I think." He made an overly theatrical display of checking his computer, bringing up the day, to affirm his absolute innocence. Overly theatrical and probably totally unnecessary for the day before yesterday but a game often played. "Ah, yes, Monday. Here all day from 8:30 until 5:00. Popped out for a sandwich at 1:30."

Carmichael beamed a self-satisfied grin. *Pick the bones out of that one, copper!* Daley's first impressions had been confirmed. Carmichael was smug and secure in his skin. The fish happily swimming around as the angler set about his cheese and pickle sandwiches, each aware of the other but content to co-exist, the pike oblivious to the fly being wound and the line being prepared. Carmichael's office was his patch of reeds, and, underneath the carefully arranged clutter, it was pristine and organised, a bolt hole. It was up to them to wheedle him out.

"...And returning when?" asked Daley. A momentary flash of irritation crossed Carmichael's face. Resenting the implied doubt, that this was more than a Q&A session. Inwardly satisfied, Daley watched Carmichael's expression. The hunt was on. The psychological equivalent of tugging the line, teasing the fly across the water, making the ripples dance across the surface, or setting one's chair slightly higher, leaning across the desk. For now he was happy for the gremlins of uncertainty to scamper through Carmichael's mind.

"Around 2 o'clock, if I recall. Maybe slightly before or after. Why, is it important?"

"Just building a timeline, Sir." Daley caught Carmichael's eyes flitting from himself to Whetstone and back again, knowing the process that was going on in his head, a re-evaluation of the situation, reviewing the degree of safety or danger. He was formulating a timeline of his own, affirming his alibi, or creating one where there was none.

Having cast a few mealworms across the water, a few innocuous questions across the desk, Daley knew Carmichael's interest had been piqued and he had swum over to investigate, inquisitive but still wary of the colourful nymph lightly skipping on the plane above.

"Tell me about Monday." Daley swiftly changed the subject before Carmichael could delve too deeply into Dawn's death. Not that he would divulge any more, but leaving that edge of mystery helped with the dynamic too.

"Well, what can I say? It was like most Mondays. In the morning I had client meetings and in the afternoon I dealt with matters arising from the morning. Then after work I spent a couple of hours with a group of friends. We meet most Mondays, give or take."

Carmichael's voice tailed off leaving Daley to dig a little deeper.

"And Dawn was part of the group?"

Yes. There's a whole gang of us. Fortunately, two of our number own the Plough & Harrow in Ealing. On Cordon Street, just by the Green. Bit of a jaunt from my house but we tend to meet after work, so it seems like good idea. And there's usually some free food so there you go!" Carmichael let loose a forced chuckle, toasting his own good fortune at the odd meal *gratis*.

"So who's in the group, apart from Dawn and yourself?"

"Well, there's Marcus. Marcus Balfour. He's a doctor up at Ealing. There's Shelley Nugent and Finn Byrne. They're the ones who own the Plough & Harrow. Convenient, huh?" Daley nodded and even forced a minuscule twist of the top lip that in a good light might have passed for a smile. "Then there's Guy, er, Guy Higson. Oh, and of course Dawn."

Faint recollections flitted through Daley's mind. The group became hazy, half-remembered faces that would become clearer as he reread the case notes on Rachel Jones, visited their faces and gave them dimensions. Carmichael scratched his chin.

"Hang on, there is Alice of course. She's part of the group from way back but she doesn't often turn up on Mondays these days. Not since Christmas, really... I think she moved out of the area."

"Alice...?" Whetstone let the name hang, dismissing the presumption that she should divine the surname from the stifling, mote-strewn air of the office.

"Alice Bown. Sweet girl. Very self-contained. Plain. Smokes like a damp fire. Never got close to that one. Bit of a prick-tease, if you know what I mean, Inspector."

Whetstone raised her head and shot Carmichael a withering glance, which struck around the right temple, as he was too busy aiming his chauvinistic matey smile towards Daley. All pals together, the line was being played out and Carmichael was dancing with it.

"Sir, is that tease with an ee-ay or two ees?" Carmichael turned his head towards the Sergeant and the smile drained from his face and pooled in his lap, replaced by a slightly sheepish smirk.

Daley was starting to understand Carmichael. In this office, clients would hang on every word and laugh along with the staged humour. He held the upper station. Even now he assumed he had an advantage over the two police officers. Daley kept his eyes firmly on Carmichael as he pulled himself straight in the chair. Perhaps he did need to make the guy sweat a little.

"So, apart from Ms Silverton, were you all there on Monday?" Beneath the surface the fish was happily gobbling the wriggling mealworms as they writhed down through the water, it was swimming around the hook, ever more content, growing more oblivious to the game.

"Well, there was Marcus and I. Of course, Shelley and Finn were there. Shelley was mainly in the restaurant. Oh, and Guy came later, probably around nine."

"But not Alice, er, Bown?" Whetstone checked her list.

"No - but as I say, that's not unusual these days. The thought of Dawn lying dead while we were all laughing and joking makes me go cold." Carmichael once more stared into middle distance, lost in some thought, becoming distracted from the chase. Daley decided to throw his line out further, if only so he could yank it back once Carmichael had a firm hold.

"We're not certain of the exact time of death at the moment, Sir. We have to await the results of the post mortem to give us a clearer picture. At the moment we are focusing on afternoon and early evening."

"Well, I left here around 6:30pm. I walked around to the Plough & Harrow. I got there around 7:00pm."

"Mr Carmichael?" Deb laid down her pen and looked across the desk. "Are you aware of anything that might have been troubling Dawn?"

Carmichael made an overly grand gesture of pondering the question, scratching the bristles on his chin with his thumb and forefinger. "No, not that I am aware of. She was finding the housing market a little slow. I wouldn't say she was a particularly good saleswoman, but I did my best to help where I could."

"So you can't think of anyone who would want to harm her?" Deb held eye contact, watched the momentary glance to his right.

"No, not that I know...no! Everybody loved Dawn."

Daley took up the reins once more. "There are lots of entries in Ms Silverton's diary with your name against them, but she had some kind of code, so we don't really know what they are about. For example, this one on the nineteenth..." Daley proffered the book over the desk to Carmichael, who scanned it rather more studiously than Daley thought necessary for such a recent appointment. Within a second or so, the book was passed back.

"Oh, they are just business appointments," he said dismissively. "Dawn recommended her clients to me. You know, a bit of mutual back-scratching. Like I said, I did my best to help her out." There was a complacency to Carmichael's tone, which Daley had met many times before, but now which sparked an inkling of a memory from four years previous. A dismissiveness that masked evasion. It had then, and almost certainly would now.

"That explains it, Sir. Maybe she was handing out your cards and using the diary to remind herself that she should let you know in case the buyer called." Daley beamed a smile of gratitude across the desk at Carmichael. "But what about the others, 7:15pm last Wednesday, 8:00pm on Friday, 3:00pm on Sunday, and then at 12:30pm on Monday, the day she died. Were they all business meetings too?"

"Well, I suppose so. I can't recall every meeting, every appointment." Irritation soaked into Carmichael's tone, and his expression was as a child who had been playing *Hide and Seek* and been caught hiding in the most obvious place.

"Sorry, Mr Carmichael, I must have misunderstood. You said a moment a go that you and Dawn last met four or five weeks ago, but her diary suggests that you saw each other a lot more recently. You also seem to phone each other quite a lot. Twice in the week before she died. What were the calls about, if you don't mind me asking?" It pleased Daley that Carmichael obviously did mind. It pleased him further, as he watched Carmichael's eyes darting about and his mouth flapping, that what followed would be worth listening too but most likely, complete bollocks.

"I, I don't recall off the top of my head... What I meant was that the last time we met *socially* was around four or five weeks ago. The nature of our business, things just crop up, so we met to sort out issues as they arise, that's all. There were a lot of issues in the last week or two." Carmichael's eyes swivelled in their sockets as he scanned the room for inspiration, finally settling on the computer screen. He irritatedly shuffled the mouse, waking up the screen and he searched the diary. "They were about No. 53 Chapel Rise. We'd been having trouble getting the sale through. I was helping Dawn make it happen..." Daley drew in a little more line, pulling the gaudy lure towards him, enticing Carmichael to follow.

"On a Sunday?"

"Well yes. It must be the same in your line of business. Criminals don't work 9-to-5, nor do financial advisors. It's a 24-7 world. People expect you to be available to suit them." Carmichael's face was plastered with relief as he appeared to have freed himself from the hook, but Daley was only taking a rest allowing the line to slacken. It had not escaped him that Carmichael had unconsciously likened himself to a criminal, an impression that Daley had shared since receiving a bill for his recent remortgage following the divorce.

"What about the entry for Monday? That one's easy to decode but not easy to interpret. '*Drew Fuck fuck,*'...er...'*fucking hell*'". He enunciated the words precisely. "Now I have not studied the diary in any great depth, Mr Carmichael, but the only swearwords that seem to appear are against entries involving you. Does that seem odd?"

Carmichael shrugged and raised his hand in an appeal. "OK. Look. Dawn and I were not actually seeing eye-to-eye at the moment. We were having a lot of business dealings and some of them weren't the easiest in the world. It's a difficult market. No. 53 Chapel Rise was a pain in the arse and she had spoken to my boss, Gerald Thornton. I felt that she was going to start up again over No. 57. I was none too pleased so I tore her off a strip."

"No. 57 was her first viewing on Monday afternoon. So you *did* see her on Monday? When exactly was that?"

"Like I said I went out for lunch. We had coffee. I don't know, around one fifteen, maybe half past."

"And how was that?" The atmosphere in the room prickled.

"Well, actually we argued a bit. About Chapel Rise. Nothing serious, all sorted out there and then."

"Did this argument turn physical?"

"I am not sure I am happy with the implication..."

"No implication at all, Sir. This is a murder enquiry. Sometimes the questions need to be direct. So, did it turn physical?"

"Well, not really physical. I did catch hold of her and stop her walking away at one point. But, you know, not really physical. As a matter of fact, it was she that got physical with me." He proffered his hand. The wields on top of his wrist were still red but paling and less angry. "Kneed me in the groin too."

Whetstone smirked to herself as Daley sucked air in through his teeth. "It does seem that she was rather upset with you. And then what happened?"

"Nothing *happened*. We discussed her conversation with my boss, how we were going to deal with it later, and then she left. It was all a fuss about nothing, really."

"But I am sure you realise, Mr Carmichael, you may have been the last person to see her alive."

"Except for her killer, surely!"

"Well, yes, except for her killer. Oh, and those scratches. There were skin fragments under Miss Silverton's nails. Would you consent to us taking a DNA swab for elimination purposes? We would just like to confirm they are yours - from the altercation you mentioned."

Carmichael made a reflex move with the other hand to cover up the scratches. "Oh. Yes. I suppose so."

So why did Carmichael not mention the Monday meeting with Dawn earlier? Unless it was a case of Occam's Razor - the most obvious explanation being the truth. Whetstone had told of her meeting at the Estate Agents, how Jane Wright had been sure that the relationship was once more failing. Perhaps the phone calls and texts in the last weeks were frantic attempts to end the relationship and Carmichael was having none of it. Perhaps, his relationship with Dawn would never have truly been over.

Or maybe there was another dynamic at work? Maybe *we argued a bit* had been more than a bit.

Whetstone decided she might as well be hung for a sheep as a lamb and broached the other question that she knew Daley was holding up his sleeve for another day.

"Mr Carmichael. Do you remember Rachel Jones?"

Carmichael swivelled his chair so he faced the Sergeant and

leaned back, folding his arms across his chest. The look on his face turned quizzical, momentarily motionless, processing his next move as a chess player studying the board, assessing the remaining pieces, seeking to avoid humiliation. *They know something I don't. What's their game?*

"Rachel Jones? Yes, a long time ago, now. Funnily enough, she was..." His eyes narrowed to slits and he peered back at Daley. "Ah! Now I remember where I've seen you before."

Without another word being spoken both Daley and Whetstone knew that Carmichael had made the link between Dawn Silverton, estate agent and one-time girlfriend, murdered a couple of days ago and Rachel Jones, estate agent murdered four years ago. The link between a quiet Detective Sergeant who took copious notes and the authoritarian Inspector on the other side of the desk.

Carmichael's eyes shot to the artexed ceiling and he ran his hands through his hair. Recomposed, his delivery was business-like and measured, back in a groove. He spoke to Daley.

"So, you think the person who did this to Dawn is the same one that killed Rachel Jones all those years ago?"

"Too early to tell but it's a strong possibility, Sir." Whetstone answered, ignoring the snub. If she had been in on Daley's piscatorial analogy, she would have yanked the rod from his hands and started to beat Carmichael with it.

"Well, I hope I am not going to endure the same bully-boy tactics as last time. If you'd spent less time hounding me and more time looking for the killer, maybe Dawn would still be alive." Carmichael eyed Daley with more than a hint of threat. Whetstone pressed ahead.

"Did you ever have a relationship with Rachel Jones?"

"She wasn't my type. Well, when I say 'No', we went out a few times, but it was nothing. She was just a bit of rough, and she was already seeing someone else. You know, it just happened. She was a distraction, OK for a good time if it was getting late and there was no-one else in the frame." Carmichael was still conversing with Daley as Whetstone continued.

"And this would have been how long ago?"

"Well, it was just before she died. But look, you already know all of this, surely?"

"It was exactly fours years ago, Mr Carmichael." Whetstone said.

"Hang on a minute... what, you think I had something to do with both of their deaths? Bloody Hell! Haven't you got anything better to do with your time than to go about slinging accusations?"

Daley raised his eyebrows and stared at Carmichael. "We're not jumping to any conclusions, just yet, Sir. To be fair, you do seem to have been seeing both of the two women at the time of their respective deaths. Sooner or later, once our wheels are in motion the truth will out. At the moment we are just fact finding, no more."

Daley was tired of this pompous, overbearing prick, so he decided wrest the rod back from Whetstone, to play out the line and hook this sucker once and for all. "Mr Carmichael. We're not trying to trick anyone. This is a murder enquiry and we have to explore every avenue. It's still very early in the investigation, but you have to agree, it's interesting that Rachel Jones and Dawn Silverton were both killed in the same way - I mean *exactly* the same way and *exactly* four years apart, and you appear to have been in a relationship of sorts with both of them around the time they died."

Carmichael smiled sardonically. "That is a bit of a stretch, Inspector. As I told you, it was all strictly business with Dawn. Had been for a couple of years."

"So, as your relationship was strictly business, and maybe a few Monday night drinks, were you aware that she was pregnant?"

"Pregnant? What Dawn?" The face exploded with incredulity, but the eyes were the windows to quite a different soul.

"Yes. Estimate is around twelve to fifteen weeks. Would you have any idea who the father might be?"

"Well, how would I know? Like I say, strictly business for some time. A lot longer than twelve to fifteen weeks anyhow. Inspector, it seems we are travelling down a familiar route to that which we travelled four years ago. And look where that got us." He pressed the intercom button sending two short bursts down the corridor. "Anyway, if there's nothing else, Mrs Hughes will see you out."

Daley took the cue to leave and held out a hand. "Thanks for your time, Mr Carmichael. It's been really helpful." Daley flourished a business card and laid it on the desk. "Oh, by the way. The name Watkins. Does that mean anything to you?"

But by now Carmichael's patience had been thoroughly depleted. "Nothing whatsoever, Inspector. Now, look. I am a very busy man, so you really *will* have to excuse me."

As they left Barraclough and Leavis, Daley glanced at Whetstone and they both raised their eyebrows. Carmichael had been economical with the truth. Why, Daley was not yet sure but it was in some way connected to the phone calls and diary entries. Whatever the two were up to in the days before her death, he knew it must be significant. Was it about the baby? If that had unbalanced Carmichael, the mention of Rachel Jones had sent him reeling into an instinctive counter-attack. The fish had been lured, and now he left it curious about the hook. It would only be a matter of time before it was flapping on the bank, gasping for air and awaiting its fate.

***

The walk back to the station was only a short distance. The meetings with Gascoigne and Carmichael had eaten most of the morning rush but Daley was still forging a staccato path through pedestrians who all seemed to be walking the opposite way. Gascoigne's findings gave grounds to bring someone in. He just had to figure out who. Team Brief was an hour away and in his head he rehearsed his lines. Yet another opportunity to make a bad impression. Now his accelerated trot drove him back to the station to start piecing together a coherent story he could confidently put to them. But it was the weapon that occupied his thoughts. There were many instances of the same gun appearing in two different killings. Guns change hands. To his knowledge, there had never been a case of a sword being wielded so precisely on two different victims by two different murderers.

So Daley was satisfied that a new shadow of doubt was forming around Carmichael and that meant another session with Allenby. Another career limiting argument, dredging up past mistakes, airing dirty linen. Yesterday, the whole bear-pit had paused, or typed more quietly, to overhear the row between the two officers, muffled through the glass walls of the goldfish bowl. Allenby had made it absolutely clear that something more substantial than Carmichael's name in Dawn's diary would be needed. He had reminded Daley of the shit-storm that had descended from the top floor when they had investigated the Rachel Jones Murder and Carmichael had been leaned upon. Heaps of circumstantial evidence but nothing concrete. If Daley wanted Carmichael in an interview room, then he had to build a more solid case than Allenby had, otherwise the investigation would become a fiasco.

Deb did her utmost to keep pace with Daley's purposeful stride, performing an odd staggered three step dance to remain within communication range. But she struggled to keep pace in other ways too. She was sceptical of Carmichael's guilt, especially since their interview earlier. As she scuttled behind him, she kept reminding him of the need for an adequate motive, means and opportunity to square Carmichael into the frame. For her, process was everything. Where corners are cut, something won't fit. She could not simply trust, like Daley, that the detail that would come out in the end.

Finally, as Daley paused to ascend the steps into Lambourne Road, Whetstone was able to shuffle in front of him. He had a determined blaze in his eyes that would mean only one thing in the Team brief - trouble. She held out her hands to halt his progress as he made to cross the lobby. With a bee the size of a Harrier jump jet in his bonnet, it was going to take some serious persuasion to convince him to slow down, take a breath. And even more to convince him it was his idea.

"Gov, Don't you think it's strange that Dawn was pregnant yet Carmichael never mentioned it? Do you think Dawn had actually told him?"

Daley paused mid-step and sighed deeply. He and Deb Whetstone had worked together for around two years and he had to admit that they made a good team. When Daley's impetuousness got the better of him, Deb was the one to drag him down to earth. But that had its downside. In every investigation, there was a point where he had started to knit the strands together, and Whetstone began picking at the stitches almost immediately till the case unravelled. And the self-doubt would creep in, niggling and tugging at his confidence.

As the evolving address to the Team Brief evaporated from his mind, he cocked his head sideways and glowered distractedly. "No idea!"

"Carmichael didn't mention it. The girls at the estate agents didn't mention it either. You would have thought that she was bursting to tell them - *oh, by the way*... Christ, if I knew I was that far gone, I'd want to tell someone. Right now, I'd want to break his bloody nuts as well!"

"You heard Gascoigne. She was still in the first trimester. Loads of pregnancies end before the twelfth week. Maybe she was erring on the side of caution."

"Really, Sir? Dawn Silverton doesn't strike me as someone who would keep quiet about something like that."

Daley dodged around Whetstone and headed off again, leaving her staring at empty space. She needed to persist, make him reconsider entering the Team Brief with all guns blazing. His bias against Carmichael was based on history rather than facts. She turned and scurried after him.

"Unless of course he was the last person she wanted to speak to about it. What if she hadn't told him on purpose? What if the baby was a problem?"

Daley's attention was finally grabbed. "Exactly what are you getting at?"

"What if the baby wasn't Carmichael's?"

"So what? There could be any number of reasons, she wouldn't have told him. Maybe she was waiting for the right moment. Maybe this audit business had made her wait until he was in a better mood."

"OK, Sir, but if I got pregnant, not only would it be a miracle given my sex life, but also I'd have to think about the effect on my job, all sorts of things. What about the rent, the mortgage, the car payments? Maybe a baby right now would be too expensive. I would have to go on maternity leave, and then there's the cost involved, turning the box room into a nursery, buying cots and nappies and shit. Surely a trouble shared...?"

"Maybe she was afraid to tell Carmichael in case he flipped his lid and hacked her head off with a sword. Whoa. Maybe, she did tell him over lunch. Maybe they had words, a struggle?" Sarcasm was not a good look on Daley.

"That's just my point, Sir!"

"Ah, there is a point then!"

Deb parried the remark. "Dawn finds she is pregnant. She has bills to pay. Surely the first person she needs to talk to is Carmichael. Well-off, successful. He would help her out, given their past relationships. Even if it wasn't his, he would help her as a friend."

"Really, Deb? Does he strike you as a philanthropic sort of guy?"

"And there is the point, Sir. He's unaware she is pregnant. She hasn't told anyone, so if the baby is the reason she was killed, then someone else did it. Reading the statements last night, I seem to recall that Rachel Jones had also been pregnant and had an abortion. Both cases a pregnancy involved. In both cases we don't know who the father is. Think about it, Sir, I tell you I'm pregnant and it means I have to give up my job..."

"I'd just get another Detective Sergeant. One who doesn't bicker all the time."

Deb cast him a scornful look, but at least she had his attention. "Yes, but suppose I am and I did. It just doesn't fit the profile. If you feel that strongly about it, you would come home and strangle me, or knife me, or beat me senseless. I'd be lying on the floor of Copley Close bleeding everywhere, or on the phone sobbing to my mother. Or you would have found a skip to throw my cold dead corpse in, you heartless bastard! You wouldn't have arranged to meet me at a house under an assumed name and then decapitate me. It just doesn't work for me. We see domestics all the time. Doesn't sound right."

"OK, so Carmichael didn't know about the baby but what about Dawn's diary? There had to be something sinister going on, surely." Frustration was creeping into Daley's voice. Not fifteen minutes ago, he had a perfect set of circumstances to bring Carmichael him in, and he was ready to go cap-in-hand to the D/Supt and beg forgiveness for his transgression the previous day. And already the worms of doubts were burrowing through his brain.

He had to admit that Deb was right. If Carmichael had murdered her at Chapel Rise, then it was premeditated and that seemed to rule out the pregnancy as a reason.

49

Daley scratched his forehead, and screwed up his eyes. A myriad disjointed pieces of data swam around like pollen on a millpond, waiting for that one breeze to drift them into a discernible stream of information. He needed the team to come through and hoped that they had turned up some new lines of enquiry. Leaving Deb in the lobby, he took the stairs two at a time, barely noticing the effort. Maybe the strands would start to draw together as he related them to the team. Maybe they would tighten the noose on Carmichael, or place it around the neck of someone else.

Scanning the Team Room as he heaved his way through the double fire doors, Daley took a deep breath and composed himself. For three weeks it had been his goal to avoid the lift whenever possible. His thighs ached with lactic acid and his lungs struggled to recover from the two minutes of leaping up the stairs two steps at a time...but he was buggered if it was going to show.

***

Spinning his chair on its axis, Carmichael distractedly rescanned the scant list of appointments for the morning. Carol had done an excellent job of shifting meetings to accommodate the police. Much too bloody good a job as they had left within forty minutes and his next punter was not due in until 10:30.

Which had given him far too much time to dwell on their visit.

The Inspector - he cast a glance down at the card on the desk - *Daley* - knew more than he was letting on. Questions about the entries in his diary, the texts and phone calls to Dawn, especially the ones the previous week. It's true that some were about 57 Chapel Rise and some were social, but the rest were not. He racked his brain to remember the calls, to piece together a conversation spread over several days. Had the police retrieved the texts, seen transcripts of the calls? Had he given anything away? His mouth parched. He reached for his empty coffee cup, cursing under his breath. Holding down the intercom button, he watched the orange light illuminate and waited for the voice to answer.

"Carol, get me another cup of coffee. And this time make it a mug - a big mug, please. And none of that instant shit."

50

Dawn Silverton, the smile disconnected, still stared lifelessly from the newspaper on his desk, forcing him to acknowledge the mounting sense of loss. He remembered his last words to her as she fled down the Alley - *You have messed me about for the last time, Dawn* - and hoped he had not been overheard.

Did Daley know of his little financial scheme? If he had read phone transcripts or spoken to Thornton, then he must suspect. Carmichael had never expected the phone calls to be recorded, so he hadn't bothered with any codes or pretexts. He had been a fool to involve the Monday Club in his scheme. If he was discovered, the money would be lost, and he would have to answer to them all. Shelley and Finn would almost certainly lose the pub. Guy and Marcus would be after his bollocks - or worse. His only hope would be that he would be found guilty of something and the beak would lock him away for a while until the heat died down.

Or he could keep the account hidden.

Then most of that Inspector's questioning had been about Dawn and Rachel. Obviously, Dawn had just died - been killed. But they had picked up on him very quickly. Damn Dawn and her diary! He could only surmise what she had confessed to it but it must have placed rather too much emphasis on his relationship with Dawn and seeded the Inspector's fertile imagination.

Then there was Rachel! Surely that was pre-history by now? It was that dyke sergeant who had mentioned her. The quiet ones are always the worst. What connected him with Rachel? True, they had screwed a few times but that was just sex, just convenient for both of them. Rachel could separate the physical from the emotional. It had all gotten a little messy before she died. Then after her death the police had hounded him into the ground but, with the help of Edgar Sampson, the family lawyer, he had been able to keep himself out of the investigation, to keep the real truth about him and Rachel hidden. It needed to stay that way.

Searching the contacts on his computer, he found Guy Higson. He had already called Shelley and Finn - well, Shelley - those two were joined at the hip. You couldn't fart by of one of them without the other smelling it. It had been a difficult phone call. She had not seen the picture in the paper and as per usual had started wailing and moaning.

And that's when, like a predatory beast emerging from the mist, a long-forgotten memory resurfaced in a perfect storm of names - Dawn, Rachel, Shelley. Was that the subtext to the policeman's questioning? Had they had made a connection after all this time? Surely no-one was interested now?

Unless someone had talked.

Maybe that was it? A tawdry attempt by one of the Monday Club to up the ante, to dig their snout deeper into his trough? He had told Shelley to keep quiet. Had she even been listening? There was malice in her voice as she blamed him for everything that was wrong in her life, when she blamed him for leading Dawn and Rachel to their deaths, when she told him that someday he would pay. Maybe this was when he started to pay?

The earpiece burred as Higson's mobile chimed a mile away but the sound of the lilting voice that followed was his voicemail greeting.

"Guy, it's Drew. It just gets worse. If you haven't looked at the papers, you need to." He paused. How can you describe something like that? "Well, anyway look at the papers. I know you say you have sorted everything, but I need to be sure that we have taken care of business - *all* of the business. I can't talk on the phone, so call me back. Let's talk A.S.A.P. Right?"

Another call for the police to transcribe. Another meaning to construe.

A soft knock came from the door and Carol entered with his coffee. He studied her as she tidied up, his eyes scanning her face and the deep curve of her chin, porcelain skin, the shadowed v-shaped indentation at the base of her neck, the sternal notch, he believed it was called, emphasised by the slender gold necklace which dangled loose as she stooped. He thought how much more comfortable his life would be if he could simply keep his work and love life separate. And it occurred to him that even at thirty-five he was too old for most of the women he met - most of the *girls* he met. He wondered whether those that slept with him did so out of sympathy.

"Did the police speak to you before they left?"

Carol raised her head at the question, sensing the sudden gravity in his manner.

"Only for a moment, Mr Carmichael. They took my details, asked to see the desk diary. They asked me about Ms Silverton's visit."

Carmichael invited Carol to sit in the chair that Daley had left askew. He kept his eyes on her face as she crossed her legs and her skirt rose over the nylon sheen of her knees. There was a time and a place.

"Did they mention the accounts at all?"

"No, they only seemed interested in that visit on 20th of March. I left it to Mr Thornton to fill in the details when they speak to him."

Carmichael shifted in his seat and rubbed the scratches on the back of his hand. "That's what I am worried about."

Chapter 10

Replacing the handset in its cradle, Shelley Nugent watched Carmichael's number disappear. She caught her reflection in the mirrored glass behind the optics. Tears had already tracked through the thin makeup and crested over her high cheekbones, usually crimson with laughter or embarrassment or joy, but today devoid of any colour. They had pooled in circles onto the smiling face of Dawn Silverton, distorting the newsprint into damp ridges of grey. Tasting salt in the corner of her mouth, she fumbled beneath her blouse and into her jeans for a tissue. She cursed as the stone of her ring snagged on the hem. Across the bar, the two morning cleaners, unaware, giggled and prattled as they prepared for lunchtime. Behind her the fridges hummed and clinked and motes of dust played in the strands of mid-morning light peering in from the street. However much energy she devoted to polishing the aged surface of the bar she knew she could never recapture the lustre it had when it was new. She thought of life with Finn, once so full of love, but now dulled to a life of duty towards each other and to this place. And the loss became ever deeper.

Having not read the days papers, Carmichael had called and demanded she look. As the eyes connected with hers, she was transported back four years to a similar photo, a similar woman and the depth of her loss had returned fourfold. She had laid out the paper on the bar, to prove that this was a different Dawn, not the same Dawn whose hand she had let slip as they said their goodbyes a week before. The same Dawn who had flicked a small wave over her shoulder, whose ponytail had bounced to and fro as she walked away.

Starting momentarily, she spun on her heels as Finn Byrne peered curiously around the door. He was so attuned to her that he had heard the plaintive cry over the clinking of glasses and roar of the vacuum cleaner.

"What's the matter, love?"

Since meeting at University over a decade and a half ago, Finn and Shelley had been inseparable. She had tamed the tall,

54

impetuous man from Ballymena and he had melted instantly at the playful, ebullient girl from Nottingham, whose mindless chatter he would never tire of. Her froth of brown curls and matching eyes, her ever smiling face, ensured that he had never looked at another woman since, or she at another man.

She showed him the paper, and watched his head tilted inquisitively as he read the headline and studied the picture. He too felt himself drawn back four years to a similar picture and a similar situation. For Finn, the memories were different. They were not about the loss of Dawn or Rachel but the loss of Shelley to her secrets, her depression and to Carmichael.

"Bloody hell! Dawn? Dead? Shit!" Finn was a man of few words and those he chose were usually colourful and apposite.

"Murdered, Finn. Murdered. Just like Rachel." She peered over Finn's arm at the smiling face, noticing the aubrietia in the background, heady and sweet, mottled and grey in newsprint, hearing Marcus Balfour pleading for them to keep still as he framed the shot. Seeing the hand on Dawn's shoulder. Knowing it was her own. Dawn would never be still when the girls were together. First there were three, then there were two and now there was one. A chill of isolation bit through her and she extended her arm around Finn's back, drawing him closer.

"First Rachel. Now Dawn." She chewed her thumb, eyes flicking left and right, trying to hide the insidious terror that was creeping over her.

Finn screeched out a chair from the nearest table and dragged out another for himself, flattening down the page. He frowned and scratched his brow. "Tough neighbourhood, I suppose. By our age, Law of Averages that someone's gonna die." Given the circumstances, this was his best explanation, pathetic and trite.

"Come on, though. Both murdered. Both amongst our closest friends. And look at the date. Exactly four years since Rachel died. Not four years and a week, or three years and fifty one weeks, but exactly four years. That's not the Law of Averages." Just as with Rachel, Shelley had begun to make the connections back to 1997. Connections that had been buried deep, rippling to the surface four years ago, and now re-emerging once more. She knew Finn would not speculate. He had the business head that had made the Plough & Harrow a success.

"Law of Averages sometimes gets skewed, that's all." He ran his fingers over the tear spots, almost dry, the ink barely leached.

"Rachel, Dawn. I'm the only one left, Finn."

"What about Alice?"

"Alice has never been one of us." It was true. Alice was part of the group, one of the girls at Coventry University, but she was been as close as Rachel and Dawn, never part of the real gang.

"For God's sake, Shelley. Let's not go over all this again." Finn exhaled deeply, feeling her anguish, anticipating the sense of separateness that her depression brought.

Since meeting on the steps of *FiftyFour*, a Students Union hang-out, a few weeks into his first semester, they had forged an instant bond. Both leaving to escape the incessant thump of the disco, they had ended up in Finn's room in Priory and the most enjoyable six months of both of their lives. Until that one night in the spring of 1997 when everything changed for them. She had never revealed to him what had happened that night before she returned, beating at Finn's door in Priory hall.

Then, years later, Rachel Jones' death had hit Shelley hard and for months she had succumbed to the black dog that had been her dark companion since University. For months the radiant energy she had exuded became a facade and only he saw the demons when they surfaced. Now, once more he felt excluded. He turned and looked her straight in the eyes, taking her clenched hands in his, praying she would not sense the exasperation in his voice.

"Please, Shelley. You can't think like this. You've never been alone. Why can't you accept that? This is not some vendetta. No-one is coming after you. I have always been here by your side and I'm not going anywhere now." A familiar frustration resurfaced, as inside he knew he was reaching the end of his patience. With Shelley, with her mood swings and with the exclusion that her inevitable descent into depression caused. And now once more it was tearing her to pieces and he didn't know if he had the strength left to hold her together again.

The anger threatening to consume him, he knew there would need to be a reckoning.

Chapter 11

As 1:00pm arrived, D/Supt Bob Allenby dragged out a chair from the edge of a desk by the mobile whiteboard. The pandemonium generally eased a little with his presence, but only a little. The team room was charged. Nerves were on edge as everyone wondered if it was their turn for a bollocking, privately questioning their abilities. Allenby loved the energy at the beginning of an investigation but was relieved to be a spectator. His stresses were altogether more manageable. It had been over forty hours since the body had been found and he was anxious to hear what Daley had pieced together. A new day had dawned and the evidence in the Dawn Silverton murder case was beginning to fade.

The story had already hit the papers, such was the curse of the Capital, and the Twittersphere was buzzing. The press had already contrived links back to Rachel Jones, speculating with what scant information they had, and a lot they had invented. At least they had spelt her name correctly, but other than that details were sparse and inwardly he commended the work of the team for keeping them so. These days, a celebrity puking in London can be seen on YouTube in Sydney within seconds. Where they obtained the photograph that was emblazoned across the tabloids; the same photograph that Whetstone had shown him earlier, no-one was sure. It would not be long before the postman, or one of the attending officers, yielded to the relentless pressure and let something slip. By separating the evidence from the chain of witnesses, they had hoped to keep the number '2' and the sword out of the press. He sipped at a coffee, some instant that one of the constables had found in a skip, his head pounding again. The parallels with the Rachel Jones inquiry had meant a disturbed night's sleep. He worried about Daley, his ability to cope, but mainly he worried about his own failure in the Rachel Jones case. With so many obvious similarities had he missed something? He also worried about what he would say in the press briefing later.

Daley nodded nervously to the D/Supt as he, Whetstone and

Corby entered from their conflab around the lift. He raised his hand and the room stilled.

"Ladies, gentlemen...and D/Supt Allenby." An awkward, polite, almost embarrassed rumble of laughter pulsed through the room, more in deference to Daley than in amusement. Allenby smiled broadly. "Dawn Silverton was thirty-four, lived alone in Copley Close, West Ealing. She was a high-end estate agent working at Parkin-Wright on the High Street. The postman found Ms Silverton at around 11:00am yesterday morning inside No. 57 Chapel Rise, an empty property up for sale. According to the victim's diary, the viewer was a 'Watkins', gender unknown, meeting arranged for 2:30pm the previous day. The preliminary Path report suggests that she met her end then or soon afterwards. We have a few witnesses who describe her client as between 5-2 and 6 feet tall, male or female - one or the other - wearing a greatcoat or mac, which was either black, brown or dark blue, or maybe green. Oh, and he or she had a hat, or a hood which obscured his or her face." He paused for ironic effect. "Good luck with that! It appears that she was decapitated with a single blow from a Japanese samurai sword which was thoughtfully left at the scene – Sergeant?" Daley introduced Dave Monaghan with a sweep of his hand.

"Sir."

Monaghan was a slight wiry Irishman with aquiline features, a tufted moustache and a stoop from too much desk work. The eldest of the team, he had a quiet unexcitable manner and a legendary memory that made him a great guy to cosy up to when picking teams for Quiz Night. Above all though he was methodical and rigorous, putting a check on the teams more fanciful speculation and bringing them back to the facts.

In the manner of a hostess from *Sale of the Century*, a show that he was sure, he alone would be able to remember, Monaghan stood and raised a clear polythene bag presenting it for the room to see. The sword inside looked cheap and unspectacular, but the blade lustred keenly in the strip lighting. He set about enlightening the room in his faded Wicklow brogue.

"Right Guys, pay attention. There will be a test! This is a genuine Japanese Type 98 shin guntō military sword, more familiarly known as a *katana*."

"Like the motorbike, Sarge?" Monaghan cast an eye around the room but failed to identify the culprit.

"Yes, like the motorbike, but you probably have more chance riding one of these through Brent on a Friday night, without getting it pinched. It was issued to non-commissioned officers of the Japanese Imperial Army. It is *not a samurai* sword, *Sir...*" He stared scornfully over his spectacles at Daley who held his hands up, suitable admonished, "...a fact which we will keep between ourselves, please. The shin guntō was made between 1935 and 1945, but the Imperial War Museum dates this one towards the end of the war. Japan was running out of materials, and bullets and tanks outranked swords, so the fittings are cheaply made out of iron and copper. However, take a good look at the blade." He wielded the sword, still in it's bag, in two handed Samurai fashion. "Slightly curved upward and bloody sharp, even after 70 odd years. They would be carried into battle but rarely used in combat, unless the owner ran out of ammo. Usually they were used for beheading, as a form of execution. Three things to note:" Monaghan gingerly replaced the sword on his desk, as if it were a live stick grenade, and went over to the whiteboard and retrieved a blue pen, writing as he spoke.

"Firstly, the gash on the wall was made by that sword." He pointed to one of the photos attached with magnets. "The end is blunted and Forensics confirm that plaster found on the tip was from the wall. Secondly..." Monaghan traipsed back, wielded the sword and feigned a slow, shoulder-high sweep. "...assuming that the slice was like this, given the height of murdered woman's neck and the height of the gash in the wall, we can reliably estimate the height of the murderer at five feet six inches tall, about two inches shorter than our victim. Thirdly, according to Professor Gascoigne, the decapitation was carried out in a single action. Whoever did this knew exactly how to do it.

"Forensics confirm time of death of around 11:00 to 17:00 on Tuesday. So 14:30, her appointment at that house, sounds like a reasonable time."

DC Smollet piped up. "That's quite a skill, Sarge, you know, chopping a head off with a single blow, and you would have to be fairly strong and damn accurate to miss the shoulders, or not just bounce off the back of the head. Are we assuming that the killer was a man and that he knew about martial arts, then?"

"No we are not. Fifty years ago, these things were the preserve of Japanese males, but I did some digging and it seems nowadays Japanese martial arts, like Kendo – which uses the *shinai* - a piece of wood - in place of a sword, is increasingly popular with women. It's a common misconception that you have to be strong to decapitate someone. Weak and clumsy, you could be hacking away for ages. The executioner took three swings at Mary Queen of Scots, and then he had to finish the job with his knife, and her head was resting on a block. Jean Rombaud, the executioner of Anne Boleyn accomplished the task in a single stroke as she looked around before she placed her head on the block. It's all in the technique - the speed and angle of the blade. Given the right training, the right motivation and a strong stomach, anyone could have done this. Even you, Smollet."

Daley interrupted. "The fact that the sword swiped the wall may be significant for a couple of reasons. Firstly, if you think about it, the force of the swing would have to be considerably greater for it to graze the wall and still have enough momentum to deliver a clean blow, and secondly, the depth of the graze is shallow, so it could indicate that the killer had a long reach, and that may indicate a male, someone with martial arts training, or even someone in the military." Daley glanced over at Allenby, who was frowning; he had picked up on the inference. "That said, I agree with Sergeant Monaghan, with the right motivation and a bit of skill, anyone could have done it. So don't get hung up on gender, or hobbies or past history. These are things to bear in mind during the investigation. The sword, Dave, is it rare? I mean, can anyone get their hands on one?"

"You would think so, Sir, with the Internet and all that, but this is an old one, an original, not a modern replica. My expert says that there would be thousands in The States but only a few hundred would have made it to Britain from Burma or Malaya and most of those are in private collections and fairly well documented. He is looking up the serial number of this one and should get back to me.

"What he *did* say was that there should be a scabbard. They rarely ever turn up alone, because they were difficult to carry without."

Daley resumed the briefing. Monaghan took the hint and sat

down.

"So we think that as our victim went through the front door, she was hit from behind with that sword, decapitating her and killing her instantly. Then the killer took a permanent marker pen and drew a number '2' on the forehead of the head as it lay on the ground...", Daley paused for the inevitable gasps and murmured comments, "...then it appears the killer sat inside a cupboard and cleaned the sword with surgical spirit. The killer then stripped off an outer layer of clothes, which were placed in a polythene bin bag, leaving it gently dissolving with the sword under the stairs where we found it."

"Sir. Why would anyone clean the murder weapon and then leave it and the other stuff behind? Seems pretty stupid to me."

"I kind've agree. Think of all of the potential evidence. You tell me, Smollett?" It was an invitation to add to the briefing. Smollet, who was always ready with a question, also knew it was a chance to make a fool of himself in front of his peers.

"Maybe it was left behind as a statement. I dunno, flipping the bird at us, Sir, letting us know that they were sure they would get away with it. Or they couldn't take it with them. Perhaps it was too risky once the murder had been committed?"

"Or maybe..." suggested Daley, "...they have finished with it now. Those of you with longer memories may remember Rachel Jones? Killed in Wembley, four years ago? As it happens exactly four years ago...to the day. And she was decapitated by a single blow from the same sword. In fact, the M.O. in both cases is absolutely identical. Both women knew each other. They went to University together in the *Nineties*."

The room lapsed into silence, lost in thought as Whetstone attached crime scene photos to the whiteboard with magnetic clips. She threw in a question to fill the void.

"Sir, we're talking about killer in the *singular*. Are we sure that it was one person, and they were working alone?" With two almost identical murders, right down to the number on the forehead, it was a good question. Four years ago to the day, Daley, in his first murder room as a DS, had attended a briefing just like this. After weeks of house-to-house enquiries, local and national television appeals, poster campaigns and countless interviews, every lead became a dead end, every alibi remained watertight. Now today, Daley was here pondering whether it was a killer, or killers, and again there was no categoric evidence to support either. His gut still told him that a single twisted individual had carried out both murders. The psychopathy of a serial killer was complex, but an interval of four years was rare. What could have happened to start him killing again? And how was he connected to Rachel Jones and Dawn Silverton? Whoever carried out this latest murder almost certainly knew both women - how else could the M.O. be so similar? Or maybe the M.O. was the same but the murdered women were completely random?

"OK. So let's look at the wider picture. Two females who knew each other are killed in the same way nearly four years apart. Each victim had a number drawn on their forehead with a marker pen, and I have just been told..." he waved his mobile in the air, "...that there is a high probability that it was the same pen. So what about the two victims? Deb?"

Whetstone grabbed an A4 notepad from the desk, opened it and stood.

"Rachel Jones and Dawn Silverton were roughly the same age. They lived and worked locally. Rachel Jones had recently undergone an abortion and Dawn was in the early stages of pregnancy. Sergeant Monaghan and I have done some digging to try and connect the two people. The two women certainly knew each other and were probably friends. They were at Coventry University together in the late nineties and have apparently kept in touch since as part of a group of friends who called themselves the Monday Club, along with Andrew Carmichael and five others - Marcus Balfour - doctor, Guy Higson - accountant, Finn Byrne and Shelley Nugent - who run the Plough & Harrow on Cordon Street in Ealing, er, Alice Bown - a sales clerk at Johnstones in Brentford. Both Rachel Jones and Dawn Silverton were, or had been at some time, in a relationship with Andrew Carmichael, who is a financial adviser in Ealing. He was ruled out of the Rachel Jones enquiry for various reasons, not least that he claims to have a couple of witnesses who placed him in the Plough & Harrow on Cordon Street at the time. Still being verified, but at the time of Dawn Silverton's death he was in his office seeing clients."

"So", resumed Daley, "these people all knew each other and now two of them have been murdered. Which are quite high odds in anyone's book." He swung a hand towards the list on the whiteboard. "Maybe the killer is in this group, or connected to it?" Out of the corner of his eye Daley noticed Allenby shuffle uncomfortably. "There is nothing at this stage to indicate the involvement of more than one killer, however, like I've already said, we need to keep an open mind."

But this was not what Daley's gut was telling him.

"However, I think we have to at least consider that these crimes may be connected. The victims knew each other; they went to the same University at the same time, and all belonged to this *Monday Club*. And factoring in the number on the forehead we have strong evidence pointing to a single killer, or a close-knit group of killers, who struck once and for whatever reason have struck again. But now he, she - or they - *have* struck again, and if we count Rachel Jones, that's two in a row. We have to assume he's out there looking for victim number three right now."

"If he hasn't already found him or her, Sir." Deb Whetstone was ever the optimist.

"So, are we formally linking this death with Rachel Jones, Inspector?" Allenby's words tumbled like lead turds onto the carpet in front of Daley and room hushed awaiting the response. For three years, the trail of evidence had been colder than an Icelandic fridge and each night the lifeless eyes of Rachel Jones, once so bright and vivacious, returned to him as he shut his. She was the last person to speak to him every night and he hadn't forgotten the promise he had made to her. Whatever it takes, however long, I'll get him. So he disregarded his gut and said what Allenby wanted to hear.

"Sir, Monday was the fourth anniversary of Rachel Jones' death. That has to be significant somehow, but it's not enough. Look, guys, no assumptions. Let's just keep digging shall we? Treat them separately until we can positively link them. DC Taylor, you take video duty. DC Corby has rescued a back-up of the DVR unit from the Church at the top of Chapel Rise. It's a long shot but see what you can find. We had three camcorders ourselves when we arrived, but there may be others. Anyway, let's get to it. The full Pathologists report is due later today and the preliminary examination of the scene is here." He waved a sheaf of papers in the air and deposited them on the front desk.

"Make a date – same time, same place tomorrow unless..." and the whole room lazily joined in a chorus of "...*you have anything interesting to share.*"

Whetstone began to assign tasks around the room. Corby was to co-ordinate interviews of all of the bystanders and neighbours. His detailed mind, along with those of three other constables on the team would help to collate a picture both before and after each of the events. DS Monaghan and DC Taylor, as team geeks, would work the various data sources at their disposal to find a pattern. Monaghan, with his wealth of contacts, was given the task of investigating the University connection and the Monday Club. They had already isolated Facebook and LinkedIn accounts for Dawn Silverton, and were busy looking for connections with the other members of the group. Daley and Whetstone were to concentrate on the murdered woman's life and immediate contacts, starting with Shelley Nugent and Finn Byrne.

As the gaggle dispersed, Allenby rose from his chair and approached Daley.

"Scott, my office for a minute, would you?"

***

Daley let the smoked glass door latch with an ominously final clunk. He could feel the accumulated eyes of his team boring into the back of his head, as D/Supt Allenby groaned himself into his chair.

"I've had Edgar Sampson on the phone this morning. I don't need to tell you we have to tread carefully here, Scott, do I?" It was more a statement than a question, imbued with a significant degree of threat. Clearly he felt he did have to.

"Of course not, Sir."

"Andrew Carmichael."

Daley sighed rather too audibly as Allenby prepared his rake and sized up the four year old ground. "Sir?"

"What you said out there, the suggestion that the Dawn Silverton and Rachel Jones murders are linked. Sounds pretty much like you have your sights on Carmichael again." He paused and fiddled with papers on the desk, before looking Daley directly in the eye. "We need to be sensitive to what happened last time."

Annoyed, Daley reflected on the Rachel Jones investigation, his vague memories of Carmichael. Whilst unsubstantiated, the *gen* was that Carmichael had been the mysterious boyfriend and father to Rachel's aborted baby. At the time of her death, his alibi was suspect, corroborated by friends, but there was no solid evidence to placed him at the crime scene either. For months, Allenby and Daley had pursued Carmichael, seeking chinks in his armour. The press had gotten wind of it and billed it as harassment. Eventually, with no conclusive case for the CPS, the SIO, more mindful of his pension than catching a murderer, had told Allenby to lay off. And Allenby had laid it firmly at young Sergeant Daley's inexperienced door.

"We did everything we could last time, Sir. There was no-one else. He knew both girls at the time of their deaths. Surely, that gives us much better odds this time. You have to admit it's looking more like we let him get away four years ago."

"More like *I* let him get away."

"I didn't say that, Sir. *We* let him get away. We were a team. Look, last time we built a strong case against him...

"...circumstantial case. Didn't impress the CPS. They made that abundantly clear."

"Yes, but now we have another girlfriend, another identical death. They have no choice but to listen this time, surely? We will have his DNA from the scratches on his hand and we can match that to the baby as well as the skin fragments under Dawn Silverton's nails. Maybe we can match it to samples taken off Rachel Jones too."

Allenby scratched his chin, pondering. Then he raised his head and eyed Daley gravely.

"I need you to leave Carmichael alone."

Daley threw his hands in the air. "Sorry?"

"Look, if you can build a convincing case, we'll bring him in. Otherwise, leave him alone. At least for now."

"What, you think the case isn't compelling enough already?"

"Come on, Scott. You remember what happened last time. We thought we had a compelling case then. The guy was practically hanging a noose around his own neck before that whole bloody harassment thing blew up in our faces. Then, somehow he's got the Press on his side and the whole PR machine started moving in his favour."

"With all due respect to Carmichael," Daley pleaded, "we can't let the Press dictate how we handle a case. We were so close last time, I'm sure of it."

"Well, they did. They blamed us for bugging Carmichael to the point of harassment. They blamed us for letting the real killer go while we had our thumbs up our arses chasing him. But at the end of the day, it doesn't matter what the Press think. I have to answer to the Chief Constable and, in case it has escaped your notice, that's the same Chief Constable Summerhill who was the senior officer back then. So unless you have more - a lot more than last time - leave Carmichael alone!"

"Surely, this is different! Surely the Chief Constable can see that?"

Allenby struggled to contain his impatience. "You know as well as I, that as soon as the Press learn we are going to bring Carmichael in, they'll dig up that whole can of worms again. I've already had Summerhill on my back and the woman is hardly cold! Apparently Carmichael's boss Gerald Thornton belongs to the same golf club."

"But Sir, same boyfriend, identical murders, dodgy alibi, pregnancies. Surely that's enough for the Chief Constable to see that Carmichael needs to be pulled in?"

Allenby angrily pushed his chair back from his desk and strode round to the goldfish bowl window. He glared at the team outside as he closed the blind. Daley remained motionless. He enjoyed a good working relationship with Allenby as long as he didn't overstep the line.

A line that he had just ground into the pile of the carpet.

Allenby swung round. His eyes were blazing. He pointed a finger at Daley.

"Now, you look here! It's alright for you to go stamping around with your size-fucking-nines. It's me that has to answer for the mess you cause. Summerhill blames me for not casting the net wider, for pestering Carmichael last time, and he knows, as well as you and I, that if we had laid off Carmichael he would have incriminated himself somehow sooner or later. Instead he shut up shop, like Petticoat Lane on a Bank Holiday Monday, and started bleating about the pressure we put him under. He's no fool. He will just do the same all over again."

"How could that possibly be our fault, Sir? He had a good solicitor, that's all."

"I don't care..." Allenby's bark rattled the blinds. He continued in a subdued rasp, "...I don't care whose fault it was. That lawyer, Sampson, ran rings around us last time, bringing in internal affairs, crying to the papers. I am telling you. Unless there's a witness who saw him there, or fingerprints on the handle of that sword, or he spills his guts voluntarily, leave Carmichael alone! *Is - that - clear?*"

"Crystal, Sir." Daley stared at Allenby for a long moment then looked down at his shoes, tired, scuffed and dull. He knew the feeling. He felt suitably admonished and utterly frustrated. Allenby strode back round his desk and slumped in his chair.

"I need you to bring me some solid evidence. Some solid facts that connect Dawn Silverton to her killer. Something tangible that I can give to Summerhill that can prove my faith in you - *his* faith in you. If that points to Carmichael, then all well and good. Take your own advice, Detective Inspector. Keep an open mind. He might very well be banged to rights, but follow procedure and you'll get him. Otherwise, we'll be off on a wild goose chase like last time and I can't afford another one like that. You'll be back giving directions to tourists and God knows what they'll do with me."

Daley held Allenby's gaze until it became uncomfortable. "Yes, Sir." He stabbed out the words in frustration. The hackles on the back of Daley's neck had risen and he squeezed sweat between his thumb and forefinger. "Like I said, we'll look into Carmichael but I won't get fixated by him. But now he has been linked to two separate cases so I have to do my job and investigate."

Allenby rubbed the tension, which was growing in his neck. "Look, it's early days. We haven't got anything because it's less than 48 hours since the body was found, that's all. It's always a struggle at the start of an investigation. You know that. At least, that's what I am going to tell the press conference in..." he glanced at his wristwatch, "...fifteen minutes time."

The air in the room was charged and suffocating. Allenby

nodded and Daley left the room, letting the door swing shut a little too hard. Allenby sighed deeply and picked up the departmental budget forecasts from the desk, reassembling the pages into order before scanning the first page. This ground he was more comfortable with.

***

Unbeknown to Alice Bown, her world was to change in the blink of an eye. For now, though, she would remain blissfully oblivious, the minutiae of her life utterly and breathtakingly constant. As every other day, the alarm had turfed her out of a dream-filled half-sleep and into a shower which shot spiteful needles at her flesh. She had trudged through a bowl of muesli and, after a familiar age searching for her phone and her keys, had run for a bus that arrived four minutes late. Sales Administration was endemically monotonous; her day had dragged anonymously by, a small mercy these days. So anonymously that she was straining to remember a single notable task. In fact this Wednesday was proving itself to as uneventful as any other Wednesday.

Uneventful except for the phone call.

Alice's phone was a decoration, a distraction to prevent her fingers from idly drumming on the desk. Something to scrutinise aimlessly as she huddled with the other windblown nicotine addicts. For all its features, it could have been a wart on her hand, but she felt mysteriously lost without it. That the phone had rung at all was, in itself, was an event. In the eight months since it's purchase and nearly two hundred and fifty pounds of her unlimited everything contract, the calendar was empty, the contact book barren, her inbox filled only with junk. She shared the trivia of her existence with Merlin, her cat, who himself paid it barely any attention, except where food was the expected outcome. And when the phone did ring, every call was a call she expected to receive.

Until today.

Out of the blue, as the treacherous wall-clock inched towards lunchtime, the phone had buzzed insistently in her hand, sending tiny fibrillations through her bra and left nipple, an enjoyable sensation she had few opportunities to experience, despite folding her arms that way habitually. After six rings, as she peered furtively down, the call dropped and she pushed it out of her mind, dragging herself back to the monotony of the sales huddle around her. But the call irritated like an unpicked scab and she had peered down once more, surreptitiously, as a card player checking the hand close to her chest. But her curiosity piqued when she spied the name 'Carmichael' and the flashing voicemail icon. For the next three minutes, she mused as to why a person she openly despised would be calling her. Perhaps 'despised' was too strong a word for how she felt about Carmichael. Perhaps ambivalent and disinterested pretty well summed it up.

In the Nineties, University had been an escape, and at Coventry she felt free. Striking up an immediate and enduring friendship with the other girls in her wing of Priory Hall - Shelley Nugent, Dawn Silverton and Rachel Jones - they had joked about the smell of disinfectant and cabbage which hung about the corridors, ogled male students and drunk themselves into oblivion when the grant cheques arrived. The four had become part of the small group that hunkered into in the same alcove in Browns. She drank the same drinks, smoked the same weed and woke the next morning with the same sense of awkward guilt that eased by the evening when it would start all over again.

Drew Carmichael was in the year above, and partly through his own arrogance chose himself as leader. The group did not disabuse him of this, leaving him to command and them to go along for the ride. Also leaving him to amass his conquests, hitting on with anything that moved and a few that, by the end of the evening, did not. In two years, he had hit on Alice many times, advances which might have succeeded in sweeping the average bimbo, air-head into his bed, were wasted on Alice and a source of copious amusement between the girls. Admittedly, he was handsome in a gentrified, pompous way, but hers was a very different type of man. Paradoxically, that dubious honour had fallen to Carmichael's wing man, Marcus Balfour. She had met him part way through her first year but it had withered and died in the coldness of the spring.

Since then, they had both become a memory, until by chance two years ago, she had met Marcus and been invited along to the

Plough & Harrow. But even the novelty of meeting her old friends from University again had worn off and the effort of dragging herself back out on a cold dark evening began to take second place to a carry-out and a DVD.

The flame that burned for Marcus had never really died, but could never be rekindled until Marcus renounced his friendship with Carmichael. Not since 1997.

As the sales stand-up adjourned, the craving for a cigarette was biting. The phone was abandoned to the miscellany of her handbag, voicemail unread. Much as Tuesday had, and as she fully expected Thursday to, Wednesday resumed it's role in Alice's life as just another day.

***

When Daley and Whetstone arrived at the Plough & Harrow, they were ushered through to a corner booth in a sparsely filled lounge bar. Shelley Nugent had set out a plate of sandwiches and Finn Byrne had brought over some coffee in readiness for their own lunch. Despite their better judgement both police officers politely refused and told them they should go ahead as they talked.

As Daley dealt with the pleasantries, Deb cast her eyes around the bar, large and empty, subdued after the bustle and noise of Cordon Street. There was an old world charm about the decoration, although it had obviously been recently refurbished, a fact betrayed by the smell of new laid carpet and fresh wood varnish. Somewhere behind one of the mock brickwork pillars, a fruit machine trilled inanely and there was a vague hum of air conditioners under a background of piped music. It was a warm, homely room in which Deb could quite cheerfully have spent the afternoon dozing or reading a book, blissfully unaware of the passing of time. She smiled professionally at the two people opposite her as they smiled back. Shelley Nugent, hands on her lap, seemed to bob as she spoke, one of those irrepressibly genial people that breathed life into a room as they entered, transforming dreary days into the warmth of summer. Her cheery smile beamed from beneath a froth of curls and every word seemed to be a melody. It reminded Deb of Snow White in the Disney animation. Improbably twee and perfect. But although the irises were a deep hazelnut brown, the pupils were

70

empty and cold. It was a darkness that Deb had seen many times in the eyes of her mother, in those of bereaved parents. It told of abject and irrecoverable loss, of the struggle to take one day at a time. It was a look that greeted Deb most mornings when she looked in the mirror.

"We need to ask you a few questions about Dawn Silverton." Daley began "I believe you both knew her?"

"Yes...Inspector?" Daley nodded and Finn continued. "We've known her a long time. It's come as a considerable shock to us both."

Outwardly, Finn Byrne was very different to Shelley. Measured and quiet when he spoke, yet emphatic, every sentence imbued with deep consideration. Like Shelley's, his face beamed a superficial geniality, but the eyes were exacting and studious scanning and assessing. His whole demeanour was protective and, in Deb's view, secretive.

"When did you last see her? I believe she came here often?"

"Well, I wouldn't say often. A group of us get together on a Monday, you know, share a few drinks, have a chat, that sort of thing."

Daley felt this was going to be a long drawn out affair. Byrne was only yielding what he had to, forcing Daley to extrude the words, like the mental strain of willing a stammerer to finish the sentence.

"But not last Monday...the Monday just gone?"

"No. She wasn't here."

"Sometimes she just wants to go home after work." Beyond the pleasantries, it was the first time Shelley Nugent had spoken. Tears were welling once more behind the effervescent facade. Finn reached out and took Shelley's hand, holding it a little too tightly. Controlling her, a steady hand on a tiller.

"So the last time you saw her was the Monday before?"

"Oh, no. I saw her this Monday, around 10:00am." Daley noticed Byrne's eyebrows turn down into a momentary frown before snapping back. Maybe she hadn't mentioned this to him? Cracks appearing so early on. Shelley continued. "It was only a flying visit. She had some papers to deliver locally and parked her car around the back of the pub. She just popped her head around the door, to say 'Hello', let us know it was there."

71

"And did *you* see Ms Silverton, Mr Byrne?" Deb asked, if only to resolve the conflict on his face.

"No, no. At 10:00am I would be in the cellar checking the barrels, cleaning the pipes, same every day. God, that's a shame. If only I'd known. Why didn't you tell me, love?"

Shelley shrugged. "It didn't matter at the time. It was just a normal day."

Deb paused as she made her notes. There were so many small details that didn't matter at the time. Dawn's new pregnancy, a stupid spat with Carmichael, a fleeting 'hello' on a doorstep. So much day-to-day trivia, which might yet prove important. Did that account for the fleeting confusion behind Finn Byrne's concerned expression?

"So what did you and Ms Silverton talk about?" Daley was eager to keep them on message.

"It was just hello, really, five minutes if that." Shelley half smiled. "We spent some time talking about something or nothing. She had had her hair tinted, and I made some remark about how nice her suit looked, you know normal girl-stuff. She always dressed so smartly."

"Did she seem distracted, or worried about anything...her job, home?"

"Well yes, a little. She was having a few problems at work. No-one buying houses. There had also been some trouble with the financial people they dealt with. Which didn't surprise me really, considering."

"Considering?" As the word came from his mouth, Daley noticed Finn Byrne let go of her hand and cross his arms, sighing audibly. He would need to steer that particular course later.

"Well, she puts a lot of work through Barraclough and Leavis, through Andrew Carmichael. He's someone we all know from way back, keep it amongst friends."

"I'd hardly label him as a friend." It was Finn, arms still folded, staring at the table, a barely perceptible flinch as the words had spilled out unchecked. To Daley, it seemed Andrew Carmichael had few allies. With so few people willing to speak well of him, sorting the truth from the bile might prove difficult. Shelley cast Finn an admonishing glance and continued.

"From what she had been saying, Drew had been very good at solving financial problems and moving her sales along, but she was worried about his unorthodox methods. She said she had spoken to him on the QT, but that it had still carried on, so she was going to stop feeding him clients."

"Did she say what these 'unorthodox methods' were?"

"Not really, but it always seemed to be around holding back payments, you know, putting the squeeze on people as deadlines loomed, making them sweat. She said she nearly lost a couple of sales because Barraclough and Leavis held on to funds longer than necessary. Dawn just wanted a quiet life. She just wanted to do her job well and keep her clients happy. But rather than oiling the wheels, making the process smoother, Drew Carmichael always seemed to be in the way, if you ask me. I don't think it was a very good business relationship."

Unorthodox. Not dodgy, not crooked. Unorthodox. In Daley's mind, when used in association with 'financial problems', that meant only one thing - someone was on the take. Maybe it was insignificant. Petty pilfering versus cold-blooded murder. He needed to retain a focus, but it was another strand of the victim's relationship with Carmichael that would need to be drawn into the fabric of the investigation at some point.

"In her diary, there was an appointment with Carmichael at 1:00pm on Monday. Did she mention that?"

"Yes, but only in passing. Something along the lines that she was going to have it out with him once and for all. But I just let it go over my head. Those two have been best of friends and worst of enemies for as long as I can remember. It would have been something or nothing."

It was never something or nothing on the day she was brutally murdered. Daley pictured the two women chatting breezily, remarking on Dawn's new hair and the well cut skirt and jacket she had been wearing and he tried to drive from his head the image of her ponytail matted in blood and the skirt sodden and stuck to the floor. And once more Drew Carmichael had appeared centre stage. Maybe there was something in Deb's sixth sense?

"So do you know what time she came back for her car?" Whetstone took over from Daley, as she could see he was corralling his thoughts.

"Not really. It was still there at twelve-thirty. I saw it from the upstairs kitchen window."

"And it was gone shortly after 2:00pm as I went out with one of the bar staff for a chat while he had a smoke." Finn Byrne was still leaning back, arms folded. The stable door was open and the horse had bolted. No amount of tugging on the harness would bring it back. Now he could only hope to control the path it took.

"Ms Nugent. Did she mention anything about a baby to you?" Whetstone put the question, aware of the impact, a blunt instrument delivered with as much professional compassion as she could muster. Shelley Nugent's expression turned inward as she tried to process the significance of the question.

"You mean Dawn was pregnant?" She turned and looked Finn square in the eyes. Finn, impassive, just shrugged. She turned back to the policewoman her eyes appealing for detail, for context.

"Less than three months apparently. Maybe she hadn't told you yet. We don't think she had told many people."

"My God, that's terrible!"

"Would you have any idea who the father might be?"

"No idea at all, if it wasn't Carmichael himself." Finn spoke, taking Shelley's hand and holding it tight. She looked down into her lap, words stifled before they could appear.

"Tell me a bit more about Andrew Carmichael, about his relationship with Ms Silverton, about their business together. You say you've known them for a long time. How did they get on - really?" Whetstone had aimed the questions at Shelley Nugent, but it was Byrne who again sought to answer.

"Andrew Carmichael is a shit, basically. I don't think there is a better way to put it. He was with the rest of us at University and has been a pain in the arse ever since. You know, he is one of those people who knows how to use you, to manipulate you. Yes, I think *shit* is a good word."

"So you don't get on?" Deb felt she had mastered understatement.

"It's no secret. Not to anyone. It was only ever Dawn who couldn't see it." Byrne was almost spitting out the words. "When we were at Uni, she was all over him like a rash. It was almost obscene. And then something happened and they went their separate ways for a few years. He settled down for a time with someone else. Then there was another fling with Dawn a couple of years ago, which fortunately fizzled out. And then off and on ever since."

"So you never heard her complain of him being violent towards her?"

Shelley looked aghast at the suggestion, as if someone had spit-roasted a poodle in front of her. "Oh, no, no, no! There was never anything like that. They had their ups and downs but nobody can hide something like that!"

Daley wondered if Monday afternoon was a case of history repeating itself. There seemed to be threads that looped back on themselves. Mistakes of the past forming actions of the future. He seized the opportunity to poke the open sore that Byrne had exposed earlier.

"Mr Byrne. You don't get on with Mr Carmichael. Why is that?"

"Like I said he's a shit of the first order." A censored response. Restrained but suitably pithy. Carrying the message but not expanding the meaning behind it. It was like a chapter of a book with the last few pages torn out.

"But you all seem to keep in contact with him. Surely, if he was that bad you would cross the street to avoid him? But still you see him most Mondays, and Dawn Silverton had a relationship with him right up until her death. That seems rather strange, don't you think?"

"Relationship's a bit strong, Inspector. Maybe in the past, yes."

"But even so, Mr Byrne. There were a lot of texts, phone calls and they met up on Monday, shortly before her death. They did seem to be seeing rather a lot of each other. Were you not a little curious?"

Daley let the question hang in the air like a pawl of smoke, letting them inhale it and assimilate it, process the inference. Since leaving Carmichael's office he had sensed there were secrets. And nothing since had changed that view. There were certainly financial improprieties. Maybe Carmichael was in financial difficulties. Maybe he owed money to Dawn? Shelley

Nugent and Finn Byrne were exchanging glances, and each appeared to be willing the other not to speak. Whatever the secret was, he had yet to hear it, and they were closing ranks. After a long moment Daley thought he needed to prompt them.

"In my experience, there are a few reasons why people stay in our life past their sell-by date. Some are just there as noise in our lives. We say *hello* and *goodbye* and pass on the street but they don't really feature; they are just there. Others are our friends, whom we love or are deeply attached to. We can't bear to think of life without them. They enrich our existence. Then there are the spongers, the leeches, the scroungers, the blackmailers, those we owe something to, or who want something from us. The only reason they stay in our lives is because we can't get rid of them. There is an outstanding obligation. Which of these groups would Mr Carmichael fit into?"

The expression on Shelley's face had changed, a barrier drawn up and Daley knew he had hit the nerve again, but once more Finn Byrne was holding her hand, this time more tightly. The curtain of silence draped heavy and there was no more to say on the subject. Daley signalled to Whetstone that it was time to leave and he rose, offering a card and his hand as he did so. Shelley Nugent and Finn Byrne both stood and Byrne reached out to Daley's hand. As he did so, Deb Whetstone provided the Columbo moment.

"Ms Nugent. There is one thing that's bothering me. This girl, the one that Carmichael settled down with for a time. Was that Rachel Jones?"

The colour, what little was left, drained from Shelley Nugent's face and she gave a weak nod.

"What has that got to do with the price of fish?" Byrne snapped defensively. He put his arm around Shelley, who was visibly shaking. "Look, I am sure you know that Rachel, Shelley and Dawn had been good friends for a long time. And now two of them are dead. Murdered. How the hell would you feel if somebody came poking their great size nines in? Have some bloody compassion, will you?" His eyes were wide and the anger burned across his face, but Daley still had the feeling there was another dynamic at play. What it was he was unsure but what he *was* sure of was that Nugent and Byrne were using every trick in the book to keep him from discovering it. He let Whetstone repair the damage.

"I am sorry if we caused any distress, but this is a murder investigation, and we have to explore every avenue, especially as Rachel's murder is still an open case. I hope you understand." *Just doing our job.* The old trite excuse for running a train through someone's life.

Chapter 12

Merrill and Goodman, Chartered Accountants were doing very well. That was obvious to Deb Whetstone as she trotted up the steps of the stately Georgian terraced house that overlooked the Green in Richmond. As her eyes grew accustomed she was, as always, disappointed to find the interior freshly decorated and disingenuously modern, converted to offices. A woman behind the expansive beech and smoked glass desk beamed a plastic smile, only to raise her eyebrows as the warrant card was unfurled.

"Guy Higson, please."

"Take a seat. I'll check he's free." The girl crouched down and peered at the hidden monitor behind the desk, her long straight auburn hair falling across her face and being brushed away countless times. Why was there never a *scrunchie* around when you need one? She raised her head and smiled. "Would you come this way, please?"

The girl led Deb through a set of period double doors, which had survived the post-modernist massacre, and up a flight of stairs to the first floor landing, where she knocked once and entered an office the size of a small country. Behind the desk, a man rose to his feet and reflexively buttoned his jacket before extending a hand across the desk.

"Hi, Guy Higson, and you are?"

"Detective Sergeant Deborah Whetstone, West London Homicide." She held the hand a long moment, resisting the vice-like grip. Guy Higson was a tall athletic man; slim at the waist but with unfeasible wide shoulders. Under a crisp white open-necked shirt, a rounded sculptured chest flashed a tantalising wisp of hair and biceps that filled his sleeves. His face was round and rugged, the eyes warm, engaging and genuine, hemmed in by a close mop of naturally curly brown hair, with grey peppering the surface here and there. Now here was a man that Deb could really find a place for. Strong, successful, really good looking, in a risky sort of way, except he was so obviously gay. Down Girl!

"Homicide! That sounds dark. Please sit down. Coffee?"

Deb did as bade but declined the coffee. She would hate for the girl to spill tell-tale drops up the tidy beige stair carpet. Instead, as the door closed, she got straight down to business.

"We are investigating the murder of Dawn Silverton. I believe she was a friend of yours?"

Higson nodded sombrely. "Yes, Dawn. I can't believe it. Are you sure it was murder?"

"Oh, yes, Sir. Very definitely murder." An interesting first question. Not how did it happen but was it murder. "When did you last see her?"

"That was a week last Monday - the 16th. In the evening. I go around to the Plough & Harrow in Ealing for a drink with some mates and she was there. Mind you, I've spoken to her on the phone a couple of times since."

"So how did she seem when you saw her that Monday evening?"

"She looked a little under the weather. Compensating with make-up. A cold or something, maybe. There was something on her mind, but she wasn't very forthcoming. Drew Carmichael - that's another one of our mutual friends - said she was on his case about something, but that was nothing new. She was always picking a fight with him. Best of friends and worst of enemies. Dawn was quite hard work at times. They both were."

"And you say you phoned her a couple of times since?"

"Well, to be precise, she phoned me. Purely business. Merrill and Goodman look after the accounts of a number of firms around here, not least Parkin-Wright where Dawn worked and Barraclough and Leavis, where Drew works. She was just nagging me about a few loose ends on some house sales, that's all."

"And her relationship with Mr Carmichael generally? You said *best of friends and worst of enemies.*"

"If you ask me, they were an old married couple without the ring and the mortgage. They were always having spats, and then making up. They needed to get a room and sort it out once and for all."

"And lately? Worst of enemies?"

"Perhaps not the worst of enemies, but the detente was uneasy. She sells houses and Drew does the financing. She wants to sell them faster than he can process the money. She's always after him to hurry up, pestering him to move faster, but I am sure you know, there are a number of set stages in a house purchase and the system likes to take it's time. I don't like to speak ill of the dead but I think Dawn was overly optimistic about what Drew could actually achieve."

"So you and Mr Carmichael know each other fairly well, too?"

"Drew, yes. Actually I've known him longer that I've known Dawn. We became friends at University. We see each other two or three times a week on average, you know, socially. He's a great guy."

Here was someone who actually had a good word to say about Carmichael. Maybe he saw Dawn as competition? Deb made a mental note. "Tell me about Mondays, this get-together."

"Oh, that. Yes, most Mondays since the Nineties when we were all friends at Coventry University. A lot of us just happen to live near each other so we sort of continue a tradition. Back then it was more of a club than it is nowadays. These days we just chew the fat and drink."

"And who else is in this group?"

"Well, apart from Drew, myself and Dawn, there's Shelley Nugent and Finn Byrne. Now they really are an old married couple. They own the Plough & Harrow, where we all meet. There's Marcus Balfour. He's a doctor at the general. Then there's Alice Bown, she works at Johnstones in Brent, if I remember correctly."

Whetstone scrawled down the list of names for the second time that day. "Seems a little unusual that so many of you have stayed together after all this time, even moving down to the same area of London."

"I suppose it does. I can't speak for the rest, but for me it was luck that an opportunity opened up here, no more than that. Drew moved here shortly afterwards and he dragged Dawn along with him. As for the rest, I wouldn't like to hazard a guess."

So the congregation of the group in this quarter of Greater London owed more to serendipity than to planning? Deb was doubtful. What was it that bound them all together? Nugent and Byrne had been very uncomplimentary about Carmichael, yet still hosted the Monday Cub. Everyone else to whom they had spoken, either openly despised Drew or, as Higson had put it, found him hard work. Except for Higson himself.

"And Dawn, you said you thought there was something on her mind. Do you know of anyone who might want to harm her, of any trouble she might be in?"

"No, not at all. Everyone loved her." But once more, Deb picked up on an infinitesimally small change in expression, which said otherwise.

"Were you aware she was pregnant?"

"What, Dawn? No!" Higson's eyes cast about the room, as if searching for an errant sperm donor. "Wow. That puts a whole new light on things. Maybe that's why she looked off colour when I last saw her. Mind you, wouldn't surprise me. Couldn't keep it in her knickers."

"Could Mr Carmichael be the father?"

"Drew? Oh, no, definitely not! Well, not intentionally. Drew is a little too self-consumed to have room in his life for a baby. As for the rest of us, I am certainly off that list. Lovely girl, but most definitely not my type."

Deb smiled sympathetically, but not without a hint of regret. What a waste! "Might he and Dawn have slipped up, or perhaps she had gotten pregnant to force him into some kind of commitment?"

"I really wouldn't put it past her but, no, Sergeant. Drew is a very careful man. He would not allow something like that to happen."

"So you have no idea who the father might be?"

Higson shrugged noncommittally and shook his head. "Unless, as you say, she had intentionally gotten herself pregnant to move things along a little. Dawn could be a little manipulative at times."

Deb gathered her things and rose to leave, offering a card and an eternally open door should anything else spring to mind but she knew nothing would. It felt obvious to her that

Carmichael was far closer to Higson than Dawn Silverton. Perhaps Higson had seen Dawn Silverton as a threat? Clearly Carmichael and he were never going to be an item, but maybe Higson had always resented Dawn's appearance in Carmichael's life. Perhaps, he had known of the pregnancy and taken drastic steps to remove her from it?

For that matter had Rachel also been a threat? Had he taken similar drastic steps before? With a single shake of a limp hand, she once more looked at Higson's frame. Powerful and honed. He could certainly wield a sword but had he?

Throughout the whole of the time she had been there, she could almost hear the cogs meshing and a story being roughly machined out of nothing, or maybe being crafted to mask the real story. There was a superficiality to everything Higson had told her, a superficiality also apparent when they had interviewed Carmichael earlier.

Roughly machined but a story nevertheless.

***

The journey back from Nottingham coincided with the agonising rush hour crawl, but Daley's driver deftly negotiated the heaving streets and he made the standard class seat that had been reserved for him with time to spare. The two hour journey passed with him lost in his own thoughts.

Aspley was a smart suburb to the east of Nottingham and the sun had been blazing down on the airy, neat cul-de-sac in which Doreen and John Silverton had spent the morning and most of the previous day weeping. There were around thirty houses in the winding close, all identically built forming an honour guard for the unmarked police car and shepherding it dutifully to the house at the end. The front door was opened by a stunningly attractive *Family Liaison Officer*, rendered plain by the stricture of the uniform, but who's sympathetic smile somehow helped to make the duty he was about to perform slightly easier to bear.

Inside, the house had smelt of beeswax and lemon, overly sweet and cloying, obsessively cleaned by Doreen Silverton, taking her mind off the enormity of the catastrophe that had befallen her. Daley was ushered through to the living room, awash with photos and reminders of their only child. They sat, each self-contained, hands in laps, both staring through the expansive bay window, the sun etching shadows on their faces. Mrs Silverton was clutching something - a memento, a small toy but Daley could not make it out. The room screamed silently a deep unremitting and unfathomable misery that only a bereaved parent could hear.

In a practiced yet hollow speech, he had apologised for disturbing them at this time, expressed his sorrow for their loss and apologised once more for having to bother them now but there were a few questions that he had to ask. It was John Silverton who had answered him. Matter-of-fact and business-like, the face he reserved for the office, the daily disguise. Daley asked all of the standard questions - *When did you last see Dawn? How did she seem? Can you think of any reason...? Do you know of anyone...?* But he knew the answers lay in London. He knew that her life here had ended when she had left for *The Smoke*. He pointed to the photographs staring from the mantelpiece, asked permission and the father nodded. Save for a single picture of their wedding day, standing proud, unaware of the heartbreak almost forty years later, every picture was of Dawn; the baby cradled, the awkward teenager and smiling graduate. He had sat as John Silverton had reminisced about a holiday in Jersey, evenings waiting in the car outside a guide camp, or a disco, or a million and one other chores that a dutiful father does not realise he will one day miss. He proffered his card and he clasped the outstretched hand. He had promised that if there was anything he could do, they only had to ask. John Silverton had answered simply and forceful *'You just catch the bastard so he doesn't do this to anyone else'.*

He had bid them an awkward goodbye, but it felt like a desertion, hoping he hadn't betrayed his relief as he left.

Speeding back toward St. Pancras, a setting sun had burned his eyes as he watched the rhythmic wave of wires bouncing from pole to pole, lost in thoughts that other passengers, scanning papers, tapping at computers, could not even imagine. The horrors that lurked in the catacombs of his soul, now compounded by the expectations of a bereaved father and his devastated wife.

As the immense grey-brown sidings heralded the approach to St. Pancras, Daley stuffed his notepad into his battered satchel. There were too many co-incidences between this murder and that of Rachel Jones - the neat beheading, their jobs, the grotesque marking on their foreheads, the untouchable Andrew Carmichael. Even the crime scene was similar. Someone had done their research. But more, that a group of friends from university nearly fifteen years ago, should still be such close friends, bound by something more than friendship, something he had yet to discover.

The appearance of the sword. That was different. Maybe they can find Rachel Jones on it, even after four years. So the most likely scenario was a single killer who took a four year sabbatical. Although not the only scenario. Perhaps the details of the Jones murder had slipped out and some whack-job decided to masquerade as the original killer? Or a team or two disparate people. If it was a serial killer, murder number three may come quickly as the compulsion takes hold. If this were one person, it would be someone connected to both Rachel and Dawn. If that connection can be found, the rest will follow.

Maybe that person was Carmichael? However that was dangerous ground after the pummelling from Allenby. Of course, there was an off-chance the Super was right, God forbid! This time, he would be more circumspect, make it count.

That morning, as the car had made its way along the Westway, the traffic had afforded him an easy passage. It seemed like a lifetime ago, and now, drawing back into St. Pancras, Daley was no nearer to assembling the jumble of facts into any cohesive form. In his mind, Carmichael was still the favourite. There was something deeply disquieting about him. Something that begged Daley to look more closely at this self-centred, pumped-up prick.

***

With the number of customers in the Lounge dwindling, the Plough & Harrow endured the graveyard shift before the onslaught of the evening. Finn cast his eyes about the cosy bar. The air was sterile, esters of expensive perfume and the flat undercurrent of dust from the upholstery, occasional wafted smells of cooking from the kitchens behind the bar. Of all the changes the licensed trade had seen, the smoking ban had had the most impact. Not so long ago the room would have been thronging with afternoon drinkers, thick with smoke, and the motes of dust that darted like angry fireflies would have struggled through the clouds of grey. It was the smell of a pub. The air would pall with a heady air of alehouse and tobacco smoke that had all but disappeared. Finn was old-school and missed it. Looking at the newly laid patterned carpet and the comfy seats, this room could have been a retirement home with a bar and a fruit machine.

The booth that the Monday Club usually sequestered was towards the back of the room and rarely used due to its distance from the bar, unless the Plough was particularly busy. A trellis screen and some faux shrubbery afforded a degree of privacy. Seeing the empty seats, he thought of Dawn, of Shelley and he busied himself behind the bar rather than succumb to the building anger. He caught his breath as he counted how many would be there, and the sum came up short.

This was the evening when it would be all sorted out.

When he had returned Carmichael's call, Shelley was already in the throes of an uncontrollable episode of melodramatic grief. Finn figured this had more to do with her feelings of abandonment, now that Dawn had joined Rachel in the great beyond, than it did Dawn's actual death. Shelley was an accomplished drama queen; letting moments like this feed her anxieties until they burst. When Carmichael had demanded an audience, Finn had half a mind to tell him to fuck off, but then he reflected that Dawn's death, the heightened state that everyone was in, might just be his opportunity to shake things up a little. Maybe even to teach the prick a lesson. Perhaps tonight he would tease out a few secrets, find out for certain what skeletons were in his closet. He decided he could safely entrust the remainder of the day to his staff and concentrate on making sure Carmichael got his comeuppance.

But first there was Shelley.

Just behind the bar, a staircase snaked around a dogleg, transforming itself halfway into the living accommodation above the restaurant. Finn raised his eyes towards the first landing, sighing deeply, remembering an evening four years ago. Why was this first step such a problem?

The previous Monday night, perhaps the last for the eponymous club, was a blur, as more nights tended to be lately. The whisky had started its inevitable trail of devastation through his mind, so only snatches would come back.

They had congregated as usual in that same booth, same seats, but that Monday night the Plough had been busy, so Finn had watched the group from the bar. Marcus and Alice were maintaining their oh-so-polite conversation with prolonged bouts of radio silence - nothing new there. With Dawn away, Shelley hadn't really engaged with the others, spending most of the evening in the restaurant. So Carmichael and Higson were left to amuse themselves. Usually, Higson was an attentive and gracious listener, which was just as well as Carmichael was a good talker. But on that previous Monday, Carmichael seemed pre-occupied so Higson had been doing the talking, low and conspiratorial, and Carmichael seemed to be the begrudging and less than gracious listener. Only in hindsight did it seem strange and incongruous. So whilst attendance was sparse, there had been no inkling then that last Monday could potentially be their final gathering, that within eighteen hours the space between them all would widen still further.

Reaching the top of the stair, it was dark beyond the effervescent prickling of Finn's eyes. He could just define her silhouette in the bay window overlooking Cordon Street, the glistening silvery trails down her cheeks lit by passing headlights. He knew that once more the depression had taken hold; the bigamous black dog that had cuckolded him since that day in Coventry when she had hammered on his door. Then, as now, she had stared out of a window, transfixed by the lights of the passing traffic, a superficial distraction to mask the turmoil that was consuming her. Over the years, he had learned that was how she coped. Then as now, he lost himself to drink. And with every passing year, every descent into uncontrolled despair, she was drifting a little further away, and he was ashamed that he cared a little less about getting her back.

Then as now, Shelley's troubles began and ended with Drew Carmichael. For fifteen years, Shelley had protected him telling no-one, not even he, Finn, what had happened on that night. And when Rachel had been killed she had held her tongue, Surely Dawn's killing would be one death too many, enough for her to break her silence?

***

Reversing the Mercedes out of its parking space, Carmichael slapped the steering wheel with the flat of his hand, the horn protesting at the unwarranted violence. All around him loose ends flapped like bunting at a church fete and he struggled to figure out how to tie them all down. The rest of the Monday Club were a waste of time too. Not a single one had answered their phone. Yet more messages for the police to unscramble.

With the exception of Finn. Out of the blue, the *Mick* had returned his call, demanding that they meet in the Plough & Harrow that evening. He was ranting about Shelley's depression, about co-incidences, about Carmichael's unwarranted intrusion into all of their lives. At first Carmichael had wanted to suggest he go do one, but Shelley was a cannon so loose she could easily flip and blow him out of the water. However, the Irishman was dog with a bone. Give him his due. He had stuck by that neurotic bag of nerves through thick and thin so he was unlikely to let go now. He would need to be managed carefully, and through him Shelley kept quiet, especially if 1997 was exhumed after all this time. Carmichael had convinced Shelley to keep her mouth shut, and Finn was just flying a kite. He knew nothing. She and Finn would need to tow the line now, if they expected a return on their investment into Carmichael's financial scheme. Blackmail was a tawdry word for it, but if he went down, so would they both, and with them the fruits of ten years labour.

When Finn's ranting had finally run out of steam, Carmichael had immediately phoned Balfour and demanded he attend the Plough too. He kept quiet about Finn Byrne. He would keep the two away from each other; if possible feed them different lines. Divide and rule.

However, the most important task was to garner support from Guy Higson. He had been particularly elusive earlier and Carmichael had filled his phone with voicemails, as yet to no avail. Desperate times called for desperate measures, so he set the *sat nav* for Richmond, pressed the button on the steering wheel and demanded that the Bluetooth call Higson again.

***

Meanwhile, around 6 miles away, Sergeant Dave Monaghan rubbed damp sweat from the side of his neck as he cradled the phone. He was in no doubt that three hours of phone chasing had been worthwhile. Tearing the sheet from his A4 pad, he set it geometrically parallel to the pad. Symmetry mattered. It would organise the scrambled notes into a cogent sequence that he could present to Daley. His email pinged and he briefly glanced up. Another piece of a complex puzzle falling into place.

The University connection had made his collator's itch flare up. Recalling his days at Aston University, fresh across the Irish Sea, and basic training in Hendon, he could scarcely remember a single face or name, except for Ed Harrison, who by fluke, had ended up at Lambourne Road too. Even then, Monaghan and Harrison had little to do with each other. So how come so many of Carmichael's contemporaries had migrated to dwell within a five mile radius of each other?

Hunting in his desk drawer, he retrieved the business card for Billy Davies, a Collator for West Mercia in Coventry, whom he had met months before at a conference. Like Monaghan, Davies was old school, from before search engines and databases. It took a special skill, an innate talent, which Monaghan had in spades. He had emailed Davies the scant details of the Monday Club and followed up with a call, which the duty officer had promised to pass on. All he could do was wait. Monaghan was an old hand. Sharing Daley's view that solving a crime was a long, rocky road. DI's come and go; some in a blaze of glory, some in a shower of shite. Daley, at four years, seven months and three days, was by far the most enduring.

Not that he was counting.

And being a Sergeant, he was fairly immune from the sort of bollocking that the DI had received from the D/Supt earlier. Burying himself in facts, he could only work as fast as the computers he was using or the evidence coming in. Not for him the perils of deduction, simply a cold, hard chain which led from A to Z and all points between. He rarely saw the subjects of his work, they were just names on a pad. All he did was piece together the evidence into a cogent, tangible, believable structure. The DI could then deduce all he liked.

Right now, the evidence was flooding in. Starting from a hypothesis - to be proved right or wrong. His premise was that Andrew Carmichael was nowhere near Dawn Silverton when she died, giving Carmichael the benefit of the doubt, but that was a coin flip. If he disproved the hypothesis, Carmichael would still be there to explain anyway. Now, he just needed one piece of information to do that.

But then there had been the CCTV. Taylor had spent much of the previous evening and most of the morning yawning as the humdrum of Ealing passed by, a greyscale checkerboard of jumpy images from the cameras on the Broadway. They had both huddled over a monitor and watched Dawn Silverton enter the Costa coffee shop, leaving twenty minutes later, closely followed by a man. Taylor had flicked to another camera and watched them both walk through the alley to the side of Costa's. He noted the index of the tape as the two had merged into a single, indistinct blob and then as they separated, angry arms flailing at each other. Then they watched the man, Carmichael, head back down the alley, where Dawn Silverton had exited two minutes previous.

The camera on the church was not so fortuitously positioned, concentrating on the lych-gate and the path leading to the main entrance. However, the top corner of the shot had picked up the rear of Dawn Silverton's blue Mini as it arrived and her legs as she strode towards Chapel Rise. The time tallied with the time of her appointment. Then they watched as, five minutes after she had gone, another car pulled up alongside and a man left the car to follow her. They had stilled the frame and played with the resolution but the recording was indistinct. They could only see the rear quarter of the car and a set of legs belonging to a tall man, but Monaghan was sure he had seen those legs before.

He opened his desk drawer and drew out a packet of mint humbugs. He checked the best before date to ascertain that they were OK to eat. There weren't many days when all of the pieces fitted, when all of the strands start to knit so closely, so he rarely had the opportunity to kick back and enjoy the sweets in full knowledge that he had done a good job - good enough to satisfy himself, that is.

Scooping up his printouts, he scanned his organised list of notes. With a nod of satisfaction, which only he saw, he gathered them into a neat pile and found DI Daley's number on his mobile.

"Gov, Andrew Carmichael's alibi for the time of the murder is shot to pieces."

Chapter 13

There was a biting breeze scything over Richmond Bridge and Guy Higson pulled his jacket about himself. Gazing at the launches and open boats messing about on the water, he stamped his feet as much in discomfort at the chill as disgust at being made to wait on Carmichael...again. As usual, his friend would have a plausible excuse for using up his lunch hour on some fools errand.

The seven voicemails were the only reason he had paid any heed at all and the girl in the office to pop out for an *Observer*. Perhaps the only reason Dawn's smiling face had made him catch his breath. But the visit from the Police had changed all that. So he had reluctantly persuaded Drew to pick him up, to drag him to a place of neutrality and explain the urgency.

He turned as the Mercedes E-class drew up to the pavement. Smartly, he dived into the comparative shelter and was whisked away to the complacent bongs of the seatbelt alarm.

"So did you actually read the paper, Guy?"

Higson rolled his eyes. Typical Drew. Straight down to business. No small talk.

"It was on BBC London this morning. I caught the 8:30 news over breakfast but the name didn't click. It was a real shock when I saw the paper."

"Yes, it was a shock for me too, but at least the police haven't been crawling all over you."

"That's what you think. A sergeant, this morning."

"Probably the same one that saw me. Woman. Dark hair. Face like a depressed baboon." Drew turned the car off the road, into the small car park fronting the Athletics Ground. Killing the engine, he turned and faced Guy for the first time. "Look, this spells trouble with a capital 'T'. We have to make sure we have our ducks in a row."

Higson kept his eyes to the front, aimlessly watching a motley selection of footballers cavorting to and fro on the pitch. "*Ducks in a row?* Drew, this isn't some kind of business meeting. Speak

English for God's sake...and what's all this *'make sure we have taken care of business'* malarkey?" A pregnant pause descended. Guy turned his head towards Drew, whose eyes, wide and incredulous, stared back.

"Jesus, Higson. Must I spell it out for you? Murder? The police? Our financial scam for Christ sakes!"

"What? Your ex-lover off-and-on for fifteen odd years is murdered and all you're worried about is some dodgy deal? God, you're one sick bastard, Drew Carmichael!"

"You didn't have to endure a grilling by some hairy-arsed copper before your coffee this morning. If you had, you'd know exactly what I am talking about!"

"Hairy-arsed. Sounds right up my street, Drew. Tell me more."

"This is no time for some shirt-lifting, fudge-packer fantasy, Guy. Concentrate on the business in hand. This is serious!"

Guy distractedly returned his eyes to the football match, to the men in dirty shorts and the toned pumping legs. "Get to the point, Drew. I have a client at 3:00 and I can't tiptoe around your sensibilities."

"The accounts, Guy. What happens if they find out about the accounts?"

"Must we go through this again? Three times today already! Me and that secretary of yours, Carol. We spent a lot of time together protecting your cute tush in that department. That bloody woman stirred up enough trouble when she was alive and now she's doing it again even from the grave!"

"But they knew something. I'm sure of it."

"Look, Dawn's dead. Good Riddance! Surely that's enough right now? Do you really think that a day after they found her, the police have dissected her life to such a degree, that they know about one of her friends who happens to be embezzling clients' money? I should think they have enough to worry about, just figuring out who killed her."

"How should I know how much they have figured out?"

"Enough, Drew! Just...shut up for a minute!"

Lately, Drew had become too much of a problem for Guy. At Uni, they were almost inseparable, each acting as the others wingman. But that was a lifetime ago, and since, they had drifted into a casual friendship, parallel lives linked only by the odd get-together, five minute catch-up calls, and the occasional business arrangement.

And then Drew had asked for his help.

Specifically, he required Guy's financial expertise to start the Fund, to organise the mechanism, keep it hidden. Initially, Guy had refused point blank. A blossoming career, the chance of a partnership, there was too much to jeopardise for a shady get-rich-quick scheme. But, finally, he had relented. Whether it was the incessant pressure from Carmichael or whether Guy had always been a sucker for a sob story from a good-looker like Andrew Carmichael, he wasn't sure. So he had set up a series of accounts, which automatically moved money around, gaining a little interest on the way. Periodically, the accrued interest transferred into the main Fund account. Because the Fund largely looked after itself, quietly, anonymously, Guy had all but forgotten it. Until Dawn Silverton had entered Carmichael's orbit once more.

No sooner had the two met than Drew had touted the idea to Dawn. Whilst the extra investment was useful to increase the balance, it also drew another partner into the close circle that knew about it, another flapping mouth that could get them all arrested. Guy had advised Drew to exercise caution and, with typical Carmichael self-assured arrogance, Drew had ignored him and their friendship had started to fray at the edges. The calls became more frequent as that bitch got her claws into him, and Drew's whining and mewling about his troubled relationship started to grate. Then providentially Dawn and Drew had split up...again. In fact they had been separate for nearly two years when, out of the blue, Drew had called Guy in a blind funk jabbering about audits, and fraud, and that Guy had to help him, that they would all go down together. So, once more, against his better judgement, Guy masked the accounting anomalies and covered the pert rounded rear of his friend, whether to keep him out of jail, or from some misguided loyalty, or just as a hostage to his feelings for Drew, he wasn't sure. From firm friends at Uni, they had rode the roller-coaster until now, Guy despised Drew for the tightrope he had been forced walk and for the shameful way that he had allowed himself to be used.

Higson took a deep breath. "Did the police actually mention the money at all?"

"Well, no, but surely that's just a matter of time. Surely they..."

Higson raised his hand, stopping Carmichael mid flow. There was no time for histrionics. For the police to latch onto Carmichael so quickly, there had to be something that had piqued their interest. "Concentrate, Drew. Just for a minute. Shut up and think carefully! What exactly did they ask you about?"

Carmichael braced both hands against the steering wheel and pushed himself back into the leather, collecting his thoughts. "They wanted to know where I was when they think Dawn was killed. Around 2:30pm on Monday afternoon."

"Naturally. What else? What specifically were they interested in?"

"They had her diary. That woman had kept a record of every phone call, every time we met. They knew she had seen Thornton. They knew that I saw her, Guy. Dawn and I met up before she died. So we had a row, but how should I know that she was going to be topped?"

Guy turned and peered at Drew. The two had met on the day she died. "So she had her diary on her and your name featured heavily. Are you surprised? Doesn't mean they know about your sordid financial affairs, does it? What else did they talk about?"

"They asked about the Monday Club, who you all were and who was actually there on Monday evening. Then they started asking about Rachel Jones, bringing all of that back up again. They knew about Rachel and me. They knew I was shagging Rachel and now they know about me and Dawn."

Rachel Jones? That was a different angle. The sergeant hadn't mentioned Rachel Jones earlier.

"What, and they think you had something to do with their deaths?"

"They didn't actually say that, but they certainly implied it. They say Dawn was killed exactly four years after Dawn - *exactly* four years."

Higson pondered for a moment. The police could not be interested in the money. Not yet, although if they got to hear about it, there would be a mighty powerful motive for murder. But they were interested in the tangled, messy relationship in which Dawn and Drew had been embroiled, not to mention his *carryings-on* with Rachel.

There had been a similar melt-down when Rachel had been found dead, similar theatrics all geared around putting Drew's self-preservation ahead of his friends. There had been no real concern for Rachel, as there was none now for Dawn. Maybe for the police, the money was secondary, a line of enquiry yet to be pursued? Maybe it was Carmichael's closeness to each of the girls that was the police's main focus? Maybe it was that relationship that lay at the root of both of their deaths?

Suddenly, memories of that night in 1997 came back and Guy caught his breath, making the connections back to Coventry. "Drew, do you think this is about what happened in Coventry back in 1997? That night up by the Theatre One?"

It was Carmichael's turn to catch his breath. Brow furrowed, inquiring, he turned to Guy. The colour ran from his face. "How do you know? I didn't think you knew about that."

"Look, I know, that's all. Do you think it's about that?"

"How can it be? It was fifteen years ago. Why would they be interested now? Fucking Hell. It was all going along so well. First that bloody audit and now Dawn. What next?"

It was a valid question but only one of many. When Rachel had been killed Guy had had no reason to suspect that it was anything more than misfortune, not making the connection. The wrong place at the wrong time. But now Dawn's death made him think again. Perhaps it did trace back to that night? They had both witnessed what had happened. They both had the capacity to destroy Drew, and had tried. He looked across at Drew, ashen and drawn. If this were history leaching through to the present, a case of Drew clearing up his mess, why would he risk everything to silence the girls? What would be the motive?

Surely that was obvious. A case of a woman scorned. When they had broken up, Rachel probably held that night like a knife at Drew's throat, threatening to tell all. Maybe that's why she had to go? And Dawn? The situation was identical. Surely the solution was the same?

Then Guy thought about the sergeant's visit, the revelation

that Dawn had been pregnant. Drew *had* to be the father, whether willingly or not. Surely he would have mentioned it, if he knew? Guy resolved to keep that particular card close to his chest.

But how many more would Drew need to silence?

The air in the car became asphyxiating. Guy flicked the door switch but the window didn't drop. The ignition was off. Drew was staring fixedly out of the windscreen, processing a million private thoughts. Guy opened the door and turned to sit half out of the aperture, letting the fresh breeze wash across his face. If this was about Coventry, he had to buy some time. Time to warn the others and make sure he wasn't the next to be silenced. Recomposed, he turned back into the car and closed the door with a solid, final clunk.

"You want me to explain what happens next? I'll tell you. Finn, maybe Alice or Marcus or Shelley, or even me, we get pulled in by the police and we let slip about your Fund. Maybe not intentionally, but the police have a way of making people reveal secrets. Next the police get their financial forensics people crawling like ants over the accounts of both mine and your employers, and some time later you end up in an open prison, probably in the next bloody cell to me. That's what happens next. Look, Drew. This has gone on too long as it is. Whenever there's a problem, you are always at the heart. It'll just take one well aimed question by the coppers and everything will come pouring out."

Drew felt backed into a corner. However he looked at it he knew there would be little chance of keeping the scam under wraps. Guy continued:

"Look. The Fund exists. Nothing can be done about that right now. You have to stop, decease, and desist. Leave the accounts dormant. No more investments. No more activity whatsoever. If you even think about it, have a cold shower. Just forget it exists until this stuff blows over. You understand? Listen to me this time!"

Drew nodded absently. He wasn't listening.

"When I get back later, I will clean up at my end and hide the intermediate accounts. You need to wipe any references to the accounts from your computers - all of them, home and office. Better still, go for a walk and lose your laptop in the canal then buy an old one off eBay. As long as the Police don't get wind, that should be all we need to do. Then, when the heat dies down, you can find someone else to do your dirty work, 'cos I'm out."

"But the Police? Surely they will suspect something? The audit? Dawn?"

"They will suspect nothing as long as they don't get a whiff of this. Even now, the accounts are tighter than a choirboy's sphincter. They are investigating Dawn's murder, nothing else. They won't even look at the books unless they think there's a connection."

Drew slumped forward, resting his head against the steering wheel, breathing heavily. Guy was not sure he had taken the message on-board and he needed to hammer it home, for both their sakes.

"Look, these people are your friends, Drew, but there are friends and there are *friends*. You put them in a tight spot and they'll turn on you before you can say *Parkhurst*. Just look at what Dawn has done."

"And Coventry? What are we going to do about that? What if the police find out?"

Guy knew what he was going to do. Self-preservation. He needed to look out for himself and the others that would be on Drew's list. He lied.

"Like you say, it was fifteen years ago. Another time. I only know what Alice told me that night. No-one has spoken about it for fifteen years. Why would they dig it up again now?"

"Alice? What has this got to do with Alice?"

"She was there, Drew. She saw what you did. You had already left when I came along, but Alice saw it all. It was she that told me. She has kept this secret for you for fifteen years."

Carmichael's brow furrowed. A mental card index rattled through his memories of that night frame by frame. "I don't remember seeing Alice. How could she...?"

"Look, that really isn't the most important thing right now. If you want to keep yourself out of trouble do what I say. This is your mess and you're going to have to sort it. I'll cover your tracks as best I can but as far as the others, that's down to you. Have no doubt here, Drew, you have betrayed our friendship and if it wasn't for the fact that I love you more than you will ever love me, I would have been round to the Police already, pleading to save my career."

Drew turned and faced Guy. His eyes were weary, but they burned with rage.

"You're wrong Guy. It was your own greed that got you into this. You can't simply shift the responsibility onto me. I might have led you to the trough but it was you that stuck your snout in and, let's face it, it's me that's taken all the real risks. And now you expect me just to stop? Those people have sat on their lazy, fat arses while I've worked the system. Jesus, Guy!"

Guy was tired. Tired from the day and tired of the Monday Club. And now he was tired of Drew.

"Take it or leave it. If you carry on, you've got, at best, forty-eight hours before the police start looking into the accounts. I am not going to take a bullet for you, Drew. I start planning my exit strategy right now. And if they ask me anything about 1997, I tell them exactly what I know. Exactly. And you have to deal with the consequences."

"Too fucking right about keeping my enemies close. You're as much a bastard as the rest of them. After all we have been through together. You're the one person I thought I could rely on for help. Well, I am not the only one who will have to deal with consequences, you can be sure of that. Now fuck off out of my car!"

"Only too bloody pleased, you bastard!"

Guy Higson flicked the door handle and launched himself into the daylight as tears welled in his eyes. Behind him he heard the Mercedes roar and a spattering of gravel as it was gunned out onto the Twickenham Road.

***

The half mile walk back to the office took only fifteen minutes but all the time, Guy Higson maintained his stoicism. He wasn't going to back down now. Passing through the painted Georgian entrance doors and into the foyer, he forced a smile at Vicky behind reception and asked she hold his calls for the next hour. Removing a memory stick from his keyring, he inserted it into a slot on his desktop PC and switched it on. Less than thirty seconds later a program from the memory stick had set about its task of wiping the hard drive and overwriting every memory location on it with the character zero.

As he watched the progress counter consuming ever more data, he mused over Rachel's death four years ago and was consumed by a wave of nausea. Was he really only covering his tracks or was he just being foolish? It was one thing hiding evidence from the Met's Digital Forensic Team. It was quite another hiding a double murderer. Alice had said that Dawn and Rachel had been egging Drew on that night, that Shelley had hung back. Now Dawn and Rachel were both dead. What of Shelley?

Drew and Rachel we're seeing each other before she died. That was an open secret, but one they had all sworn to keep from the police. Also Rachel had fallen pregnant. With Drew having coerced her into having an abortion, maybe she brought up that night in Coventry? Maybe she *had* held a knife to Drew's throat? Maybe he silenced her rather than live under a sword of Damocles?

And Dawn? The parallels were now even more stark, so obvious that if Rachel had tried to blackmail Drew, then why not Dawn? Surely the two friends had spoken about him before Rachel's death? Given the chaos brought by the audit, Dawn's baby, maybe she had pulled a similar stunt? Maybe she had met with a similar fate?

But now the secret buried for so long had become disinterred and was polluting all their lives, insidiously spreading a cancer through the Monday Club. Would Drew now be set on removing everyone else that knew of that night? Had Guy done enough to divert Drew from the Monday Club and back to protecting the money? Surely, no-one could be so callous as to put a few thousand pounds above his oldest friends.

As the progress bar grew ever larger, Guy fished around in his wallet for a dog-eared card from a local taxi firm. Written on the back were a series of seemingly random telephone numbers. Opening the large drawer below his desk, he drew out an old laptop, switched it on and accessed the website of the Cayman's account. Carefully typing in the numbers on the back of the card, he watched an hourglass spin. Stifling a gasp, he stared at the amount that appeared on the screen - it was a staggering amount, even when converted to Sterling. A chill of understanding ran down his spine. What happened in Coventry all those years ago and what was happening to the Monday Club today were part of a continuum. An indivisible chain of events in Drew's mind, all geared around one aim, keeping Drew Carmichael safe. It was not important whether that meant the money or Drew himself, there was no distinction. For Drew the only success was a total one.

But what of the others? They had to know what he was thinking. They had to know the lengths to which Drew was going to protect his secrets. He cast his mind back to that rain soaked street on a distant Wednesday. Surely if Rachel and Dawn had been dealt with, Shelley would be next on the list?

Then there was Chris Betts. He was there that night. No-one had seen him since. Maybe he was the first? Maybe that's why Drew felt compelled to act against Rachel and Dawn? Maybe the blackmail was more than financial?

Quickly Guy held the power button until the laptop expired with a whine. With a small screwdriver, he released the panel on the underside of the laptop and removed the hard drive. The incriminating object would be consigned to a watery grave later that evening. Then he phoned the number on the side of his desktop PC and reported a fault with the machine. It won't boot. It just won't switch on at all! No, I don't know what happened.

And Alice? Carmichael seemed genuinely unaware that Alice had seen everything, and would still be blissfully unaware had Guy not mentioned her an hour ago. Guy Higson's face fell into his hands with the enormity of realisation dawning upon him.

He had just added Alice's name to Carmichael's murder list.

Chapter 14

After a portion of Mediterranean fish heated to magma by the microwave, and a half hour quiz show to which she rarely contributed a single answer, Alice curled her legs below her dressing gown and settled down to the self-contained loneliness of evening's television and dozing on the sofa. Wednesday had continued it's part as just another Wednesday until seven minutes and thirty five seconds into BBC London's Evening News.

The report of Dawn's death had been factual and sparse. Female estate agent found brutally murdered in a house in Chapel Rise, Hanwell, identified as Dawn Silverton, 34, from Ealing... Police are appealing for witnesses... The slight woman delivering the message, her olive face overly made-up, wore a look of professional concern, her brow furrowed in formal outrage, before moving seamlessly to a piece about cuts in council funding for the elderly. Alice, staring aimlessly at a point half way between the TV and herself, started at the name. The connections began to form in her brain, and the whole sordid panorama of the City burst through the face of the news presenter and invaded her personal space. Suddenly alert, Alice had struggled to recall the details, just another murder in a sprawling city, yet shocked that this was someone she knew.

Then it occurred to her. The voicemail. A treacherous, tiny red number on her phone. She detested herself for ignoring it that morning.

Even in the mind-numbing ennui that characterised Alice's life, there was rarely a day when Andrew Carmichael did not feature. She had left him in no doubt in his final semester, that he was a boorish, bullying womaniser who, even if the world were ravaged by a killer bug and she and he were the only ones with immunity, there would be not the remotest chance of her bearing his offspring. Or as she had said to him, if he were the last bloke on earth, she'd rather shag a gorilla.

So why had he been so desperate to reach her today?

Turning up the volume so that she could hear from the

kitchen, she flounced around, annoyed, in search of her handbag. Muttering to herself, she upturned it onto the counter, spilling the flotsam and jetsam of her life, and scrabbled amongst it until the phone revealed itself. The tiny red one was now a tiny red three. She jabbed at the screen, accessing voicemail. All of the messages were from Carmichael so, sighing, she skipped to the most recent and hit the play button.

"Alice. It's Drew Carmichael. For God's sake, don't you ever pick up your calls? I don't know if you have seen the papers, but if you haven't, do it...quickly. The police have been round asking about Dawn. At first I thought they were here about the money, but then they started asking about Rachel Jones. Sooner or later, you'll be on their list too, so if you so much as mention me when they come calling - and they will... Just remember, keep your mouth shut, or you know what will happen."

Drew had always been a misogynistic bastard but this took the biscuit. Of course, she knew about Carmichael's sordid Fund, it was common knowledge amongst the group and, although she wasn't as bright as Drew, she knew it must be shady. Otherwise, he would not have cloaked it in so much secrecy. If Carmichael wanted to dig himself a hole, she wouldn't lend him a spade. He was quite capable of using one of his own.

But then she reflected on the rest of the message. She replayed the message. *But then they started asking about Rachel Jones.* Rachel's death pre-dated the Fund so why would the police be interested now? True, her murder was unsolved, but Drew had not been implicated. If she recalled, he claimed he had been in France with a rock-solid, rather voluptuous alibi. So why would the police be connecting Dawn and Drew with Rachel? And why was it so important to meet up tonight?

She stared at her face in the small round mirror that stood on top of the fridge, awaiting tomorrow's cosmetic crisis, her large grey blue eyes drawn and tired. She wondered why she couldn't have been a pretty girl like Dawn, or if not pretty, attractive in that impish, wayward manner that Rachel carried off immaculately. Alice was a short girl; her mother described her as compact, and her Americano brown hair defied any hint of a curl. Her face was pale and drained, triangular, like a Dairylea cheese but with a maroon slit of a mouth slicing off the pointed tip. Her legs were too stubby, she thought. She daren't wear jeans because they looked like two gnarled blue parsnips tapering down to her shoes. Alice often felt cheated around the other girls in the office who always smelt nicer and dressed better, no matter how little they tried and how hard she did. She viewed her profile in the mirror and cupped her breasts. At least her boobs were good, if nothing else. Her life was that of a person passed by, alone and out of sync with the world.

Scooting back to the living room, Alice grabbed her laptop and fired up the BBC London website. The headline was already halfway down the front page, unimportant in a city that lacked feeling, swallowing everyone and everything, homogenising the world. In London the mundane could rub shoulders with the bizarre and neither would notice the other nor recognise their face in the morning.

Slumping back onto the sofa, she pulled her dressing gown around her. The TV news had finished and now there were people arguing about something trivial, inane and meaningless. Should she call Carmichael? Assure him of her silence? That he had nothing to worry about from her? No. He could sweat a little while longer!

Just then her hand buzzed and the phone lit up with a picture of Guy. She smiled and put the phone to her ear.

"Hi, Guy. I was just reading about Dawn. My God. What a..."

"Alice. Just stop a minute, please." The voice was taut, sharp. It was a tone she had only ever heard once before and, subliminally, she was filled with foreboding. "I think we have a problem, Alice. A big one, and I'm not sure how to deal with it."

"Sorry, Guy, what's the matter?" He had always been a safe pair of hands. He had helped her choose her flat, even provided a reference when she took her job at Johnstones. He was probably the best girlfriend she had ever had, although in her case that wasn't saying a great deal.

"Where are you? What are you doing? Right now. What are you doing?"

"I'm at home on the sofa. Look, you're worrying me, Guy. What's the matter?"

"I think its Drew, Alice."

"You what? What about Drew? What has he done now?" Her voice, full of ennui, betrayed her irritation. Every conversation these days seemed to centre on Drew *Bloody* Carmichael.

"Dawn. I think Drew killed Dawn, and maybe even Rachel."

It took a moment or two for Alice to process the statement. It sounded so ludicrous; she had to suppress a giggle. "Don't be stupid! He wouldn't have the...Why would he...?"

"No, just hear me out. Dawn's been making his life a misery lately, accusing him of all sorts of dodgy deals with her clients. Maybe he just got sick of it? Maybe he'd had enough, thought she was going to ruin everything for him. Snapped!"

"What, you mean that stupid Fund thing of his. No way! He's a bit of a dick but really? Not even Andrew Carmichael is stupid enough to start murdering someone over a bit of money, least of all one of his closest friends. It doesn't make sense."

"OK. Fair enough." The line hushed as Guy regrouped. "What about when Rachel died? Did you know she and Drew were playing away?"

Yes...but again, isn't that just the story of Drew's life. Love 'em and leave 'em." Alice put down the laptop and trotted through to the kitchen in search of carbs. This was going to be a long one.

"Ah yes, but did you also know she was pregnant with Drew's baby, and Drew made her have an abortion? He made me sort it all out, you know, an extra degree of separation. To make sure no-one found out."

"Good job there. It was an open secret. Shelley is a professional gossip." Alice scratched her head. So Drew was a bastard. That too was an open secret. "Don't you think you're letting your imagination run away with you, Guy?"

"Maybe, but let's go with it. Rachel feels hard done by, separation anxiety, etc. She starts blackmailing Drew, threatens to expose him as a liar and a cheat. Perhaps even then he had some dodgy deal going and it slips out in their pillow talk. So he gets spooked and kills her. Then, again when Dawn starts causing trouble at his work. Maybe she has learned a lesson or two from Rachel and puts the squeeze on him? Do you know how big that Fund is now, Alice? Well, I deal with *colossal* amounts of cash and it's big enough for me to be worried. Anyway there's no way he is going to jeopardise that so he kills her too."

"What, you really think Drew would do such a thing? Surely not! Devious and underhanded is one thing, psychotic and murderous is another. However big his Fund is, its just suicide. There is no way he can get away with it! The police are sure to find out and no amount of money is any use if you're in prison."

The line went quiet, except for the resounding crunch as Alice bit into a Digestive biscuit. At first she thought she had been cut off, but she could still hear Guy breathing, pondering.

"What if there is more to it than just money?" His tone was subdued, reticent. "What if this is nothing to do with Carmichael's Fund? What if they were blackmailing him for more than just money?"

"How do you mean?" Alice clicked the switch on the coffee pot. It was Jackanory time and she was in for the duration.

"Do you remember that night at Uni? That night with Chris, Dawn, Rachel and Shelley. When I found you in the street?"

Alice's world suddenly jumped three inches to the left. Dredged from a place that she had striven to forget, a memory she had chosen to push from her mind was sucked to the surface. And it was 1997 again, the biting rain stung her face and she was utterly alone. Jackanory had turned nasty.

"Right, Guy, now you are seriously freaking me out."

"Look, Who was there that night? Rachel and Dawn. They saw first hand what he did. They kept his sordid little secret for him. Doesn't it make sense that he would do anything to stop them revealing it? Just one misplaced word and he would lose everything - the money, his career, his freedom, everything."

"Don't you think that's all just a bit melodramatic, Guy?" But Alice could smell the smoke, could sense there may even be a glimmer of flame. "If you're right, then he'll go after Shelley, too. Does she know? Surely we have to warn her?" The phone went silent apart from Guy's breath, shallow and trembling. A chill of foreboding gripped Alice. "...Guy?"

"He knows you were there too, Alice. He knows you saw everything that happened."

Alice's mouth parched.

"But I haven't said anything to anyone. How the hell did he find out?" The silence on the other end of the line was damning. "Jesus, Guy! Thanks very much!"

"Look, it's OK. I might be completely wrong. Perhaps putting two and two together and making five."

"You're a flaming accountant, Guy, and you expect me to believe you can't add up? Bloody Hell!"

"You know what I mean! Just because you were there doesn't make you a threat to him. Just calm down. I told him you've been safe all these years. There's no reason for you to change now."

"One minute you're convincing me he's a mass murderer who is going around clearing up after himself, the next you're telling me I'm next on his list and you want me to calm down? Fucking Hell, Guy. I live on my own. What can I do if he comes after me? I'd be here for days lying dead before someone noticed the smell." She looked around at the chiaroscuro shadows playing off the drab walls of the flat, imagined ominous corners dark and filled with untold terrors.

"He's not coming after you, Alice! I have already had the summons today, at lunchtime. I convinced him that, with the police sniffing around, he should concentrate on keeping his money safe. He will be busy with that for a while, so he will soon forget I even mentioned you. If he has done these terrible things - *if* - the police will catch him. If not, then, I am just blowing smoke up my own arse. He's going along to the Plough & Harrow tonight to speak to Finn, to get him onside, tell him to keep quiet, and he's meeting Marcus too. Kill two birds with one stone, er, so to speak."

"But what happens if he comes round here on the way, has a 'Here's Johnny' moment? What am I supposed to do then?"

"Now who's being melodramatic? If you're that worried, go and stay with someone else, take a holiday. Anyway, does he even know where you live?"

"Not unless you told him that as well...and we know how good you are at keeping secrets."

"Look, I told you. He's got other things to worry about. Nothing's going to happen if you keep your head down. Even if the police come round, you have nothing to say, and as for what happened in 1997, not even Drew thinks they are interested in that."

"Let's hope you're right Guy, for both our sakes, because potentially we are both on Drew's hit list now."

After Guy had rung off, her coffee cooled and the walls once more resounded to the silence. She realised she had been there, crouched in the corner of her sofa, allowing her thoughts to meander for two hours. The TV had entertained itself and now cast flickering banality outward to no-one. Purposefully, she ran through to the bedroom and pulled on her jeans, scooped the detritus of her life back into her handbag and headed out to the Plough & Harrow.

Anything had to be better than this.

***

Carmichael slammed the glass down on the counter and signalled to Finn to replenish it. His brain ached from all of the thinking he had been forced to do. He needed anaesthetic. The bar was filling with evening drinkers - young professionals with their phones and tablets, and old people pissing their pensions up a wall whilst they waited to die. He snatched up the glass even before Finn had withdrawn the bottle, sensing the other's raised eyebrows.

"Don't you bloody dare, Byrne." He prodded an index finger at the air in front of Finn. The first scotch had hit his brain, warmth spreading across his ribs, prickling behind his eyes, bolstering his bravado. Byrne, however, had perfected a supercilious detached style common to most landlords, a way of seeming to care when not giving a toss, and Carmichael knew it. He was wise to a game he often played himself. The *bog-trotter* had been itching for a fight since he had arrived. In no mood to oblige, Carmichael threw down a note before heading across the lounge to his usual secluded seat. There was a line of sight to the door, which now had a slightly fuzzy edge. He had been drinking heavily. Hell, sod Thornton. He might not even turn in tomorrow. Soon they would invent a machine to do his sodding job, make him obsolete. Anything was preferable to work, especially given the day he'd had, his mind besieged by brutal mental pictures of Dawn Silverton, counterpointed by remembered smells and touches, fading reminiscences from all those years ago, and the awful realisation that now he was the sole custodian of those memories. But his anguish had not ended there. Between the deep but manageable pain of the loss of his former girlfriend, and the mild abhorrence when he recalled the word 'murder', there was a more animal emotion. One he knew would keep him awake at night and distracted during the day.

The gripping chill of discovery.

He had reread the newspaper, painfully aware that the others would be sharing the same emotions. He had contacted as many as possible. Marcus and Alice had been unreachable, flying around like loose cannonballs, ignorant of the mayhem a misplaced word could cause. Alice was the real concern, flitting on the edge of his radar. Was it true that she was there all those years ago? He flicked through the mental card index once more but nowhere did he see Alice. The best he could do was to leave the voicemails and hope it enough to keep the shrew quiet.

From its inception as an excuse for a student piss-up, the Monday Club had transformed as they had all gravitated to the Capital. But now they had pretexts and stories, motives and secrets. They had all become millstones, even nooses, around his neck.

An interminable ten minutes of swinging doors later, the face he awaited entered and surveyed the bar before their eyes met. The newcomer wheezed anxiously, both from the relief of spotting his quarry and from the exertion of hauling his frame along Cordon Street a little too briskly. Marcus Balfour was short and stoutly built, with a round head and impossibly curly brown hair. His face was linen white, patches of red blossoming on his cheeks. In his thirties he still carried the face of a teenager, only close up the lines of worry and smoking had begun to show. The oversized jacket he was wearing flapped furiously as he raised a hand of greeting and shuffled between the seated drinkers and higgledy-piggledy chairs to where Carmichael sat.

"Where the hell have you been? I thought we agreed 7:30."

Marcus exhaled deeply. "Oh, and hello to you, Drew. Great to see you! Looking well, if a little *bloody* rude. And anyway, who agreed? You work with lawyers. I don't think a text is a contract, eh? Lucky, I'm here at all after the day I've had."

"Shut the fuck up and sit down." Carmichael grated.

"Anyway, its only 7:25 now - *Drew!*" Balfour forestalled the involuntary action of checking his own obviously inferior but probably more accurate quartz watch. Drew didn't and purposefully tapped the crystal of his *Rolex* pointedly. He had an obsession with being right, even when he was wrong, so Balfour shrugged and sat himself down. "What's the big rush anyway? Anyone would think someone had died!"

"Bloody Hell, Marcus! Show some damn respect!" Carmichael thrust the folded newspaper across the table, where the eyes in the photograph met those of Balfour. Having just pulled an all-nighter, Marcus had yet to read anything apart from some dead guys final chart and a dog-eared copy of Readers Digest from 1984. He scanned the story a couple of times, massaging his chin, whilst Carmichael frustratedly tapped his fingers.

"Whoa! That's a bummer, Drew. Jesus, Dawn. She was sitting right here only the other day." Marcus looked over to the vacant squab. "Wow. She was one of the few women who would speak to me without needing to show a faecal sample as an introduction. God, Dawn! I loved that girl. Well, I never actually had the pleasure..." Balfour uttered a grunt that passed for a chuckle, as his frame bobbed up and down like a bottle in the ocean. Looking up from the paper, directly at Carmichael, he assumed what he hoped was his most professional expression of sympathy. "You must be devastated."

"Cut the crap, Marcus. I'm not one of your grieving relatives."

"Drew! This isn't just some random girl. There was a time when I thought she was the one for you."

"Hardly! We went out for two years in, like, the 1990's." Like a teenager throwing a strop for being caught smoking, Drew's tone was casual, dismissive and to Marcus' mind totally superficial.

"Well, three years actually...and weren't you seeing each other again a couple of years ago?"

"OK, and a couple of years ago, but only for a week or two. She was just a friend."

"Jesus, I'd kill for a friend like her." He winked lasciviously at

Carmichael, whose face briefly tightened. Perhaps another misplaced quip.

"Too late. That's been done. Look, pre-history, Marcus. Get with the programme." But Drew's tone betrayed him to Marcus. Pre-history wasn't as far back as Drew would have liked.

Marcus allowed an awkward silence to descend. He shifted uncomfortably on the less than generous chair, trying to dislodge the back of his coat from beneath his buttocks. He envied Carmichael the studded fabric cushions of his allotted seat, but could not allow himself to shift into one of the girls' vacant spaces. A creature of habit. Finn arrived with a pint for Marcus. It was a familiar spot in a familiar pub, where they chose to meet each week but the slightly faded floral squab to Carmichael's right seemed empty without Dawn.

"Marcus?" Finn eyed Balfour wearily, his eyes flicking momentarily to Carmichael.

"Finn." The response monotone, a tacit greeting, appreciation for the free drink. Carmichael did not receive *that* concession at the Plough & Harrow and had not yet cottoned on.

"Drew. A word before you go?"

"Of course, Finn." Carmichael swivelled his head, waved a dismissive hand towards the dour Irishman, who hovered momentarily, his eyes fixed on Carmichael. This time more insistently. "As soon as I have finished here...honestly."

"Just make sure you do." Finn broke Carmichael's gaze and returned to the bar. Carmichael cast Balfour an insouciant shrug, a schoolboy pulled up for some minor misdemeanour. Marcus was unimpressed. Over the years, he had experienced Drew's indifference on many occasions. With little room for anyone else in that superior head of his, he had often wondered how Dawn had tolerated him. As far as Marcus was aware, she was the only girl of any significance in Drew's life. He loathed Drew his callousness, and loathed himself for remaining friends with him. A creature of habit. He took another look at the creased photograph, in his mind smelt the warm French breeze and tasted the rich fruitiness of the *Corbieres* they had been drinking and he felt immense anger towards his friend.

"You know what, Drew?" he spat, "You're a real shit

sometimes. You must have felt something for her, for Christ's sake!"

Carmichael shrugged once more. "What do you want me to say? She was a girlfriend, then she wasn't, and now she's dead. It was years ago. Look, man, in this life, you've got to live in the present, look to the future, where the money is! If you dwell in the past with your head up your arse, you'll never get anywhere. That's your bloody problem, Marcus. Always dealing with old people who live in the past. Regretting their mistakes when it's too late. You have to put your troubles behind you and move on." Carmichael drove a hand straight out, moving right on. He examined the reflections in his whisky glass. He definitely was over her. But he could still picture her perched on the edge of the bed, dark against the window, light shining through her hair and silhouetting her full breasts. He could feel her warm hands as they walked together. He could almost wipe away the tears she cried when he had moved on.

Back in the day, Drew attracted girls like bees round a honeypot. But Dawn had been different. From the start they had been touted as the perfect couple. Whenever they broke up getting back together seemed inevitable. But Dawn started making plans that Drew did not much want to fulfil. He ended the relationship, coldly and brutally in the familiar alcove at Browns on a wet, Tuesday evening. For years, their paths ran in parallel but for a brief, pointless reprise in Carcassonne, when the photograph was taken, and three reckless days in January.

She had started to use words like 'commitment' again but however much he wanted her, he wanted commitment less. Relationships were ephemeral, high points on a rollercoaster with as many peaks as troughs, enjoyed before the inevitable downhill slide. And it pained him to admit that now, the nearest he had to a relationship was the acquaintance of a raving pouf and a *bromance* with an overweight geriatrician. Rock and flaming roll!

Raising his head from his glass, he flushed his mind of the memories and leaned forwards toward Marcus. "Anyway, now it is most definitely over, like it or not. Perhaps I wasn't the perfect gentleman all the time, but, God, was she hard work, dude. I mean, great in the sack, and that arse, but real hard work otherwise. She had to go."

"So that's a '*Fine while it lasted, but good riddance*'. That is so totally unfair. Back in the day, you would use them, abuse them and discard them like an old sock. God, I wished I'd been born you then. You have absolutely no idea what it's like to be one of the rest of us. But Dawn, surely she was a keeper?"

"I seem to remember you doing OK out of it, Marcus!"

"Only your bloody cast-offs, and then only those desperate enough to settle for me on the rebound. Most of them cut their losses there and then."

"What about Alice Bown? You were always together at Uni. You still seem very friendly."

Marcus fixed a plaintive smile as the pain bit once more. "There's together and *together*, Drew. The most fantastic six months ever, followed by years of abject misery. If you'd have looked up from your harem, you'd have seen me doing all the chasing and her doing all of the running. Unfortunately, she ran better than I chased."

"Serves you right for being a fat bastard. Maybe, you'd have caught her if you'd have lost a bit of weight, and she could see your todger beneath your gut."

"I don't think that's the problem, Drew. I just wish I knew what was. Just one day, she said it was all over between us and that was that. Even now, we are always on the brink of getting back together but just never do. Not for want of trying on my part, I can tell you!" Marcus sighed and took a restorative pull from his glass. It was a pain beyond torture each time he saw Alice and each time she headed away at the end of the evening. A gulf had opened many years ago and he had been unable to bridge it. He decided the conversation needed to be steered away from himself and back to Dawn.

"Anyway, so Dawn's gone, you don't see overly concerned. So what's the urgency for tonight? From your voicemails and texts I thought nuclear war had been declared. Why drag me half way across London just to point at a picture in a paper?"

"Small print, Marcus!" Drew leaned over and prodded one specific word. "Read the small print!"

Marcus' pupils darted like tadpoles, his mouth widening by degrees, realisation slowly dawning on him.

"Murdered? My God! How awful...I'd assumed it must have

been an accident." He reread a hundred or so words that contained little of substance, then paused and reflected. After a year on a geriatric ward, Marcus had a sympathetic yet detached relationship with the reality of death and with the emotional turmoil that was its bedfellow. It was a veneer that kept him safe. "Unless of course you did it. You didn't, did you?"

Drew threw his hands into the air. "What is it with people today? Everyone keeps asking if I killed her." He proffered his hands palms upwards. "Do these look like they could strangle someone?"

"I dunno. Your tongue is pretty sharp, and sometimes one of your withering stares is enough to wind me. Anyway, who knows what you do when I am not keeping you honest. I bet the girls you sleep with could share some juicy pillow talk. Or is there a quarry somewhere where you dump 'em once you've shagged enough of their brains out?"

"Piss off, Balfour!"

"So did you?" Marcus teased.

"What do you think?"

"Ah. Thank goodness. We can all sleep soundly tonight. The world is safe."

"Some bedside manner you've got. I pity the relatives of anyone who carks it on your watch."

But Carmichael had to agree with Marcus. Dawn's murder tied up many loose ends but, today alone, there were twenty-three thousand one hundred and eighty six reasons in the Cayman Islands why it shouldn't be the end of everything. And one tragic reason why very definitely was.

Marcus cast his friend a quizzical look. Behind the brash righteous indignation, Drew was troubled.

"You don't suppose the police think that you *are* in any way involved, do you?" He held out a conciliatory hand. "I know you're not but, just saying..."

Drew leaned back and raised his eyes to the heavens. "Hooray, at last! Why else would I be at this Godforsaken shit-hole on a Wednesday? All I know is that, as an ex-boyfriend...twice, the police would want to speak to me, and guess what? This morning, 9:00 on the dot, there they were, boots blacked and pencils poised! Asked me all sorts of silly questions about Dawn, about the Monday Club. Even knew about Rachel Jones. Which means they're going to want to speak to every member of the Monday Club. And sooner or later that means you."

Balfour sat up in his chair and stroked his chin, thoughtfully.

"I hadn't thought of that. S'pose you're right." Marcus mulled over the repercussions, obviously missing something, though he was damned if he could think what. "Couldn't have been me. I was pulling a double shift again. Mind you, I suppose any witnesses will either be dead, off their face on drugs, or away with the fairies. Unless of course...one of the nurses saw me...but I don't think any of them really *see* me..."

"Marcus. She and I met up for a coffee at lunchtime just before she was killed and, well, it got a bit out of hand. There was a bit of a commotion."

Marcus eyed Drew suspiciously. "So what do you want from me? Absolution? An alibi? A character reference?"

"No...no. You're not that good a liar. The police would see through it straightaway. It's just that they seem to think I was the last person to see her alive."

"Except for the killer...?"

"Yes, yes, we've been through that charade already. Look, We met up in Costa's on the Broadway. We had a row and she walked out. I followed her and, well, we rowed more."

"And then you strangled every last breath of life out of her, and tossed her into a hedge?" Marcus' sarcasm fell upon deaf ears and then trickled to the floor defeated.

"And then she stormed off and I went back onto the Broadway."

"And you told the police that?"

"Marcus, they think I killed her. *The last person to see her alive...* OK, so we might be remembered in Costa's, but after that I can't account for the time except to say I was getting a baguette or something. I paid cash and none of the A-level rejects that work in that place would remember one guy in a suit on a lunchtime."

"It's still an alibi of sorts. Do you have the receipt?"

"Of course I do, but that doesn't account for the time

between Dawn walking off and me being noticed back at the office."

"Drew, mate. They have forensics these days. They can tell if a fly shat on you last Wednesday. When they, er, examine Dawn, they will find enough evidence to catch the chap who did it. Unless it's you, you have nothing to worry about, honestly. Then there's the CCTV. At this moment, there is probably some CSI dude following you back to the office on a black-and-white monitor."

Drew felt his wrist. The scratches were scabbed and rough. He hadn't considered CCTV.

"Look, Marcus. The police were quick to latch on to me, and invariably they'll start sniffing harder. So you have to be ready when they do."

Marcus eyed Drew warily. "Ready for what? I was an acquaintance, that's all."

"If the police delve deeper, what happens if they find out about the Fund?" He was glancing round conspiratorially, his voice a strained whisper.

Marcus had still not cottoned on. "No. You are going to have to help me, here."

"The Fund? Come on, Marcus. Who came up with the idea?"

"Oh, you don't mean that stock market thing. So I gave you a few quid to invest. What's that got to do with me?"

"Don't be naive, Marcus. You don't think it's just your money, do you? Everyone has a share in it. Shelley and Finn, Guy, you. You've all invested. Not to mention most of the clients of Barraclough and Leavis, however they don't actually know about it."

"Jesus, Drew!" Marcus took a quick draught from his pint. He leaned over the table to avoid being overheard. "Isn't that embezzlement? You can't just take other people's money, not like that, surely?"

"Marcus, nobody's taken the money! That's the beauty of the scheme. When a new instruction comes in, I channel the deposit through the Fund. Whenever a house sale completes, I just pay the money out of the pot. There is more than enough to cover the paltry interest we pay for holding it. Nobody loses!"

"But it's illegal, Drew."

"Only if we get caught, Marcus."

"Hey! Not so much of the 'We'. Devising some hair-brained scheme after a few sherbets is a long way from committing a larceny."

"Technically, it's felony, but like I say, only if you get caught, and I don't intend to. If you play dumb, neither will you." Drew's eyes grew large like a puppy in an animal sanctuary at visiting time. "Look, I may not have been the best friend to you all these years but one day when the NHS has finished with you, you'll be grateful for your little nest-egg, you mark my words." Drew leaned back in his chair, folded his arms, defiant. "You can still have everything you wanted."

"Yeah, and I can survey it all through a barred window at Pentonville!"

"White-collar, crime, Balfour. It would be an open prison, with lawns, and days out and shit. Five years at maximum."

"That's re-assuring, Drew. Only five years as Big Eric's special bitch." Marcus was astounded by Drew's lack of shame, but he was now intrigued. "This financial scheme of yours? I reiterate - *of yours*. Just how does it make me culpable? It's not really conspiracy chatting about a scam..."

Drew pulled out a folded piece of paper from the inside pocket of his overcoat and cast it across the table. Marcus picked it up, eying him suspiciously as he unfolded it.

"Fucking Jesus! How much?" Marcus started, jarring the table, the drinks slopping dangerously. The pages were a bank statement, much like the one he received from his high street bank, except there were many, many more zeros before the decimal point and the balance did not have a 'DR' after it.

"Ok, so you're rich. What does this change?"

"Look at the last sheet, Marcus. It's a copy of the registration document for the account. It's not me that's rich, it's *you*."

Marcus flipped over a couple of pages. His breath caught in his throat.

Carmichael continued. "Remember I borrowed your flat two months ago, when you were on vacation and Dawn had started becoming tiresome? I borrowed your passport and birth certificate too. Seems like you opened a couple of bank accounts. Well four to be exact. Then you took out an unsecured loan for twenty thousand pounds, which you have made one payment on so far. And also you are the proud owner of an account at Butterfield's, into which you deposited the loan, and all of the interest from your nefarious stock market dealings." Leaning closer to Marcus, Drew's tone became more menacing. "You're in this as much as I am. Probably more because if the cops find out that Dawn was involved in dodgy dealings with her clients' money, it'll be your name in the frame, not mine."

For a moment Marcus was overwhelmed by Drew Carmichael's brazenness. A thought occurred to him. He frenetically skimmed through the document again, this time searching for Carmichael's name but did not find it.

"So I have some money in a bank account? What does that prove? There has to be an audit trail back to where this money came from, surely?"

"Get this through your fat head. Those nice men in the Cayman Islands don't tend to co-operate with the UK authorities, so if my name was ever connected to the account, they'll never know." Carmichael leaned forwards across the table and eyed Balfour squarely. "All the money belongs to you, Marcus. You just need to look after it until this all blows over. If our little *arrangement* comes to light, the audit trail leads right back to you. Now, I don't know about you, but I guess that gives you a great big motive for murder, and an even bigger one for keeping your mouth shut."

Balfour felt a glow rise to his cheeks. The paper in his hands was quivering like a leaf in a breeze. Carmichael had been very thorough but would it be seen as a motive for murder? Carmichael was shrewd and skilled at self-protection, even if that meant shopping his oldest friend to the police to divert their attention. So maybe Carmichael's capacity for self-protection was stronger than even Balfour had credited? Maybe Drew was capable of murder?

"Look." continued Carmichael. "Whilst all this money is in your name, it's not in mine. That means I can safely deny knowledge of it. When all this blows over, I will transfer it all back. Until then, I am going to need a little co-operation from you."

Balfour leaned back in his chair, utterly defeated. "So what do you want me to do?"

Carmichael drained his glass. "You can get me another scotch for a start and make it a large one.

Chapter 15

There were just too many loose ends for Carmichael to be comfortable. Four years ago Rachel's death had solved all his problems in one fell swoop. He would be the first to admit that any sort of relationship with her had been a mistake. They had managed to keep it hidden from their closest friends but then the stupid cow had allowed herself to fall pregnant and suddenly the game had changed. From a bit on the side she had implored him to look after her, to become a family together, which of course he wouldn't. It was just sex. Frequent, frantic, illicit sex. There was no prospect of a long-term arrangement and he was buggered if he was shelling out for some little bastard for the next umpteen years. Anyway, there was no evidence that the baby was his. He backed Rachel into a corner and finally, with no other option, she acceded to a termination. A weekend in Reading visiting friends, returning childless and pale.

But even then there were loose ends. The stupid bitch started to wail and moan, succumbing to some kind of separation anxiety and was soon banging on his door pleading with him to make it right. Which, of course he had no intention of doing. She had gotten herself into that mess, she would have to get herself out. Undeterred, she became a regular at Barraclough and Leavis, hanging around the reception, waiting in the car park, until there were sly comments in the staff meetings and life became uncomfortable. He was afraid to turn a corner without Rachel being there.

Rachel's death tied up all of the loose ends.

Since then Carmichael had been more circumspect where women had been concerned. He and Guy had incepted the Fund, embryonic at first, small in scale but already proving it's worth. Life had settled down, Rachel drifted from the short memories of the other members of the Monday Club.

Then Dawn had chanced on Carmichael again. She had entered a bar in Wealdstone on a particularly tawdry evening and brought the sunshine with her. He was with a sinuous blonde, whose grating laugh and propensity for lupine yelps during coitus had become tiresome. He had already started working silent miracles with the Fund and before the end of the evening, she had seen the dollar signs and agreed to forward her clients to him. That night, she replaced the sinuous blonde in his bed and for two weeks after that. Then, one morning, she had stated tearfully that her life was going really well, and that deep down he knew they weren't right for each other, and she didn't need the stress that they had caused each other last time round. She had said she was sorry to let him down, and that she knew how much it meant to him. And he had breathed an inward sigh, overwhelmed with relief for the outstretched hand that plucked him from the abyss. Disingenuously mewling like a hurt puppy, he solemnly agreed with every word. The affair had ended but the clients kept coming.

Until a month ago.

Out of the blue, Dawn persuaded his boss, Gerald Thornton to call a spot audit. It had taken all Carmichael's skills of persuasion to sweet-talk Carol Hughes into discovering what was discussed, and a year's paid membership of Richmond Golf Club to convince Guy Higson, as the firm's external auditor, to dilute any incriminating evidence. But the applecart had been irrevocably upset and ever since Carmichael had been under scrutiny. He spread his accounts around the other associates to assuage Thornton's curiosity and, with Carol, spent a week re-arranging the finances, ostensibly to remove the chance of a reoccurrence, but actually to toughen up his own defences.

Still Dawn kept calling, day and night demanding Thornton reopen the audit and the heat was becoming intense. Then she too had revealed that she was pregnant. To fuck up once may be considered careless, but twice? Once more providence had come to his rescue. Maybe it was necessary to sacrifice the love of his life. Dawn was dead and with that, a load more loose ends were tied.

As he watched Balfour waddle away towards the rear door for a smoke, Drew Carmichael could not help concluding that Guy was right. The police were not interested in some tawdry financial scam; they had bigger fish to fry. The accounts were safe at least for the time being, and he was sure he could handle their questions over Dawn, just like he had with Rachel.

Which just left the conundrum of that night in 1997.

119

He pursed his lips and swallowed the whisky in a single slug, gagging as it hit the back of his throat, feeling his head lighten as the alcohol swam around his blood. Scanning the bar, he could see Finn was engaged in polite *bon homie* with a woman in a short skirt who was far too young for either of them. Perhaps she would provide the cover he needed to escape. He could talk Finn round another time. He was far too pissed tonight.

Grabbing his coat and the folded newspaper, he sidled towards the double door and the crisp evening air of Cordon Street, to be intercepted by a large hand on his shoulder.

"Not so fast Drew. Didn't I say I wanted a word with you?" Byrne loomed large in the tiny vestibule, blocking his egress.

"Come on, Finn. Not tonight, eh? I've had a shit of a day. Can't it wait, whatever it is?"

"I am afraid not Drew. This has to end now." Finn clamped his hand tight on Drew's shoulder and steered him toward a brass sign bearing the words '*Private - Staff Only*' and with a hustling of feet and a slamming of doors, they were on the other side in a cramped storeroom. The snap of a switch brought light and Drew looked about him at a motley assortment of tables and chairs stacked against the walls, and the folded arms of Guy Higson and Finn Byrne. Carmichael puffed out his frustration.

"Really, guys. What's with the cloak and dagger."

"Sit." Finn's eyes indicated a chair, which had escaped the stacking ordeal and stood isolated on the linoleum.

"Grow up, Finn. Who do you think you are talking too?" Carmichael instantly regretted the bravado, as the large hand once more impacted his shoulder and pushed him down.

"I said *sit.*"

"Fine, fine. Look, I'm sitting. I'm calm. It's all good. Now, what do you want? I am a little pissed and just want to go home."

Guy, who had been leaning against a table, rose to his feet. He was clad head to foot in his motorcycle leathers, ominous, imposing, his helmet on the table behind him. He stood beside Byrne. A show of unity.

"Just give us five minutes of your *valuable* time, Drew." There was a steeliness in Guy's voice, a hardness annealed through the afternoon since he had left Carmichael in Richmond. Carmichael felt the hairs prickle on the back of his neck. Fear dried his throat and he gulped sawdust.

Finn continued:

"Guy told me what happened between you two at lunchtime. Ordinarily, I could put that down to some lovers tiff - sorry Guy..." Higson nodded. *Granted.* "...but I think we all know there is more to it than that. Especially since you show up here on a Wednesday closely followed by Marcus, who has just gone out the back with a face like a smacked arse."

Carmichael sneered. "And your point is?"

"OK. Let's stop mincing round handbags - sorry again, Guy - straight to the point. Tell him."

Higson crouched down in front of the chair, leather creaking as his knees folded. He could taste the alcohol on Carmichael's breath. "What we talked about this afternoon. Your Fund. I have sorted it. If the police ask, you will need to tough it out with them because they will need Alan *Bloody* Turing to find any connection with me. But the others, Finn, Shelley, Marcus. Well, that's down to you to keep your mouth shut."

"I thought you said that the police weren't interested in the money."

Finn crouched down beside Guy. "Drew, we are not interested in the money. Guy and me, well, we have had a little chat and we don't think any of this is to do with the money. We are worried about what happened to Dawn, and to Rachel. What might happen to the others? Right now what use is this money if we're all dead?"

"Don't be so fucking stupid, Finn. Nothings going to happen to anyone! All we have to do is show a united front to the police and it will all blow over, just like last time."

Guy threw his hands in the air and slapped against the leather trousers, sending a crack across the room. "Last time, Rachel died. This time is already like last time because now Dawn's dead. We are talking about next time. Right now, we just need to stop *you!* We are hereby terminating your membership of the Monday Club."

"You bloody idiots! You can't terminate my membership of the Monday Club. *I am the Monday Club!* Who do you think it is who has kept you all together every week for fifteen years?

121

Without me, you'd be farming potatoes in County Clare or something, and you Guy, you'd be stuck in the post-room, wearing horn-rims and a cardie. Face it, boys, without me you're all just a sad set of individuals sitting on your jackseys waiting for someone to show you the way. Well, guess what. I am the way. And right now, I am your only hope. You have no choice right now but to trust me or face the consequences. I am going to make us all very, very rich, you wait and see."

"But at what cost?" Guy drew a hand through his hair. "On paper we are already richer because you have taken Dawn out of the equation. So what is this, some sick game of musical chairs? When the killer stops killing, the last man standing get's the cash?"

"I don't know what the fuck you're talking about. Spoils? This is a solid investment strategy. Look at this place, Finn. It's a money pit. One day you are going to be really grateful I held my nerve. We are all going to be very rich. You just have to keep the faith, honestly."

The Irishman grabbed Carmichael's jaw and pulled his face to within an inch of his own. "Honestly? You don't know the meaning. You're such a lying piece of shit. I think we have to drive the message home. From now on, we want nothing to do with you. Shelley, me, Guy. We don't ever want to see you again. If we do see you again, it'll be your picture on the front page of *The Observer*. And if you know what's good for you, you'll stay away from Marcus and the others, too. So treat this as a lesson. Just to make sure you understand."

And then Carmichael was sprawled across the floor. His head impacting the Lino, he saw flashes of blue and red, and decided to stay down. Blunt boots assailed his ribs and shards of pain shot through his torso as the air was driven from his lungs in painful rasps.

His breath sounded hollow in his ears as the door slammed and the room lapsed into silence.

***

Monaghan let out a frustrated sigh and glanced at the clock. Another plod stupid enough to be working on a Wednesday evening, when Man. City were at home to Spurs on *Sky*. Running a pen down the list of potential leads, he stopped at the entry for the University Group. He had discovered little that they didn't already know, and certainly nothing that suggested the Monday Club as anything other than a group of mates remaining friends long after their courses had finished. The University Admissions office had archived the records and could confirm little more than their alumni status, their years of graduation and the addresses they all gave at the time. And Billy Davies, the Collator in Coventry, had yet to return his call. Glancing again at the clock, he resolved to make the second half, and perhaps his dinner, if it had not yet made the kitchen bin. Margaret would be pissed off if he came home with fish and chips and there was a pork chop was on the pan. He reached for the handset to ring her, only to start as it rung beneath his grasp.

The voice was instantly familiar, despite him having heard it many months before. Seemed like there would be a pan in Coventry with a drying pork chop on it too.

"Hi Dave. Sorry to phone so late but I got your message earlier and a couple of the names resonated with me, so I had to look them up."

Monaghan sat upright in his chair and turned over a fresh page on the pad in front of him.

"No, no problem. Lucky you caught me. I was off to watch the match. I'll catch it on replay."

"Ah, Football. Since the Ricoh was sold off, I can take it or leave it. Bunch of overpaid ponces. Still, talking of overpaid ponces, this list you sent me through... I checked with some of my colleagues who were around at the time and we pretty much drew a blank, I'm afraid. Looks like most of them had an uneventful university career, or at least didn't get caught."

"That's a shame Billy. I felt sure there must be something connecting them, but hey, we drew a blank."

"Now, that's not actually what I said. I said the guys *here* didn't remember them. Anyway, I decided to go about it a different way. I plugged the names of your Monday Club members into our database, to see what fell out. As soon as I read your list, one name rang a vague bell with me but I couldn't remember why. I mean 1997 is a long time ago."

"Which name, Billy? Andrew Carmichael?"

"Oh, Bloody Hell, no! Already knew Andrew Carmichael!

Arrogant over-bearing tit, like a lot of students who think good A-Levels make them above everyone else. He was a bit of a hell-raiser when he was here. I remember having to talk him down from the Godiva statue. He was trying to cover her modesty with a bra whipped from Allders. And then another time, he was squirting washing-up liquid into the fountain in the West Orchard. Do you how long it takes the council to clear away all that foam? But it was never anything really serious. Andrew Carmichael, Findlay Byrne and Guy Higson were a posse for a year or two. Always at the centre of the student high jinks. No, the name that struck me was not on your list, but I recalled in the back of mind that he was part of the group too for a while. A weedy little chap called Christopher Betts. One of our guys looked at the list and he just said 'Carmichael. Wasn't he involved in that business with Christopher Betts?' and the whole lot came flooding back. Betts is an unusual surname and Christopher Betts just rung a bell. Anyway, when I searched for his name, there was only the stub of the case and a reference number. It's all been moved to the Data Centre Archive. Sorry."

"So what can you tell me?"

"Chris Betts was a student at the same time as Carmichael. You know about the Monday Club, a sort of students' social group? Well, there was a bit of trouble. Betts was found wondering the streets moaning and frightening the passers by. None of the guys really remember much more except that somehow Carmichael became involved and it was a bit messy for a week or two. Betts himself was off his trolley, so we passed him on. The students keep us quite busy during term time."

"Do you think you can pull those records from the Archive for me, Billy?"

"Already on it, Dave. Might take a day or two, but I've put the ticket in. Sorry I couldn't be more helpful."

"And Betts? What happened to him?"

"Haven't got a Scooby. At the time, the nut jobs were sent to a couple of assessment centres, but other than that.

"Cheers, Billy. Let me know when the case files come back, OK?"

Monaghan pressed the disconnect button on the cradle and dialled his home phone number to get that chop off the pan.

There appeared to be a new name in the Monday Club ranks that had slipped all of their minds until now.

Chapter 16

"Hiya, Marcus. You got any idea what's going on?" She asked in a matter-of-fact tone, as if asking for a quarter of brisket at the deli counter, but it still made Marcus jump.

"Alice! What are you doing here?"

Her eyes were flicking furtively between Marcus and the open fire door that led back to the pub. "I could ask you the same thing, Marcus. In fact, I think I just did."

"I got a summons from Drew."

"On a Wednesday?" Alice scratched her head. "He never comes here on a Wednesday."

"What difference does that make? When he yells, I come running."

"You could say no."

"S'pose so, but you know Drew. He can be very insistent and I am afraid I might just miss something."

"And did you?"

"If only it were that simple. It's never that simple with Drew." Marcus decided to leave the statement enigmatically vague, at least for now. Digging into his pocket, he pulled out a packet of *Superkings*. He watched the flickering amber illuminate her face as sparks danced from his lighter. "So, what *are* you doing here?"

Alice drew on the cigarette, cheeks hollowing, disappearing in a cloud of exhaled smoke, "I just found out about Dawn. I was at home in my flat and, when I heard about it on TV, I came over all cold. I couldn't stay in on my own so I came here."

"On a Wednesday?"

"*Touché.*" She flicked him an impish smile. "Well, actually, Guy phoned and scared the *bejesus* out of me. I couldn't stay in the flat on my own. Guy said that he was coming here to see Drew. Another schmuck who can't say no to a summons. I figured if Drew was here you probably would be."

"So basically you have come all this way, what five miles, on

126

the off-chance that I would be here, grasping on to Drew Carmichael's coat tails?"

"But you *are* here, Marcus."

"Hmmm. Far too predictable, that's me." He slouched back against the wall of the pub and she joined him, both gazing distractedly at the plumes of smoke drifting skywards. After a short while, Alice canted her head towards Marcus.

"You do know that, out of them all, you are the only one I really trust."

Balfour stopped picking a fragment of tobacco from his tongue, and eyed Alice curiously. She was shrouded in her fleece, about three sizes too big, just her head poking out above the collar. It was only then he noticed she was shaking. Hardly surprising, the evening had turned cold. It was the first time he had seen her since Christmas and he had longed to see her again, but their lives were concentric. She was so close that he could smell her scent on the air, he could hear the rhythm of her breath and see the rise and fall of her arms folded across her chest, but the foot or so of space between them was a chasm he had been unable to span for over fifteen years.

"Obliged, I am sure, but what brought that on?"

"I don't know. I suppose, living on my own, sometimes it's just nice to have someone I can lean on. Out of them all, I really do think you're the only one who would look out for me."

"You know I have a soft spot for you, Alice. Always have. Of course you can rely on me. Although, to be honest, I am not really sure what *is* going on, but then I am always about ten years behind the curve." Still assaulted by Carmichael's callousness, still reeling from the revelations made about the Fund, Marcus felt on the edge of everything, outside looking in. "I know one thing. Drew certainly knows how to wind people up. Apparently, him and Guy have fallen out *Big Time*. I thought those two were the best of buddies."

"Perhaps that explains all the things he was saying about Drew earlier." The sentence tailed off. It was Alice's turn to be enigmatically vague. Then, smirking, she continued, "Maybe they had a lover's spat?" But she knew it was more sinister than that.

"Maybe. Well, could you be best of buddies with him?"

"No, 'fraid not. He's rich, he's talented and quite good-looking in a self-important, pompous, prick sort of way. But no. He's one of those pretty, bad-boys my Mom warned me about. Probably screws like a stallion, though."

Marcus purged an uncomfortable image from his mind and thought back to the bank statement, to the almost infinite line of zeros. "No, me neither. He's got a hairy back. I never sleep with men who have hairy backs." He remained stone faced as Alice feigned shock. Then she shrugged and moved out of the draught, closer to Marcus.

"Just as well then. I would never sleep with a man who sleeps with men who have hairy backs." She drew another glowing lungful, exhaling a billowing cloud into the swarm of midges and night flies hovering around the light above the door, letting the inference hang in the air amongst the smoke. "Poor Dawn. Nobody deserves that."

She reached across him and dropped her nub-end in the receptacle. Then she said, "What do you think about this four years thing. Guy says that Rachel and Dawn died exactly four years apart. What would he mean by that?" She pulled the fleece tighter about her.

"Dunno, but thinking about it, it must be around four years since Rachel died. That was towards the end of April too, so maybe he's right. Maybe four years is right. So if the same person killed both Rachel and Dawn... "

"...Maybe he's got a point when he says it could be one of us? Maybe it's me and I haven't realised?" She turned to look at Marcus. "Maybe it's you and neither of us have realised?"

"Yep, definitely me. Bang to rights. You know you said I was the only one you could trust? Well, guess what?" Marcus feigned a grab at Alice's throat, and pulled back. "No! Can't see your neck in that fleece!"

"How can you joke about it, Marcus? Dawn's been killed for God's sake! Rachel's dead and it could be one of the Monday Club."

"You started it."

"Um." She fell silent for a moment, lighting a fresh cigarette, which glowed brightly as she drew on it. "Marcus. Can I ask you something?"

"Sure. How much do you need and for how long? That's all

people ever ask me these days." Alice frowned. "Sorry, fire away."

"Guy thinks Drew is the murderer, that he killed Dawn and Rachel. And he said something else which worried me."

"Oh, yes?" So it wasn't just Drew's imagination. Other people had already started to put him in the frame. He wondered what other skeletons had started to rattle in cupboards.

"He asked me if I had seen Chris Betts since Uni. Well, I haven't. Have you seen him since then?"

Marcus scratched his head and thought. Chris Betts was definitely a blast from the past. "No. Can't say I have. Mind you, why the hell would I see him? Didn't really see him back then. So now Guy is desperate to find him? Sometimes I feel like no-one tells me anything! Anyway, why are you asking?"

Alice eased her head around and peered through the slit between the fire door and the frame. At the other side of the lounge, the table where Drew and Marcus had sat was forlorn and empty. The warmth looked tempting, but had Drew simply gone to the men's room? For Alice, safety was paramount. Much as she doubted Carmichael could be the killer, she had to admit she trusted Guy Higson more, and Marcus Balfour still more than Guy. There were a lot of lingering doubts. Outside was colder but a whole lot safer. Just then, she heard the familiar sound of Guy's motorbike pull up in the car park behind the pub.

"Not here, Marcus. We need to go. I'll tell you all about it, but not here."

"Oh, so now I am not a murderer. That's rich. Shit at everything, even murder!"

"You were never a murderer. And I don't think you're shit at everything. I know one thing you're not shit at, and perhaps you haven't found any of the others yet. You're one of the good guys. Fifteen years ago, I made the biggest mistake of my life when I turned my back on you and it's taken me this long to figure that out."

But Marcus was intrigued. "So what's the one thing I am not shit at?"

"OK, so it's been fifteen years but I seem to recall it was pretty good!"

"Ah." The penny dropped. "Technique might have gotten a little rusty since then. Lack of use."

"I'm sure with a bit of lubrication we can sort that."

"Eh?"

Alice was giggling but even in the lamplight he could see she had turned a fetching shade of crimson. He shrugged his shoulders and exhaled a snaking plume of vapour, waiting for a 'but' that never came. "No idea what the heck you're talking about but, fair enough. I'm here. Nowhere better to be. Can I buy you a curry, then? Talk some more about things I might not be shit at?"

"Chinese and you're on."

He held out his arm. Alice took it and they strode around the back and out onto the street. She held him tighter than she had held anyone recently. In her mind there was only one killer awaiting the chance to get even with them all.

Chapter 17

Once the nine-to-fivers had left, Daley and Whetstone had revisited the Incident board. Billy Davies had rung when they were out fetching carryout, so Dave Monaghan had hurriedly texted his order. Margaret was used to late nights and spoiled suppers. He much preferred the company and camaraderie of *The Dispossessed* to her withering scowl. Drawing the glorious aroma into his nostrils, he wheeled the Incident board across the office and the three rebelliously sequestered the goldfish bowl for their spoils. Deb had laid sheets of A4 paper over the desk, so that the chip-oil did not mark the polished veneer. Daley, who had never grasped the idea of illicit tuck in the dorm, had liberated a plate from the kitchen. Dave Monaghan, on the other hand was old school. He left his chips wrapped, poking a finger through the soggy end of the wrap for access. Less contamination, less evidence in the morning. He could blame it on the boss.

Daley closed the blinds on the goldfish bowl, isolating it from the dark, somnolent team room.

"OK. Guys. Let's sort out this mess." He pointed at the Incident board, which resembled a map of the Underground drawn by a chimpanzee. While we're musing over our intellectual puzzle, someone out there has committed a double murder and right now may be sizing up for the next. So Dawn Silverton. Let's look at the known associates.

"Drew Carmichael. She has been in an on-off relationship with Mr Carmichael since University according to Higson, Nugent and Byrne, as well as her bosses. They all agree on that.

"But Carmichael doesn't." Deb interjected. "He was at great pains to point out that their relationship was purely business. Any other involvement was ages ago."

"Which probably means that it wasn't and he wants to divert our attention away from it. And about that business. Higson, Nugent and Byrne each remarked that Carmichael was playing fast and loose with Dawns clients, to the extent that she kicked up a fuss with his boss."

Deb spoke with her mouth full, "So Dawn and Carmichael are best of friends and worst of enemies, as Higson put it. A bit of mutual back-scratching and then for some reason, it all goes tits-up and she is reporting him to his boss."

"Which probably means it's serious." Dave Monaghan reached over and dipped a chip in Deb's curry sauce and popped it in his mouth with a nod of thanks. "Smoke and fire and all that."

"What about Higson?"

"Well, he did not like Dawn in the slightest but that could be because he had a soft spot for Carmichael."

"Unrequited love - a strong motive."

"Strong enough for murder? Especially one as brutal and premeditated." Deb looked to the ceiling and pondered. "Nah! Timing is all wrong. Higson would have done away with her whilst she was still seeing Carmichael."

Well," said Dave, "if you consider that Higson is the auditor at Barraclough and Leavis, where Carmichael is under suspicion and to whom Dawn Silverton had been complaining, then the whiff of smoke gets a lot stronger. Perhaps the problem was Higson fiddling the books and Carmichael is the innocent in all this."

"Hmm." Daley frowned. "Not so sure I would go that far. Higson already loathes Dawn because she stole his man and doesn't know what to do with him. Then she starts kicking up a fuss, which will inevitably rebound on Higson. He does his best to persuade Carmichael to rein her in, but to no avail..."

"And then he discovers she is pregnant by Drew and snaps?" Deb was dubious. She was worried that the weight of evidence was too firmly against Carmichael. Sometimes smoke will drift from someone else's fire.

Daley raised the marker pen and jabbed it at two more smiling faces on the board. "Shelley Nugent and Finn Byrne. Despite their surnames, they have been married for around ten years. In business together at the Plough & Harrow, on Cordon Street, Ealing, where they host this Monday Club. Again, they seemed to think Dawn and Carmichael were in an on-off relationship. They also remarked that there was trouble between the two at work, Ms Nugent actually used the words 'unorthodox methods' but they tried to dismiss it as just one of those things. Again they said the two were best of friends and worst of enemies, same phrase."

"Almost like this group of people had the same script, gov?"

Daley nodded. "Had occurred to me, Dave."

"Even more smoke. Whenever someone says unorthodox, they generally mean crooked." The fire, whomever had started it, was now smouldering heartily.

"Dave, take a look at this audit. See what's going on, how unorthodox the practices were." Monaghan scribbled a line on his pad.

"Funny pair, though Sir," remarked Deb "Nugent and Byrne. There was something really odd going on there." She had been thinking about their visit to the Plough & Harrow. Daley nodded. He had picked up on it too.

"How so?" It was Dave. His calculating mind still processing, forestalling the carbohydrate coma.

"Well," continued Daley, "Deb and I saw them earlier at the pub. It was all very genial, very friendly, sandwiches and tea. Obviously, she was upset because her best friend had just died, but I got the distinct impression there was a double act going on. Every time she said something she was on her guard, staying on message, and if she stepped out of line Byrne would hold her hand, or interrupt, to try and keep her on message."

"And one or two times she strayed off message and he got quite shirty."

Daley agreed. "Yes. Byrne was very angry about something and didn't hide it too well. I thought he was angry with Carmichael."

"For what, gov? Had he picked up on the unorthodox methods, do you think?"

"I don't know. He didn't say so in as many words."

"It was all about Carmichael, sir. Byrne was angry about the way Dawn was being messed about. Both he and Nugent thought all Dawn's problems linked back to the way she and Carmichael were working together."

"And Nugent." Daley shifted the marker over an inch or two. "She was on edge the whole time. I would go as far as to

133

say scared."

"Yes." Whetstone pointed a dripping chip at the board. "Those two are definitely hiding something."

"Aren't they all hiding something?" Dave waved his hand in the general direction of the incident board, leaving no-one out. "We have Carmichael, trying to hide his relationship with Dawn, as well as any dodgy dealings which might be going on. We have Nugent and Byrne apparently being economical with the truth to the point of lying for some as yet unknown reason, and we have Higson who may be hiding any amount of shady financial practices. And someone, somewhere hiding the fact that they are father to Dawn's baby."

"But none of this makes them guilty of murder, guys. All the evidence is circumstantial. Nothing points directly to Carmichael as the person who wielded that sword." Deb puffed her cheeks out and sighed loudly. Daley had erased many of the minor routes on the underground map in front of her, but there were still a few branch lines that might trip them up, or even a hidden siding that could hold the key to Dawn's death. The smoke, rather than evidence of a fire, could just be concealing the mirror of misdirection.

"So who do we think is the father of the baby? My guess is that it's most likely Carmichael. Assuming he and Dawn were more on than off. Perhaps it wasn't a slip? Perhaps she wanted to force him into a more permanent relationship and he didn't like the idea. Maybe she even told him he had to cease any nefarious financial activity and become a law-abiding and responsible father?"

"That would not go down well with a man like Carmichael."

"No, Dave. Definitely not the nurturing type. And not Higson. Clearly bats for the other side."

"Or he is a very good actor and had them all fooled."

"Take it from me, Sir." Deb trusted her judgement of men above that of Daley.

"OK, so Byrne. Just because he's married, doesn't mean to say he doesn't dabble a little."

"And Nugent seems like quite a handful. Maybe he made a mistake. Maybe that's what the secret is?"

"That just leaves..." Daley scribed a circle around the only other names on the board, "...Marcus Balfour and Alice Bown. Mike Corby visited the hospital where Balfour works but he had already left. He will try again tomorrow. I'm afraid Alice Bown seems to have disappeared off the face of the earth at Christmas. According to the letting agents, she left a forwarding address but didn't move there. We need to keep onto these two. There is every possibility that they could be our murderers."

"Or our next victims, sir."

"Ever the optimist, Deb. So let's look at opportunity. What are their alibis for the time of the killing?"

"Carmichael says he was out with Dawn shortly before she was killed but back in the office when it actually happened."

"And does that stand up? What did they say at Barraclough and Leavis?"

"The receptionist, Mrs Hughes, says she saw his car turn up in the car park behind the offices, around 2:30 - 3:00pm. She couldn't be any more precise."

"Sir, the video from the church is timed at 2:25pm." added Monaghan.

"Yes, Dave, providing it was actually Carmichael's car and those were his legs. So Higson? What about his whereabouts?"

"Got back from lunch around 1:30pm. In his office all afternoon. It's possible for him to have sneaked out the back and driven over to Chapel Rise."

"The only ones with any sort of alibi are Nugent and Byrne. Each of them claims they were with the other all afternoon."

"Which is as good as no alibi at all."

Monaghan nodded. "Much as I hate to admit it, though, Deb. He has a point. It matters not where people aren't, it only matters where they are."

"Semantics, Dave, semantics!" countered Whetstone.

"Is that what you are going to tell the CPS?"

Deb stuffed a chip in her mouth speeding up the approach as the sauce threatened to drip. "So what next?"

"OK. Speak to the other people at the office and the afternoon staff at The Plough & Harrow. Let's see if anyone signed a memo, or took an order or even wrote graffiti on a toilet wall. Anything that amounts to solid proof of their

135

whereabouts."

"And there's Higson, auditor for Barraclough and Leavis. Seems to have the *hots* for Carmichael and the *nots* for Dawn. Being the auditor, he would have the ability to make problems disappear on the financial front. Again he could have arrived back from lunch and sneaked out the back and then returned to his office afterwards, all unseen."

"Which, again, is as good as no alibi at all."

The room lapsed into a brooding silence, as the three mulled over the Monday Club and the undercurrent of deceit and evasion that seemed to permeate through it. What secrets were these people hiding? Was Dawn's death directly related or purely incidental? And Carmichael. Was he the key to the murder or were his 'unorthodox methods' just misdirection? Was the smoke hiding something much more sinister? Daley rubbed his eyes and drained his coffee. The clock above the door admonishingly told him that 9:00pm was no time to be at work. He needed to get this over with quickly.

"Right, so lets summarise. Dawn Silverton was in a stormy relationship with Drew Carmichael, who is fiddling the books somewhere along the line. She was having trouble at work, directly related to some kind of dodgy dealings that Carmichael was involved in. Added to that, she had fallen pregnant. On the day she dies, Carmichael meets her and admits the row turned ugly. About an hour later she is killed. Carmichael's whereabouts at the time of her death are sketchy. If we can tie down the evidence regarding the financial dealings, then we have a fairly cut and dried case against Carmichael."

"Too cut and dried for my liking, Sir." The sharp end of Deb's optimistic streak was coursing towards Daley's bubble. "It's all still too circumstantial, lacks evidence. Everyone else we met was singing from the same hymn sheet. Maybe they all have it in for Carmichael and concocted a tale against him?"

"Why Deb? Why would they do that?"

"Because Carmichael has stepped over the line with Dawn. Maybe he had taken money from them?"

"So to get back at Carmichael for messing Dawn about, they kill Dawn?"

"If you put it like that..."

"So Nugent and Byrne. Nugent is one Prozac short of a breakdown. She couldn't have held herself together long enough to plan and carry out such a cold blooded murder, and anyway, she was seen by the staff throughout the afternoon. I think we have to rule her out as a suspect."

"Or rules her in as a good actor, Sir."

"Then there is Byrne. He made no secret of not liking Carmichael - *'shit of the first order'*. There was something smouldering along in the background."

"What, maybe he was having an affair with Dawn Silverton under Carmichael's nose?" Dave frowned.

Deb pushed some greasy A4 sheets aside and leaned further over the desk. "Why not? Carmichael's a complete tosser. He is making life really difficult for Dawn, clients are complaining. She has spoken to Barraclough and Leavis, who pay lip service and she is at the end of her tether. She spoke to Higson but he was up to his neck with whatever Carmichael was up to. She and Byrne are close friends. Perhaps she cried on his shoulder and they got just that little bit closer?

"But, Deb, if Byrne and Dawn were having an affair, surely Byrne would have left his wife, done her in, or taken it out on Carmichael, not killed Dawn?"

Whetstone was not to be derailed just yet. "True, but what if we look at it another way. Nugent and Byrne have been married for 10 years or so. They are reasonably successful. Yet, no pattering of tiny feet. Maybe, she wanted children and he didn't? He plays around with Dawn, who drops for one, which was too much for him. He had to silence her to stop her from ruining his marriage."

Far from summing up, Daley felt himself drowning in a sea of fanciful scenarios. He needed to reach out for Occam's razor to slice through and reveal the true story hidden under layers of questions and suppositions.

"We haven't even mentioned Rachel Jones yet, Sir."

Deb was right. They had not mentioned her once, but Daley was certain that everything could apply as much to Rachel as it could to Dawn, the scene, the players, the background. Find Dawn's killer and Rachel's would be found too.

"There is one other fly in the ointment, Gov." Dave heaved

himself from his chair and took the whiteboard pen from Daley. "Christopher Betts. Apparently he was in the Monday Club at Coventry, but none of the others mentioned him."

"Yes, Dave but there must be dozens of ex-members who flitted in and out. What's so special about this Betts guy?"

"Well, Gov. Maybe nothing except that Billy Davies went out of his way to mention him. Said he had been in some trouble which caused aggro for Carmichael and that he ended up a nut job."

"Five minutes around Carmichael, I think anyone would be a nut job. Keep an eye open for him in case he crops up again." Daley watched as the name was added to the board.

At that moment there was a loud clank and an unshaven, slightly balding head peered around the door of the goldfish bowl. It was Leon, one of the cleaning staff.

"Ain't you three got homes to go to? My shift finishes at 10:00 and I need to get in here before that boss of yours see the mess you've made."

***

They had reached an area of London that was unfamiliar to Marcus, however that wasn't saying much as the only parts of the Capital he had any experience of were the hospital where he worked, the flat where he occasionally stayed and the Plough & Harrow. Their supper had been in *The Hare & Tortoise* (Japanese, Chinese - it's all the same), a table towards the back. The small-talk had been sparse and self-conscious but the portions were large so they had called a taxi. The passing streets had turned residential, dragoons of parked cars, homes dark except for the occasional flicker of the late-night film through curtained windows. The phosphor on Marcus' watch had dimmed so he had to squint under the streetlights to read it. Midnight. Except for a few meagre hours snatched the previous morning, he had been up for nearly thirty hours and his body was beginning to complain. Along ever thinning roads, as closing restaurants emptied, happy diners, lost in their evening, hugged against the damp. For the first time in years, Marcus felt one of them. He turned and smiled at Alice as she dozed on his arm.

They had met about a month into his degree at Coventry,

already under a Human Biosciences cosh, begging for the Christmas break. His route back to halls had taken him past the Ellen Terry building, an ancient cinema now the University's school of drama. Her hand had reached from a doorway, and grabbed his arm with a matter-of-fact *you will do*. She was a quirky, colourful and scatty, with a taste for flowing bohemian skirts and myriad necklaces. Waves of hair tumbled out below a tight knitted hat and around her long face and full smiling mouth. Inside facing her, press-ganged into an amateur dramatic society, he instantly knew that she was the only girl he could ever love. The society came and went but Marcus and Alice remained together for the first year and into the second until the late spring of 1997 when everything changed. Even now, he held her tighter as he recalled the phrase she had used.

It had been an ordinary night in Brown's Bar. The clock had raced to 10:30 and the bell had rung, signifying that everyone should ignore the stupid British licensing laws. But with the Monday Club, 10:30 signified the start of the evening; they would drink up and head into the city centre. Shelley and Finn, would head back to the halls to make their own fun, and he and Alice, eschewing both options, would walk back together, to one of their respective rooms. But that Wednesday evening, she had been bored by the conversation, they had argued and she had gone home alone. The next morning, Alice did not answer when he called, and purposefully avoided him for the next week. When finally he caught up with her, she was dismissive. It wasn't his fault. It was just that everything had changed; it could never be the same. So he had endured a gut wrenching year and a half, willing her think again, and sharing the pain when their paths crossed. Since graduation, whenever they met, he had kept her at arms length, content to chatter, enduring the pain because the pain of seeing her was easier to bear than the pain of not.

But today something was different and he had spent the last two and a half hours attempting to define what it was.

The meeting with Carmichael had left him in turmoil. His friend would not simply hand over such a large sum of money without some strings attached. Right now the strings were tightening about Marcus' neck. There was a pungent whiff of scapegoat, and whilst that was nothing new where Carmichael was concerned, the consequences were more serious than ever before. More serious than taking the rap for Drew's late homework, or even as an excuse when he stood up a girl. He had been transfixed by the sum of money, by the name on the account, by the unbelievable shamelessness of a person he considered, for all his faults, to be a friend.

Balfour accepted that he was one of life's also-rans, working hard and gaining little. A modest house with two empty bedrooms, a BMW with a pristine passenger seat and a fantastic hi-fi, which he listened to alone. Marcus was always Drew's fall-guy, his stooge. When it came to double dates, he always got the fat one. Balfour knew his station. It was just below, just outside, just behind.

Wasting three years on Human Biosciences just because Drew was at the same university, Marcus turned to Medicine. Finally, he had secured an internship at the Ealing Hospital, working long hours, envious of Carmichael who had been gifted his career by the kind of nepotistic serendipity of which Balfour could only dream.

And now once more he was the patsy.

One million four hundred and fifty...thousand...bloody...pounds! In the warmth of the taxi, he wondered how many of these terraced homes he could buy outright. His share alone was ninety thousand pounds and growing all the time. Even if he could manage to keep his share, would that be enough? In an age when five and a half million pounds was the new million, Carmichael's Fund was nothing. Not that he was greedy and distasteful as it may be, the Fund needed to keep growing as it was, silently, undiscovered. Within five years, there would be enough. Perhaps not the full five and a half million, but easily three. And all completely invisible.

Rich on paper. That was the killer.

Reaching into his pocket, he grasped the crumpled statement of account, if for no other reason than to affirm that it was real. A dozen or more wealthy clients moving house, upsizing by degrees. Deposits running into six figures. Transferring into and out of the main account in neat couplets. Each a client of Dawn Silverton, a murdered women from whom he now appeared to have illegally appropriated money. It amounted to a huge motive for murder.

Then there was Alice. Why had she turned up at the Plough

140

& Harrow tonight? After all these years, what had made her change her mind? Since they had broken up, he had compartmentalised his life, compact and solitary, with no cupboard space for emotional attachment. Yet now, his impetuous heart pleaded for him to trust her, to accept the moment whatever the consequences. His suspicious head urged caution. As the Monday Club disintegrated about their ears, Alice had sought him out. Surely that must count for something? He looked down at her sitting beside him, clinging to his arm. Her face was drawn and anxious, betraying something of her own inner turmoil. Right here, right now, she had put her faith in him. Maybe this was the universe finally turning in his favour? Whatever happened, Marcus resolved, he would not desert Alice, he would cling onto the Fund. His share if not the whole lot, whatever happened.

The taxi pulled up. He paid the driver, and found himself facing a large, slightly dilapidated Edwardian town house.

"This is mine. Top floor flat." She pointed needlessly towards a pointed dormer.

"Oh, er, yes. Balfour released her arm and raised his hands to the crumbling facade of the house, much like a magician revealing the dismembered assistant or unexpected rabbit. "OK then. So, er, I'll say good night then." He reached forward and gallantly pushed open the wooden gate, and apologised as she squeezed past him in the opening. He watched her walk to the door, hope drifting away with each step. And then she stopped and, half turning, she spoke.

"Er, is that your taxi heading off down the street?"

Marcus turned and saw the taillights disappear around the corner.

"Ah."

"Marcus, can I ask you something?"

He let the gate close on the spring-loaded hinge and realised he was inside. "Yes, of course."

"Do you really think one of us could have killed Dawn? I mean, we joked about it earlier but, well, I've been thinking." There was an edge of disquiet to her voice.

"What, you or me?" He shrugged. How could he answer that one? "Like I said, I know I didn't but I'm still not so sure about

141

you." Alice smiled and gazed down at her feet. Small in stature, she looked helpless and alone. Could she be capable of something so brutal and with someone she knew? Could any of the Monday Club? They had amused themselves with the game as they had eaten, but in reality, murder was a colder, harder business. It was a stab, or a garrotte, or a push. Eyes bulged, blood flowed, arms flailed, life drained away. In Marcus' world, death was an everyday occurrence but guilt was not. The law made him a murderer but compassion made him a saint. Real murder had no such moral justification. Rachel and Dawn were vibrant, vivacious people. Nothing could justify the violence they suffered. He looked at the small figure, drawing in her coat against the cold and felt overwhelmingly protective towards her.

"No Alice, you're not capable of murder, and me? I see enough death every day. I don't need to see more. I haven't seen enough of life yet."

Alice's eyes were wide beneath her auburn fringe." So who do you think is doing this?"

"Drew said the police had been round. Asking all sorts of questions about Dawn and him and the Monday Club. He must be worried about something because when she was killed, he says he had no alibi. He met her for lunch, they rowed and she stormed off."

"What, and you think he followed her?"

"I don't know but there is certainly something fishy about it. Something has got him really spooked."

She was shivering now. Past midnight there was a distinct chill in the air. Was it because he was there, or was she afraid? "I don't know, Marcus. London is full of muggers and murderers. Sooner or later, the odds are it has to be someone you know. At least, that's what I thought when I first saw the paper earlier. But now I am not so sure."

"What do you mean?" He had crossed the chasm between them and now she was holding his arm.

"Guy called me tonight and he said pretty much the same. He is certain that Drew killed Dawn, and he reckons he might have killed Rachel Jones as well."

Marcus' eyes were wide with disbelief. "Oh, come on! Isn't this all getting a little bit silly?"

"He told me to stay away from Drew, to stay at home, until it all blew over."

"Well, you're home now. Whatever Guy was afraid of hasn't happened." Marcus paused and then, as if resolved to off-load a huge weight from his shoulders, he turned to face Alice and held both of her hands.

"Look. I am going to tell you something. You mustn't breathe a word to anyone. Promise?"

She looked up into his eyes, a small child vowing never to steal chocolate from the fridge. "Of course! Get on with it!"

"Carmichael has been cooking up this stock market scam, almost certainly illegal but it's made a lot of money. I mean a *lot* of money. We all put some into the pot initially, so we are all due a share."

"I know about the Fund, Marcus. Could hardly not know, the number of times Drew has crowed about it! He asked if I wanted to 'invest' too. Fat chance on seventeen thousand a year. I assumed some of you others must have done."

"But did you know that was using the money that he held in clients accounts ready for their house move, delaying it in transit for a few weeks, artificially boosting the size of the pot, increasing the returns."

Alice's eyes sparkled as she considered this. "You know what, though. That's bloody brilliant. So people moving house happily give him money. He invests it in a high income, albeit slightly risky, scheme and then after a short, but unavoidable delay, he gives them their money back plus a little bit of the interest. And he creams off the rest."

"And the rest amount to eighty per cent of all of the interest made, because interest in holding accounts is pitiful so he only needs to give some of it back. Under normal circumstances, the size of the pool will allow for stock market losses and pound cost averaging keeps it going up."

"Wow. You've got to admit, he may be a complete tosser but that is brilliant." Alice's eyes were looking into middle distance, focussing on the floating dollar signs. Marcus brought her back to earth.

"Unless you get found out, or your source of funding dries up...or both."

143

"What, Dawn?"

"Uh-huh."

"Makes sense. Given the amount of money involved, if Dawn stopped giving him clients, stands to reason he would be a little miffed."

"All I know is that Drew and Guy have been working overtime trying to hide their dodgy dealings while Dawn was busy trying to undo all of the good work by snitching to his boss."

"But really, do you think he would kill her?"

"I don't know. He said the police asked him about Rachel Jones as well as Dawn. He seemed rattled, like *really* rattled, and it got me thinking. Let's just suppose he did murder Dawn, or both of them. Forget why. Let's just suppose he is responsible. What is the one thing that can save his skin?"

Alice pondered, then smiling, she said "The money!"

"Right. So he gets Guy to cover his tracks, moves the money somewhere he can get hold of it, and does a moonlight flit. With that sort of cash he can change his name, his face, everything."

"Sound like one of those old pirate stories, where the captain takes his ill-gotten gains to a desert island, buries it, and then kills the rest of the crew, or the evil genius who builds a secret lair and kills the architect and all of the builders."

"Steady on, now. This is Drew Carmichael we're talking about, not Ernst Stavro Blofeld!"

Alice looked a little deflated, but she was enjoying being with him. Something was stirring from many years ago. Something warm that had been missing for a long time. "So do you think that's what he's up to?

"Honestly? Well, most of it, yes. Whether he is capable of killing Dawn or Rachel or not, there is certainly a bit of financial jiggery-pokery going on. And he is certainly trying to hide the money. I know that for a fact."

"Oh, Yes? How so?" Alice was rapt by this 'Boys Own' adventure. Marcus reached into his pocket and brought out the two creased pieces of paper. As Alice reached to take them from him, he drew his arm back.

"Can we go inside and read these. I'm getting a little chilly standing here."

"Never heard that one before. Very slick." She reached down and retrieved a key secreted beneath a pot plant. "For future reference." She smiled conspiratorially.

"But hang on." Marcus held her arm. "What if I am the killer and this is all some double bluff to lure you into being my next victim?"

"I hardly think you would tell me, would you?" She gave him a wry smile. Her nose wrinkled in that endearing way that he had all but forgotten.

"Suppose not, unless it was a triple bluff."

"I think I'm safe with you!"

"I know I'm safe with you, too."

And without another word, he took her hand and followed her through the front door.

Chapter 15

The piece of paper itself was ordinary, which is why Daley, Whetstone and even Monaghan missed it. A single bookmark amongst around twelve that nestled in the pages of Dawn Silverton's diary, each marking a seemingly random page that meant something to her but nothing to anyone else. DC Steve Taylor had grudgingly accepted the thankless task of poring over the notebook, looking for anything that might shed some light on Dawn's life, or her death. He started with the bookmarked pages, scanning the roughly scrawled notes. Idly skimming the pages, he held the bookmark in his right hand, like a rule, horizontal under each line, ensuring he missed nothing and, in the many frequent breaks from the tedium, marking his place. He was about halfway down the page when it struck him that the bookmark itself was thicker than the others he had pulled out. Carefully, he inserted it back into the book and retraced his steps to the first, and then the second, and the third until finally he was back to the thick one. Each bookmark was simple and unadorned. A simple inch-wide strip torn from a piece of A4 printer paper.

But the fourth was different. The A4 sheet remained intact, folded twice; it was thicker widthways than the predecessors and, even in the dim light of the desk lamp, Taylor could see the faint image of text on the inside of the paper. Opening the paper he read the text. Then, momentarily holding his breathe, he placed the sheet unfolded into an evidence bag, sealed the plastic zipper, and marked it's position in the diary with a pink Post-It tag, and then nearly crippled himself as he raced across to where Daley was hunched over case notes.

"Sir, you need to see this."

Daley lazily raised his head and reached out to take the paper from Taylor, any malaise draining away instantly as he read:

Proposition 1 - Killing by Decapitation

Date – 8th April 1997

Proponents - Rachel Jones/ Dawn Silverton

RJ - A death is a big event, especially in the life of the victim, so it has to be spectacular, it has to violent and gory, otherwise what is the point. If one is predisposed to killing then one might as well make it good! Some of the mediaeval methods of torture and execution, which inflicted grotesque amounts of damage to the victim, keeping them alive for as long as possible, forcing them to endure the endless minutes of their termination. The sheer sadistic pleasure that one could get from administering prolonged, controlled pain to another has to rate alongside the thrill of sex. I mean remember the French Revolution. Crowds baying for the blade to fall. Blood spurting from the severed neck and the head held up to the crowd. They say the eyes would still be looking around. Cool.

DS - The rules state that the murder must be committed in such a way that the murderer isn't caught. How could you do that without anyone noticing? Setting up a guillotine at Hyde Park Corner would be a dead giveaway. Far better to lure the unsuspecting victim to a secluded place and catch them unawares.

All - How can you behead someone without them being aware of what is about to happen? You cannot wait until they are sleeping and you can't persuade them to put their heads on a block.

DS - You lure them into a private place, like a back garden or a warehouse and swing at them with an axe. Or you could use a sword like King Arthur's Knights.

RJ - Or a scimitar like the executioners of the Middle East.

Proposition Victim - Dawn Silverton

My Proposition Development - Beheading with a samurai sword. The instrument is light, well balanced and can be honed to an extremely sharp edge.

My Proposition Method - Locate empty premises. This could be a property up for rental, such as a large house, enclosed commercial property, such as a factory unit. The dimensions are important. Minimum clearance of seven feet around the victim to allow for the swing.

Select a victim. The victim would depend upon the location. In the case of a private house, select the victim by means of wanted ads in shop windows, local newspaper. Select a victim who specifically requests a non-shared letting. NOTE: Do not speak to a shop owner about an ad. Return when the shop is closed and transcribe the phone number from the card in the window.

Select a time. The timing of the murder is not important, except that there must be no witnesses. If the location is secure, then the best time is mid-morning or mid-afternoon, when most potential witnesses are at work.

Transport the weapon to the site in the hours of darkness and secure within the property or the ground. The murderer should remain on-site and await the arrival of the victim. On no account should the murderer arrive with or after the victim as the risk of discovery is increased. The murderer should remain on-site after the event for at least one hour for the same reason.

Adequate protective clothing should be worn to prevent blood transfer to the murderer. Aerial squirt has a range of around two feet laterally from the neck, so the deathblow should be struck at arms length to avoid transfer. Additionally, the heart may beat for several minutes after decapitation and thus a substantial blood pool will form.

The property should be secured after departure to reduce the risk of early discovery of the body. The weapon should be cleaned on-site in a mixture of 3 parts Hydrogen Peroxide to one part bleach to destroy any risk of transfer. All evidence should be removed.

Daley beckoned Whetstone and Monaghan over as he mounted a photocopy of the letter onto the incident board. The substance of the paper was very different to the other bookmarks, a different shade of white usually found in recycled paper, and the typeface appeared to be laser printed Arial, like a hundred million pages produced each day. However forensic examination might yield a manufacturer and anomalies in the print would act as a fingerprint to identify the specific printer used.

Monaghan began the analysis of the text.

"Basically it's a two-parter. The first part looks like someone's proposal at a method of murder and the second part is an expansion of the idea.

"Read the first bit, Dave. Looking at the initials, Rachel and

Dawn were discussing the idea and proposing a method." A cursory glance around assured him that no-one disagreed. "Between them they have come up with what they believe to be the perfect murder, according to the rules."

"So this is a game," Deb interjected, "if there are rules."

"Could be," Monaghan continued, "and then the second section looks like someone has taken the method and expanded upon the idea, fleshing it out, making it a process."

"It's a complete blueprint for the murder, Sir. It's the process we are going through now. Taylor is writing down our thought processes and will expand on his notes later, like the minutes of a meeting written up afterwards. It specifically mentions Dawn and Rachel by name and refers to 'All' suggesting that other people were present, so it's a wider group than just them."

"So why would Dawn Silverton have this in her daybook? Steve, what about the other bookmarks?"

"All the others are just strips of plain white paper. It's only this one that is typewritten, Sir."

"What about the page it was marking?"

Taylor retrieved the daybook from his desk and turned to the marked page. "On the face of it, nothing particular, Sir, just loads of notes from a telephone call in February. Can't even read some of the writing."

"So," suggested Monaghan, "could this have been left by the killer after the murder?"

Two crimes. A single sheet of paper detailing the rules to a game in which Rachel Jones and Dawn Silverton had been participants, taking the first turn, describing a murder, the augur of their own demises many years later, each marked with the number of their turn, the number on their foreheads. Was this paper left as either as a twisted tribute to their skills, or as some form of justification, an indication of why they had committed such a brutal crime?

The date was 8th April 1997 - close to the anniversary of both of their deaths. The two girls would have been at University, as Carmichael had suggested earlier in the day. It alluded to the Monday Club and the list of disembodied names that Whetstone had written on the incident board in red pen. Even though this connected the two victims, did it connect them to the killer? Daley picked up the phone and put a call through to the Cheveley Hill Storage facility and asked a surprised and rather somnolent night officer to retrieve the evidence boxes from a murder four years ago.

***

As his eyes jolted open, Carmichael became aware of a vague noise outside. A throb of traffic. His face was cold, clammy, adhering to the smooth surface. Above him a sodium light from the street bathed him orange. Slowly, painfully, he peeled his face from the dried blood and edged himself upright, his surrounding gradually coming into focus. A wave of nausea coursed through him. His chest felt like a stampede of rhinos had used his ribcage as a shortcut, and the back seat of the car reeked of vomit. After a while he realised it was his own car. He sighed. Another fucking mess to clear up. Gingerly reaching into his overcoat pocket, wincing at each flex of his torso, Carmichael retrieved the key fob and clicked the button, screwing up his eyes as the interior filled with light.

Arriving at the Plough & Harrow, he had parked up in the yard behind, as usual. Now he was surrounded by trees. They had moved the car. Out of sight, out of mind.

So now it was as clear as the maturing bruises on his body, Guy and Finn were no longer allies. Quite the opposite. They had made that perfectly plain with their boot heels. And when the opportunity arises, he would be sure to do the same. In spades. For years, he had carried that two-bit, faggot, money shuffler, a word here, a recommendation there. Higson would be nowhere without the favours gifted by Carmichael. Well, that was a double-edged sword. What is given can also be taken away. And the same applied to that bloody *Mick*, Finn Byrne and his simpering bitch of a wife. Gradually the interior light faded to nothing and once more Carmichael sat in darkness, anonymous and separate, consumed by a silent fury.

He was on his own. For years, they had been subservient sycophantic pack rats, content to follow. It would be naive to think that it was his charm and good looks that had kept them close. He had smelled their hostility before, behind the smiles, as they blamed him for Rachel's death; that her murder, whilst they couldn't pin it directly onto him, was definitely on his hands.

150

Before she had died, he had enjoyed the reputation of loveable rogue sailing close to the wind. With her death, the wind had changed, the sails had folded and the sea had become more treacherous. At first, he could handle it. *Mea culpa.* Caught in the wrong bed with the wrong girl. But the dynamic of the group also subtly changed. Far from sympathising, they had rallied against him. Double meanings when they spoke, whispers behind his back, sly glances. Publicly he had scoffed at their baseless accusations. Privately, he didn't really care. The police had investigated and come up empty. Perversely, that they thought him capable had added to his kudos. He had hunkered down and ridden the rough seas, allowing an uneasy calm to settle over the Monday Club. Turning up out of duty. As the Fund grew, it became more of a necessity, but even then he had come to the conclusion that his time with them all had run its course. When Dawn had started causing problems at Barraclough and Leavis, the whispers were almost audible, their remarks more cutting. Again, this was something he could ride. Nothing was ever gained without garnering a few enemies along the way.

But now they had finally turned on him.

Finn Byrne was just noise. Carmichael could deal with him. A colossal writ thrown his way would keep him occupied for months, possibly years. No, Byrne was not the problem. It was Guy. He would pay for his betrayal. No longer could he be allowed to continue unfettered, especially now the police were involved. The cancer was spreading through the Monday Club and had to be excised before it consumed them all. But more particularly, before it consumed him.

It was an effort to breathe but, wincing with every movement, he opened the rear door and got out of the car. He looked about him. The Mercedes was in a car park, invisible to the road, protected by an exploding laurel hedge. Across the car park was an expanse of black, a faint line of orange lights marking the boundary on the other side. Ealing Common? He pulled back his cuff and looked at his watch. Almost midnight. He climbed behind the wheel and started the engine. This was no time to pussy out because of a little pain.

So now it was clear he was on his own and he knew what he had to do.

151

When Daley and Whetstone reached Cheveley Hill, the duty officer had pulled the evidence on the Rachel Jones' case. The three cardboard crates, roughly a metre long by half a metre deep were all that testified to her life and her death. Pinging her hands into latex gloves, Whetstone watched as the duty officer cut the sealing tape with a knife and dragged off the lid of each box in turn.

The boxes contained a miscellany of dissociated objects from a defunct life. Keys that would never turn in a lock that probably no longer existed, a handbag shrink-wrapped and emptied of its contents of pens, mascara, tissues and mints. The second box made her catch her breath, as she took out the clothes that Rachel had been wearing at the time, a blue jacket and pencil skirt stained black with gore, a matching bra, slip and panties in pastel blue silk, rigid and hard with congealed blood spill, now blackened and dry.

Daley had taken the third box, instinctively, or was it through memory, knowing that all of Rachel's business documents would be in it. He lifted out sheaves of paper, notebooks and diaries, each in their own polythene bags, and set about the task of examining them.

An hour later, the duty officer returned with coffee, and started to repack the first two boxes. Daley and Whetstone continued their fruitless trawl through the endless reams of office tittle-tattle that had seemed so important when it had been committed to paper but which was now as disembodied as the rest of the dead woman's belongings. Deb started as the duty officer spoke, the volume of his voice ringing in the quiet of night, idle chatter to pass the time.

"You don't see that much any more."

Without raising her head, or even caring, Whetstone unconsciously said "What?"

"Well, the grand-kids still do it, but you don't see many thirty-somethings doing it."

Now irritated, her concentration wavering, Whetstone repeated "What, Jim?"

"Wrapping textbooks in wallpaper. You, know like covers. We used to do it at school, but I've not done that myself since I was twelve. Seems strange a woman of her age wrapping a book in paper."

Daley and Whetstone turned to the book, inside an evidence bag, still awaiting their attention. Now it had got it. Daley picked up the bag and removed the A5 bound notebook. The contents were much the same as the one Dawn had kept. It was spotless, the paper cover clean and fresh, no marks, except for the creases holding it in place, no decoration and bizarrely not even a title or the name of the owner. Miraculously, it had escaped the worst of the blood spray that Daley recalled from the original crime scene. Rachel had left her voluminous handbag, with the book, on the front step, intending to pick it up once she had entered the front door. He remembered himself carrying out the tedious task that Taylor was still carrying out three miles away, combing each page for a shred of a clue, coming up blank.

But now he knew where to look.

Easing the folds open, he removed the paper from the book and gingerly turned it inside out. He read the text, still familiar from earlier in the evening, except the type was older and bittier, as if from a different kind of printer. But the substance was the same. Word for word the same as the other. And finally, irrefutably, the link was made across the years between the deaths of Rachel Jones and Dawn Silverton.

CHAPTER 16

The end of a shift is always time for celebration. Dragging our way through the last interminable hour as the clock lollygags around to closing time, we plan our bid for freedom. Lee Smith saved that celebration for the empty streets and the bike ride home. It was a chance to burn off the pent-up energy and unresolved boredom accumulated during his tedious shift. Even before the noisy, tired Underground carriage had emptied of passengers, Lee had already bounded up the steps from the platform, and texted his girlfriend to inform her of his impromptu visit. He thrilled at the thought of ten or fifteen minutes groping and snogging, which was all he could snatch on a work night. He pumped at the pedals, his BMX yawing wildly left and right under the stress, compressing his knees and elbows, as he bobbed and weaved in and out of the haphazardly parked cars, past the courting couple paying no attention to where they were walking, past the pizza joints and chips shops and the curry house on the corner, still lit as they wearily paced and loitered, waiting for the late-nighters to piss off home.

He hit the traffic lights at Major's Lane as they changed to red, his tyres squealing as he skated to a halt a foot or so from the two adolescents crossing from *The Wheatsheaf*, not hearing the names they flung at him, anxious to set off again, imagining his hand inside her warm pyjamas, her restrained moans as his fingers probed. The traffic lights marked the halfway point in the short ride, the point at which he could put the hammer down. This new lightweight frame had dramatically increased the speed he could reach, and thus the amount of ground he could put between himself and *The Bull's Head*. To his right, he heard the deep throaty growl, and looked across to see the rider pull up as the lights started to change. He raised a hand to wave at Mr Higson, who nodded and clicked down through the box before wheelieing away. In an automatic movement borne of practice, he twisted the handgrips and felt the pedals lighten briefly as the chain rattled across the gears. His legs beat down in piston-like strokes, imagining himself clad in leather, pressed back by the night air as he twisted the throttle and a hundred and seventy-eight horses powered him down the street. The voice in his mind sang the chorus from 'You Ain't seen Nothing

Yet'; the last song on the jukebox before closing time, now piping into his ears from the iPod strapped to his arm, counting out the strokes as he attempted to beat his all-time record and reach the park gates before descending to third gear for the final push.

In his view, Wednesday night was the worst night of the week and he cursed his father for leaving home, forcing him to take a job to pay his way through college. On Wednesday night the other guys from his course descended on *The Bulls Head* and rubbed his nose in it. Of them all, only Raul understood, and that was because he was an illegal and had no money of his own. But even he joined in the mocking.

"You...ain't...seen...nothing...yet...bowm...bowm..."

Still, it wouldn't always be like this. Passing the bus stop, spooky and spot-lit by the amber street lamp, he imagined the spectres of his college buddies there six or so hours previously, laughing, and joking and passing a joint between them as he had cycled past on his way home. A penny saved is a penny earned. One's teens should be the best years of one's life, carefree and endless. A time to explore the world, to find a direction for the future. He should not have to live like this! He should be out having fun, getting stoned, getting laid! At last, he could see the outline of the church, sombre and pale against the black of the sky and beyond it the tight left into the blackness of the trees in Treddle Lane.

"You, you, you, you... ain't... seen... nothing... yet... bowm... bowm..."

He swept around the corner from the main road under the monumental overhanging oaks. His world went dark as the streetlights became obscured, flickering through a canopy of amber and olive, and he blinked in the subdued light. He was still gathering pace and the breeze cooled the sweat beneath his shirt and whooshed past his ears, as his head exploded in an electric guitar crescendo. The tyres hummed across the tarmac as the final street lamp ceded to blackness and, sensing his eyes adjust, he scanned ahead for the entrance to Lover's Lane, despite it's name inevitably deserted and the shortest route, saving ten minutes through the woods to the back of the row of houses where Lucy's moist mouth and warm breasts would be waiting. Easing on the rear brake, he scrubbed off a little extra speed, feathering the lever with his fingers to avoid a lock-up, readying himself to make the jump from tarmac to loose metalling, not wanting to come a cropper, recalling the burn of gravel rash. But the extra speed was deceptive and he was forced to apply the brake even harder. His left hand was taut, desperately willing him to squeeze on a little front brake, which would inevitably whip the front wheel away and pitch him off. The rear tyre grated on the road and the brake pads moaned. As the bike hit the gravel, it skewed sideways, the rear wheel trying to overtake the front. Despite the precariousness, Lee whooped loudly as the adrenaline coursed through him. He wrestled with the steering to pull on some opposite lock and began to breathe again as his feet skidded on the gravel, supporting the bike and keeping him upright. Inwardly he sighed as the danger passed.

Then something struck him in the neck and he felt the sting behind his right ear as he somersaulted through the air and his bike continued it's inevitable course into the gully. He landed heavily on his back and felt the breath crushed from his lungs. The sharp stones dug grooves in his flesh as he skated to a halt in a raining shower of dirt and water.

When everything came to an eerie stop, Lee carried out an inventory. His left arm was badly grazed and he'd be picking crap out of it for days. There would surely be a bruise the size of New Zealand where his iPod had embedded itself in his bicep, but it was still working, if the case was a little scuffed, and the headphone cord was snapped. He had landed badly and his right ankle, which had buckled under him, was numb. He tried to rotate it, sending spasms of pain through his foot. Only sprained though. Serves him right for trying to beat an impossible all-time record, new frame or not. A clammy wetness clung to his neck and he instinctively reached to wipe it away but just succeeded in spreading the blood across his stinging palms, forcing tiny stones deeper into the cuts. His ear felt as if it had damn nearly been ripped off. As he rose gingerly to his feet, an enormous pain shot through his buttock where his mobile had come between flesh and ground. He would have some fantastic war wounds tomorrow. Recalling the fall, Lee looked back down the lane, scanning through the dense pall of dust kicked up and hanging in the glow from the solitary street light at the entrance to Lover's Lane. The road was a landscape of ruts and small stones, nothing he couldn't handle. It was then he noticed, against the sodium orange, a fine strip of black, a dull silhouette accentuated by grey, motes of dust, bobbing and dancing. He hobbled across and ran his hand across the strip, cold and taut and his expression changed to incredulity.

What wanker would put a wire across the road like that?

A movement beyond the dust, a faint outline and then the sound of an engine. He strained to see the car as it accelerated back up Treddle Lane towards the main road.

He gingerly removed the dismembered earphone from his right ear, switched off the iPod and the echoing medley of rock music and buzzing his head gave way to an unearthly silence. It was then he heard the sound and recognised it immediately. It was a sound he had envied, that had excited him from the first time he had heard it. Four cylinders, water cooled, revving at over twelve thousand, but now just ticking over. Steadily throbbing away further down the lane he could hear Mr Higson's Honda Fireblade. He strained in the direction of the sound and saw the red taillight peering out through the hedgerow, like the eye of a beast of the night, growling and skulking. The bike was canted at forty five degrees suspended in the ancient gnarled hawthorn, suffused in a pink mist of exhaust smoke and dust, as the rear wheel turned aimlessly. It took him a moment to make sense of the situation and then he felt a trickle of blood course down his neck and instantly knew. About ten yards nearer lay a crumpled bundle, which Lee took to be Mr Higson. He wasn't moving. Wincing with every step, he dragged himself over to the body, and then felt the bile rise to his throat as he saw the black congealing gore and the ragged edge of flesh under the helmet. He knew that Guy Higson was dead.

Chapter 17

The roads at that time of night were empty and deserted. Although technically it was morning, Daley might well have kicked anyone in the nuts if they had attempted to correct him. But no-one would, as no-one else was stupid enough to be around at this insane hour. Except the police, a certain Forensic Pathologist, an injured cyclist and yet another dead guy.

Paradoxically, Daley loved the early hours. During his time on the beat, this was the time before the boredom started to bite and when the tiredness of the day had lifted. The time of spirited humour with cafe owners, of harmless meandering drunks.

He reached Whetstone's house in minutes, arriving as she was leaving, wrestling an outdoor coat over her arms like a scarecrow caught in a gale, none too happy with being hauled from her bed at such an ludicrous hour. She threw herself heavily into the passenger seat with a sigh of unmitigated disgust. Daley had already started to drive away.

"This better be bloody important or, senior officer or not, you are a dead man."

"Why? Did you have other plans?" The look she returned threw daggers. In the glow from the dash, accentuated by infrequent passing cars, her face was pale, sparse make-up, a rush job. She always found time to put on the mask before she faced the world.

"Gascoigne rang my mobile. Why'd he do that? He has never done that before." She held up a black blob, which Daley took to be the offending phone. She concentrated on the minimal cosmetic improvements she could make in a moving vehicle, and on the business in hand.

"What did he tell you?" Gascoigne had rung Daley twice. The second time had succeeded in rousing him. The half-hour of semi-conscious dozing would be all the sleep he would be able to glean until much later the next day. The call from Gascoigne had been terse and staccato, to a background of moving vehicles and the muffled buffeting that indicated he was making the call outside.

"Nothing. He was just pissed off because you didn't answer.

I told him you were at home as far as I knew and he said he'd try again. He *did* say that he was freezing his 'nads off whilst we were tucked up in bed and that I should go and kick you until you woke up. I told him that contrary to gossip we lived several miles apart. Why, what's it all about?" Whetstone knew that murderers did not respect her free time, or that of Keith the Uniform, who was, at that moment, completely pissed off and dressing to leave. The weather had taken a turn for the worst and spits of rain mottled the windscreen. A cold night, standing around would chill her to the bone and she would invariably be sniffing for the whole of the next day and probably the weekend.

"Another suspicious death. After he'd finished having a go at me, Gascoigne said he thought it might be one of ours. That's all he told me."

They were at the scene in a matter of minutes, the road deserted of all but the hardiest of night owls and the loneliest of vagrants. At the top of Treddle Lane a single bobby kicked his heels against the early morning chill. They parked up with a flash of the warrant card and trotted briskly towards the floodlights and the noise and the ribbons of blue and white tape hanging limp in the still damp air. Gascoigne was in an inflatable ribbed tent, the lights inside casting unnatural shadows that rose and fell against its skin, like a developing larva inside an egg. Warned by a WPC, they ducked under the tripwire, Daley casting a bemused glance back as he rose on the other side, a knot in his stomach as they neared the tent.

"Ah, Scott, Deborah. Glad you could make it at this ungodly hour." Gascoigne's head appeared through the unzipped aperture as they approached. A man lay in the starkness of the artificial room. He was lying on his back; his leather jacket rucked up behind his head, which was canted at an abnormal angle. A straight red line ran from his Adam's apple to just behind his right ear, and the balance of his body's blood had soaked into a blackened stain below him. Gascoigne had already removed the helmet, which had been bagged and taken away. Deb gave a gasp as she looked into the eyes she had seen earlier that same day.

"That's Guy Higson, Sir." Instinctively she put her hand to her mouth, her gorge rising.

"What, the accountant chap. Carmichael's friend?" Daley

159

scratched his head. "They're dropping like flies!"

"Need him on the slab to be sure, you know, rule out MI, stroke, epilepsy, but it looks like death was exsanguination due to the laceration across the carotid artery and jugular vein on the right side of the neck. Probably caused by that trip wire across the road. Middle to upper register Piano string, I would guess. Most likely unconscious or winded from the fall and bled out." Gascoigne pointed rather unnecessarily with a pen towards the obvious wounds and then in the approximate direction of the wire, invisible through the opaque tent. "There is a severe blow to the back of the head, a broken left collarbone and forearm probably sustained in the fall off the motorbike. Time of Death? Very recent, say about 10:30 to midnight, judging by latent temperature of the body, and the complete lack of lividity or rigor. Although complete exsanguination cools the body more rapidly, I am fairly satisfied with that time being 12:07am because his watch broke on impact. Shame. Quite a nice one. Would have taken him around a minute to die, poor sod, so if he had regained consciousness, he might have seen the killer."

With his gloved fingers, he tilted the head to the right. On the left cheek, in black marker pen, was scribed a number '3'. Fortuitously, Gascoigne had been on rotation and was called out to examine the body. "I know this may sound stupid, Patrick," Deb used the first name and rode the look that Daley cast her, "but did you find anything odd, such as a piece of paper, probably folded, stuffed into a pocket?"

***

Proposition 3 - Killing by Decapitation (2)

Date - 10th April 1997

Proponent - Guy Higson

GH - The great advantage of decapitation is that it is quick and relatively painless, although it has it's drawbacks.

For one thing, it requires that the person wielding the weapon is swift, strong and above all accurate. If the blow is too weak, or off the mark, then a catastrophic injury may occur without the victim dying, leading to the potential for discovery. For another, as you are actually present within feet of the victim, it increases the potential for transfer of evidence, for example

160

blood onto the murderer, and of other trace evidence onto the victim.

Me - That breaks the rule of anonymity. Any exchange of evidence would need to be prevented.

All - *(General agreement)* So what do you suggest?

GH - I like the swiftness of death that comes with decapitation, and I like the ghoulish prospect that the victim sees their murderer, even if only very briefly before brain function ceases. What must go through their head at that precise moment?

DS/ RJ - You're sick Gxxxxx. (The two girls grimaced at this point).

Me - So what do you suggest?

GH - Now if you could achieve the beheading from a safe distance. Just near enough to see the blood spurt but not get drenched in it! Maybe a swinging axe similar to *The Pit and the Pendulum* by Edgar Alan Poe. It could be suspended from the ceiling and triggered by, say the victim opening the door.

Me - The speed of the drop and the weight of the axe would need to be extremely precisely matched to achieve the desired effect. Also the height of the person in relation to the swing of the axe would need some maths. But it is plausible.

GH - Alternatively, if the cutting surface was stationary but the person was moving, one could more precisely control the impact and subsequent beheading. Like the old films where a rope is tied between trees when a rider comes along and is knocked off his horse. Well, I ride a moped, and I once saw a TV crime drama where a moped rider was decapitated by piano wire strung between two trees on the route that the rider always took.

DS - Not very original then, GH.

GH - Where in the rules does it state originality?

Me - Originality is not a rule. Originality is a discretional requirement in order to increase chances of winning.

Proposition Victim - Guy Higson

Proposition Development - Use of piano wire (NOTE: Check gauge of piano wire. Lower scale strings are round

161

wound, which might render them ineffective. Upper strings are fine gauge, which might render them too fragile and liable to snap). Potential high tensile wire from another source - research required.

My Proposition Method - Locate the site. This would need to be a private road, or another route that was rarely frequented, in order to reduce the risk of an unintended victim. Additionally, it must be possible to rig the wire rapidly around the time of the arrival of the victim, so suitable trees, street lamps and/ or telegraph poles should be located. A wire stretcher, such as 'Bulldog' by Herdsman should be sought.

Select a victim. The victim would depend upon the location and by definition they must be a bicycle or motorcycle rider. May require significant research to isolate a suitable candidate.

NOTE: Care required during research in order not to be seen. For suitably isolated properties, it may be possible to 'case the joint' using a ruse such as a lost cat or wrongly delivered post, however care must be taken to ensure the victim is alone and that one is not spotted by neighbours.

Select a time. The timing of the murder is important, to ensure that the subsequent crash of the bicycle or motorcycle is not seen or overheard. Where there is the potential for the incident to be seen, care should be taken to select a victim with a regular motorcycle trip carried out under cover of darkness.

Ensure leather faced gloves are worn prior to touching the wire or equipment, as the sharpness of the wire may cause cuts and transfer of murderers DNA to the wire.

Prior to the murder, secure the wire around the first upright with a Gripple T-clip. Feed the wire to the second upright using the wire stretcher to achieve tension and a second Gripple T-Clip to secure. Tension on the wire should ensure less than 10mm deflection at the centre, given a span of no more than 10 metres.

Subsequent to the murder, the wire may be left in place. Due to the nature of an outdoor site, footwear should be purchased for the event and disposed of following the event.

***

Did Guy not realise that he would need to be stopped? Had

it not occurred to him that our collective secret would require me to take these steps? Yet still he had persisted with his threats to reveal everything. He must have known that as soon as he started playing his games, he would force us to act? Once an ally now an enemy. How could the worm have turned so quickly?

Notwithstanding, he was next on the list and it was only a matter of time. The wheel is inexorably turning. Our sequence had been ordained a long while ago. They were all there that night, gathered for the cabaret, baying for blood and together, they all bore witness, they all became a hostage to the secret and to the unspoken vow to keep it hidden. To keep us hidden.

The preparation had been meticulous but in the end, it was a close run thing. The best laid plans. Once more your iniquity threatened to be our undoing, as you languished in your own vomit and pity. I had to claw back time, get the plan back on track. The wire stretcher took every ounce of your strength to draw the lethal band between two sturdy ash trees, biting into the bark, leaving vicious gashes. We struggled to remove the device, to load it back into the boot, wood chips on the boot floor. We were lucky he didn't see us as his headlight scoured the lane, the faintest sheen of silver before the resonant thud, the incongruous pirouette, the spattering of stones and the subdued purr of the engine as the bike rested down the lane.

How long must I be your moral compass? How long until you acknowledge that I am right and your path is the one that leads to destruction? Why do you not know I am here, a footfall in your shadow, a whisper on your breath, a tiny glimmer of guilt behind your callousness? Is none of this percolating through to you? Can you not hear me screaming at you?

I have become the terror that haunts your nights. Your vestigial twin, a parasite, a prowling, unseen beast that lurks in the recesses of the mind, venturing out to play when the darkness descends. For too long now, I have floated at your shoulder, just beyond reality. I have loitered in the shadows awaiting my opportunities.

I have become the terror that haunts your nights. And now it is night.

Chapter 18

The door of the apartment was ajar and Finn inhaled the pungent aroma of ground coffee. For a heartbeat it could have been any other day, except for the redness in his knuckles. Seated at the table, elbows on the melamine, Shelley held the buttered toast at eye level before she chowed down on a bite. She was immaculately made up and her hair was a festoon of auburn curls. She was wearing a crisp white blouse with a pleated front, a black skirt that hovered around her knees, which in itself was a miracle given that she normally wore a tracksuit until opening time. Only the faint greyness under her eyes betrayed the effort it had been. She pushed a cup of coffee across to him, the saucer jarring, quivering waves across the surface and shards of steel through his brain.

"I can't go on like this, Finn. Not anymore."

It was a conversation he knew would have to come. In the four years since Rachel's death, their marriage had taken a beating, talking less, arguing more. When they spent time together they were still alone. They both knew a change was inevitable.

Finn swallowed the coffee, scalding his mouth, searing and cathartic. "So what do you want to do?" He had been over the options a million times. They would lose the pub and the restaurant; have to start over, a mountain of debt. To part would destroy them both.

"I don't know but I can't carry on like this. I can't wake up each morning afraid of the day."

"Do you want to split up? Is that what you're saying?"

She raised her eyes to his, wide and earnest. "Oh, no, Finn. If life has been this tough with you in it, how tough would it be if you weren't there? No Finn. I want to start again. I don't know what that means but something has to change. Two of my oldest and dearest friends are both dead and I have almost driven you away. I am afraid to turn a corner for fear of who I might see. Apart from you there is no-one. I don't want to be alone, Finn."

164

Her eyes glistening with tears.

Tentatively, Finn placed his hands on hers. "I keep telling you, you have me. Haven't I always been here for you? Day and night?" It exasperated him that she always wielded this weapon whenever she descended into a depression.

"You have been here, Finn. Physically, in this house by my side but however much you tried, you have never truly been here with *me*. There are times I needed you and you simply weren't there to help me, to understand how it felt to be me."

Finn pondered what she was saying. Could a man truly understand any woman? "Look, I know you've had it bad, but I have never let you down, not once. I've kept this place going when you couldn't. If it's really what you want, we can put all of this behind us, move on. I'm sure we can. This place is ticking over nicely. At last we are making some money, covering our debts. Hey, look, maybe we can take a holiday; get away from it all for a week or two. I mean once Dawn's funerals out of the way..."

Shelley held up her hand to silence him. He sensed the determination in her manner and realised she must have lain awake working on the words.

"I need to tell you something, Finn." She lifted her cup and paused, summoning up the courage. "You know we lent that money to Drew three years ago? Invested money into his scheme?" Finn nodded, remembering the arguments and finally the silence, before he relented and they joined Drew's Monday Club scheme. "Well last year, I borrowed against the pub and gave him more."

Finn sat down opposite her and looked at her aghast. He saw the fear in her eyes, a secret now exposed.

"How much?" When Drew had first approached the Monday Club, as Finn and Shelley had the Plough & Harrow, he had pitched in at a colossal fifty thousand pounds, laying on the flannel - *speculate to accumulate, an offer like this does not come along every day*. He had promised that the business would be mortgage free in less than ten years. It had taken Finn all of his powers of persuasion to convince Shelley of the risks, and eventually, as much to appease her as anything else, he had relented and fifteen thousand pounds had been borrowed against the Plough & Harrow and handed over to Carmichael. He had all but

165

forgotten the scheme, instead being beset by the fallout from Shelley's nervous episodes and frequent bouts of depression. And now it occurred to him that the scheme was probably the reason for them all along.

"Another thirty-five thousand."

His eyes remained firmly fixed on her for a long moment, composed, besieged by a million and one emotions. Her deceit, the extra burden on their already stretched finances and the explosive rage he still felt towards Drew Carmichael. He lowered his eyes to his bruised hands as they cradled the lukewarm coffee cup. He noticed they were shaking.

"When was this?"

"About a year ago. You were staying overnight in Sheffield visiting the Brewery. He came round, showed me the statements from the fund, how much it had grown in the previous couple of years. How much we had accumulated. He showed me how much we would have had, if we had invested the whole fifty grand. Finn, we would have doubled it in two years."

Finn raised his eyes and hands to the ceiling as if seeking divine intervention. "How could you do that - go behind my back like that? How did you get the money anyway? There's nowhere near that much ready cash in the business."

"I took out an extension on the mortgage. I phoned them up while you were away."

"But you couldn't just arrange it like that. I mean, it's in joint names, you would have needed my signature at least."

Shelley lowered her head. The catharsis she sought was dragging its heels.

"You forged my signature...? Shelley, for God's sake! What the hell did you think you were doing? What if someone were to find out? For God's sake!" Abruptly, he stood and hurled the coffee cup across the kitchen.

She started as the cup exploded in a burst of white shards and dripping brown but the fell motionless once more, breathing heavily, trying to forestall the tears. With a deep exasperated sigh, Finn righted the chair, sat back down and cradled his head in his hands. They were teetering on a precipice, either side a chasm, where the only safe course of action was to continue along the knife-edge. Down one sheer side lay financial ruin.

Down the other lay pain and heartbreak. A whole life spent choosing the lesser of two evils, where the difference was infinitesimally small and the burden unbearable. He was tired of making crucial decisions, of carrying the weight. He just needed it all to be over. And now he stood on the banks of his own personal Rubicon deciding whether to cross.

Rising from his chair, he poured fresh coffee. The success of the Plough & Harrow had buoyed them. Shelley's depressions had pulled them down, the new restaurant hauling them back up again. And now Dawn's death. He felt like Stretch Armstrong in an unending Tug of War. Sitting back down, he placed a finger under her chin and gently raised her head until he could see those vivid, fathomless brown eyes.

"You said you want to start over." She gave the tiniest of nods. "Let's just...try and think of all this another way. Can we afford the mortgage payments?" Again a nod.

"So right now, sitting here, just you and me, that extra thirty-five thousand is not causing us a problem?"

Another weak nod.

"Well, this is the first day of starting over. Firstly, I am going to get our money back, and then the whole of the Monday Club can go and do one. I don't want to see or speak to any of them ever again. From now on it's just you and me, right?"

She mustered a weak smile and clasped his arm. Quietly, she answered, "Right."

"From now on, no secrets, OK?" She nodded, but the knife-edge was a path full of pitfalls, and the chasms either side beckoned him to fail. He had to build foundations on the crumbling ground. "You need to tell me. What was it that gave Carmichael such a hold over you? What happened that night when you came back from Browns?"

He could see that the pain of the last great secret still eating away at her, but no secrets meant no secrets. She had to tell him. He was insistent.

"Please, Shelley. If we going to start over."

And coldly and dispassionately she began to relate to him the story of that April night in Coventry. The one secret she vowed would never tell.

167

Chapter 19

Though she managed the dampened cloth with tenderness, Carmichael still winced each time Carol Hughes dabbed at him with whatever unctuous crap she had found in the first aid kit. He yanked his jaw from side to side, still tasting blood. It hurt when he breathed. Painful but he would live. Apart from a bruised rib and a cut to his face, he had survived. The journey to work that morning had been a trek, though practically only a short distance from the car park on Ealing Common. Fortunately he kept another suit and a clean shirt in the office, although his underpants would not bear close scrutiny after the beating he had taken. A quick call to Carol's mobile had persuaded her to come in early. God! He must have sounded rough.

"Drew? Can I ask you something?" He looked up, her face serious and business-like. She turned his head back and kept dabbing. He nodded almost imperceptibly. "They said in the paper she was murdered. Did you kill her?"

Such a direct question spelled danger. Carmichael measured his reaction, neutral, expressionless. An image flashed through his mind. An inky black pool, a rattling death rasp. Again he turned to her but her face too was stone, non-committal. Did she believe him capable? God knows she knew he was capable of just about everything else. He chose evasion. "What do you think?"

Momentarily she was conflicted. "I don't know. There are a lot of rumours going around. They say there's no smoke without fire. Is there any truth to them?"

"You know as much as I do. Dawn and I were strictly business." He needed her to believe him, but he knew she would have to reach that conclusion alone. Her face remained unconvinced. He continued: "Carol, I am no angel, I admit it, but do you really think I am a killer?"

For a long moment, they lapsed into silence. Her pendant swayed and beyond it, her blouse fell away yielding to the darkness of her chest. Her perfume filled his nostrils and the silence became uncomfortable. Dawn and Rachel had been consigned to history. Carol was an undiscovered country, which he yearned to explore but might still never visit.

"Well, do you believe me?"

"I thought I'd worked here long enough to figure you out, when you're being economical with the truth. But today, Drew, I am afraid. I have no idea where you were half of Monday afternoon, and then this." She gestured at the wields on his cheek. "If it's nothing to do with you, why are you so worried about the police? They are probably only doing some background checks, building a picture of Miss Silverton's life."

Carmichael was barely listening. His mind filled with scenarios, which he could unfurl to counter her doubts. Explanations of his whereabouts on Monday, his whereabouts on a similar afternoon four years ago, or even long dormant alibis from fifteen years ago, but at this moment there was only one issue that concerned him.

"And the police? Did they ask about the accounts?" After all, that was why Dawn had visited Barraclough and Leavis last month."

"No, Drew. They didn't ask about the accounts." Her tone was one of annoyance, an emphatic maternal tone, chiding him for not listening carefully. But all he heard was the soft Tyneside intonation and the words 'today I am scared' resonating in his brain.

Just then the intercom buzzed. Carmichael made to press the button, but Carol intercepted it before he could. It was Reception.

"Yes, Rebecca?"

"That policeman is back to see Mr Carmichael. Shall I send him through?" It was the gangly YTS.

"No, just ask him to take a seat. I'll be out in a minute." She released the button. "I don't know how many times I have told her never say an associate is in his office."

"I can't see him looking like this. God knows what he'll make of these bruises."

"Don't worry, I'll get rid of him in a while."

Drew appreciated Carol's efforts to shield him from the

police even if only to protect her share in the Fund. The weight of his secrets hung heavy, the isolation of not sharing. It was a risk but he needed her on his side.

"Look, Carol, You need to know about me and Dawn." She tilted her head slightly, inquisitively. The hair fell away from the side of her cheek and her earring glinted. "But I have to know you are with me on this one. I will be honest if you promise to back me up." She nodded.

"Dawn Silverton and I met at University and were a couple for a few years before we split. I met her again more recently, when she started passing me clients. It was like old times for two or three weeks but that was over ages ago. Since then, I have just seen her socially, with friends, nothing else. I swear I had nothing to do with her murder." Carmichael held his hands up. "OK, I admit I was working the client accounts, but you know that already. I'm worried that if the police find out about the accounts, they'll put two and two together and make a million, and all of a sudden I'll be chief suspect."

"Drew. We all knew that you and Miss Silverton were in a relationship. You know how women gossip! Why should the police connect the accounts to her murder? Why would they? There must be a dozen ex-boyfriends. Any of the partners in this practice could have fiddled the books. Why would they think you any different from the rest? And anyway the audit was clean."

"But the texts and phone calls? The police seemed very interested in those."

"So you were doing business together! Of course they need to know about them. So what if you had been in a relationship. They say the last person to see the victim alive is the murderer. Where were you when she was killed?"

"I was in Subway getting a sandwich, I think."

"Did she die in Subway?"

"Not that I am aware of."

"So stop bloody worrying! You're in no fit state to work. You get off home, and I will get back to what I am paid to do - tidying up your mess."

***

170

Like most visitors' chairs littered about many receptions, this was an excruciatingly uncomfortable one. The chrome steel tubes that imitated arms drilled into the underside of Scott Daley's elbows and the seat was as soft as a granite ironing board. He felt the pain and grudgingly accepted it. The snap team session earlier had been a sombre affair, everyone curt and to the point. They had failed Guy Higson and Daley's stomach knotted as Deb lifted the pen to the incident board and struck through his name. More progress should have been made.

As erstwhile boyfriend of the two girls, and clear contender for Dawn and Rachel's murders, they had concentrated the majority of their effort on Carmichael. Guy Higson's death brought a new set of dynamics into play.

Paradoxically, now that Higson was dead, he had to be treated both as a potential murderer and a victim, stretching lines of enquiry, and the team, still further. Potentially, he may have killed Dawn and Rachel, only to be murdered himself by an accomplice. However, the number on his cheek and the paper in his pocket had made that scenario unlikely.

OK, so Deb and Dave had agreed that Higson's specialist financial skills gave him a motive to silence Dawn, but bulk of the evidence, even if circumstantial, was stacked up against Carmichael. No matter what Allenby thought, he should have had a tail on Carmichael.

There had, however, been some positive developments, although as with many, there was a disappointing twist. Responding to a text from Patrick Gascoigne, Daley had made a quick detour to Loughton Street on his way in. The Professor was ensconced in his customary spot in the cubicle off the main theatre.

"Ah, Scott. Tea?"

Daley waved a hand; he was swilling in the stuff. "What do you know, Patrick?"

"If life were long enough for me to impart all I know... However, we inhabit this earth for but a short time, so I had better stick to this case, eh?" The bushy eyebrows danced above an impudent wink. "Firstly, I have the preliminary results from the samples from the house in Chapel Rise. As I feared, the mixture of bleach, hydrogen peroxide and surgical spirit used to clean the weapon has destroyed any blood evidence on or around the cupboard. The blood marks on the doorway were the victim's, and we know she was there. So then we turned our attention to the plastic bag containing the overalls found in the cupboard. Although they too had been well doused, the liquid had not permeated through the whole of the fabric, and a significant part of the overalls remained dry. Which meant Simon was able to extract some hair fibres and skin cells caught in the elasticated wristbands. Patently the killer put on his or her gloves after they put on the overalls."

"His or her?"

"I believe this is my thunder, Scott. Please be good enough not to steal it." Gascoigne pressed a button and a projector cast a logo onto the opposite wall. "We can tell an awful lot from hair fibres. Take a look at these..." Gascoigne tickled the computer mouse several times and the wall filled with the magnified images of two filaments side by side. It was clear that they were very different.

"There were hair fibres from two people on or in the overalls. Here you can see a sample from each of them. The one on the left is rather rough; also the light from the microscope gives it a translucent appearance. This tells me three things. Firstly the hair is quite old and degraded - you can see the structure is fractured. Secondly, this is undyed blond hair, and thirdly, although this is just an educated guess, he was a male. Traditionally, us blokes tend not to take particular care of our hair. Conditioner was not regularly used, evidenced here by the roughness of the hair shaft. Hair products tend to stick the flaky bits back down, or prevent them from occurring in the first place.

On the right is a much smoother hair sample, which shows up darker against the slide. So if I were to make another educated guess, I would say a female who dyes her hair and takes better care of it than her male counterpart. Of course it could be the same person who has two distinct hair colours, and who has recently decided to take more care of him or herself, but if we compare the actual hairs..." He clicked the mouse and the projected image subtly changed the position of the hairs in relation to each other. "...I would wager they are from different people."

Daley scratched his chin and stared at the images for a long moment. "So potentially, the overalls were worn by two people; one who had left trace evidence a while ago and one more recently. "Could these be the overalls that were worn for the Rachel Jones killing, do you think?"

"That thought had occurred to me. Older hair fibres left in the overalls four years ago, and then added to last Monday. Potentially yes."

"Pointing to two killers rather than one."

"Entirely possible, but as yet conjectural. No evidence to prove it conclusively."

"Can you prove it?"

"Given sufficient time and an infinite number of monkeys... Simon extracted epithelial samples from the hair fibres and I have sent those off along with some of the skin cells to ask for DNA analysis. The older hairs were quite degraded, so the lab may have trouble extracting sufficient DNA, and as you know the process will take some time..."

"Patrick, we don't have a lot of time..."

"But... following the unfortunate demise of Mr Higson, the lab has relented to the overtime and should have preliminary results in the next day or two. These should positively affirm the gender of the people who shed the hairs at least."

"I'll take anything I can get right now, Prof. Thanks."

On the drive over to Barraclough and Leavis, Daley had mentally revisited the list of potential suspects. The theory of two killers still seemed rather fanciful. The older hairs on the overalls may be coincidental, a stolen garment, the hairs from the previous wearer. Secondly, the inconsistencies between the hairs, different colours, different quality, perhaps even different genders. Dawn and Carmichael had different hair colours; Carmichael was blond and Dawn dark, and it was she that dyed her hair. The same could be true for Rachel and Carmichael, although four years ago, both may have been different. Finn Byrne had a rough mop of dark blond hair and Shelley Nugent's was a lustrous bottle brown. Maybe the overalls had been stolen and the hair samples were irrelevant?

The older of the women, Mrs Hughes, Daley remembered from his previous visit, had returned to the reception. She cast a nervous glance at him and ducked down behind the desk. She

173

whispered something to the young, rather gangly girl, who disappeared into a side room with her tail between her legs and now Daley could just see an occasional elbow move as the photocopier burnt another hole in the ozone layer. As the silence again descended, Daley felt discomfited. So as not to arouse suspicion, least of all with Allenby, he had decided a softly, softly approach might be best. Meet Carmichael on his own turf; invite him to attend the station. But it seemed he had been rumbled.

"Inspector?"

Daley snapped back to the present as Mrs Hughes addressed him. Ignoring the phone buzzing in his pocket, he picked up his PVC folder and made for the desk. The woman's face had turned to a concerned frown.

"It seems Mr Carmichael has had to go out this morning. I've rung through to his office and he isn't picking up, I'm afraid."

"Out? What, like just now? Oh, come on!" Daley puffed wearily, the frustration showing through.

"Unfortunately something urgent has cropped up." She flashed him an insufferably patronising smile.

"What, something urgent like me, I suppose. So, has he actually been here this morning?"

"Oh, yes, Inspector. Shall I make you an appointment for another day?"

Daley knew when he was being played. He knew she had tipped Carmichael the wink. He rounded desk and made for the connecting door. "Buzz me through." He leaned on the door, which did not give. "Buzz me through!" The door gave way and Daley half stumbled into the familiar corridor and located Carmichael's office where he cranked the handle to reveal, as he had expected, an empty office. Except for the soothing hum of the PC and Daley's own rasping breath, the room was quiet. Wheeling round, he bounded around to the back door and pushed the bar that yielded to the rear car park and an empty space bearing the name 'A. Carmichael'.

CHAPTER 20

"What the Hell did you say to Allenby this morning?"

Daley, still sore from losing Carmichael, now stung from the arse-kicking Allenby had meted out upon his return to Lambourne Road. Cresting the top of the stairs, he had been intercepted by the D/Supt just inside the team room. Deb was hiding behind her monitor, like a kid who had been caught scrumping next doors apples. With a hushed team hanging on every overheard syllable, he had followed the senior officer into the goldfish bowl. Allenby had proceeded to replay selected highlights of a phone call with Edgar Sampson, Carmichael's solicitor, which had consumed the last thirty minutes of his life. The words 'harassment', 'heavy-handed' and 'groundless' featured prominently. His attempts to reason with Allenby, to expound the theories of financial impropriety, of Dawn's obvious involvement with Carmichael and the unwanted pregnancy had been met with indifference, even hostility. He reiterated the similarities to the Rachel Jones case and laboured the closeness, both personally and professionally, of the deceased Guy Higson to Carmichael. He emphasised how much Carmichael had to lose and counted off the people who potentially stood in his way that were now dead. But it had all fallen on deaf ears. The upshot had been that, unless he had blood dripping from his hands, Carmichael was out of bounds to Daley. One more incident of this nature and the case would be farmed out to DCI Wilson and Daley would face suspension. The anger in Daley was reaching volcanic proportions, and he had decided that Whetstone was a suitable target.

"Nothing, Sir. I promise. Nothing that I didn't already say to you. He just came in and asked me where you were. What was I supposed to say?"

Deb sighed and slouched over her desk. She had magicked up some paperwork to make herself look busy but now she just shrugged her shoulders. She didn't really care anymore. Following Daley's ill-judged hunches and the bollockings she had been forced to share, she was again wondering whether the moody, impulsive and somewhat insane DI was good for her career. Even though she was a team player, she wondered how

175

long she would continue to take the shit that inevitably followed him around. Wanting out of the conversation, she grabbed her cup and headed away.

"What's that supposed to mean?" Daley pursued her to the kitchen area and rounded to face her. He was steaming. This had to be finished here and now.

"Look, Sir. Like it or not we have to stay away from Carmichael. Don't forget, even if his relationship with Dawn Silverton was on-off, it's off for bloody good now. That's going to really mess with his head. As soon as we come within a hundred yards, he will start blarting, claiming victimisation in his hour of pain. He'll click the speed dial to that solicitor of his and you and me will be up in front of the P.I.C.C. begging for our badges."

"What? Is everybody blind around here? When we brought him in for Rachel Jones, everybody did there utmost to put us off the scent and yes, on that occasion, they succeeded and guess what? Another girl has had her head cleaved off her shoulders and the self-centred, arrogant bastard who happens to have had affairs with both of them is playing us like idiots. And now, another slab of fresh meat, who just happens to be a friend of both the dead girls and Carmichael. Still no-one is prepared to admit that he may have some questions to answer. How the hell does he do that? Come on, tell me that? How the hell does he always come up smelling of frigging roses?"

Deb pushed past and clicked the button on the kettle before squaring up to Daley, fire now burning in her eyes and her heart racing. After a long night of poking in the guts of yet another corpse, when she could have been wrapped up in a warm duvet with Keith the Uniform, she was tired and hungry and spoiling for a fight. Time and place was everything when arguing with your boss but there was a red mist now, eating away at everything rational. The kettle wheezed as the thermocouple clicked off, demanding at least a few millilitres of water, buying her a few seconds of thinking time while she filled it. She decided that mending fences would achieve more than throwing Scott Daley headlong through them.

"Scott, Scott. Listen to me." Daley, taken aback by his first name, found himself dredging his mind for the last time Whetstone had used it. "You and I both know that Carmichael is guilty. It all over his face as if, just like Dawn and Rachel, someone had taken a Sharpie pen to him. He is a bastard. From the very first second we saw him, we knew he was guilty. But you know what? Maybe he didn't kill Dawn or Rachel. Maybe what he is guilty of is entirely separate. Have you even really considered that? In my opinion, we're just wasting time fixating on him when the real killer is still out there."

"Oh, come on, Deb! The guy had no real alibi for Rachel. What was it? He was on his way back from France; a journey that seemed to last three hours longer than he could account for. And now some bloody cock-and-bull story about a quick lunch and back to the office. But again no way to account for the actual time he was missing." Daley was not going to be convinced. She would need to try harder.

"OK. Let's try it a different way." The kettle clicked off behind them but by now they were oblivious, and it cracked and plopped its displeasure. "If it was just a simple matter of two women murdered in cold blood and we had nothing else then yes, perhaps I would be pointing the finger squarely at Carmichael and I would be arguing with Allenby right now. But it's not! It's about Dawn Silverton, Rachel Jones, Guy Higson and Andrew Carmichael. It's about all of them and the whole Monday Club. Any links between Dawn Silverton, Rachel Jones and Andrew Carmichael are purely coincidental right now. It's a fact they were all in the Monday Club. It's a fact that Carmichael is a philandering bastard and, I'm sure it's a fact that he knocked both of them up. But none of this proves he's a murderer."

"What about those documents, Deb. Surely they make the link. I am sure of it. They were identical. And again, Guy Higson. Another identical piece of paper."

"And who wrote them, Sir?" Deb leaned against the counter and took a breath. "If we assume the documents are genuine, it smacks of a lot of planning. The date on those documents goes all the way back to 1997, when these people were at University. Whoever is doing this has been brooding on it for years. Those documents go into a lot of detail. I mean, I struggle with meeting notes and if the witness forms didn't have lines on them I'd be fucked. OK. So Carmichael's an educated man but would he really plan a series of murders fifteen years ago, to the nth degree of detail, keeping them on ice and then pull each one out of a hat when coincidentally the proposed victim just happened to piss him off? Come on, he's a manipulative son-of-a-whatsit, but do you really think he would plan his revenge like that, and in that much detail? Do you think he needs to be that clever? Either he is an absolute genius pretending to be a plonker or *he - didn't - do - it!*'

Daley exhaled and leaned his arm against the wall. She had a point, well several, but he was buggered if he was going to concede it just yet. The one thing he couldn't argue with was Deb's passion. With all of the terrible things to which her job had exposed her, all of the cruelty and the inhumanity, she was still able to see the goodness in everyone. She was still able to find some small corner to fight however stacked the odds were.

"Look, Deb, someone has to be killing these people. Someone in the Monday Club, or pretty damn close, and I still think the favourite is Andrew Carmichael. Now Guy Higson has been killed, who else could it be?"

"That's not the point, Sir. Even if Carmichael is our man...and I really can't see it...even if he is our man, we have to let him come to us. Reel him in slowly. Because when we are not there in his face, keeping him on his guard, he is going to slip up. I've seen it a million times at Stockwell Green. We'd stake out some warehouse because we got a tip-off only to find the place would be done over two days later. Nothing is ever going to happen whilst you're looking at it." She cast about for an analogy. "Take this kettle. It didn't boil while we were watching it, er, did it? We were so busy arguing it just boiled behind our backs."

"OK, OK. Enough of the crap analogies. Let's get back on this. I am going to look over the Rachel Jones files again. See if there is anything that makes more sense now than it did back then. You...you...keep on at Monaghan. And find out about that University group, especially that new name, Christopher Betts. If I have to ditch the idea that it's Carmichael, then you need to bring me someone else."

He swung around and slammed through the swing doors, the coat stand teetering like a drunken giraffe as he grabbed his overcoat.

"Glad I kept out of that one!" Steve Taylor flicked the switch and made them both a cup of tea. Steve was one of the good guys. He was more like an IT geek that a policeman. He was tall and slim, his thickset mop of black afro-textured hair blending down his face into a stubbled beard which tried it's best to hide his kindly brown face, and a slouch which matched the contour of his badly adjusted chair. Rarely wearing a suit, generally in jeans and a cardigan, it was unusual for him to stray outside the team room, unless it was to the canteen or the bogs, and Deb was not sure she had seen him in either of those places.

"Yeh. Sometimes I wish I could too."

"You want to talk?" He placed a hand on her shoulder. His eyes were earnest behind the black-rimmed spectacles.

"What?"

"Do you want to talk about it? You know, a trouble shared..."

"Are you making a play for me, DC Taylor?" She instantly hated herself as he mumbled his denials, abject apologies and gathered his tea, his eyes searching around for an escape. What exactly was wrong with her that she had to be such a bitch?

"Hang on Steve, I'm sorry. It's been a tough morning already." But the moment had gone and Taylor was already scurrying back to the relative sanctuary of his HP Desktop. Deb fished out the teabag and watched as it dangled above the cup, spinning and dripping, and she mused on the conversation she and Daley had just ridden roughshod over.

Daley had warned off Carmichael. She didn't believe he was guilty anyway. There was nothing to pin him to the scene. In fact there was nothing to pin him anywhere. And then there was motive. That was weak too.

So who could be capable of such meticulous planning apart from Carmichael? Who could be capable of such brutal murders?

Fishing in her pocket, she retrieved a pound coin, which she used to liberate a Mars from the vending machine. Then, bearing the placatory gift, she headed off towards Steve Taylor and Dave Monaghan.

***

Through leaden eyelids, Alice stared sleepily at the ceiling rose. Cobwebs festooned the decoration and the drop lead, and down to an incongruous maroon pleated lampshade. She wondered how it was that spiders weaved their webs over such distances, vast to them. Someone, probably Carmichael, who reckoned he knew everything, had once told her they just let themselves drift on the wind, reeling out a strand of web until they reached the next solid landing. But there was no wind in this room so how did that happen? Perhaps they just cast themselves off and trusted to serendipity.

Behind her, Marcus lay pressed against her back, cocooned in a duvet which felt orders of magnitude softer this morning than it had on every other cold empty morning when the alarm had roused her to the silence of herself. His breathing was steady and shallow as he dozed, her left arm cool against her breast, but warming since it had ventured out to kill the raucous alarm. She reached behind her and placed a hand on his thigh and he nestled his head deeper into the back of her shoulder. Comfortable and safe.

Last night, as the front door clattered shut behind them, it had felt like that first time in Coventry. Two people who knew each other but were still strangers, tentatively exploring before yielding to an overwhelming physical desire borne of the moment, wrestling with the door to the flat, wrestling with each others clothing, wrestling with an uncomfortable sofa and an unfamiliar process. But after that first eager, clumsy time, after the sweat had cooled and the moment had passed, he had awkwardly held her, and she had sheepishly asked if he wanted to stop over, and they had both self-consciously made their way to the bedroom and slid under the covers. Where they lay warily on their backs, like two teenagers unsure what to do next, unsure how to cross the cold foot of no-mans land. Finally his arm had reached across to hers and they had fallen together into the deepest sleep either of them had experienced for fifteen long, lonely years. And now, as the cobwebs fluttered and danced in the draughts, she felt that she was casting herself off and trusting to serendipity.

Half an hour later, she was tucking into toast in the kitchen. Marcus had finally prised himself from the absolute comfort of her bed and made his way through to the kitchenette, dressed only in her pink flannelette dressing gown and looking absurd.

"I can't find my underpants, Alice," his tone matter of fact, as she stood at the table, mouth open, a half-eaten slice of toast poised mid-bite.

"I think they went under the telly, Marcus, or maybe the sideboard. I wasn't paying much attention."

"Me neither." He disappeared back around the doorway.

Alice fed the toaster a couple more slices and poured out some coffee, and mused how life can change in the blink of an eye. She recalled the sales stand-up the previous morning and the interminable sameness of it all, the innocuous damning voicemail which had languished unread for hours. She was horrified when she heard the news of Dawn's death, but it didn't really affect her. Even Guy's call and the fears he had voiced, whilst it had concerned her, it had not really changed anything. Guy was normally trustworthy, but on this occasion she thought he might be being a touch fanciful. But it had piqued her curiosity.

No, her life had changed in the split-second she had rounded the corner to find Marcus on the back step of the Plough & Harrow. In that instant, she had resolved that if Guy's fears were grounded and Drew was a threat, she needed an ally who could look out for her. If the whole business revolved around Drew's dodgy financial dealings, then Guy was as implicated as Drew. Neither could be trusted, at least for now. If it was all bollocks, there was still Marcus.

But seeing him again, separated from the Monday Club, away from Drew Carmichael, had dragged many suppressed emotions to the surface. Too long she had kidded herself she could ignore them. For years she had felt wretched about the way she had split with Marcus, casting him adrift without word or explanation. He had followed her around for months pleading with her to reveal what he had done, how he could make amends. In the years since, she felt ashamed that she didn't have the courage to tell him the truth. Relationships had come and gone but for her never had there been that special feeling she had when she had been with Marcus - that feeling of coming home. Now she was certain that Marcus was the only one she ever wanted to be with. He had been the only person she could ever really trust.

And she never wanted to be alone again.

The toaster popped, bringing her to the present as a slightly more soberly appointed Marcus joined her at the table. He took a scalding sip of coffee.

"So, how was it for you, Doll-face?" He beamed a wide grin at Alice, who scowled back.

"Don't Doll-face me or you will be wearing that coffee." But the fire in her cheeks told her she had blushed a deep crimson, and the smirk on his face told her he had noticed.

"Alice?" Marcus, pensive, placed his cup on the table. "About last night..."

She rested her elbows on the table. "It was great, Marcus. A bit frantic, a little lacking in finesse admittedly, but great."

"No, no, no. Not that. I am far too grateful for the opportunity to ask for a score out of ten. No, I mean that whole business with Carmichael at The Plough. I meant to ask last night but, well, we were kind of busy. You mentioned Chris Betts, that Guy was asking if anyone had seen him."

Alice shuffled her feet and played with the handle of her cup. Mentioning Chris Betts had been a mistake. Oceans of water had flowed under the bridge since then, and it had all flowed unseen past Marcus. How could Chris Betts be relevant now, least of all to Marcus?

After University, they had all gone their separate ways. Not surprising as they all hailed from different corners of the British Isles, pursuing different careers, different interests, the only thing in common those three years at Coventry a lifetime ago. So why did they lead their separate lives so close to each other? For Alice the answer was simple. The job she now trudged through every day just happened to be near the supermarket where she had chanced upon Carmichael one day. But for her, Carmichael, the Monday Club, all of the others, even the money, were incidental. They had exchanged mobile numbers and he had returned to the night bearing beans and bread. It had been a while before she had met Shelley in the Plough & her staccato attendance of the Monday Club had resumed.

OK, so that could be marked down to serendipity. She had cast her web out into the breeze and alighted here in Ealing by pure chance. And Marcus? He was glued to Carmichael's coattails and would have followed him to Timbuktu if he had bid him so. That would have to stop! But what of the others?

Guy Higson, an accountant. You can account for stuff anywhere. And Shelley and Finn? That pub-restaurant must be infinitely more expensive than one outside of the Capital, so why choose that one? And Dawn and Rachel? They had all converged on that small corner of the UK, all still under the spell of the Great Drew Carmichael.

All except Chris Betts.

Undoubtedly, Drew Carmichael commanded power. She herself had seen his power make women weak at the knees, although for her, it tended to be her bowels that loosened. She had also seen his superlative business prowess, a subtle art of persuasion that owed as much to threat as it did to coercion. But had Carmichael really turned threats of loss of wealth, loss of kudos, to threats of violence, even death? Had his bluff been called by Rachel and Dawn? Had he then taken the threats to their extreme conclusion?

Guy thought that Rachel and Dawn both had reason enough to force Carmichael's arm up his back, to then suffer as the arm came back around their throats. Why not Chris Betts? Her mind drifted back to Cox Street, to Drew and to Dawn and Rachel and Shelley, and the last time she had seen Chris, on that dank, humid night in 1997. She knew that he was the key to all of this, to the murder of the two women and for Carmichael's resolve to keep his friends close, especially now that the eyes of the police were trained upon him.

But what should she tell Marcus? With Marcus so close to Drew, how much could she safely reveal? Once more she cast herself off and trusted to serendipity.

"Yes, Guy mentioning Chris Betts like that, after all these years, that was interesting. Do you remember? It was that night in Coventry back at Uni. The night I dumped you and flounced off back to my digs like a big girl."

"Well I wouldn't exactly call you a *big* girl, but if the cap fits..." Alice glowered and Marcus shoved toast into his mouth, where moments before his foot had been. "You never told me what that was all about. However many times I asked. One day we were an item and the next it was all over. Even now, I have no idea what I did wrong."

"You've never really asked," she lied.

"I did nothing but ask for three or four months, and then I just gave up. It was tearing me apart."

He stared across the kitchen lost in a world of pain, a world of fifteen years previous that no amount of contrition from Alice could cure. She reached a hand across the table and laid it on his arm. "I am so incredibly sorry, Marcus. You have to believe me. Something happened that night. Something so dreadful that suddenly everything changed. My whole world turned on its head. I just had to stay away from Drew. It wasn't you Marcus. It was what happened that night. Surely Drew has told you about it?"

"No! This is the first I am hearing about any of this. I just turned up at Priory the next day and you didn't want to know me. Point blank. When I asked Drew, he probably just shrugged and made a pre-menstrual joke, but he didn't tell me anything. Then after that no matter who I asked, nobody said a word. Talk about Monday Club more like *Shtum*-day Club!"

"Drew was the problem, Marcus. After what I saw, I just couldn't bear to be anywhere near Drew Carmichael, and you and he came as a set. I don't actually think they knew I was there that night. Of course neither was Guy. He just came along afterwards and helped to sort it out. But Chris was right at the centre of it. Rachel, Dawn, Shelley and Chris, they are all implicated and now Rachel and Dawn are dead. Chris is nowhere to be seen. He simply disappeared after that night. The hoo-ha died down and there was barely a ripple left."

"What, and you think Carmichael did them all in? Surely not!" Marcus frowned, a goods yard of wrinkles crossing his brow. "I've known him for years. It's just not his style."

"He's got a lot to lose and no real conscience. Why not? Maybe Rachel was not the first. Perhaps, Chris grew a pair of balls and decided to stand up to him. Maybe the reason we have not seen Chris since is because Drew silenced him all those years ago."

"That's a little bit of a stretch. Surely Chris' body would have turned up, Guy would have let something slip. Dawn and Rachel were found pretty well straight off."

"Do you remember that game we used to play when the Monday Club started? *Where would you hide a body so that it would never be found?* Think of the suggestions we came up with.

Perhaps he is in the foundations of the new science block they were building, or wrapped tight in cling film on top of a crusty old corpse in an old Mausoleum. All I know is that Guy came round the next day and swore me to absolute secrecy, and I have never spoken a word of it, not even to you, until last night."

"Bloody hell. So Carmichael offs Chris Betts to protect himself and conspires with Guy to keep this whole 'thing' hidden for well over a decade, until presumably Rachel opens her mouth and he offs her as well?"

"Why not? There was that palaver about the abortion. It's an open secret that it was Drew's. Maybe she got all hormonal and threatened to spill the beans?"

"And Dawn started getting jumpy about the money, so now he has gotten his hand in, he deals with her too? You know what, Alice Bown? You have a vicious imagination, but it does have a ring of truth to it. There is just one thing..."

Alice took a gulp of her now tepid coffee. "What's that?"

"You never did tell me exactly what happened on that night in Coventry."

Chapter 20

"Gov, over here." It was Monaghan. "Just typed in *Betts, Club, Coventry, 1997* and this was on the fourth page of results. Take a look..."

Instantly, both Daley and Whetstone were transfixed by a page entitled *Phantom Memories of FiftyFour* by a blogger called Rod Stanway.

"It's easy for the bored mind to embellish the past with whatever rose-tinted view sits best with the humdrum world of today. They say life is for living but many of us live in the past for fear of accepting our present. Such is the case with most of us that have at one time or another attended University. Fun days, wild nights and lost weekends. At least, that's how we remember them. Of my three years in Coventry, what do I remember? The smell of disinfectant in the corridors of Priory. The endless rumble of cars on the ring road. The proud ruins of the once grand cathedral, its skeleton standing defiantly in the post-Hitler modernistic apocalypse that spawned its hunched ungainly neighbour. Maybe the cubic entrance hall to Coventry University, a door I entered but once during my tenure? Or maybe, as in my case, it's the Student's Union that I remember most. Especially, as I spent a whole lot of days and a huge number of nights there, it became my second home.

Nowadays, with The Hub, you lucky people have a whole new place to fritter away the hours considering whether you want to attend lectures or just crib the notes off your best friends for the cost of a pint at Browns, but back in the day, the place to be, or not as the case may be, was FiftyFour, a grotty Student's Union dive on Cox street. In bold silver Roman numeral's the sign over the door yelled 'LIV' but inside the building it was too late even for Doctor Frankenstein to work his dubious magic. Maroon walls and sticky laminate floors, not to mention the motley selection of chairs and stools which one was often afraid to sit on. Boasting not one but two stages, FiftyFour played host live music most nights, even if it was just a second-year with a guitar, but most people just went in there for the cheap beer and even cheaper conversation. In the late Nineties, I wiled away many a grant cheque - oh, yes, children, that's when the Government used to pay for your education - sitting around getting drunk and people-watching.

Removing my rose-tinted spectacles for a while, squinting in the sunlight of this brave new world, I often wonder what happened to the people I used to know, especially the ones too lazy to keep in touch or just too damn sensible to 'friend' me on Facebook. For example there was a strange character called Lenny Green, who, a child of Two-tone, sported a sharp white suit and black shirt at all times, doffing his trilby, much to the amusement of the girls he smiled at. And then there was Christopher Betts, a shy boy with quite enough friends in his own head not to bother with too many of the rest of us. I also recall the legend that was the Monday Club, an institution in the SU at that time, fronted by the equally legendary Drew Carmichael. What a man, or as he used to say when he saw me - 'What, a man?' Drew was the chick magnet of my time at Coventry, and to paraphrase Eric Cantona, we followed Drew Carmichael because we expected hot and willing girls to be thrown. And sure enough for two brief weeks, I caught one of his cast-offs by the name of Rachel Jones. Rachel, if you're reading this and you remember that fortnight, don't cry baby, Uncle Rod is now happily married and over you!

I never managed to persuade Drew to let me into the Monday Club. It was a select group, who used to hunt as a pack. They had a pastime they called 'The Murder Game' where special guests were invited to make up the most outlandish ideas for killing someone they could think of. The only rules? There were no rules. Well actually there were. Firstly the idea had to be murder, secondly it had to be possible and thirdly, you had to be there when it happened. Break these rules and rather than drink your pint, you would end up wearing it.

The Monday Club were the celebs of the informal social scene. They would be seen everywhere together, and if they weren't seen, it wasn't worth being seen. And talking of being seen, the place they were seen was the scene - Bar 54, the smaller sibling to Studio 54, complete with scarlet walls, faded pool table and the cheapest alcohol around, especially on Monday evenings.

Back in the day when time was plentiful, I used to spend it lolling about in FiftyFour, buying a snack from the cut-price on-site cafe and generally hanging out trying to get noticed by the chicks that never did take any notice..."

And on went the reams of rhetoric about the salad days of higher education. But no-one was reading anymore. Daley looked at Monaghan as he bookmarked the page and dragged the text into a separate file.

"We need to know more about Betts and what happened to him after University. That's twice in as many days his name has come up in connection with the Monday Club and Andrew Carmichael. Not to mention Rachel Jones." Daley rubbed the back of his neck. "How long do you think it would take to find this Rod Stanway character?"

"Dunno, Gov. If he's on any of the social network sites, it

187

shouldn't be too difficult. There can't be a great many people called Stanway who were at Coventry in the late Nineties. As long as he wants to talk to us, that is."

"Do it. Use your charm. I think we need a chat with Good Ole Rod. See what he can remember. And while you're at it, chivvy up that chap in Coventry."

Chapter 21

By the time Carmichael arrived home, it was 11:15am and there were five messages on the answerphone, each from Carol and each increasingly more anxious to confirm he had arrived home safely. Each deleted without being fully played. It had taken a Herculean effort to drive home and he gingerly placed himself into a corner of the couch. He knew he shouldn't have driven given the state of his ribs, but hey.

On the journey, he had rerun the whole situation. He was sure that nothing led directly back to him. Since Dawn had first started bleating to Barraclough and Leavis, everything had been done to make her accusations groundless. Surely there was nothing he had missed?

Unless the police forensic computer experts were brought in. Would they be able to unravel the tangle of debits and credits, account changes and repostings that Higson had instructed him to perform?

But why would they look? It was a huge leap even to think that the police would be so interested that they would discover some anomalies on her clients' financial adviser's computer. Too many degrees of separation. Her employers were unaware and no cash had gone missing. The balances were consistently in credit. If the police needed to examine Dawn's professional life, they would simply see a large number of her clients using Barraclough and Leavis, and particularly Andrew Carmichael. Was that so strange? Old friends, a little mutual back scratching? How else would anyone become a member of the bar, or an MP, if not for reciprocal favours?

Or Marcus opened his fat mouth. That was more likely. It was inevitable that the police would interview the corpulent fool. The way he was blubbering yesterday evening, that was more likely. He had never shown any backbone before. When the going got tough, Marcus got a burger, took a gargantuan bite and hoped everything would just go away. He would let slip some minor detail, the police would start delving deeper and he would fold like a straight dick in a Gay Bar. Once they started

189

along those lines, innocuous professional back-scratching would become a conspiracy and they would descend upon him, poring over the paperwork and eventually hoisting him by Marcus Balfour's petard. Right now, the fat fool would be looking to save his own skin. It would only be a matter of time before it all went tits up, and that could not be allowed to happen.

As usual, it would be down to him, Drew Carmichael, to sort it out.

With effort, he dragged his way into the kitchen, his head thick and woolly, and his ribs seeming to fold as he breathed. He threw a teaspoon of filter coffee on top of the clotted dregs from the previous day, added water and waiting a beat for the rasping sound of percolation to begin. He could not allow Marcus to destroy three years of work building the pot. Moreover, he needed another three to grow it large enough to be a meaningful sum. The thick liquid started to dribble into the brown stained jug, and a hard aroma hit his sinuses. A watched percolator never fills, no matter how much you swear at it. He poured the unctuous sludge into a cup and sighed.

Moving through to the hall, he hauled himself up the stairs to the office in the front bedroom. He flipped open his laptop. The coffee had scalded his tongue, leaving it numb and feeling like parchment, but had already started to clear his head. He always did his best thinking when he had a good caffeine buzz going on. Opening up his contacts folder, he paged through searching for anyone who owed him a favour, anyone whom he could put the screws on to rid himself of the problems that bitch Silverton had created. The shrill warble of the desk phone made him start, wrenching his ribs. He peered at the tiny screen. It was the office calling. He felt a pang of guilt but quickly dismissed it. Guilty people are weak people. In his condition, he deserved one day away from the donkey pump, surely? As like as not, he was in serious shit with Thornton but sod it, the old bastard needed him and would have to handle it. And right now, he had neither the strength nor the inclination to deal with such trivial distractions. There were more important fish to fry.

On the other hand, pissing Carol off might not be such a good strategy. Having helped Higson with the audit and shown herself loyal by turning the odd blind eye, she may be his only ally. She *was* just admin, however, she knew where the bodies were buried and that must count for something. He would have to eat so much humble pie when he saw her in the morning.

His desk phone lit up once more; again it was the office. He should have switched it off. Reluctantly he clicked the green button, lifted it to his ear and announced himself with a single word - *Carmichael.*

"Mr Carmichael. Drew. Are you OK? Did you get home safely? I have rearranged today's appointments and Tom Cramer has handled Mr and Mrs Bellfield."

"Yeh, I'm sorry, Carol. "I'm actually feeling pretty sore."

"I will inform Mr Thornton, log you in as sick. Is there anything I can do to help?"

He knew she was playing along. Her tone lacked sympathy. Maybe she could be overheard? But for Carmichael, loyalty was an unwritten pre-requisite, expected, but never acknowledged nor recognised as she cleared up his messes, organising the minutiae of his work life usually unnoticed.

There were three other girls working in the practice, all of them hardly old enough to be out of school, dressing in a way that perplexed him. No pretence to decency, high skirts and revealing tops. God knows what their names were, or what they did, but generally they were quiet and unobtrusive, which suited him well. Carol Hughes was slightly older than him. Older women exuded maturity and worldly-wiseness. Not for her the crop top and t-shirt, nor the absurdly short shorts over flesh coloured tights that made them look virtually naked. He imagined her in his bed, a consummate sexual skill that could only be drawn from experience. Indeed maybe she could teach *him* a thing or two. He felt himself firm and smiled to himself as the silence was broken by her voice on the line.

"Are you sure you're alright?" Her maternal tone had returned. He decided to play along. He could do with some company tonight, if only to ensure she was an ally, on-side.

"Well, as a matter of fact, I'm not doing so well. My head aches. My ribs ache." Steady, Carmichael. Don't lay it on too thick!

"Do you not think you should go down to A&E? Get yourself checked out?"

"That's the last thing I should do. Just think how the police would interpret that." Reflexively, he massaged his aching ribs, hoping the discomfort would show in his voice. "Look, I just need some time that's all. A day or so to clear my head." *And to try and sort out the awful bloody mess that Dawn has left me in.* "All this on top of that audit. What must you all think of me?"

"Mr Carmichael, I am pretty sure that Mr Higson and I handled the audit to the Board's satisfaction. There's nothing to worry about, there. What makes you think there's a problem?"

"It's not that I actually think there's a problem. It's more that *her* death might make people ask uncomfortable questions - you know, the police?" He paused for a moment. "They might ask *you* some uncomfortable questions."

The line decayed into silence again. He could hear her breathing over the static. It was she who spoke first.

"I am not stupid, Drew. I had to weigh up the situation. I earn twenty five thousand pounds a year. Might not be much by your standards but I need this job. If your little scam had come to light, we would have all been in the shit. The girls are already talking about what is going to happen when Thornton retires. We all think he may close the practice and this might just have twisted his arm. You don't realise the consequences of what you have been doing."

Paradoxically, Carmichael felt no guilt. If the practice closed, they would all just be incidental casualties, so much jetsam discarded en route. Carol was a smart cookie, though. She would survive. There were plenty who would take her on. The only person that needed help now was himself. Not to save his own skin, or help to forestall any threat to his livelihood, but to ensure that the Fund he had amassed was spirited away successfully before the ship sank. As for the rest of them, *fuck 'em, fuck 'em all.* They could fight their own battles from now on. Yes, Carol was a smart cookie and he needed to keep her close for now. At least until this thing blew over or the money was safe and the hole closed up behind him.

"I don't think you should be on your own tonight, Drew." As he heard the words, he felt the familiar frisson. "I am worried that you may have broken a rib or two and if you don't want to go the A&E..."

"But what about you? I couldn't ask you to put yourself out like that."

"I insist. I've got nothing planned and I am sure you have a spare room."

He considered for a moment. Perhaps he could combine some business with pleasure. "I am going to need you to bring some things with you. We can work here. Make sure that the money is sorted. Make sure *you* are sorted." Drew kept his tone flat, no particular inflexion, letting her make the interpretation. Letting her make the next move.

He wedged the phone between his shoulder and ear, gathered up his cup and painfully made for the stairs. He needed more coffee to get his head straight. She was right about being alone. However he rationalised his feelings for Dawn Silverton or diminished their relationship, he always came round to an uncomfortable truth. He had cared for her. She was gone and that was a harder truth. Now there was a decision to be made. Whether to trust Carol Hughes beyond the bounds of associate and office manager, or to keep his cards close to his chest until he could use her to find a way out of this mess. He had never been denied anything, and right now he would not be denied the chance to be rich, the chance to hide the proceeds, and no, regardless of the pretext, he would not be denied his chance to have Carol Hughes.

***

Lee Smith lay on the sofa wrapped in a tartan blanket. It was clear he had slept, or lain awake, there all night, His face mottled with salt stains and his eyes bloodshot, he looked small and frail and a lot younger than his eighteen years. DC Mike Corby nodded his thanks to Lee's mum as she placed a cup on the table. Lee gazed up to her as she smiled sympathetically back. In Corby's opinion, he was milking it for all it was worth. Often sleep allows the brain to organise thoughts that could not be brought to mind at the time, but similarly, it allow the mind to synthesise and manufacture, to fill in the gaps and envision, so it was not such a bad thing that he had lain awake shuddering to the gruesome images which prowled the dark of the previous night.

"So tell me Lee, you said that after falling off your bike, you looked around to see who had played the trick on you. Did you see anything, you know, dog walker, courting couple?"

"No. Doggers don't go to the park that way. It was quiet. My headphones were broke so it was like the noise suddenly stopped. I had forgotten how quiet it was at that time of night."

"And then you heard the motorbike?"

"Yeah. I didn't know what it was at first. I thought it was one of my fuckwit mates making sure I'd come off. Then I saw the taillight of the Fireblade and heard it ticking over. I could tell it anywhere 'cos it's, like, a tiny, square light. I couldn't understand why Mr Higson would leave it there, running. It was, like, ten metres from his gate. Then I saw him. I nearly vommed."

"What did you do then?"

"I went back to my bike. It was lying in the road and I didn't want it run over. That frames magnesium. Cost over a grand. I got my phone out to call Mom and Dad but it was smashed when I fell. I went back up to the end of the road, under the wire to ask the man in the car but he just drove away."

"Yes, you said about the car. Can you remember anything else?"

"No, just that the bloke was bastard. All he needed to do was make a call. He must've seen what had happened."

"And..." Corby referred to his notes, "...you say that you didn't get a look at him. Has anything else come to mind since last night?"

"Not really. It's like I told you then. It was sort of cream or white but the streetlight made it look orange. When I walked towards it, the lights came on and blinded me. Then the guy just started up and sped off back up Treddle Lane. Cunt!"

"And the driver. You keep saying 'he'. How do you know it was a man?"

"Because the car is a man's car, like a Merc or a Lexus. A big car. Women don't drive those. Well, usually they don't."

"No-one else in the car?"

"Not that I could see, no. Unless she was bent over blowing him or something."

Corby sighed, closed the notebook and took up the coffee, taking a swig and rolling it around his mouth, to assuage the creeping fatigue. It had been a long night and was looking like an even longer day. One of the forensic robots had taken a cast of the tyre track in the detritus where Lee said the Merc or Lexus or whatever had been parked and it had turned out to match the tread pattern for a Pirelli Cinturato P7, of a size fitted to the Mercedes E Class. There were also some distinctive wear marks, but short of examining every E Class in the London area, these would be useless. Pirelli Cinturato P7 could also be fitted to a Lexus, like the IS250E, which would be the most likely blokes car, or to a dozen other different makes, and there were a fair few of those in the Capital too. He rose to leave, struggling hard to hide the frustration of a wasted visit. The boy had been dazed by the fall and succumbed to shock when he had found Higson's body but, notwithstanding, there was probably nothing more to tell. Could have been a Merc, perhaps not. Could've been a man, maybe not. Corby left his card and thanked Lee and his Mom, and was shown to the door.

***

Forty-five minutes after replacing the phone handset into it's charger, Carmichael had mixed feelings about inviting Carol Hughes back to his house. His home was a sanctuary, a retreat. Few people at Barraclough and Leavis knew, or even cared where he lived. Which meant now he was making an exception. As office manager, she must know his address. He could only pray that she would keep tonight's extra-curricular activity private. He had quite clear plans for what he wanted to achieve. Even if it was at the expense of bringing a potential enemy into the camp.

Over the last fortnight the other partners had been crawling like termites over his files as they searched for evidence of some petty misdemeanour or minor legal infringement. But no matter. Those dip-shits couldn't find a hole in a barrel of arses. Some sandal wearing geek might eventually find it but not these plodding bean counters. Which left only the transfer out of and back into the client accounts each evening and morning. He had that covered by using a dozen different accounts to funnel the money through and several different intermediate accounts in the names of unsuspecting friends and relatives. Again, a forensic computer cop might be able to follow the smoke trails but the only common point now was that bimble-head Marcus. It would be he who received the knock-knock-knock from the

195

plod if they ever figured it out, and who would need to explain the healthy nest-egg garnered for his retirement.

But the visit from the police had spooked him and he needed to be sure.

His car had been stationary outside Richmond Tube station for twenty minutes and the air-conditioned warmth had dissipated, leaving his knees stiff and aching. He stretched them as far as he could in the confined footwell, and then pressed a switch, making the seat glide backwards on motor driven runners.

After an age, Carol Hughes emerged from the gloom beneath the severe *Art Deco* clock. She was carrying the box file that Drew had asked her to bring. It contained the last incriminating paperwork from the office - the enciphered passwords to the Cayman account and the dealing services. She saw the car and she smiled, a fleeting enigmatic smile, hiding a multitude of emotion, still professional and detached. A tremor coursed through his body in anticipation of the coming hours. He always thrilled in that first unconscious, subliminal awareness that the niceties of social communion could seamlessly move into the realms of sexual intimacy. Carmichael wondered if she had realised that the work was a pretext. Had that smile betrayed her? Her hair was up and her naked neck was caressed by the collar of a camel hair coat which parted as she walked, offering a glimpse of the long legs he had admired for so long, and with which he hoped he would make a better acquaintance later.

Chapter 22

Unfortunately for Carmichael, the next morning came all too quickly. Before long he was back in the office staring down at his desk, irritatedly biting the quick around his thumbnail. It was only 9:00 and he was already he was pissed off with the day. The insincere smile he would need to chisel onto his face at 10:00am was looking more and more impossible. Still reeling from his beating, he had been popping Ibuprofen like Smarties, which made the pain in his ribs slightly more bearable. The Hang Seng had taken another lurch overnight and the account had grown significantly. They would all be lucky to see a penny of it now, though. He would lie and say the stock market had tumbled. They would be too stupid to prove otherwise. He may pay Marcus back his investment. He owed him that much. Again he would lie, shed a few crocodile tears and say that out of loyalty he was paying Marcus out of his own pocket because he felt bad about it. The fat bastard would squeal but he would buy the sob story and piss off too. As for that traitor Byrne, if he thought he was going to get away scot free, he had another thing coming.

Then there was Carol. Another bloody disappointment. A literal anti-climax. Sticking to her guns, she spent the entire evening on the accounts, with this cross-posting and that double-entry until his head was spinning. And all the time, across the dining room table, he was turning hornier by the minute. It was not until 9:00pm that he finally convinced her to take a break.

To be fair, he had struggled to maintain even a modicum of interest, between the pain in his ribs, and one of a different kind elsewhere, transfixed was he by the way her tongue brushed her teeth as her lips parted. Eventually, using the time-honoured tactic of alcohol, he had lured her to the sofa, and that had loosened her up a little, revealing a few chinks in those armour-plated knickers. He learned a few juicy titbits about her, which was great intelligence in the long campaign she was turning out to be. Firstly the wedding ring, a big obstacle but not necessarily insurmountable for a man with his charms, a keepsake from a long-dead marriage. Then there was the family. Was there a whining brood at home, or worse still, an elderly mother who can't crap for herself? Jesus. He would sooner not know where those hands had been. But it turned out there was no family. Parents both dead and a brother, dead also. News met with a suitable amount of sympathy, which he hoped did not come across as disingenuous.

By degrees, he had even managed to slide closer across the sofa, but a hand on her knee had been the zenith. No sooner had he paved the way to her knickers, than she had locked the gates on him. Somehow, the talk had turned to his relationship with Dawn. He had found himself defending it, and the accounts and that whole damn mess with the audit. The atmosphere became strained and tense. Breaking the standoff, she had made coffee before she decamping to the spare room. This morning, she was gone, leaving clouds of her glorious aroma when he tidied the sheets, and she had affixed a note to the fridge - 'Don't beat yourself up. You have had a hard day. See you at work later.'

To add insult to injury, it had been that beanpole spot farm Wendy who had brought in his morning coffee earlier so he had yet to make amends.

Just then, the intercom buzzer sounded. He pressed the switch and Carol's voice came across. There was an edge of nervousness to it.

"Mr Carmichael. I have a Mr Byrne to see you. I said you are busy but he is fairly insistent. I'm afraid he's coming down now..."

A lump lodged in Carmichael's throat and for the first time in as long as he could remember, a true terror gripped him. But before he could regroup, the door burst open and Finn Byrne loomed large in the doorway with Carol close behind, a look of mild panic on her face. Finn was flushed and his hackles were up. He pointed a finger at Drew.

"We need to talk...now."

"What, and you think I want to speak to you after your performance the other night? You can piss off! Carol, call the police. This man is not welcome."

Finn swung round, finger still raised and now aimed at Carol Hughes. "Belay that order. All your man's going to be hit with today are a few home truths."

Carol's eyes darted from Byrne to Carmichael, seeking a direction, seeking absolution should it turn nasty.

Drew arose from his chair and scooted around to the door. "OK, Carol. I'll deal with it. I'll take Mr Byrne at his word. Right Finn?"

The Irishman nodded tersely, a bull enraged and pawing the ground. Carmichael closed the door behind Carol and returned to the meagre protection of his desk. Things might get ugly like Wednesday night, and the less anyone knew about it the better. He proffered a hand at one of the guest chairs, retaining as much of an air of calm as his racing heart, parched mouth and aching ribs would allow, hoping he could appease Byrne's temper. The bull steamed and panted.

"My office, my rules. Now sit!"

Byrne eyed Carmichael suspiciously but took a seat anyway, crossing his knees, his gazed firmly fixed on the other.

"OK Finn. Talk. I'm listening."

Finn let out an exasperated sigh, turned his head and stared out of the window, seeking inspiration, where to start. Clearly he hadn't thought he'd get the chance. Drew poured a couple of glasses of water, holding one out to Finn, who took it distractedly.

"When we had the police round on Wednesday asking all sorts of absurd questions, I managed to field most of them. The ones about the problems you were causing Dawn at work, about you seeing her on Monday, how you two had a stand-up row on the day she was murdered. Basically I just played dumb, said we had seen her car around the back of the pub but didn't know when it came or left. Thought we would be generous and give you a little wiggle-room with that flimsy alibi of yours."

"What, and you expect me to be grateful or something after the kicking you gave me? You think I need an alibi?"

"We really only have your word for that, though, don't we? The police say you could probably be one of the last people to see Dawn alive. They said you had lunch together on the day she was killed. So I guess an alibi would be quite useful, don't you?"

"Why is it everyone thinks I killed her. Look, Finn, despite the killer *usually* being the last one to see the victim, it isn't always the case that the last one to see the victim is the killer."

199

He scanned the desk for an analogy that wasn't there.

"Were you screwing Dawn again? Was that it?" Finn smiled at his own cleverness. "That's it, isn't it? Shelley thought there was something going on between you two a couple of years back. She thought you were rather close again. What happened? Did she threaten to end it all? If you couldn't have her, no-one could. Is that it?"

"No, Finn...look, OK. We were seeing each other, but it was only sex. It was three or four months ago. It just sort of happened, you know, old times sake, a quick drink, some food. Anyway, I decided to end it, not her."

"What, she comes over all lonely and you give her one to make her happy, but it's alright because you felt like a shit for doing it? Bloody Hell Drew! What sort of man are you? Did you know that Dawn was pregnant?"

Drew recalled her face in Costa's, her face in the alley, the fire in her eyes and pressure of her grasp about his wrist.

"So did you know?" Finn was leaning across the desk. "More to the point, was it yours?"

Drew rallied. He was not going to get drawn into wordplay with this jumped-up publican. Not in his own office.

"Yes, I knew, but what difference does it make? She could have had an abortion, anything."

"Yeah, so it was yours, then?"

"I don't know. I didn't even know about a baby until... If she had've said anything to me, I would have sorted it, but she didn't."

"You are a piece of work, Drew, you really are. You do know the police are connecting Dawn's death with Rachel's, don't you?" Byrne kicked the chair back and began pacing the office. "You haven't got the slightest idea of the situation you have put us all into. We are all covering your arse, even lying to the police, and I have no idea why."

"Situation I put you into! It's not you who is watching the police rake up all sorts of muck on you. And now they are going to drag up the whole business about Rachel."

"This is not about you, Drew. This is about me and Shelley and all of the others. Can't you get that through your thick skull?

Do you not realise the impact you have on people? You just drive on through their lives, leaving a trail of devastation behind you. We are quite likely to lose the Plough & Harrow, lose everything we have worked for, all these years, and it's all down to you, to your greed and your...disregard for the rest of us. We're all just expendable casualties of war. Well, guess what? We have our own games to play.

"Yes, Finn, this about you and Shelley and the others, and hell yes, it's about me. Whether you like it or not, we are all in this together and someone has to get us out of it."

"Aw, c'mon, Drew, less of the *we're all in this together.* This is something between you and Dawn and we are all just collateral damage."

"Just sit the fuck down, will you, for Christ-sake!"

Byrne threw his arms up. He was tired of arguing. He took the glass from the table. After a long slow pull of the water, he deliberately placed the glass back on the table and rested his hands on his lap, linking his fingers.

"So tell me about the money. Tell me *all* about the money. Tell me why we are *all* in this together."

Carmichael weighed his options. He was stuck in an office with a fiery Irishman who had the capacity to do him great harm. He could lie his way out and watch the lies unravel later or he could be straight up, tell him the truth, as economically as necessary, and deal with the consequences. There were two ways out of this office, excluding headfirst through the window. Either he left under a hail of abuse and possible violence, or they could strike a deal and leave peacefully. Carmichael knew which he preferred. Over the next few minutes, he brought Finn fully up to date. He told him the size of the Fund and how he had grown it. He showed Finn the stock tracker and together they watched other investments as they gained and lost but inevitably rose. And he showed Finn the paperwork bearing Marcus' name.

"And Marcus is cool with this?"

"Well, not exactly. He didn't really have a choice."

"And Dawn? What has this to do with Dawn?"

Carmichael outlined the part Dawn had played. All the time, Finn sat motionless, his hands in is lap, giving Carmichael enough rope, and once he had lapsed into silence, Finn leaned forwards and rested his elbows on the desk and took a hold of the noose.

"The way I see it is, for once...and I'm saying this through gritted teeth...you are right. This is not about the money." He held a hand up as Drew went to speak. "No, this is where you shut up and I speak. Someone killed Dawn. Probably the same person who killed Rachel. Now, you have my word that it wasn't me, for as God is my witness, if it was me, I would have gotten to you first and you would still be begging me to finish you off. But when push comes to shove, I can't really be sure it wasn't you. I know about Rachel, and the abortion. Maybe Dawn wouldn't have an abortion, perhaps that's it? Maybe you killed Rachel because she got rid of the baby? Maybe you killed Dawn because she wouldn't? I wonder how many other people you have driven to the brink of bankruptcy or suicide, how many beyond the brink. Well, guess what? This is my life to break not yours and you are sure as hell not going to take Shelley and me down with you. Is that understood?

Carmichael remained unmoved in his chair, hoping his look of contrition was sufficiently genuine. He could take any amount of mud-slinging. But Finn hadn't finished yet.

"Tell me Drew. There's one more thing, isn't there? All those years ago. That night in Coventry when Shelley came banging on my door. That night when she saw something so terrible, she wouldn't even tell me. So terrible that when you go behind my back asking for money, she just pays you out. 'Cos for me, that's when it all started. That's the night when you took your hold over us, and whether I liked it or not, you have been the other man in Shelley's life. So tell me exactly what happened that night? I want to hear it from you."

The colour drained from Carmichael's cheeks and he had to suppress a quiver in his arm, as the memories of that night appeared again like wraiths. The knife and the blood, the pleading, the desperate minutes of confusion and indecision. He spoke but no words came, as the memories could not be formed into words.

"You know what, Drew? I don't need to know. You can let it haunt that fetid mind of yours because you know what? Shelley has finally opened up to me and we can finally move on from all that."

Finn rose from the chair and drank the remaining half glass of water; his head clearer than it had been in a long, long time. He placed the glass on the desk and pointed a finger at Drew. And with fire burning in his eyes, he spat his final words through clenched teeth.

"I don't want to see you, or speak to you or even see your name written in an obituary, ever again, or so help me I *will* kill you. End of next week, and I am being charitable, I want our money back. All fifty grand of it, and interest, call it a round seventy-five. No. Let's call it one hundred. A good will gesture, eh, Drew? You know where it came from so you know where to return it. One hundred grand by next Friday in the Pub current account, or I will blow this whole scam of yours out of the water. And everyone will know what you did that night. I will see you hang, whatever the cost to Shelley and me."

***

Five miles away, as Carmichael had cowered in his office, DS Monaghan had let out a sharp, self-conscious shriek.

The previous evening, Lambourne Road CID had settled into a graveyard hush and he and Steve Taylor had spent their valuable drinking time locating people with the surname Stanway and the popular variations on the first name - Rod, Rodney, Roderick, Rhodri and even, and as it happened fruitlessly, Ormerod. They had searched Twitter, Facebook, LinkedIn, Pinterest, Google+, Grinder and Tinder and a few smaller social media sites. The list had been surprisingly short with just fifteen people, and then only a single individual who had attended Coventry University from 1996 to 1999 and would have been contemporaneous with Drew Carmichael and the others. Taylor had left a message on LinkedIn, Facebook and Twitter, all of which showed the same round faced, balding man with overly large glasses, asking him to contact them urgently when he received the message.

And then, because everyone else had, they shut up shop and buggered off home.

Friday morning turned out to be a sombre, unproductive morning so far. The rest of the team were out interviewing or poring over files. Documented history of the Monday Club or even of the Murder Game was non-existent beyond the blog by

Stanway. Dave had identified a million different Monday Clubs around the world and at least ten based in Coventry, although all of these involved senior citizens and either tea or dancing. His current search threw up 19,637 results which purported to have some tenuous connection with the words 'Monday Club, Coventry, 1997, Betts, Carmichael'. Idly he paged through the references, until the words started to blur and the screen fizzed in front of his eyes. Maybe, the single hit the previous evening was all he would ever find. Time for a brew.

Grabbing the handle of his mug, Monaghan's eyes were drawn to the small yellow envelope in the task bar, which indicated yet another email had fallen into his metaphorical lap. He replaced the mug, double clicked the icon and let out the sharp, self-conscious shriek.

Hi, DS Monaghan and DC Taylor,

I received the emails and tweets you left. You have indeed tracked down the right Rod Stanway. These days I live and work in Cairns, Queensland, so I am afraid I can't come to see you in person. I will spend the next hour or two writing a few notes about my recollections so feel free to give me a call at anytime. Due to the time difference, I may be a little grumpy, but I'll take the call.

Tapping Taylor on the shoulder, he spun the screen for him to read, ordered the junior to get the brews, whilst he commandeered the PC in the video conferencing suite.

"What is the time difference between here and Australia, Steve?"

Taylor paused as he crossed the office. "Ten or eleven hours in front, Sir, depending where he is, East or West. Queensland is East, I think, so probably about 10:30 -11:30pm."

"Shouldn't be too grumpy then. Friday night. Tinnie-time." Dave smiled broadly and shooed Taylor towards to kettle. Within a few minutes, they were in the video suite staring at a Skype window.

The ringtone boomed around the room as the line connected and soon the wall screen filled with a shadowy face resembling the one from Facebook the previous evening. With a whirr, the video camera in the room turned to aim at the two officers. Monaghan spent the least time he could with pleasantries and dived straight into his interrogation.

"Good evening, Mr Stanway. Really appreciate your time. I'm Detective Sergeant Dave Monaghan and this is Detective Constable Steve Taylor. We're currently involved in a murder enquiry here in the UK, and we believe you may be able to helps us with some background information."

"Good to meet you, Detectives. The arm of The Met has an extremely long reach. Better be careful what I say. Mind you, already been transported, so can't get much worse, eh? Bet you haven't got a view like this in Blighty." The picture on the wall blurred and the screen was filled with a view of the esplanade with the sun burning the horizon as it lazily sunk into the millpond of Cairns Harbour. Then the screen was once more filled with a smiling Rod Stanway. "I was really taken aback when I saw your email. You know that feeling you have when a part of your past that you have almost forgotten comes back to bite you? I must have started that blog post ten years ago, back when I thought you could post any old crap and instantly become an Internet millionaire. That page was probably written in 2004 because I mention Facebook. Needless to say it didn't happen. Haven't even opened that blog for a good six or seven years. Buggered if I can remember the login details, even. I am in real estate over here. Still not reached a million dollars but well on the way, thank the Lord."

"We're just pleased you would take our call, and sorry it's so late."

"Ah, it's not that late, mate. For a Friday!"

"Anyway, we've read the blog post, and we have spent quite some time searching the Internet but there seems to be no other information on the Monday Club. I wonder if you can fill us in a little, give us a bit more background?"

"Yeah, when I wrote the post, I was going through some rose-tinted nostalgia phase. Uni was a long time ago and I though all my old friends would pick up on the post and immediately, it would be as it was then. But no-one left comments, none of them so much as emailed. It was shortly after that I looked into emigrating. In a way they did me a favour.

"I started at Coventry in September of 1996, studying of all things Business Management and Politics. Needless to say, it bored the tits off me, so I ended up at *FiftyFour* and Brown's rather a lot. Andrew Carmichael was already installed and lording it over his little coterie of acolytes, and for a week or two, I sat around that hallowed table. But either I got sick of them or they got sick of me and I decided *The Kasbah* could do a better job of dulling the pain."

"What do you remember of the Monday Club itself?"

"Not a fat lot to be fair. It was mostly a vehicle for Andrew Carmichael's pomposity and I really couldn't be doing with that shit. You know, pissing in the fountain or stealing traffic cones, painting a cock-and-balls on the flyover. It was all a little juvenile for me. Did cop off with a couple of girls though. There was one called Alison, no Alice. She was in the frame for a weekend or so, but then she dumped me for one of the blokes in the gang. There was also Rachel Jones, but I guess you know that from the blog."

"And Andrew Carmichael? What do you recall of him?"

Stanway's hand raised to his nose and a finger aimed at the bridge. "I recall he gave me this scar. I don't know whether the camera picks it up, but it bloody hurt at the time. Fair play though, I muscled in on Rachel and he was none too pleased. Caught me with my pants down, so to speak, coming out of her room. Laid into me hard and I ended up at the bottom of the stairwell in Priory, counting my teeth. I kept my distance from then on, you know, two tables along, just in case Rachel was a fan of scars, but she had already moved onto the barman and Carmichael had moved on to Dawn Silverton."

"You mention *The Murder Game* in your post. What can you remember about that?"

"I thought you'd ask that. And this morning, before I got the email, I would have to say nothing, but I've given some thought over the day and bits and pieces have come back. It started as a silly game. Imagine you had topped someone. Where would you hide the body so it was never found, that sort of thing. If you couldn't think of a decent answer in your turn, you got the next round in. They would tip all the dregs into an empty glass, and if Carmichael didn't like your answer, or he was trying to impress Dawn, or there was an 'e' in the month, he would declare that you had to down the dirty pint. Like I say, just a silly game. I think I said something so obviously flawed that they just took the piss out of me. Needless to say, my idea got me the pint and the slow handclap until I puked all over the floor. But at least that let me off being Carmichael's stooge for the rest of the year. I got it easy."

"How so, Mr Stanway?"

"Rod, please. Well, by Christmas in my first year, they had started to play an altogether different game. Same penalties for failure, same line of wannabe Monday Club members, but different rules. Like I said in the post, they moved onto the whole process of the murder, rather than disposal of the body. Suppose you need to murder someone - how would you do it without getting caught? It had to be obvious to anyone that a murder had been committed, and you had to be present when the deed happened."

"Sounds a bit dark, Rod."

"Maybe, for you, Sergeant. You probably see far too much death, but for a bunch of naive students, whiling away the evenings, I suppose they thought we were being clever, intellectual. It did take a much darker twist, in my opinion, when they started to write them all down. They persuaded one of the would-be members to make notes and there was to be a competition at the end of the year.

"The guy they chose was Chris Betts. He was a bit special. I suppose you'd say these days. Autistic or Asperger's or something, but what it did mean was that he could sit there all evening and then go home and transcribe it all from memory. Which he did. From then on, he was always hassling Carmichael to read his Murder Book."

"Did you ever see this Murder Book?"

"Yes, on many occasions. It was just a loose-leaf folder with loads of punched pages in it. Betts used to bring it into *FiftyFour* or *Brown's* for Carmichael to check his work. I suppose seeking his approval but all they ever did was rip the shit out of him. Must have gone on for weeks. We could see Carmichael becoming more and more annoyed with Betts, with the continual interruptions. He used to follow him around like a tame puppy, which of course just made Carmichael, even angrier. Everyone started asking where his poodle was, until one day he went completely off his block and made Betts down the dirty pint. After that, it kind of fizzled out."

"What, the Monday Club?"

"Oh, no. That continued but it was a much tamer affair. No, I mean the whole Murder Game stopped. Betts stopped chasing Carmichael around. I got the distinct impression that something had happened. Maybe Betts had reported them to the Dean, I don't know, but it all became a lot more civilised after that."

"What can you remember of Christopher Betts? I'll level with you. We can't seem to find much about him apart from a name. We would really like to speak to him."

"Christopher Betts should never have been at University. I suppose it's what you Brits call *Care in the Community*. He had a whole load of friends in his head and he used to walk around chattering away to them. He was afraid to go outside on his own and would only venture out if he could tag onto a group of people. It was a bit creepy but we all knew he was harmless so we cut him some slack. He just disappeared. The word was that after the incident with the dirty pint, he had just quit and gone back up North but that was only a rumour. Many of us preferred to think Andrew Carmichael had taken a page out of the Murder Book and done away with him."

The two detectives shared a quick glance. Many a grain of truth lay in idle speculation. Perhaps Chris Betts was the first? Long before, Rachel, Dawn and Guy. Perhaps, the book just provided the mechanism each time Carmichael's fuse blew?

"Do you mind me asking what this is all about? You mentioned a murder in your email. I know you can't give too much away but is Carmichael in trouble?" Rod Stanway scratched the scar on his nose, self-consciously. "I would hate to dob someone in here, really I would. Especially if it was Carmichael - *not!*"

Dave Monaghan sighed and shifted in his chair. "I have to tell you that Dawn Silverton was found dead last Tuesday and her death points to murder. At this stage we have sufficient reason to link her death back to the murder four years ago of Rachel Jones. And last night, Guy Higson, who you also may remember from Coventry University, was killed in suspicious circumstances."

"Jeez, guys! There won't be a lot of them left at this rate."

"Indeed, Mr Stanway, which is why we are eager to get in

touch with Christopher Betts before anyone else meets the same fate."

The blurry pixelated image threw its arms in the air. "I can't help you at all, I'm afraid. Like I say, something happened and it all fizzled out. Betts must've crawled back under his stone and Carmichael resorted to different ways of torturing his posse. I moved out here in 2006. Haven't heard a word since." Stanway eased back in his chair and rubbed his hand across his face, as if trying to take in the enormity of what he had been told. The microphone roared with the ambience of the seafront bars and late evening traffic. Finally he said, "I am not sure what else I can tell you, really. I hope that's been useful."

Monaghan raised his hand and gestured toward the camera. "Rod, that's been great. We really appreciate you giving us your time. There is a lot of background for us to digest. Is it OK if we get in touch with you again?"

"Yeah. No worries. Use the email. Comes onto my phone and my Mac. Anything I can do to help, you just ask."

"And if you think of anything further, however trivial..."

"Goes without, mate. Goes without."

As the screen blanked and the camera parked itself, the video suite fell into a pensive silence. Without a word, they gathered their papers and scooted back to their desks.

Daley needed to hear about this.

***

"Plough & Harrow, Shelley speaking. How may I help you?" Her face beamed a welcoming smile, an autonomic gesture that affixed itself during the hours of work. The voice lilted gaily in a practiced dance, warm and empathetic. But her eyes were dead, the pupils voids. The absolution she had prayed would come from her confession had not materialised, instead yielding to a deeper more profound degree of guilt. Her secret now exposed to the world, or more specifically to Finn, would now take all of her efforts to contain. Until now, she had been able to keep the lid firmly on, to keep the shame hidden so that the only person who needed to confront it was herself. And a lifetime of internalised anger and depression were the price she had paid.

Finn had listened intently and in silence. This was his way.

His face had fixed upon her, the only expression in his eyes; a kindly, almost sympathetic expression, the only clue that he was even listening. She told him of the day that everything had changed. A cold April night when the thrills and excitement, the exuberance of her carefree youth, had turned in on themselves. As the memories of that evening had returned pin-sharp, she also revisited the fear and panic which had filled her and the shame and anger which had ultimately turned to an all-consuming guilt.

She had felt a brief catharsis, a small weight lifting, relieved that another person, beyond those who were there, knew the story. But her relief had turned hollow, as she realised that she had simply transferred the weight to Finn as guilt and shame for having done nothing then, nor in the days, months and years since. The world still turned beneath her and the sun arched across the sky above, leaving her confession a Pyrrhic victory against her demons.

When she had finished, he had remained quiet, mulling things over for probably three minutes before the silence had become too much.

"Well?"

His response, imbued with care and love but above all a deep sense of incredulity, was matter-of-fact. "I can't understand why you haven't told me this before. Fifteen years, for God's sake! Why have I had to watch you slowly self-destruct? As dreadful as you make it sound, it's not as if you actually did anything."

And he had probed right to the nub of it.

"I should've at least tried. And afterwards. I could have told someone, the police, even. Every day, when I thought about that night, it just became more difficult to justify my silence, why I allowed Drew to get away with it."

"Look, love, What's done is done. It can't be changed. Anyway, apart from you, who is going to care after fifteen years, except maybe me?" Finn was ever the pragmatist. He had moved behind her and was clasping her shoulders, his strong hands massaging the flesh, in an attempt to exorcise the demons, show her their impotence against the overwhelming power of his love for her.

"I care." She had reached her hand over and taken hold of

his.

"I know you do, love. But from now on there are two of us who care. And if it's the last thing I do, I am going to make Drew *Bloody* Carmichael face up to his responsibilities. He is going to make it right by us!"

"No, Finn, just leave it. There's no sense in bringing it all up again. Nothing to be gained from it."

"Oh, but there is a whole lot to be gained from it. You and me have had fifteen years of this secret, whilst Carmichael has been carrying on as if nothing happened. You know, I doubt he even remembers. No. I think it's time for payback, don't you? It's time he started to give back a little of what he has taken from us all these years."

Shelley had seen the steely resolve on Finn's face. Yet, as if a switch had been thrown, the day had resumed its normal pattern, and no more had been said. A man of quiet determination, when Finn set his mind to a task he rarely failed to achieve it. He had turned the ailing spit-and-sawdust alehouse into a thriving business. The Plough turned a steady profit but scarcely any was left once they had met their obligations, so much of it burdensome repayments on a mortgage taken out to acceded to Carmichael's blackmail. She knew that eventually Carmichael would pay, Finn would make sure of that. They had spent the rest of the day lost in chores; fresh wind in their sails but Finn's mind had been elsewhere, planning and scheming. When he had finally crept under the clothes beside her that night, he had pulled her to him and, for the first time in years, she had yielded to his lovemaking, strong and dominant and she had exploded in an ecstatic crescendo she had not known for many years.

"Shelley, it's Drew." Shelley snapped to the present at the sound of the voice. It was short and sharp. There was anger behind every word. Her response was equally curt.

"Drew?"

"I thought I told you to keep your mouth shut?" He was direct and challenging.

"What makes you think I haven't?" She was non-committal, in no mood to play his games.

"I'll tell you what. I have had that bog-trotting ape of a

211

husband of yours around just now sticking his size nine's into my business, threatening me with all sorts if I don't pay him off. We might not have seen eye-to-eye over the years but at least there has been an uneasy detente. Now, all of a sudden he's bursting in here all guns blazing. Why, *all of a sudden*, would he be doing that, eh? Unless of course you had been blubbering to him again."

Briefly, she felt her resolve weaken, the wiry fingers of her demons pulling her down. She wanted to blurt out her apologies, promise to make it right, vow that it would never happen again. But deep within her, that faint, subjugated part of Shelley Nugent, held hostage for so many years, strained at the chains until the links began to fracture. She would no longer be silenced, and she heard her voice saying:

"Yes, Drew. I told him absolutely everything. All of these years I have been afraid of you, of the power you've had over me. No more! I told him what happened in Coventry fifteen years ago. I told him about the money, about what you threatened to do if I didn't pay up. Well guess what? I don't care what happens now, as long as you start to get some of your own medicine. Finn and I will make it our personal quest to make sure you are brought to book..."

"I am warning you, Shelley..." Carmichael's voice was quavering. She had seen him angry before, watched his features harden and his eyes narrow, and she had heard his voice tremble. But this was different. He was afraid.

"*You* are warning *me*? You are in no position to warn me. We both know what you did, what you are up to now. How dare you warn me?"

The line went quiet, except for the rasping of Carmichael's breath, slowing, ominous.

"Now you listen to me, you bitch. I am going to say this once, and you are going to listen. You and that man of yours need to keep your mouths shut. And I mean shut. You don't even mention a word of this phone call to him otherwise you will pay. I am not going to let you jeopardise everything now. Do you understand?"

"Go take a flying fuck, you arrogant bastard!" And, as she spat the last word from her lips, she slammed the phone into the cradle, sending a resounding crack across the empty room.

Slowly, as if every remaining ounce of strength was ebbing from her body, she slid down the wall until she was sitting in a small corner behind the bar, foetal and drained. The crushing weight of one and a half decades fell from her shoulders in that instant. The tears welled up in her eyes, and she let the tears flow uncontrollably, conscious that the fear she had of retribution from Carmichael was far surpassed by the pride she had in herself for finally standing up to him.

***

Carmichael rolled the receiver in his hand, agonising over which buttons to press next. Bastard! How dare that potato-crunching moron threaten him? What had he said? 'One hundred grand or I will kill you'. That was definitely blackmail...and a threat. Fucking Mick! And one hundred grand! Just let him come and take it. As for Shelley, how that simpering worm had turned. They might think themselves a formidable team, but he, Drew Carmichael, would show them just where the power lies. They would both regret the day they decided to turn their guns on him. He could dial Higson's number but he knew he wouldn't answer. By now the voicemail was probably full anyway.

Who else was there?

The net was closing in, tightening around him, and choking the air from his body. None of them would get their money now, nor could they risk going to the police. Even Finn Byrne understood that the police would hold them all to account if they found out about the scam. But then the police might naturally happen upon the Fund. Once they got wind of something dodgy they would pursue it to the bitter end. They had resources. Their specialist financial fraud investigators who would destroy all of Guy's handiwork in an instant.

If the police found out. More likely when.

When that time came, the Fund would be seized, his career would be finished, his life over. The Caymans account would fester for years quietly growing whilst bigwig lawyers squabbled and bickered, dragging their heels, gradually garnering their own accounts until the whole fund was subsumed, like some Victorian Chancery Court. That couldn't be allowed to happen. He would need to secure the money quickly and ensure that when the police finally arrived at his door, he was no longer there. There would be expenses. A new life, a new identity, maybe even a new face. The police would put a watch on his finances, maybe even sequester them. Even his meagre inheritance would be blocked. They would know if he so much as printed a balance slip from an ATM and hunt him down.

His finger alighted on the zero and he held it, hearing the faint, insistent howl of the buzzer outside and down the corridor. He needed Carol to cover his back while he considered his options.

"Mr Carmichael?" The voice was immature and bored. He guessed at the skinny one with the lank hair and pinpricks for breasts, and he stifled a curse, tempering his voice.

"Hello, er..." He had no-idea of the names of any of those pimply, sour-face kids they employed on YOPS or YTS or whatever it was called these days. "Is Carol there? Mrs Hughes?

The line went quiet and he could hear faint noises-off, a few voices. He could hear Carol talking to someone. His minds eyes imagined her standing behind the counter top, her skirt rising as she stood tiptoed, leaning over the desk. He could not discern the conversation but then he caught his name and recognised the voice, struggling to visualise a face. A bus went past and drowned out the voices and then Carol was on the line.

"Mr Carmichael. The police are here again. They are asking to speak to you. About Mr Higson."

Carmichael sighed rather too deeply and caught the rasping sound of his irritation fed back through the speaker. He glanced at his watch, cursing under his breath. About Higson? There could be only one reason why they would be asking about Guy Higson. "I've got enough on my plate without him. What have you told them?"

"Drew. Guy Higson has been killed. Wednesday night, apparently."

Carmichael's pulse quickened. The familiarity of the office, the hum of the computer, the chirp of the clock, the creaks of the floorboards in the corridor outside suddenly seemed so alien, threatening. The air in the room had grown cold, or was it the chill of discovery? In his mind, disconnected images swam and he could smell an odour of damp and the sweet sooty fumes of the motorcycle's exhaust, he could picture the black contorted figure at his feet crumpled and broken.

Rubbing his hand across his neck, he felt the dragnet closing in. First Dawn. Killed after she had complained to his boss about improprieties in the accounts. Now Guy, who had managed the accounts. And then there was Rachel, seemingly dead and buried along with her corpse.

But there are two sides to every story; it all depends upon your viewpoint. A scheming financial advisor, killing off his girlfriend because of the pillow talk, killing off another girlfriend because she was too close to his shady ways and then killing off the auditor who knew where the financial bodies were buried. Regardless of the truth, which was most plausible? He had to buy himself some time to think. Time to phone his solicitor Edgar Sampson and plan a way out of this mess.

"Tell them I am out, I didn't arrive this morning. Tell them any fucking thing. Just don't bring them in here."

"Mr Carmichael?"

The question in Carol's voice spoke volumes. What could he tell her that she didn't already know?

"I can't see them. Not here. Not today."

The police would be looking for the rest of the University crew. For Finn and Shelley, for Marcus and Alice. Maybe this *was* payback for Rachel?

"Come and look for me. Give me a minute to leave out the back. Say I must've nipped out for breakfast or something. Just...just give me five minutes."

"And then what?" Carol's voice was low now, barely a conspiratorial whisper. Carmichael pictured that fool detective sitting in the reception and Carol hunched over the receiver. "Jesus, Drew. We used that excuse yesterday, for God's sake!"

"Just shrug your shoulders and flash your eyelashes, I don't know!"

***

With Finn changing sides and Guy out of the picture, Carmichael knew there was only one who would offer him any help now - Marcus - but only because he still had the screws on

215

him. Ealing General was busy when he arrived. He had had driven straight home and dumped the car on the drive. The police would have circulated the number by now so it was a miracle that he had not been stopped on the way. He had thrown a few things into a holdall, locked the house and hidden the keys in the garden. If they went to the house, they would find the car, the house empty and a whole world in which to search. And that would buy him some time.

The hat could have been a mistake, and maybe the coat but the less he looked like himself the better. The hospital was infested with cameras. Rounding a corner, he spotted the door to a laundry store. He and Marcus had met there before when he had needed to put the fat fool right about something. This was the one blind spot in the CCTV coverage. He checked his watch. 11:30am. Surely it must be about break-time. This was the NHS. Lazy and work shy, everyone always had breaks, all the time. He had to wait another fifteen minutes before he was rewarded.

Marcus Balfour scurried desperately toward the laundry cupboard and eased the handle down. This was a familiar respite from the wards, for a crafty fag when no-one was around. If the door was unlocked the room was his, at least for the next fifteen minutes. He slipped his less than slender frame through the smallest gap and closed the door, only for it to open into his face as the stranger forced his way in. Balfour stifled a yell as he recognised the intruder. He dug into his ward coat pocket and locked the door using a key he had long ago purloined from the cleaning staff.

"Drew! You can't be here!"

"Well, look at me. I fucking-well am!"

"You do know the police were round this morning, don't you? Did you know Guy is dead? They say he's been murdered too. They asked if I knew where you were. What's going on Drew? Come on, I'm starting to get a little jumpy now." Balfour dug into his coat for a pack of *Superkings* and hurried over to a window where he coaxed a cigarette into life, suppressing an involuntary cough at the first sharp inrush of smoke.

Drew followed him and spun Marcus by the shoulder, looking him straight in the eye. "What did you tell them, Marcus?"

216

"Nothing! I had no idea where you were until a few moments ago. As for Guy, what could I say? I was almost sick, still feel rough now - *as a matter of fact.*" Marcus took another huge drag and watched the flickering amber devour several millimetres of the cigarette paper. "What's going on Drew? This is freaking me out, now."

"Don't be such a pussy, Marcus. The police came to see me as well, but I gave them the slip." Drew mustered all of the bravado he could. He hoped it would be enough. There would need to be an upper station in this conversation and he wanted to occupy it.

"You *gave them the slip*! Why on earth would you do that? No wonder they came to see me here - *at work*. No wonder they are asking so many questions. What have you got yourself into, Drew? And more to the point, what are you getting me into? What do you know about Guy?"

Drew irritatedly wafted the smoke away through the window.

"Guy bloody well deserved everything he got for not picking up my bloody calls. That's what I know."

Marcus paused mid drag. He realised the cigarette was quivering and the taste was stale in his mouth.

"There's not an ounce of compassion in you is there, Drew?" He eyed Drew askance. Were these really the eyes of a killer bent on self-protection? He thought back to Alice's revelation about that grim night in 1997. Could it be that Drew himself was slowly exterminating the witnesses, maybe removing the blackmailers? How long would it be until he rounded on Alice? The cramped laundry cupboard suddenly seemed stifling and hot despite the breeze though the window, and Drew's frame seemed all the larger between himself and the locked door. Perhaps the best approach would be to appease the beast rather than antagonise it, at least until he and Alice were well away from the Capital. "Sorry, sorry. Look it's been a hard day and it's not yet noon."

Extinguishing the butt against the window frame, Marcus tossed it into an ever-growing heap on the ground outside. "Look Drew. This is getting out of hand now. The police asked all sorts of questions about Dawn and Rachel, about you. Did I know where I was when Dawn was killed. I actually have no idea where I was. I know I was at work, but you know what? We are all zombies in here on a Monday because the weekend is such a hard time. If I had sodomised a registrar between the beds on Addison Ward, I bet no-one would remember - not even me! Then they told me Guy had been murdered on the way home on Wednesday night. And you know what? Again I couldn't tell them where I was. So I had to lie. Yes. *I* had to lie to *the police*. They asked about you. How well you got on with Dawn. When did I last see you. Come on, Drew. There is something very wrong here. Exactly what is this all about?"

Carmichael decided that economy was best. The less his friend knew the better.

"I don't know, Marcus. I genuinely don't know." Then a thought struck him. "Anyway, what do you mean, you had to lie? Where were you on Wednesday night?

Marcus threw his arms in the air. "*I was watching some late film eating a sad-bastard-meal-for-one* or *I was asleep in the nurses day room.* Which would sound the most convincing to you, Drew? If you must know I was with a woman. I know that's hard to believe, but it's true and the last thing I want is for her to be involved in all of this."

Whenever Marcus lied, there was an air of theatrics that surrounded the lie and Carmichael could see through it. "C'mon, Marcus. Never try and kid a kidder. This is the police we are talking about. It's one thing for me to embroider the truth a little, but they will find you out as sure as you can say *fit-up* and before long you'll be in an interview room trying to remember the name of a good lawyer. Think of the money. The more evasive you are the more chance they will dig deeper. Why didn't you just tell them where you were?"

"Because I am scared, Drew. First Rachel, all those years ago. OK, statistically unfortunate. Then Dawn. That was tough, but again four years after Rachel, just a blip. But when they told me Guy had been killed and they said it was definitely murder... They are all our friends, all members of the Monday Club. Shit Drew, even you must see that someone is working their way through us."

"Don't be such a bloody idiot. You're just hysterical. Just tell them where you were and let them sort out the truth from the lies. If you have a *sad-bastard-meal-for-one* wrapper in the garbage then the story stands up. Just because no-one saw you eating it, doesn't mean you're a murderer."

Marcus recalled Alice's warm bed, the comfortable scent of her neck, the lingering glow of intercourse, and the pain of nearly fifteen years of separation. No-one would know. This was his chance. His new beginning. And no-one was going to ruin it this time. Not the police. Not Drew. Not even a killer.

"That's OK for you to say. You know what? You are an infinitely better liar than me. And yes, you probably could get yourself out of a locked room with a few charming words. But me?"

Carmichael shifted his weight, the Dexion frame cutting the blood flow to his forearm, urging him to flex his fingers against the *pins-and-needles*. But what of his own alibi? What of his whereabouts? What of that Monday afternoon, filled with rage at Dawn's insubordination, consumed by the need to silence her? He remembered driving up and down the streets, the rows of parked cars flashing by like sentries on parade. He desperately tried to recall where he was, exactly where, before he arrived back at work late in the afternoon.

And yesterday. He remembered Carol and the wine. But it was only half a bottle and she drunk most of that. He recalled them discussing the audit, some stupid row about Dawn and Guy, but of the night, a vague recollection of the cold air, of condensation on the windscreen, of waiting under the street-lights, of his head sinking into the headrest as the car accelerated away. And he recalled the searing warmth of the blanket as he crawled back into bed. Did he take her home after all? He must have done. For a short while, he stuttered, trying to catch memories as they skulked away to a darker corner of his mind.

"Yes, I...I was at home, I think." He was gripped by an urgent need to speak to Carol.

Once more, Marcus flounced theatrically. "You *think*? So you have no alibi either? Bloody Hell, Drew. I was at least hoping there was a Judy or a Trudy in there somewhere." He spun and stared out of the window, rubbing a hand across the back of his neck, bending his head back against the building tension. Either Drew could not, or would not, confirm his innocence. But did that in itself make him guilty?

"This is now starting to seriously freak me out. Jesus! What happens if Guy and Finn were right and it is you playing some kind of sick double bluff game with us all? Perhaps I better look around for some sharp objects, bits of rope, bottles marked poison!"

"Don't be so bloody melodramatic, Marcus. If it was me, I would kill you here of all places. Far too public and, anyway, on the basis you have just admitted having no alibi, would I just not get you to vouch for me, and me for you, concoct some drunken night in a pub together? Pull yourself together. If I am right...and I usually am, this is about that Monday Club fund. Someone, and I think I know who, is trying to get their hands on all that money and deprive us - deprive you, Marcus - of it. This is *all* about me and the money. Don't you realise? Every one of you has a vested interest in the money and in bumping off the others, and each time the individual share increases. Which means it's someone who knows about the money. And that is becoming an ever shorter list. And you know what? It could be you next, Marcus. And then me."

Marcus' eyes were starting to shine as he processed Carmichael's rhetoric. There was a simple truth. One by one, they were being exterminated, and whoever was responsible, whatever the reason, whenever it was going to happen, Alice was on the list. And he thought of the previous night, of the warmth of Alice's arms and of the alibi he would never give.

"For Christ's sake, Drew. Look, I'm scared mate. Just tell me what to do?" He was grabbing at Carmichael's sleeves, his voice was earnest, imploring.

Carmichael looked Marcus in the eye, still trying to process the intangible memories floating around his head, the vague feelings of rage, of horror and the emptiness, fading like vapour trails along the paths of his mind.

"I know, Marcus. I just don't know."

CHAPTER 23

When Daley and Whetstone reached Carmichael's house in Richmond, it was almost noon. The Mercedes lay askew in the drive, the gravel viciously grooved, intimating that the nature of its arrival had been somewhat hurried. Feeling the bonnet, Daley estimated an hour, no more than two. The uniforms from the mobile unit confirmed the house locked up and empty.

Once Corby had confessed that Carmichael had again given them the slip, Daley had radioed the station and now the quiet close, normally a morgue during the day, played host to Whetstone, Corby, three uniforms and a forensic monkey with a keen eye for tyre tread patterns. At that point, their phones had both lit up like Christmas trees, with both Monaghan and Taylor anxious to impart the information that Rod Stanway had disclosed. And now they were all sitting in the pool Insignia with Dave Monaghan on speakerphone.

"OK. Look, apart from Carmichael, we're running out of ideas here. Let's look at the rest of the people we know. Dave, who's on the University group list?"

"There is a Dr Marcus Balfour, works at the Ealing Hospital..."

"Yeah. I saw him an hour or so ago." Corby flipped open his notebook, skimmed the notes. "He was working on Monday with a hundred witnesses, and last night he says he was alone watching TV. I asked to see the rotas and they check out. I asked what was on TV and he said he couldn't remember. He said he was probably asleep."

"Well, check it out anyway. Was he seen by a neighbour, the chap at the corner shop, anyone? What car does he drive?"

"Black BMW. Looks like it hasn't moved for weeks."

"So who else have we got, Dave?"

There was a hesitation on the phone line and a clicking of keys. "There's Alice Bown, Sir. Uniform visited her last known address but she moved around Christmas and as she lives in the rented sector we are struggling to find a forwarding address. Electoral Roll hasn't been updated so we are searching some other databases; see if she has insurance, whether she changed her bank details, who her employer is. And then there is Christopher Betts. He also seems to have slipped off the grid years ago whilst at University, and no-one has seen him since."

"Keep on it, Dave. We need to find them. Anyone else?"

"No, Gov. Apart from Andrew Carmichael that's about it. I have a call out to the University and they are sifting through their records, see who else might have been part of the group but not part of the current gang, so to speak, and I am also waiting on Sergeant Davies in Coventry. He has promised me some news later."

"So based on our Mr Stanway and loads of circumstantial evidence, and whether D/Supt Allenby likes it or not, it all points to Carmichael. If what you were told is right he could be behind the disappearance, not to mention the murder of, Christopher Betts, in addition to the murder of Rachel Jones, Dawn Silverton and probably Guy Higson."

"All because of a Murder Book created in 1997? Seems a bit far fetched to me, Sir." Deb scratched her chin and peered aimlessly out of the window, before turning back and facing Daley. "Why would he want to draw attention to himself by leaving pages from a book? Surely he knows we would make the connection eventually?"

Daley sighed openly at her insurrection. "No idea. Perhaps he is still laughing at his in-joke. We didn't find it on Rachel Jones. We didn't find it on Chris Betts..."

"We haven't found him yet though, have we, Sir. And why would an intelligent bloke like Carmichael leave clues?"

"I don't know. Maybe he's not as clever as he thinks he is. Maybe we are cleverer than he thinks we are. Maybe it's as simple as *look at what I can do!*"

Deb slumped back in her seat, conceding the point for now. There had been enough arguments with the boss for one day.

"Mike, I need to know if that tyre tread matches the one found in Treddle Lane." Corby nodded.

Daley pondered, hearing Monaghan's breathing over the phone line. The Merc was light coloured, matching Lee Smith's less than precise description. Carmichael now appeared to have done a runner. Like it or not Allenby was going to have to accept it.

"Right! We have to treat Carmichael as a serious suspect now. We speak to him on Wednesday and by Friday another person is dead and he has done a bunk. And there is CCTV which puts him at the scene of the Silverton murder, and a witness who claims he was at the Higson murder."

"Agreed, Sir," chipped in Dave Monaghan from the tiny handset. "There was certainly something fishy going on between Dawn Silverton and Andrew Carmichael at work too."

"Yes, I know." interjected Daley. "Deb and I picked up on that when we spoke to Nugent and Byrne yesterday. Carmichael said there had been some trouble over clients that Dawn was passing to Carmichael. Shelley Nugent corroborated that apparently he was hanging on to the clients for longer than necessary, almost losing her sales. According to Carmichael, they had rowed about it on the day of her death and it had got ugly."

"I followed it up with Barraclough and Leavis. Dawn Silverton spoke directly to Gerald Thornton, slinging accusations around right, left and centre, claiming client funds were being misused.

"And were they, Dave?" Deb asked pointedly. Another piece of circumstantial evidence stacked up against Carmichael.

"Well, they ran a full scale internal audit. They found one misposting of a hundred or so quid which was down to Carmichael, or rather the office manager, Carol Hughes, clicking the wrong keys and that was remedied as soon as it was noticed. Apart from that, nothing. In fact, Thornton himself was surprised that it was only a hundred quid that was misposted. Usually a couple of grand can be lost in the system. As he said 'we are solicitors, not accountants'."

"So, on the face of it, there is no motive there for Carmichael to kill Dawn because she grassed on him to Thornton?" Deb scratched her scalp, hoping to trigger some mental connections.

"No, Deb...or maybe not on the face of it!" Static on the line suggested Monaghan was reaching for some paperwork. "Just give me a second. Here it is. Yes. A couple of interesting things about Guy Higson, our motorcyclist. Firstly, he was the accountant looking after the Barraclough and Leavis company accounts. Also he was a close friend of Carmichael, Silverton and the rest through this University group. No surprises there. But when we look at his billable hours for the last three months, a large proportion of them are at Barraclough and Leavis, and most of those happened on or around the time of this internal audit."

"Well, that figures, though, doesn't it, Dave?" Daley stated the obvious. "Internal audit, looking through the accounts. It would pay to have the accountant on hand."

"Yes, Sir. That would figure - see what you did there - figure, accountant." In the car they looked at each other, Daley shrugged. "Only, except for 8 hours or so, all of the billable hours are *before* the internal audit started. Maybe there was a little tidying up done first?"

"Nice one, Dave." Deb nodded her head. "So maybe there is a motive? Maybe Carmichael is abusing the company funds, Silverton finds out and grasses him up, but not before Carmichael and Higson have tidied up, as Dave so eloquently puts it? And then Carmichael has it out with Silverton behind Costa's and not satisfied with her response, he tops her."

"Or something like that." Daley interjected.

"But I don't get Higson." said Corby, chewing his pen, looking puzzled. "I can see all of this - the embezzlement, the audit, the anger and Carmichael killing Silverton. But surely Higson is the hero in all of this. He just got Carmichael's balls out of the fire. If we are right, Carmichael was bang to rights without Higson.

"And who penned the Murder How-to documents we found on the bodies? Carmichael doesn't strike me as someone who would draw any more attention to himself than necessary, especially if he was embezzling money. I mean business is business."

Daley asked Monaghan to get a detail outside Carmichael's house, a warrant to search the inside and a trailer to take the car away for examination. After Monaghan had rung off, the three sat in the car, each lost in a myriad of ideas and suppositions.

From a single murdered woman, a pattern was forming. And with mixed emotions, Daley conceded that it stretched further back than Rachel Jones towards Christopher Betts and was now extending it's tendrils forwards into the remnants of the group.

But, like a fractal in its early stages of evolution, the fingers were stretching in different directions, growing and forming yet to betray the pattern, yet to reveal the next twist or turn.

Which just left the Murder documents. Seemingly derived from a parlour game over a decade ago. But it was these documents that convinced Daley that there was a pattern emerging. The pages connected the murder and they connected the killer - a serial killer. Each an augur of murder, narrated by the victim. Individual scenes of a drama where the denouement had yet to be revealed. They told a story only part way through, that would not end until the finale was over, until all pages had been read, until all of the characters killed. He knew the sleepless nights, lying awake, trying to expunge the grisly images from his mind were nothing compared to the ever increasing guilt he felt for not being able to prevent Guy Higson's death, and for the gnawing horror of knowing that out there, probably less than five miles from where they sat, another paper was being printed, another death was being planned and he was powerless to stop it happening.

Chapter 24

Balfour slouched at the window, the chair bobbing and groaning under his weight, the rhythmic creaks slowly dissipating into the background murmur of the busy corridors outside. The staleness of the laundry room testified to one of its alternative uses, helping junior doctors and willing nurses through long night shifts. The room's other purpose was as his sanctuary, time out from the constant maintenance of a caring facade. He dragged a hand across the thinning bush of hair behind his already receded hairline. He shouldn't have to feel so tired all the time. There had to be better ways to serve the apprenticeship that would lead him to a lucrative consultancy.

He lit another cigarette and adjusted the opening in the window to scavenge the smoke he exhaled. Lousy habit, but the stress would kill him long before the smoking, that was for sure. Less than two hours into the afternoon, with another seven ahead. And to tip him over the edge, that bastard Carmichael!

Taking a cathartic drag on the cigarette, watching the orange tip, he held the smoke in his lungs for as long as he could, tasting the cool bitter softness, feeling the burn give way to warmth and the mild electricity as the nicotine hit his brain. The plume surfed out through the window before being buffeted by the breeze and fragmented into nothing.

Through the angular slit at the side of the window he could see a patient strolling aimlessly in deep conversation with a relative. It should comfort him that people turned to his noble profession in their hour of need, but he despised them. For every genuine, deserving patient there were three more who saw the National Health Service as a necessary evil, a drain on the public purse, and the staff within their own personal whipping boys. He loathed patients from the neck upwards. They were rancorous and unappreciative and from the neck downwards they were just malodorous machines, neglected and malfunctioning, and, in age, often filthy and repugnant.

A loud crash outside the door brought him out of his daydream. The handle bobbed up and down and a voice swore. The door was locked and everyone on the floor knew what that meant and resented it. Balfour tossed the nub end out of the window now spent but barely smoked, almost two inches of ash bursting like chaff as it hit the breeze.

So he was rich on paper and implicated by it in the scam. A scam that Carmichael had convinced him was failsafe, that hurt no-one and exploited a loophole. In recent months he had all but forgotten the scheme until Wednesday, when it had resurfaced with a vengeance. He had watched Carmichael down a neat double Scotch in a single draught, off-loading the problem, as he always seemed to, and he despised him as the question that Carmichael would never in a million years even think to ask, had hung in the air.

So how am I going to avoid going to prison here?

Right now, it was he who was custodian of a very large pot of very hot money, which Carmichael assured him could never be traced. But that's what the police did! Soon their specialists would be finding connections and pursuing them, and the paper trail led straight to him. So it was he with a massive motive for murder.

It was a busy hospital, ward rounds, the afternoon dementia clinic he had run. Someone would be a witness to him being there. But even that sliver of salvation had been snatched away as Carmichael went on to expound a new theory.

"Would you really murder her yourself, though, Marcus? Would I, for that matter? Far better to get someone else to do the deed, for a share of the proceeds, don't you think?"

"What proceeds? I didn't even know how much there was until just now! You work with legal people. You have far greater knowledge than I do in that department. And far more connections. If anyone hired the hit-man it was you!"

"You forget Marcus, that I have to remain solvent and free from significant debt because my personal accounts are vetted regularly and even after the audit, I am personally squeaky clean. So as far as anyone is concerned, I am as pure as a virgin angel. Whereas you. You have access to drugs, you work in a busy hospital where you could get lost in a crowd, 'I think I saw him getting some water from the machine, or taking a slash. He does go for long smoking breaks. Come to think about it, perhaps I can't be sure...' Even if you didn't do it, the money will be the clincher for the police. Junior doctor, mountain of debts, no way out. Might even add

227

'bit of a loner, keeps himself to himself'. Hit-man or not, Marcus, they're going to do you for the money. You can kiss that consulting post goodbye."

Balfour's mouth had parched. Even aware that Carmichael was playing him, he had begun to doubt his own innocence. Carmichael offered the hand once more.

"There's only one thing for it. If we find the killer first we can the tip off the police and let them follow that lead instead."

Find the killer before the police?

Another solution that was fantastic on paper, but just how was a junior doctor and a financial advisor meant to stay one step ahead of the combined resources of the Metropolitan Police?

Balfour had cut directly to the chase. Now was the time for more than an empty gesture. Carmichael had to find a way to protect them both. After all the shit he'd fielded in the past, it was payback time. After all, there was always the possibility, Balfour had threatened, that he would crack under pressure and they would both go down for embezzlement. However good Carmichael had been with his financial housekeeping, Balfour felt sure the Met's guys were better.

Carmichael had relented; whether as a line of least resistance or from uncharacteristic concern for his predicament, Balfour wasn't entirely sure. It was in both their interests to find a way of keeping a lid on their little business arrangement, and it would have to be done quickly.

And then there was Alice.

Just to think of her had brought butterflies to Marcus' stomach. Fifteen years rewound in an instant. She had constantly been in his thoughts and there was no way that he was going to lose her now.

Drew's financial dealings were inevitably going to become police property. Carmichael would sell his granny to save his own arse and it would always be Balfour's arse in a sling when the police came knocking. A leopard like Carmichael doesn't change its spots. Deep down, Balfour knew that all Carmichael cared about was self-preservation. He was a user, a philanderer, a liar and a cheat, but was he also a murderer? Could he rely on someone like that to find him a way out?

Balfour flicked another unsmoked cigarette through the gap in the window, purposefully brushing the back-blown ash from the lapels of his white coat. There was no way he would swing for Carmichael. Not now he had found Alice again. Enough was enough. If all that remained was to find the person responsible then that was what had to be done...and the police could do that. He was having nothing more to do with any of it.

Well, except for one and a half million small details which would receive his unremitting attention.

Standing up, he smoothed out the creases, drew in a deep breath and made for the door. Within twenty minutes he was AWOL, on the Tube and heading home.

***

When the door eventually opened and Gerald Thornton eased his way around it, Daley noticed a slight hesitancy as the eyes first alighted on him. A momentary pause as the owner of the office broke stride and sized up the visitor on the leather chesterfield clutching a battered satchel. He must have known Daley was doing the same.

Thornton was taller than the smiling head and shoulders photograph in reception implied, the head appearing at well over six feet, followed by a torso and a pair of arms, which fluidly closed the door and extended in greeting. There was a firmness in the grip, a sighting shot, *don't mess with me, I have had a hard day*. The face, behind a billboard smile, said nothing. The eyes were cold and emotionless but impressed upon Daley that Thornton was still on duty, that his brain would process every word that was exchanged. But tall as he was, Thornton was thin and his suit, not drastically expensive but serviceable and hard wearing left him looking gaunt and weary.

The office was substantially larger than the one hurriedly vacated by Carmichael and the decor more opulent. The walls, though painted the same magnolia, were less tired and were panelled to a dado rail in a cherry mahogany; a deep maroon carpet studded with ranks of silver *fleur-de-lys* gave it the appearance of his old grandma's front room. In place of the eighties cream and brown filing cabinets, there were deep cherry coloured wooden affairs at six times the price and bedecked with polished brass fittings. The desk was also larger, regency styled

229

with a huge studded red leather executive chair behind it. And all of this splendour was let down by the ubiquitous piles of manilla folders tied up with ribbon. Bounteous, but still less than in Carmichael's office. Yet another perk of leadership.

"Right, Inspector. Let's get this over with shall we?" The marker set down, Thornton placed himself on the adjacent sofa, disregarding the relative safety of the office chair. "What can I help you with?"

"As you know, we came here on Wednesday to speak to Andrew Carmichael about the death of Dawn Silverton. I believe you know Ms Silverton?" The nod was almost subliminal. A lawyer, much less eager to dispense information than to elicit it. Daley prompted. "Can you tell me about that?"

Thornton sighed and rose from the sofa, crossed to the desk and poured himself a coffee. He watched the swirls on the surface as he rested his spoon onto the saucer.

"Yes. Ms Silverton was an associate at Parkin-Wright, and as with a number of local estate agencies we have an informal arrangement whereby our card is passed to the prospective buyers. If instructed, we assist with the conveyancing and completion, and in turn Parkin-Wright receive an introduction fee. And up until a month ago, that arrangement was working satisfactorily."

"So then what happened?"

"Well, it was strange really. I had picked up on a number of complaints from clients regarding the length of time taken to process their sale, or the size of the deposit they had to find up front, or extra funds they had to seek. Of course I have to treat these complaints seriously as referrals are our bread and butter. And whilst one of our other associates had received a single complaint, which turned out to be a simple misunderstanding, impatient buyer not being aware how slowly the wheels turn, there were five or six complaints against Andrew Carmichael that couldn't altogether be explained away. However, I satisfied myself that business does not always run smoothly and afforded Carmichael the benefit of the doubt. His portfolio of clients is sizeable and worth a good deal to the company and I suppose the bigger the portfolio, the bigger the risk of receiving complaints."

"So what changed that?"

"It was Ms Silverton. She came to see me and made an outright accusation against Carmichael, suggesting he was playing fast and loose with clients money. I asked her for evidence to support her allegations and she gave me a list of clients and properties, which she claimed, had been problematic sales. I investigated and, yes, the sales had been problematic but there was no evidence of any wrongdoing. When I spoke to Ms Silverton again, she was insistent, and so I asked our internal auditor to inspect the accounts. I told all this to your Constable earlier."

"Yes, sorry I'm making you repeat yourself. We are covering a lot of ground very quickly. So the audit found nothing?"

"Nothing. A handful of cross postings; mistakes which were easily resolved."

"And that was the last you saw of Ms Silverton?"

"Saw, yes, but she did phone me at the office last Friday. Complained once more about Carmichael and a particular property, Chapel Rise, which she felt he had been dragging his heels over. I told her I would ring her back and, after an hour or so for Carmichael to find the details, I was able to confirm that everything was sorted."

"And did she seem satisfied with that?"

"Not really. I think she was gunning for Carmichael. You know, *hell hath no fury...* I wondered if the breakdown of their past relationship was getting in the way of their professional one. I promised her that I would have a word with Carmichael - which I did, first thing on Monday morning. Carmichael assured me there was no issue, and as far as I was concerned, that was that."

"And how was Mr Carmichael, generally? How did he seem over the last month or so?"

Thornton lowered his head and peered at Daley over his spectacles. "You have met Andrew Carmichael, Inspector. He is overbearing, arrogant and a little too cock-sure of himself. But, that is exactly why I employ him. He exudes a confidence that makes clients feel comfortable. But over the last year or so he has become a little pre-occupied. I have noticed him being a little more, er, abrupt than usual. And maybe more self-contained, more secretive. Notwithstanding, his work has been

231

exemplary, except for the few complaints which, in the final analysis, I could only conclude were down to his thoroughness. There is no reason to suspect anything dishonest."

"Except for Ms Silverton's complaints."

"Well yes, that did set the cat amongst the pigeons for a while but that was all resolved. Mr Higson came in to assist the auditor, show him through the accounts and that was that."

Thornton settled down onto the sofa and sipped at his coffee. Daley followed suit, perturbed by this man who seemed to have all of the answers, even if they were superficial and non-committal. Almost as if they were prepared, an errant boss drawn before a Parliamentary Select Committee, primed with the answers to the most obvious questions. But behind the eyes, there were the stirrings of disquiet, as if Thornton was refactoring his ideas on Carmichael. Daley decided that he would make the man sit longer in his unease.

"Up until last Monday that was that. But now, surely? Do you not think it strange that Ms Silverton sparks an internal audit, but the accountant comes in before the audit for an extended period?"

"Maybe, but that would have been March - end of the financial year."

"Technically the end, but surely the year isn't closed off precisely on March 31st. It can take a few weeks to finalise the accounts. And in that few weeks, Mr Higson only booked a day with you, yet spent seven billable days between Ms Silverton's first visit to you here, and the day you instigated the audit. Does that not seem odd that the audit occurs on accounts that have already seen a weeks work on them by the firms accountant?

"I couldn't possibly comment. Mr Higson has our utmost..."

"Had. Mr Thornton. Had. Guy Higson was found dead early on Thursday morning, in suspicious circumstances."

Thornton clasped a hand to his mouth to stifle a whimper. Daley took the reaction to be genuine.

"So please indulge me in a little fiction for now while I put a timeline together? For some reason, Ms Silverton and Mr Carmichael have another falling out. Maybe it was personal, or maybe Ms Silverton was getting too much grief from moaning clients. Anyway, she confronts Carmichael and he decides that

232

she is serious. So he calls another best mate, Mr Higson, and together they set about taking the wind out of Ms Silverton's sails by some kind of cover-up. Ms Silverton complains to you, and lo and behold your auditor finds the accounts so squeaky clean even you are surprised. You would be foolish to trust the whining bitch again. But Mr Carmichael hasn't learned his lesson. He keeps on doing what he is doing, and clients keep moaning to Ms Silverton. So she rings you up again. You decide to have a word with Mr Carmichael, who in turn, decides to have a word with Ms Silverton on the very day she dies."

"Wild speculation, Inspector, surely!"

"Indeed, but let's carry on the fiction. My Sergeant and myself pay Mr Carmichael a visit and we get the distinct impression he is hiding something. We figure it's something personal between him and Ms Silverton. There's no direct evidence and we weren't looking in his direction. But we have caught his attention now and being the neat, orderly person he is, decides to remove the only other person who could implicate him in whatever little scheme he is involved in. Guy Higson."

"For goodness sake, Inspector. I have worked with Mr Carmichael for a long time. There is no way he would harm anyone, let alone kill them."

Daley countered. "But he did assault Ms Silverton on the day she died. We know that."

Thornton was momentarily taken aback but immediately rallied. "What? Did he slap her? Shake her? We both know the word assault covers a continuum all the way from inappropriate touching to GBH. Assault doesn't equate to murder. And anyway, to carry out two murders in the space of three days. Surely that would take a good deal of premeditation? I can accept Mr Carmichael becoming annoyed with Ms Silverton. I myself had become frustrated with her unrelenting phone calls. But annoyance, frustration, neither of those are sufficient motive for murder, surely?"

"I agree, Mr Thornton, but my Constable turns up this morning, bright and early and completely uncharacteristically, Mr Carmichael disappears out of the back, while we are waiting out the front. For the second time in as many days. From where you're sitting, does that sound like a man with nothing to hide?"

"Well, no, it doesn't but again, *nothing to hide* is a broad

233

continuum from some minor misdemeanour right the way up to genocide. I genuinely believe that if Andrew Carmichael is hiding something...and I am not saying he is...that it is towards the minor end of the continuum."

"Were you aware that four years ago, a Rachel Jones, another acquaintance of Mr Carmichael's, was also killed in strikingly similar circumstances? Both women were estate agents, both were having an affair with Mr Carmichael, and we believe both of them were pregnant by him around the time of their deaths. And you will have to take my word for it, Mr Thornton, but the way the two women died was practically identical."

Daley let the outer door of Barraclough and Leavis swing shut, the latch pinging as the glass made contact with metal. There was a cool breeze traversing the afternoon traffic and the sun had retreated behind brooding clouds, yet he was relieved to be out of the cloying atmosphere of Thornton's office. He mused on the attitude of Thornton towards Carmichael, and thought of his own relationship with Allenby. Would the D/Supt have backed him so staunchly in a similar situation? The way Thornton had defended him, Carmichael was a paragon, whilst she had been painted as some kind of harridan. Daley couldn't help but conclude that the tail was wagging the dog.

***

Thornton poured another coffee, but it tasted sour and he rattled the cup onto the tray irritatedly. There was no doubt about it, Carmichael was becoming unmanageable. His head was reeling with the wild suppositions of this policeman. A flight of fancy, surely, but it was his experience that there was no smoke without at least the orange of an ember. The smoke may be a precursor to a blaze, or the smouldering ash of a tragedy, either way it spelled danger for Barraclough and Leavis. He could count the days until his retirement - four hundred and sixty-eight, no, seven. A successor had more or less been chosen and the greens of Sunningdale were over the horizon. The decision had been difficult. Townsend, with his dependable, often boring view of business. Solid, faithful, trustworthy, but conservative. How long would the business continue with Townsend at the helm? Constant, never changing, always with an eye to the past, overtaken by the times.

And then there was Carmichael, brash, confident, modernising in his views, able to think outside the box, able to take a few measured risks. Thornton had been sure *he* was the man to inspire the next generation of employees. To move the business forwards where he, Thornton, had not.

He turned and gazed out of the window, a single space in the car park stark and empty. Maybe the decision was presumptuous? Whatever was happening in Carmichael's life at the moment could be damaging to Barraclough and Leavis. He needed to take steps to stop the rot.

Chapter 25

Carmichael had paced the platform at Ealing Broadway for an hour before Carol finally debarked through the scuffed red, blue and grey doors into the growing gloom of the afternoon. He had almost turned himself inside out to remain unobtrusive and anonymous. After just a quarter of an hour, he had started to panic, fearing he had missed her. Three times he had fallen under the gaze of an inquisitive guard, three times he had visited the toilets as a pre-text. Had she arrived whilst he was in that filthy, flatulence filled midden trying not to touch anything? As she stepped from the carriage, she was wearing the same camel hair coat as the previous evening but her hair was down and she had an entirely different expression on her face. Impatiently, he hastened over to her. He made to speak, to express his relief, but she looped her arm in his and continued walking, dragging him through the burgeoning late afternoon hubbub and out of the station.

Abruptly she stopped and pushed him against a creaking gate, chains rattling and hinges complaining, and planted a hand against his chest.

"What on earth were you thinking? Do you realise what's been happening while you have been gallivanting around?"

Briefly winded, Carmichael peered urgently around, hoping that she had not drawn too much attention but in London, the most uncaring of cities, the world barely noticed. "I didn't know what else to do. Until I know what the police are up to, I'd be stupid to go anywhere near them. God knows what that Inspector would pin on me if he had the chance."

"Just shut up for a minute, will you. We are not at work now. Let me speak for a change." Her eyes were steely, her features stern and determined, and just a little scary.

Drew caught an exasperated gasp and nodded solemnly. "OK. But not here, please. Over there." He gestured towards a Starbucks and soon she had hauled him to a seat towards the back of the cafe, where the clatter of the baristas covered their voices.

"Look, I'm sorry, Carol. I'm just not sure what is going on

right now. I mean, the beginning of the week was just fine, until lunchtime on Monday, and then everything changed."

Carol looked up suddenly from her coffee, momentarily lost, and then she said, "Too right, everything changed. The police have been around three days this week and a squad car is stationed across the road. I have had to worm myself out of some really difficult situations, no thanks to you. Like, I know I am paid to do that, but come on Drew, you are stretching loyalty a little too far. That bloody policeman came back, gave me the third degree about where you had got to, and then barged into Gerry Thornton's office, which of course went down like a lead balloon. After that, he sent all of the temporary staff home and got Joel from IT to switch off the server. They are speaking to a judge or someone right now about a warrant to search the offices. Do you know they have a policeman outside your house? Yes, Drew, there is a very nasty looking copper in your front porch, just waiting for you to show your face."

Drew peered around. The cafe had become ominous and claustrophobic. He imagined the eyes of the dispassionate clientele, sneaking glances, hazy recognition, '*Is that him off the news?*' "Fucking Hell, Carol. What am I going to do? Perhaps, I should just give myself up, here and now." He proffered his mobile in the air, willing her to take it, to end this ever-deepening crisis, whatever the personal cost.

Laying her hand on his, she pushed the mobile to the table. "Get a grip for goodness sake...and stop attracting attention to yourself with that stupid bobble hat. We are going to sit here like civilised people, work colleagues or husband and wife, even total strangers, and we are going to finish our coffees as if we have just done a hard days work - and boy, Drew, have I done a hard days work today! And then you are going to come with me and do exactly what I tell you."

Drew sipped at his coffee and looked at Carol. Her eyes were unsmiling, her expression stern and stolid. It was the sort of look he had only seen her fire at the work placement girls when they had transgressed her parochial rules. Only a day ago he would have found it irresistible. Today, the look turned him cold.

"Look, Carol. I'm really sorry about all of this. I don't know what to say. It's just a matter of time until they put two and two together and find out what I have been up to." His face was a picture of contrition. He wondered whether he was wearing that particular expression out. Carol returned him a sombre glance.

"Remember, at least ten per cent of that money is mine. I've earned it and I am not going to bloody lose it now. If we keep a low profile the police can go whistle for a bit."

"So you're not mad, then?" Drew looked puzzled. He had the distinct feeling he had missed something.

"Mad, I am flaming furious! You are such a disruptive influence on my life! Why on Earth did you have to get *her* involved with your little fiddles in the first place?" She spat the *her*, leaving Drew in no doubt what she felt about Dawn.

"Please, Carol. Give me a break. Just for this evening? I am sick to death of explaining myself, of running away and having to hide."

For a long moment, she paused, eying him over the rim of her coffee cup. Then she relaxed. "Fair enough. I'll give you a break, but first, you owe me an explanation."

Drew nodded. "First, you tell me something? When did it occur to you that I was using the client accounts?"

Carol looked towards the ceiling, her mouth turning into a contemplative frown. "Well, I've been with Barraclough and Leavis for just about five years and it was pretty soon after I joined."

Carmichael was dumbfounded. "What? There's no way you could have picked up on it that quickly. Me and Guy were really careful."

"Yes, Drew, but Guy was the problem. Remember, I process the supplier invoices and much of Guy's time seemed to be off the books, which made me smell a rat. I only really cottoned on for sure when you told me to assist Guy with the audit. I knew he must have been tidying up by the way he was organising automated cross postings."

"So why didn't you speak to Gerry Thornton, there and then?"

"You really want to know? I thought it was quite cool, manipulating the client accounts, creaming off a profit and nobody loses. It's victimless and really quite clever. Added to that, I though there might be a bob or two in it for me eventually...and I was right."

"So there's my point. Dawn already knew about the scheme and that sometime in the near future she was going to be quids in. All she needed to do was play along and no-one would have been any the wiser. But what does she do? She starts blarting to Gerry Thornton, taking the moral high ground. Did she really believe that the way to climb the greasy pole is by shitting on the people around her?"

"But couldn't you have talked her round? Used your charm?"

"Christ, where do I start? She's a... she *was* a manipulative bitch. She knew she was playing me off against Thornton. She knew that the only way to a partnership was to keep Thornton sweet, and that in turn meant keeping her sweet.

"Look, I admit I was a little rough on Dawn. I needed that money to grow the fund - our fund. She stood to gain as well. But the bitch just wouldn't see it that way. The slightest whiff of, shall we say, dubiousness she demanded that I stop what I was doing. How the hell did she think I had made all that money - Salvation Army collections? Then, like some whining teenager, she starts moaning at me again. But this time she goes to Thornton. You know the rest.

"So on Monday, I go to have a quiet chat with Dawn. To re-orientate her thinking, shall we say, before she gets us both sacked. But it got a little heated. Suddenly, she's dead; the police put two and two together and make five. And for some reason I am the prime suspect! I promise you, I grabbed at her arm, maybe shook her a little, but nothing else. For fuck's sake, there must be some forensic stuff - a hair follicle, a skin cell, whatever - that will point them to the real killer."

"Maybe there is, Drew. Perhaps they are still processing it. These things take time."

"So why the hell won't they leave me alone until they actually have some solid proof?"

"Because, *durr*, now Guy Higson is dead too, maybe?" She stared earnestly at him. Her eyes were wide and dark in the amber light, so wide he could have dived right into them. So dark they could have been a home to sharks.

"Exactly!" There was irony now in his tone. "So now I am a hardened killer. I have strangled Dawn and now I am on the

239

prowl for my next victim. For some reason, which escapes me, I choose Guy Higson. One of the oldest friends I have."

"...Who has helped us cover up the dodgy dealings which got Dawn killed, and is therefore top of the list to go spilling the beans to the Feds!"

Carmichael rubbed a hand across his stubbled chin. "But the police don't know that. They can't know that, can they?"

"They know something is wrong at Barraclough and Leavis." Carol adjusted her seat, leaning down closer to Carmichael, sending a zephyr of scent across the table. "I don't know, Drew. There must be some reason why they figure you are their prime suspect for Guy Higson. Or maybe, it's just a lack of anyone else to concentrate on." She pondered for a long moment and added, "So, if it wasn't you, who could it be?"

"I have no idea."

"But didn't you say that you and Guy argued on Wednesday. Came to blows, almost? Surely someone might have mentioned that to the police?" Carol's interjection gave Drew a little time to think, the connections a little time to form.

"Yes, but it was nothing. Just old friends getting maudlin and deciding that someone had to be to blame."

"But didn't he beat you senseless the same day...just before he was murdered?"

"Well, yes but..." The case for the prosecution was becoming more compelling. "So, I kill Dawn to protect the fund and now, after the argument with Guy - an argument where he specifically threatened to go to the police himself - I shut Guy up to stop him squealing. Or at least that's what the killer wants the police to believe."

"It's possible, I suppose." Carol stared at the ceiling for a long moment. "It doesn't look good at the moment, does it? But we can ride this out. If they can track you down, their beady suspicious eyes will almost certainly fall on me too - so from now on we have to work together, to keep ourselves off their radar until they find someone else to pin all this on."

Carmichael bowed his head into his hands. How did it come to this? How could a world so ordered, so predictable turn diametrically in such a short period of time? More to the point, how could he turn it back? He let his frustration boil over. He

240

pointed an angry finger at Carol and rasped: "You know, that bitch Dawn had it coming to her. It's a bloody vendetta, just because I ended our relationship. She started this whole thing to get back at me. Am I the only one who can see it?"

Carol scanned the coffee bar anxiously but no-one was interested, Carmichael's voice lost in the hubbub. "But she didn't murder herself to get back at you!"

"I tell you what, if she wasn't dead already, then I would bloody kill her myself!"

Carol leaned across the table. "That's not helpful, Drew."

"Maybe not, but it made me feel a whole lot better."

"Right now, how you feel is not important. What is important is how we get out of this bloody mess."

"Hang on a minute, that's not fair! It's not all down to me. Everything was going OK until that bloody woman got herself killed. There is absolutely no connection between me and Dawn Silverton's death - *none!*"

"How bloody naive are you really, Drew? How long did it take the police to connect you with Dawn, eh? As long as it took them to read her diary! You were plastered all over it. Did you really expect them not to ask why?"

Carol was correct. The diary had irrefutably connected him to Dawn. But it was far from evidence of murder. Then Carmichael had a damning realisation.

"Shit! What about my computer?

Carol reached out and laid a hand on Carmichael's arm. "Look, don't worry about the office computer. Before the police got there I powered it off. Your transactions are all on-line, and when it is powered off the Internet history is wiped. To be honest, I was more worried about the stuff we were working on last night. Which is why I kept them with me when I left your house this morning. They're in my handbag. What about your laptop at home? Is there anything on there we should be worried about?"

Drew shook his head. On the way over to the Tube, his personal laptop had met with a watery end beneath a jetty on the Thames.

"Ok. So if we do nothing, what happens to the money?"

"It just cycles between the Fund and three different accounts - the Cayman Islands account and investment accounts in New York and Hong Kong. I rarely look at the accounts themselves, I just look at the closing prices and that tells me how much I have made. The whole process is automatic."

"So, basically we can forget the money for the moment." Drew nodded.

She paused and slowly she leaned over and clasped both of his hands in hers.

"Look, Drew, I think you have to accept the very real possibility that as far as the money goes, you will never see it. As soon as the police find out about it, they will put a hold on the accounts and there will be no chance of getting it back."

Drew lifted his head and stared at Carol. Even in the dimness of Costa's his face had paled but there was an acceptance of the inevitable. She chivvied him to finish his coffee and once more they ventured out into the evening air. An orange hue suffused the roads as street lamps began to burn. The approaching darkness heralded an anonymity, which Drew welcomed, but he still wore the stupid hat, just in case. Turning right, they re-entered the Tube station, where she bought tickets to Northfields, and an obedient dog, he followed her in silent supplication, changing at Acton, until eventually they left the station and he found himself at the front door of an imposing Edwardian terrace.

***

Drawing the huge Arran cardigan tighter around her, Alice curled herself up in the chair and threw the remote down beside her. She was not cold. The room was warm from the late evening sun, which cascaded through the voluminous bay window. But she was scared. She took in the aroma of the cardigans collar. It was a mixture of musk and tobacco, of Davidoff Cool Water and comfortable memories. It was old and worn and missing half of the large wooden penny buttons, but it belonged to Marcus and she felt safer and warmed by it. His shift at the hospital would soon be over and he would be there to warm her himself.

London Tonight had just reported Guy's accident. The police had not ruled out murder and the walls had started to close in on her. She thought back to the last time she had spoken to Guy. His impassioned phone call on Wednesday night, his concerns over Drew, his fears for her. At the time she had been dismissive, finding the thought almost laughable, but four hours later he was dead. As the early evening game show counterpointed the silence, her mind began to drift. Wild, disconnected ideas, dredged from her past, her future, her imaginings. She saw herself and Dawn and Rachel and Shelley, she saw Drew, his head arched back as he laughed manically and one by one the girls disappeared until only Carmichael was left, the laughter turning to a howl, it's pitch deepening like a tape recorder being slowed, becoming a rumble and a growl as the eyes turned to her, the grin now replaced by a lour of vehemence and a finger pointed at her.

She knew he was coming to get her.

And then, starting from the nightmare, her whole world shifted sideway by a couple of inches, suddenly out of whack, and she wondered if she was the only person in London who understood the significance of the murders. She felt her gorge rise and bolted for the bathroom, vomiting into the lavatory bowl and hanging there, hearing the echoes of her breath drawing in and bellowing out, tasting the rank acid and smelling the pungent odour, replaying the news report in her head, rehearsing the voicemail. She dragged an icy cold flannel across her drawn skin, flecks of water dampening the triangle of white T-shirt that showed below her neck, and the face she saw wore an expression of abject terror, pleading for help from a reflection which pleaded back. She alone understood the significance of the demise of two estate agents four years apart. Alone except for Carmichael. She surmised that even the police would be unaware of how close she was to Dawn Silverton; but without her, Alice Bown, coming forward, they may never make the connection between the two. Then even if they did make the connection, there was nothing to link them all back to that evening in Hillfields when it all started. Nothing except Carmichael and The Book.

The Book.

Such a distant memory from a different life. A macabre island in a sea of ordinary experiences, remaining lost, even purposefully forgotten. Now surging to the surface unexpectedly, like a volcanic island thrust into the daylight after eons submerged and unknown beneath the waves.

Alice ran to the bedroom and drew out a shoebox from under the bed. It took her several minutes to locate the CD amongst fifty or so, all in plastic wallets but the instant her fingers alighted on it, her mind filled with smells and scenes, images and people, as if being beamed directly into her mind from the mirrored tracks on the disc. Dropping the box on the bed, disturbing a comatose Merlin, she rushed back to her laptop and inserted the CD, trawling through the folders of data until she found the folder she needed. Called '1997', the folder contained her journal for the year and it took her several minutes paging through entries until she located the day she was looking for. An event so shocking that she had wanted nothing to do with Dawn, Rachel or Shelley for many years afterwards. So awful that all she could write on that day had been their names - Drew, Dawn, Rachel, Shelley, Chris and a single short phrase - everything changes now.

She hauled her mind back fifteen years to the day, straining to keep a handle on recollections, which had faded to images, incidents which she now only half remembered. She remembered how far she had run just to be away. From the deep recesses of her mind, dusty corners in which she had stored those events in the hopes she would never be able to find them, the full horror returned and once more her diaphragm spasmed. She hurried to the bathroom, her head down the toilet retching until her ribs ached. Her bottom jaw was trembling and she was sobbing quietly to herself, her mouth emitting a plaintive warble, a plea to no-one as there was no-one there to hear. Returning to the living room, she snatched up the laptop and surfed to the *BBC London website*, finding the headline, similar to the one she had seen the other day, halfway down the front page, already becoming old news. And above it she saw the smiling face of Guy Higson and the tears streamed down her face. The day Dawn had been killed was the anniversary, not only of that terrible night, but also of the death of Rachel Jones. Once more she thought of the Book. Wiping spit from her mouth she poured a large measure of scotch into the teacup that lay beside the sofa, kicked over in her rush for the bathroom, a snail trail of tea soaked into the carpet. She took a large swig and washed it around her mouth, feeling the tingle and then the burn as she swallowed. Paradoxically, her head began to clear and her shaking subsided.

Searching the CD again she finally located The Book. Not the actual Book. Someone else had that. But the rough notes she had scrawled as they all spoke, the recollections she had added afterwards. She began scanning the hasty notes, of the drunken nights in Browns, of the juvenile games and vile plans and of the dreadful culmination, an event that changed everything. The notes were buoys floating on the surface to mark the evil that lay deep beneath. She recalled the night that the Book had come about. Students getting drunk, and getting high in a student bar, wild nights and even wilder ideas, and the one who took their insane ramblings seriously. She read the details of Rachel Jones murder, neat tabulated text, a study in death nearly a decade before it had happened. She remembered Dawn and Rachel conspiratorial and conniving, planning the murder, unaware that one day it would be their own. She read about Guy Higson and the outstretched wire and wondered if it were true. And then she read about the next murder and shook uncontrollably as she realised that it was her own.

Did he know where she lived? Did any of them? Since she had moved to this flat the previous September, she was sure she had not given her address to anyone. But Carmichael worked with solicitors. He would have resources. He would be able to find her.

Returning to the kitchen table she scrabbled amongst the contents of her handbag for her address book and began leafing frantically through the pages, the whisky blurring the names and numbers into a morass of meaningless symbols and faceless names. And she slumped into a chair and stared at the kitchen clock measuring the seconds of her life as they ebbed away.

The room assumed a gothic terror as the lights danced and played off the walls and shadows filled every corner. After two hours, she had read and reread her notes on the Book, she understood the course of events that was unfolding as the murderer replayed their ramblings from all those years ago. Still she was no closer to understanding why this had all started, why the time for the story to continue was now. She was no closer to finding the killer before he found her.

She scrolled through the scant contact list and realised the name was not there, just a number in her recent call history. She hit redial and waited for the ring.

Chapter 26

As the front door latched behind them, Drew flopped against the wall, struggling to regain his breath and his composure. The walk from Northfields was short, but she had made it brisk and he had forgotten what it was like to walk. The Mercedes had left him soft and his calf muscles burned. When all this was over he would do something about that, even if it were a smart lap of the exercise yard. He watched as Carol leaned her hip against the door and yanked the deadbolts into place.

"Wait here." she barked, circling around him. A light came on in the living room. He heard her draw the curtains. And then she was in the doorway. "Well, what are you waiting for? Come and sit down."

The front room was bathed the weak glow of a standard lamp. It was a tall Edwardian room, the high ceiling skirted by ornate floral mouldings. Otherwise it was modern and sparse. He fell onto a huge soft leather sofa, which looked blood red under the orange light. There was a table small and lost in the centre of the floor and a television perched on a grotesque chrome and glass stand in the corner. The room was scant and bare - it looked as if he were the first person ever to have used it.

"You might be here a while so make yourself comfortable." Carol wafted through the doorway and placed a tray on the minuscule table. The maternal, benevolent smile had returned. He obliged, removing the overly large coat, like he was freeing himself from a collapsed tent, and she whisked it away to some unseen hook in the hall. "Look. There's nothing we can do tonight. Nobody knows you're here. Why don't you go and have a shower? There should be some of Peter's old clothes you can borrow in the back room and a towel in the airing cupboard. I'll go and make some supper."

Drew could not help noticing the change in her demeanour now they were both safely behind her front door. She was perched on an easy chair at right angles to the sofa. The dour features of a woman scorned had softened. She had removed her coat and kicked off her shoes. The shadows played on the length of her crossed knees and disappeared into the darkness of her skirt.

Wearily, he dragged himself up the steeply raked stairs. In the back bedroom, he found a T-shirt, jeans and sweater, none of which he would ordinarily be seen dead in, which therefore were perfectly suited to a man incognito. Fifteen minutes later, descending the stairs, the house was filled with the homely aroma of herbs and tomatoes and the television was chattering away to itself in the corner of the living room. A red wine was left to breathe in the centre of the table. As they both sat to eat, it suddenly occurred to Carmichael, just how hungry he was.

He became aware that she was looking at him and he raised his eyes to meet hers.

"Why did you never marry, Drew?" Carol was leaning back on the sofa beside him, sipping her wine, her lips moistened, watching him eat. "There must be women queuing up to bag themselves an eligible, up-and coming financial advisor."

"I suppose the right girl never came along. Or I was too busy to notice when she did."

"Dawn - was she the right girl?" Carmichael thought of the times that he and Dawn had shared; mornings he had woken up to her smile, and that final stolen week in Languedoc when love had turned irretrievably to hate. And it hurt so much that he avoided the question.

"What about you, Carol? What's your story?"

"Me?" She placed a hand on her own neck, genuinely surprised that the question had been asked.

"Yes. What brings you down to the big bad city?"

"Hey, less of the bad! Newcastle is pretty shite as well, you know. I came down to look after my brother, Kitt, four years ago. He has always had problems, but he was having it tough, so I moved down here to care for him."

"And is that when...?"

"Me and Peter? Well, partly. He stayed behind because of his job, but the distance took its toll and the weekend visits became less and less. Eventually, we had grown so far apart divorce was a formality. For a while, I resented Kitt, his anxieties, and his illness. He had changed so much from the person I had known as a boy. Then when Peter and I split, I hated him even more. It took a long time for me to accept we were just victims of circumstance. He had always been a victim." Here eyes were moist flickering sparks reflecting from the tears.

"I'm sorry, Carol." Drew reached across and took Carol's hand. "That was insensitive of me."

"No, not really, it's just the way these things go. You can choose your friends but not your family. When Peter and I divorced, Kitt and I moved into this place. It's expensive, but with the settlement..."

"And your brother?"

"His sickness worsened after I moved down here. He died." She turned her head to face a middle distance as the painful memories resurfaced. She quickly worked to supplant them with happier days.

"He was my little brother, five years younger. It was magic as a kid having someone to boss around. Everyone called him Kitt, except me mam. She used to call him Kit-Kat. Whenever he was naughty, or noisy, she used to shout 'Give me a break, Kit-Kat' and he used to take not a blind bit of notice."

"So what happened?"

"Well, it was just one of those things. He was a sensitive child. Always in his own world, happy with his own company. He never cried or fought back. Until one day. We were on holiday in Skegness and they had made a mess of the bookings. Kitt was about fourteen, I think. Dad had to book another room for him down the corridor from us. He couldn't cope with being separate. He smashed the place to pieces. They had to call the police. He was crouching in a corner, snarling like a wild animal."

"Bloody Hell!" Carmichael held her arm. She turned and laid her hand on his, a hint of a smile on her lips.

"They sedated him and took him to St. Nicholas'. They filled him full of antipsychotics and he eventually came out of it and seemed to have got better. They told us he was bipolar and to make sure he took his medication. After that he was perfectly normal, except for a couple of episodes. He had come down to London and had a job working in a bookies, you know, setting the odds - he had a brilliant mathematical mind. He was so clever.

"We heard nothing from him for a long while. We kept

expecting that one day he would walk through the door back in Newcastle and introduce a bonny lass he had met. Announce to the world that he was getting married. Give us all a chance to buy a posh frock."

"So what went wrong? I mean, if it's too painful..."

"No, it's alright. Do you know, you're the first person I've really talked to about Kitt?" She poured out the last of the wine, equally between the two glasses. "One day, I got a call from the Police in London. They had detained him under the Mental Health Act. Apparently he had stopped taking his medication and gone berserk in the Westfield. He had trashed a clothes shop and ripped a whole bank of sinks off the walls in one of the toilets and was just sitting there in the water on the floor. He was admitted to Park Royal and after a few months, they told me he was responding to treatment, so they let him out. I don't know why they do that. It was clear he couldn't cope on his own. I came down here and looked after him, and when Peter finally got sick of the situation, I rented this place so we would be together. I did some temping. We got by.

"And then one day, I came home from work. It was a Friday and I had stopped by the chippy on the way back. I let myself in and the whole place was in darkness. I assumed he must have gone out for a walk or was upstairs asleep. So I went into the kitchen to warm some plates, left the supper in a low oven and called for him up the stairs." Carol's eyes were glassy and her lip was trembling. The memories were painful. "He was lying in the bed, the cover drawn right up under his chin. They said he had just taken all of his pills, climbed into bed and fallen asleep."

Drew threw his arms around her and she buried her head into his chest and the tears flowed unabated. For the first time in a long while, perhaps for the first time ever, Drew was gripped in a deep, gnawing sympathetic sorrow, a consuming hopelessness, unable to do anything more for her other than hold her in her pain. Unable to do anything more for himself than to accept that Dawn was gone.

Freeing an arm from his embrace, she reached inside her pocket for a tissue and dabbed, smudging her mascara, leaving a small comma across her cheek. Carmichael smiled, took the tissue and gently wiped it away, before leaning over and, hesitantly at first, kissing her. A tentative, gentle meeting.

Drawing back slightly he looked in her eyes and they were deep and yearning.

"I couldn't save him."

Drew shrugged. "Maybe no-one could. I believe that somewhere out there, there is a bullet with our name on it. We can dodge and weave, keep ourselves fit or drink ourselves into oblivion. It really doesn't matter. When your time comes, your time comes."

"But it's so unfair. He had so much to give."

"Where in the contract does it say life is fair?"

"He was just so terribly lost. This world ate him alive. I made all those sacrifices to try and save him, gave up everything I had. And now he's gone and it's me that's lost."

"We are both lost at the moment. With everything that's happened this week, maybe it's right that we have found each other, now?" He shuffled over until their legs touched and he pulled his arms tighter around her, her head on his chest. Her hair smelt of gardenia. How long they remained like that he was unsure; the television jabbered through countless commercial breaks, her breathing slowed to a regular beat. As the lack of blood to his arm made his fingers turn numb, he gently roused her. She raised her head and looked into his eyes, and they exuded a calm and warmth. And he kissed her again.

"It's been a long day. Let's get you to bed. We can talk more in the morning."

Tenderly, he took her hand and led her up the stairs. She closed the door behind them, her body striated by the light from the window and he rolled the sheets back and tucked her in, her face consumed by the darkness. As he edged out through the door, she called quietly after him.

"Drew. Stay with me tonight."

He made his way back to the bed and he ran a hand across the shadow that was her cheek, soft and warm. For all the months of trying to seduce her, for all the opportunities missed and the advantages taken, he had longed for her to want him as strongly as he wanted her. But total advantage now would be wrong. A woman needed to be chased and caught, grounded and defiled, to be taken and defeated. To be seduced. He could not simply invite himself into her bed and make love with her -

he had to make love *to* her.

"Don't worry, I'll stay. Where else can I go?" He kissed her lightly on the lips. "I'll be in the back room, don't worry."

"No, stay with me here. I need you to be here, with me. No strings. I just need you here, all night."

And this time it was she that kissed him, and this time, it was stronger and more passionate and she held him in the kiss for what seemed like an eternity. He walked around the bed and climbed in beside her, feeling her warmth within the sheets, and as she turned her back to him, his arms encircled her and he felt the erectness of her nipples as his hand fell between her breasts.

Chapter 27

The clang of the litter bin still echoed around the team room. Daley ducked guiltily as admonishing scowls were cast his way from the other members of *The Dispossessed*. Still, with no sign of Carmichael and an ever-increasing list of questions, his frustration had inevitably boiled over. Having abandoned the uniforms outside Carmichael's house, he and Whetstone had returned to process the search warrant. At present, a remorseful DS Allenby was communing with a particularly uncooperative magistrate, who felt that the murder of three close friends, evading the police and absconding was not enough reason to break Carmichael's door down on a fishing trip. So they were left to await Carmichael's return to the house, or hope any of the beat officers, who may be half looking, would pick him up.

Daley held up a hand of apology and scooped the spilled detritus back into the bin, cursing once more at some sticky residue adhered to his fingers. It had been a day of annoyances and frustrations. The death of Higson had diverted resources away from the Silverton case, diluting the effort before the trail had even started to cool.

And at present, Andrew Carmichael was the largest of those annoyances.

Carmichael was universally hated by his so-called friends, enough so that they made it plain in interviews with the police. Still, after a long association, they met with him most Mondays and maybe a couple of nights in the week too. In Daley's eyes, this smacked of one thing. Dependency.

And without the evidence of drugs, dependency usually meant money.

The Office Manager at Barraclough and Leavis had also given him the run-around, compounding his frustration still further. She had obviously tipped off Carmichael, allowing him to slip out of the back unhindered, and then when he had tried to vent his spleen on the cow, she had pleaded the fifth and gone off whining to Gerald Thornton. He had insisted one of the associates sat in on her interview, rendering it pretty well useless.

Even then she had intimated that she had worked with both Carmichael and Higson on the accounts before the audit, and still more with Higson during it. But none of this was sufficient for a magistrate to issue the search warrant.

However, what he had secured was the desktop computer from Carmichael's office. He had set Dave Monaghan the task of examining it, only to find that the Internet History was cleared on shut down. Not the end but another frustration to the day.

The sight of members of his team donning their coats and merrily heading home for a night of warm food and TV had made him all the more frustrated. He implored the gods of the suspended ceiling to give him one iota of comfort to lull him to sleep tonight.

"Dave, what do you know?" Monaghan had removed the hard drive from Carmichael's PC and jerry-rigged it to his own. A disk examination program revealed both the many hidden files, as well as those that had been recently deleted. Whetstone was looking on, chewing a pencil, completely confused by the two columns; one that Dave had told her was hexadecimal, and the other a textual representation of the contents of the file. When viewed this way, most files are a collection of compiled code and appear as gibberish, even to the trained viewer, but some files that contain data, particularly textual data, can reveal concealed information. One such file, as Dave Monaghan had told them two hours earlier, was *index.dat*. There were many *index.dat* files dotted around a hard drive, as many applications created one, but the ones that Dave was interested in were the cache *index.dat*, the history *index.dat* and the cookies *index.dat*. Even if a user sets out to delete all traces of their activity on the Internet, these files remain as tell-tale breadcrumb trails of everything they have ever done, including those sites they have visited and sought to erase from their computers memory. And despite Monaghan actually pointing out the contents of the *History* version to Whetstone, she was still in awe of his black arts.

"It's good news and bad news, Sir." Monaghan craned his neck round as Daley approached his desk.

"Which means?" The furrowed brow and challenging eyes persuaded Monaghan to hurriedly turn back to his screen.

"Well, ignoring the law related sites, eBay, PayPal, LinkedIn, Facebook, there are five sites which were accessed on a frequent basis. One of them is a stock tracker, three of them relate to the Hong Kong, New York and London Stock Exchanges and one of them is a site, which I cannot readily identify by name. Unfortunately, when I enter it into a browser, it comes up forbidden as it needs metadata."

"Ok. So that suggests in the recent past Carmichael has looked at a number of stock market websites, and has used a stock tracker. In common with half the city, I wouldn't wonder. The last bit was Klingon, I think, so you might have to translate."

Monaghan sighed. "Imagine you get an email from, say Facebook, and it tells you that Auntie Joan has just posted a picture of her on the beach in Margate. Being the thoughtful nephew that you are, you would immediately click the *View Comment* button in the email, which would open up your browser and reveal the posting that Auntie Joan made. Doesn't she look stunning in that floppy hat? Well, if you look in the Address bar at the top of the screen, the normal address for Auntie Joan's page is followed by a string of characters." He pointed to the address bar on Steve Taylor's machine. Following the traditional website address was a string of characters including equals signs, ampersands and numbers, which Whetstone now knew were in hexadecimal, whatever that was. "It's these characters - the metadata - which tell Facebook to go not just to Auntie Joan's page but to this specific entry on Auntie Joan's page. Added to that they also identify *you* as the person who wanted to look at the picture." Monaghan allowed himself a self-satisfied grin.

Whetstone felt her brain starting to knot. "So what your saying is that we know which pages he visited but not what he looked at because we haven't got the metadata.

"Top marks, Deb and thanks for listening!"

Daley exhaled deeply. "Another dead end then?"

"Not exactly, Gov. At least not yet. Carmichael, or one of his clever IT bods at Barraclough and Leavis has used standard Windows settings to clear out browsing history each time the computer is switched off. In this case, it deletes all references to websites, all cookies and any temporary Internet files on the computer when it is shut down. And as we know, when files are deleted from a computer's hard drive they are not in fact deleted, but just not referenced in the directory."

"Meaning...?"

"...Meaning that as the computer was not switched back on, none of the files have been overwritten, and so, given a little more time, I should be able to discover what that forbidden site was and what metadata was used to access it. Same goes for the other sites. I should be able to isolate exactly what information he was looking at."

Chapter 28

The sharp rapping noise startled her, and Shelley filled her lungs and puffed her cheeks out in an overly dramatised harrumph. Why she did this, she was unsure because she was alone, catnapping in the sitting room above the pub, so she smiled to herself at the futility of the gesture; just like so many gestures and acts and anxieties which had defined her over the years.

Friday night was hers. It had been an unwritten tradition since they had opened the pub, that the world should bugger off and leave her alone on Friday nights. And in the last three years, it had actually happened a few times. The evening would start at around 7:30pm when Finn hollered a cheery goodbye as he trotted down the stairs to spend a long evening in the company of other publicans in the area, supposedly discussing trade matters, but probably indulging in a legitimised piss-up. Then having run herself a bath and poured herself a large glass of *Pinot Noir*, she would indulge in a prolonged soak in a room full of steam and the aroma of roses.

And tonight, for the first time in all of those three years, she had surrendered herself to it.

There was something hedonistic, about indulging oneself whilst others worked, and the sensual warmth of the water had cosseted her for over an hour, with the occasional luxury of a top-up, both of hot tap and *Pinot Noir*, before she had reluctantly drawn herself out, donned a bathrobe and proceeded to doze in front of the TV.

Glancing at the clock, she was perplexed, her short snooze having lasted a good three hours. The TV was playing a random cooking programme and the sounds downstairs had long since faded away to a midnight silence. The restaurant had closed an hour before and the waiting staff had finished tidying the tables. Declan, the sous chef, had performed his usual cursory clearing of the kitchen. The dishwasher made an ill-tempered rumble somewhere below, disgusted at being the only one working at this ungodly hour.

As she had lain there, in a rich post-bath warmth, she had

drifted into a half-sleep dream state, a miasma of weird disconnected notions and bizarre images, seeded by half heard dialogue from the television, annoyingly punctuated by an alien rapping sound which, incongruous in her dreams, had metamorphosed into staccato applause, then to flamenco heels on a wooden floor, until finally, her subdued consciousness had clawed it's way to the surface and convinced her that the noise was something she should pay heed to.

Wearily, she hauled herself from the sofa, muted the TV and listened in the near-silence, tutting loudly as the beer garden gate rapped against the kitchen wall. Which idiot had left it unbolted this time? At least on Wednesday night, Finn's gallantry had saved her a trip into the cold garden. She reminded herself to have a stern word with Marcus next time she saw him. Descending the stairs, she could hear the various hums and clicks of the electrical equipment in the downstairs rooms. Checking the alarm panel, she could see it was unset; Finn would be out for a few hours yet. Boy, how those guys can drink! Safe in the knowledge that she was not going to be assailed by cacophonous sirens or, more to the point, two burly policemen from Ealing Police station, she eased her head round into the restaurant. The street lamps snaked through the slatted venetian blinds, casting their dull fingers across the tables and up the walls but everything was still. In the kitchen, the dishwasher was still moaning and the fridge was adding a low humming accompaniment. Similarly the bar was still, dark and quiet. Letting out another deep roaring sigh, Shelley knew it fell upon her to traipse out across the beer garden and secure the catch.

Above the rear door, the automatic light flooded the back yard with a blinding white sheet and she paused whilst her eyes adjusted, squirming as she realised that apart from the fleecy dressing gown, which struggled to make its way down to the middle of her thighs, and pair of fluffy pink bunny slippers, she was utterly naked and the breeze had picked up, chilling her in places that even she rarely admitted having these days. Maybe a couple of burly policemen would be a welcome distraction with Finn out? Her mission had better be swift. She threw the catch to prevent the door from locking behind her and jogged across to the gate. She peeked outside but fortunately there was no-one passing to see the rather too prominent cleavage, now sporting goose bumps as big as her rather solid nipples. Quickly, she latched the gate and leant her back against it and, for the first time in many long years she giggled to herself. Not just at the incongruity of the situation, the pink bunny slippers, the cream dressing gown, the chill of the air, but at the lightness of it. No more fear of the future, of the fate of the Plough & Harrow, no more anxieties over Finn's love for her, and no more cowering childishly behind the sackful of neuroses she had dragged around for too many years. And if Carmichael were here now, she would tell him to fuck off again too! She held her shoulders high and sauntered back to the rear door, her hands in the dressing gown pockets, flapping the hems as she walked, almost enjoying the cold wisps of air between her legs. As she slid inside the doorway and the warmth of the interior swathed her, she turned her back to the door, lifted her dressing gown, revealing her rounded backside, and shouted for all to hear "Andrew Carmichael. From now on you can just kiss this!"

But she did check to make sure she wasn't being overlooked!

***

It was almost three in the morning before Finn climbed aboard Asif's Toyota Corolla to avoid the short but unsteady walk home. Asif was always in the rank. He had three girls to support but then as now, Finn was far too drunk to really listen. Asif's voice ambled along in concert with the rattle of the diesel for the seven minutes of the trip, as Finn catnapped in the back. It had been an enjoyable evening amongst men with similar problems, a similar sense of humour and, like him, a weakness for the drink and the cards. There was something soul-destroying, knowing the more pickled he became, the easier his poker face was to read and, how much lighter was his pocket by the time they wrapped up. However, tonight had been different. He had been on his game. For most of the day he had been working on balance sheets and cash flows, taking a closer look at the accounts himself rather than simply handing them over to Guy. Since Dawn had started to raise questions regarding Guy and Drew's handling of the Fund, he felt he needed to check Guy Higson's handiwork. Seeing how much cash flowed through the business, he had resolved to take a little less stake money with him...at least until Carmichael coughed up. Maybe, despite his moaning, Asif had got it right. Finn envied him children. Shelley and he had planned so many things that had been side-lined in favour of the business. Things would be changing from now on.

"Fukin' Hell, Guvnor! Look!"

Finn lurched forwards, the seat belt biting into his shoulder, as Asif drew up sharply alongside the Green, wound down his window and pointed. Finn, bemused at what could excite this small, cheerful Bangladeshi, slid across the seats to peer through the off-side rear window and followed the finger to the flickering reddish, yellow lights playing on the upstairs windows above the bar. For a second, the lingering veil of alcohol and tiredness fogged his mind and he could not register the significance of the shimmering leaves of gold until he was snapped aware by a soft pop and a shower of glass onto the street below.

Yanking on the stretched seat belt, fumbling with the catch, Finn yelled at Asif to call the fire brigade. He tumbled into the street before vaulting the small fence and spanning the fifteen yards of the Green to the crackling flames, the alcoholic torpor lifting with each stride. Racing around to the back gate, he tried the handle, frustratedly flicking it up and down, cursing under his breath. Eventually he backed up and shoulder charged, feeling the lower half cave under the pressure, but the gate remained latched and his shoulder burned. As he took a second run, he sensed Asif by his side and under their combined weight the wood yielded and they toppled into the garden beneath a shower of splinters. Almost before he had landed, Finn was back on his feet and leaping towards the rear door, with Asif dragging at his coat and pleading for him to wait for the fire service. Straining with every fibre of his being he steadied his shaking hands, the end of the key playing with the lock until it finally found the void and turned. As the door opened, a rolling fog of thick unctuous cloud stole the breath from his chest and he gagged. Turning away, took in a rib wrenching lungful before launching himself inside. Immediately he was consumed by the billowing ink, unable to gain his bearings. He could see nothing except the falling folds of gunmetal smoke and his nose burned with the chemical soup it contained. As his eyes began to stream, Finn squinting to the ceiling, picking out the eerie green of the emergency sign pointing back towards the door and by degrees, as if wallowing through a pond of grey, rolling molasses, he fell to the floor and crawled commando style until he felt the bottom of the stair. Grabbing a duster from the hall table, he tied it as best he could around his face before exhaling every molecule of the last good breath he may ever take. As his lungs refilled he wretched and coughed, as much from the rancid odour of polish on the duster as from the air, foul and noxious. Behind him, he vaguely heard Asif screaming for him to come out, to leave it to the professionals but in his mind he could see Shelley in the bedroom, alone and afraid, waiting for the amber tendrils to reach in and draw the life from her. A thousand Asif's could not stop him from trying to reach her, however slim the odds. Grasping at each step, Finn dragged himself on his stomach up the stairs, peering under the surging murk, advancing step by step, feeling the oxygen lessen with every breath he rasped until his mind swam and his eyes clouded with firing patterns of red and green. Reaching the top, he looked left at the wall of flame, growling and popping, as the living room door, agape, rippled in a florid blanket of flame. Turning right, he felt around the corner and grabbed the architrave, and hauled himself up into the gloom, robbed of every inch of vision groping for the door handle, twisting it frantically. He called her name but even though his mouth was wide, the words played only in his head. The inside of his lungs were burning now and his mind swam. Beneath him his knees began to buckle as the last remnants of oxygen were scoured from his blood and the world around him began to prickle and be subsumed by the darkness. He placed his cheek against the door and prayed to a God that had long ago deserted him, that she would be behind the door, a few millimetres away, and that even if she were to die too, that at least she would know he had come and that he had kept his word to always be there.

Chapter 29

The trees were trembling in the breeze, like a Hula dolls on the dash of an American sedan. The grey turned to black as the besom branches swept away the moonlight, their arms pawing at the air around Carmichael. Through tight closed lids, the shapes blurred into waves and sounds echoed in his ears. A voice barked, or was that the sound of his own breath in the hollow chimney of his throat, howling and moaning? He was floating and he knew that it was a dream, aware of the impossibilities and the implausibilities, smiling at the surreally, a monotone world just beyond his fingertips. He sensed he was looking about, breathing in the smells, to define the scene, to name the players, the faceless extras with whom one shares the abstract narrative of a dream. And the voice in his head resonated a million miles away, words disappearing on the breeze, turning up through the rustling leaves and alighting on his ears. The words were spoken but he struggled to discern them. Like a familiar tune playing in his head.

Look at him. See what you have done.

At his feet lay Guy, his arms by his side, his legs together, standing to attention, lying on his back but his head, shrouded in the shiny black of the helmet, turned to one side. *Eyes Right!* And there was a laugh, a long groaning laugh as he realised that Guy's new trousers were muddy and the voice inside his head was saying:

Now she has to die and he will go with her.

And the man in the helmet was pushing them back, eyes bulging like the eyes of a fish, flicking left and right as the streamers festooned blue and white, the hand pushed on his chest and the grip on his arm resisted. The men in green carried the glistening chariots to the waiting doors and screamed blue and black into the night.

Carmichael was sitting upright as the last bounce creaked and the mattress stopped hard and still below him. The voice echoed inside his head, a scream bursting through into the harsh light of morning. He brushed a hand across his face to sweep away the lingering remnants of sleep, clinging to the dream as it sifted away like the sand through his fingers, and the images dissolved from his mind.

"Are you OK?" It was Carol. She was standing in the doorway She was wearing a salmon pink satin nightdress and her hair was wet.

"Yes, Yes. Just a bad dream that's all. I saw Guy - dead, well, it was as if I was standing over him, watching him die." For a moment he was perplexed, gazing around the room, the double bed, Guy staring lifeless through the open visor, Carol in the doorway, a soup of images that bobbed to the surface and then sank to be replaced by others. Weird faces appearing through the inky window of a Magic-8 ball.

Carol scrunched her nose up and smiled. "You have some seriously weird shit going on in that head of yours. Now get dressed and come downstairs. Breakfast is on!"

"Your hair? It's wet."

"And? Some of us have a life to lead, even if we are harbouring fugitives. It's seven-thirty and I have a hair appointment at nine, so shift." She disappeared and the door shut with a rather final clunk, leaving motes of dust eddying and dancing in the shafts of light from the window.

Carmichael looked around him. The bedroom seemed different in the light of day but still stark and utilitarian. His clothes, or rather those of Carol's ex, were heaped on the floor, cold, flaccid and abandoned, which to be fair was exactly how he felt.

He struggled to recall the previous night, the memories of Carol, the warmth of her back against his chest and her breasts firm and full as his hand nestled between them. He tried to imagine pulling her onto her back, the deep and consuming kiss as their lips had met and the rush of absolute surrender. He tried to imagine... but there were no memories. Perplexed, he grabbed his clothes and made his way to the bathroom. The air in the bedroom was rank with the odour of unwashed male and by comparison, the bathroom positively reeked of roses, of gardenia, or some other girlie smell. Condensation clung to the mirror, concealing from Carmichael the hideous apparition to which Carol had just been subjected. He wiped away a circle and peered at the reflection, distorted and unshaven.

263

Jesus! Not even I would shag that.

Spruced up, washed and dressed he made his way downstairs. In the kitchen, Carol had laid out a breakfast, which he attacked with relish. His mouth tasted as if he had been gargling sawdust and he felt like he hadn't eaten for a week. By the time she came downstairs, he had demolished two bowls of cereal and was sheepishly indulging in a third.

"Wow! Someone's got an appetite this morning!" She was wearing a pair of tailored beige chinos and a white T-shirt bearing a Varsity slogan. Her hair was simple and swept back into a ponytail held in place by a blue elastic band revealing a pair of tiny pearl earrings and a silver chain which disappeared into the T-shirt; a tiny lump protruded where Carmichael assumed a locket hung.

"Certainly have got an appetite. Especially after what we got up to last night. Remind me again, what did we get up to last night?" He furrowed his brow in mock confusion, which only served to hide the very real bafflement he felt.

She smiled as she took the seat opposite him and picked up the cafetière. He pushed a cup across.

"Well, you got up to first base - this one, if memory serves...", she cupped her left breast and hoiked it a couple of inches, "then I got up to freshen up and when I came back, you were out like a light. So basically we slept together, with the emphasis on sleep."

"You're joking! Not even a grope, a crafty fondle?" She shook her head and clucked as he scratched his scalp, dredging his mind back to her warmth and the soft animal smell of her neck, to the cold of the pillow, but then nothing. He imagined her breast in his hand but try as he might he had no memory of it.

"Don't worry, pet. It's not the be-all-and-end-all." She smiled, again that infuriating motherly smile that could make an erection wilt in an instant.

"Trouble is, I am not really sure why it didn't happen. Lets put it in words of one syllable. We were both well up for it last night, surely!" He looked at her earnestly across the table and she smiled and then took a sip of her coffee, her tongue darting across the sheen of her lipgloss.

"Two syllables...or is it three? 'Surely' has either two or three syllables, depending on your pronunciation."

"What?"

"You said words of one syllable... never mind." She reached across and took his hand. "Drew, I was very vulnerable last night. I revisited a lot of painful memories. Despite your reputation I invited you back to my house. Even though the scale of your conquests is legendary, I led you on and then I took you into my bed. You had every right to exploit my vulnerability and I would probably have refused you nothing. But you know what? I am so glad you didn't because that would have betrayed the trust we need to have between us. You have trusted me with sorting out the issues at work and I have in turn trusted that you were not responsible for those two girls. Perhaps the time just wasn't right to trust ourselves to each other?"

Inwardly stinging from the slight on his reputation, Carmichael took the compliment and filed it away under accidentally received and not deserved. He smiled and nodded. It was slightly confusing that he had not pursued his long held ambition to bed her. The signals couldn't have been clearer if they had been sky-written by the Red Arrows in fifty foot letters.

She rose and swilled the cup under the tap and his eyes fell on the well-rounded half-moons of her buttocks held tight in her chinos, taut and curved as she bent to fetch a towel. How in the world did he manage to let *that* escape for a second night running? "Now, I'm off for a couple of hours pampering of a Saturday morning. God knows I deserve it working for you. I should be back by lunchtime and I'll bring a razor. You look like a badger's arse - not that I've seen one, but well. You stay here and watch telly or something. Don't forget, there are a lot of people looking for you, so, in words of one syllable - don't go out, stay here 'til I get back. Savvy?"

Drew watched as she raised her arms to put on her jacket, her breasts fulsome, shapely and prominent in the tight T-shirt. If only he could remember the moment of embrace, the slightest brush of flesh, perhaps just the uneven tautness of her areolus, anything. He smiled what he assumed to be a grateful smile, grateful for her hospitality and her kind words, even for letting him down gently from an embarrassment of which he had no recollection. She disappeared and the house fell silent to the falling latch of the front door.

Immediately, stir-crazy, Drew decamped to the living room and switched on the television. There had to be something that could take his mind off her. Unfortunately all he saw badly drawn cartoons shouting inanely. Irritated, he fired the remote up button. A buxom, drug-ravaged children's presenter appeared. She was only marginally better than talking sketches, and she had better tits. He flicked again and again, past the kids channels and endless disingenuous cooks and their gullible guests. Then he alighted on the BBC News channel and was transfixed by the image.

"...and is believed to have been started in the early hours of this morning. There were two people in the building at the time of the fire but as yet we have no information on fatalities."

Drew's mind played images of blinding blue flashes, shadows dressed in black with white helmets, he smelled the caustic smoke, heard the smack of the hoses as they filled and stiffened. He felt the pressure on his chest as the huge fish-eyed man drew the tape down in front of him. He wrestled with the images. How could he know this? Had she left a morning paper? No! This was the early hours. It would have missed this morning's papers.

A face labelled Leading Firefighter Matthew Pridden spoke against a backdrop of devastation as the dawn was burgeoning. "We suspect that the fire was started deliberately and has destroyed the upper storey of the Plough & Harrow and most of the rest of the building has sustained water damage. I can confirm the use of an accelerant and, subject to confirmation from fire investigators, we will be asking the police to investigate. We have recovered two persons from the scene, but I cannot give any more details until relatives have been informed." Carmichael was rapt by the replay and again the images from his dream filled his head. How could he have known? And the recollections of Guy lying in the dirt. Were they any more real? Was any of it real? He reached down to his ankle and raised his left foot onto his knee. Of course the leather was dry, barely any residue from his trekking across town yesterday. Certainly no evidence that he had been standing next to the effluent from a burning building.

266

Disoriented, unable to process the mounds of conflicting truths, he fired the remote and killed the pictures. A cloying silence descended on the small sitting room, stifling, consuming the air. He returned to the kitchen and grabbed another coffee. He needed to think.

How could the images from his dreams seem so real? No-one had released details of how or where Guy had been killed. Perhaps it was an unconscious manifestation of the guilt he felt for treating Guy so badly?

And the Plough & Harrow? Dropping his head to his hands he forced himself to recall the dream but only snippets would come. The howling ambulances, the acrid smoke and the streaming hoses. The recollections were so real, they had to be memories.

Then it occurred to him. What if they are all right? What if he was the killer? Had he suffered a breakdown from the pressure Dawn had put him under? And Rachel? Had she been the catalyst that had set him off on this manic killing spree? He had heard of hysterical amnesia, of brains wiped clean of events too traumatic to deal with. But could he simply flip, like Dr Jekyll and commit such barbaric crimes under his Hydean alter-ego and then flip back, completely erasing the memories? His mind was playing too many tricks on him lately, leaving him torn between truth and fiction. He needed to see the Plough & Harrow for himself, be certain that the dreams were just vivid horrific coincidences and not grotesque remembrances burning through the hidden walls in his brain. Racing into the hall, he retrieved a baseball cap and greatcoat from the hangers. Then he fished around in the hall drawer for keys, and finding a bunch, he tried each one in the front door lock until he found a match. He donned the greatcoat and cap, removed the key from its ring and disappeared out through the front door.

***

The bed was comfortable and warm, enveloping him like a cocoon, a womb; every part of his body so perfectly held that he couldn't feel a single part of his skin. The wisps of gas tasted of plastic and rubber and were chill against the lining of his nose but, notwithstanding, Finn was more comfortable than he could ever remember being. So he kept his eyes shut, listening to the voices as they communed and discussed notes. There was a sonorous staccato beep and his breath made a rhythmic drawing sound, which served only to relax him further. He heard a name and he knew it was his but he had no inclination to heed it further, such was the state he was in. Another name. He knew it was she and he felt a deep, dragging despair that took a moment, maybe a minute or an hour, to process. Clawing his way to consciousness, he latched on to the voice, frostbitten fingers grasping at a ledge, the rather hard, tired female voice that was rooted in his past, a voice familiar from just before. Just before it happened. Before what happened?

Deb Whetstone stopped mid-sentence and swung around to face the prone figure of Finn Byrne, watching the spasmodic jerks, the nurses running to remove the mask, to check the machinery, press the buttons and summon help. After a moment she tentatively approached the bed, keeping out of the way, wires and tubes being drawn back.

"Is he OK?" She peered down between the pastel blue shoulders and glimpsed a face wracked with pain, eyes reddened and sore, skin dry and cracked. His hands were packed into plastic bags against infection and dehydration.

"He's crying, I think." The nurse laid a gentle hand on his shoulder. "Mr Byrne. My names Belinda. Time to wake up now." Tenderly, she dabbed the swollen eyelids with moist cotton wool and the eyes opened, blinking against the neon harshness, turning to face her.

"My wife? How is she?" Belinda shuffled her feet, turning away, adjusting a pillow. Deb leaned over.

"Hi, Mr Byrne - Finn." A brick lodged in her throat momentarily at the cruelness of the fireman - *Who'd have thought it, a man named Byrne in a fire* - perhaps that was how they survived. "Finn, it's Sergeant Whetstone - Deborah. We met on Thursday. At the pub?"

"Shelley?" The word was half croaked, like the rusty hinges of an unused gate, but a single word embodied a universe of meaning.

"She's in the next room, Finn. The doctors are doing everything they can." She struggled to keep her emotions in check as Finn Byrne's lower lip curled and quivered. A single tear tracked its way into the hair around his ear.

"I wasn't there when she needed me. I should never have left her alone." He raised a wrapped hand to his eyes and unashamedly wept behind it. Deb watched a man so powerful and self-reliant, so dependable, now so helpless and desolate. The firefighters had found him unconscious against the bedroom room, the skin of his finger melted to the peeling paintwork. He had guided to them to Shelley, as she lay on the other side, her fingers bloodied as she had tried to scratch her way through the wood. She now lay in an induced coma, machines scrubbing the carbon monoxide from her blood, but who knew what noxious chemicals were still poisoning her. The odds were poor. No matter how many times Deb had been faced with life-changing events, it never came any easier.

"She's alive, Finn. She's very poorly but right now she's alive. Because of you." She laid her hand on his shoulder. "You *were* there when she needed you. You nearly died making sure you were there."

Finn removed his hand from his eyes and laid it upon hers. Sorrowfully, he looked up at her. "But where have I been for the last fifteen years?"

***

Daley slumped over his desk, his face in his hands. The wetness of his tears squeaked between his palms, salt stinging the flesh under his eyes. The tears had only come briefly, helped by the relative isolation of Saturday in the team room, a barren tundra where only the hardiest, the loneliest, or in his case most desperate, of coppers scratched an existence. Between the veneer of capable self-assurance and the core of self-doubt and ebbing confidence, there was an ever shifting mantle of uncertainty and anxiety, which heaved and flowed. For no reason his defences were down and the full weight of the previous days had descended unmercifully to exploit the weakness. He heard his breathe rasp between his fingers, his body ached with tiredness and his soul was torn by guilt. The body count was stacking up and soon Allenby would want to see tangible evidence that any slight progress was being made to stem the tide of carrion.

In the early hours of Saturday, the shrill, insistent squeal of his phone had awoken him from his fitful doze on the angular

269

sofa that formed the majority of the furniture in his spartan flat. Uniforms on the scene had called in the fire and Harrison, who seemed to always inhabit the comms. room, had come up with names from Daley's investigations.

And the drama had begun. He had roused Whetstone, ridden the inevitable abuse and driven around to Hammersmith Hospital, to begin a test of patience and time. Emerging finally from the Emergency Room, into the grey half light of a dawning day, he was none the wiser. Neither casualty was in a fit state to talk. Given the smoke inhalation, and the massive amount of toxins in their bloodstreams, it was touch and go as to whether either of them would talk again.

Not twenty-four hours before, staring dispassionately at the corpse of the dead motorcyclist, he could chalk him up as a statistic, planned long before the call had come through about Dawn. And then, he had been standing in the ambulance bay at Hammersmith Hospital, the silence broken by the clattering of gurneys against kerbs and doors slamming against stops, as a train of green and yellow hastily arrived with the prone figures of Shelley Nugent and Finn Byrne. He had flashed the warrant card and been ushered in to stare through a window, helpless and frustrated. These were people he knew. He had seen the colour of their faces, heard the lilt of their voices and formed part of their memories.

Leaving Whetstone at Byrne's bedside, he had headed for the scene and, despite arriving at 7:00 o'clock on a brisk April morning, there was already a crowd of ghoulish rubberneckers and other weirdoes, garnering a macabre delight from the misfortune of others. Beyond the cordon several appliances were jetting water through the smoking sockets of windows. Tired firefighters wearily slouched, black-faced, staring into polystyrene cups. On the corner, a cluster of white light shone on the bottle-blonde roving reporter practicing her detached outrage before the guy with the camera started beaming misery to the masses. Daley had a quick chat with the uniform who was rubbing his hands together at the front doors of the pub, peering suspiciously up at the strings of murky water raining down from above. And then, scanning the line of blue flashing lights, he spotted the white helmet and introduced himself to the man in charge.

"Hi, Detective Inspector Daley, Lambourne Road - Scott. I've just come from the hospital. What do we know?"

"Hi, Leading Firefighter Matthew Pridden - Matt. Not much at this stage. We're lucky the fire was contained upstairs. The bar and restaurant are a bloody mess from the water and smoke though. The fire probably started in the living room at the front..." He pointed a finger towards the corner of the building over the entrance to the bar, "... and tracked it's way along the hallway."

"Could this be an accident?"

"No, mate. Definitely not! An accelerant was used. There are the remains of a couple of car tyres in the living room and the place reeks of petrol. The sprinklers have been turned off at the mains too. Someone deliberately set out to kill whoever was in there. Forensics are on their way. We should know more by the end of the day." Pridden scratched his chin, the detached air of a professional supplanted by concern. "How are they? The two we found?"

"Dunno, Matt. According to the doctors, the man should be OK. He inhaled a lot of smoke but given a couple of days he should be out of hospital."

"And the woman?"

"Not so good. She was locked in the bedroom. Apparently she had been unconscious for a lot longer before you arrived, taken in a lot more of the smoke from the fire, and the chemicals from whatever was burning. The doctors say it's a waiting game with her. She could recover from the effects of the smoke, but never recover from brain damage caused by the toxicity. They've put her in an induced coma."

"And what was that number all about? At first I thought it was a tattoo, but then I could see it was permanent marker."

"Look, you know what it's like with a criminal investigation. There are some things we have to keep back.

"Bloody Hell. What? She's number four? Christ!"

"We need you to tell your men to forget they saw it for now. Can you do that?"

"Yeah. They'll be solid. You need to talk to the ambulance guys too, though." Pridden looked up at the smouldering remains. "Do you know, he was *that close*..." Pridden indicated a

271

millimetre-wide gap between thumb and forefinger, "...to her. If he had arrived home ten minutes earlier, he would have probably got her out before the fumes started."

"Or been locked in the bedroom and died in the fire with her." Daley was convinced the timing was no accident, that Nugent was the intended victim and Byrne just a casualty of war. Byrne had no number.

Daley decided he could do no more at the scene, and thanked the tired fireman, handing him a business card. He slowly spun through 360 degrees, squinting past the street lamps and up into the horizon of rooftops and trees, counting five cameras trained on the pub, silent witnesses to the event. At least some of them must be functioning, and at least one of *those* may have seen something. With any luck, and plenty of coffee, Corby should be able to find it.

Reaching the office, Daley had headed up the back stair to avoid the front desk. He was in no mood to speak to anyone. Then as he had rested his elbows on the desk, the veneer of self-assurance had given way. Tiredness had overwhelmed him and he felt himself unable to stem the flow.

***

Proposition 4 - Killing by Fire

Date - 27th April 1997

Proponent – Shelley Nugent

SN – OK. So it's my turn. I've been thinking about this. The one thing Rachel and Dawn's ideas share with Guy's is that the actual murder is sudden and unexpected. One second the person is alive and the next they're dead. They wouldn't have a clue what has just happened to them.

RJ – Well, not quite. Like I say they say a decapitated head looks around and speaks for a bit afterwards.

SN – Yes, but that hardly counts as knowing what has happened. The head would be in shock and the movements may be automatic. What you need is for the murder to be slow and drawn out. For the victim to know they are going to die before it happens and have plenty of time to think about it. Imagine what it must be like to be in an aircraft that is plummeting thousands of feet a minute, knowing that you are going to die.

GH – Yes, but you're not proposing that to kill one person, you would sabotage a plane and kill the other three hundred at the same time, are you?

SN – Why not? I saw a film once where a murderer killed a string of people to hide the fact that he was after just the one.

Me – We need to stick to the point. What is the murder and how does it happen (Shelley looked strangely at me for suggesting this).

SN – OK. What I propose is that you select your victim and follow them to somewhere quiet and then you drug them with ether or chloroform or something.

DC – Ah! The rules state no poisons.

SN – Not a poison Dxxx. Just to incapacitate them.

DC – Fair enough.

SN - Then you take them to an abandoned warehouse – there is always one in Scooby Doo, you tie them up, wait until they come round from the anaesthetic and set fire to the place.

GH – Surely you would die in the fire too?

SN – Not if you made sure there was an open widow and stood outside watching. Obviously, you would need to be careful of the fumes, and careful that the fire wasn't discovered before the person could die.

GH – But wouldn't the victim pass out before the fire got to them?

SN – And? Before they passed out they would know that they were going to die.

Proposition Victim – Shelley Nugent

Proposition Development - There is no rule that states that the murderer has to watch the victim die; only that the murderer must directly inflict the death. The building needs to have a lockable door, or an internal room with a lockable door, in order to prevent the victim from escaping as they come round from the anaesthetic. Any windows in the room should remain locked although internal ventilation is required in order to promote free movement of fumes.

The use of a suitable sedative is suggested to ensure the victim can be managed in the chosen location.

Additional to the fire is the use of a suitable accelerant.

My Proposition Method - Locate the site. Whilst the murder of other people is not forbidden under the rules, the purpose is to murder a single individual. Therefore the premises should be a property occupied by a single individual, such as a house where a person lives alone or a property where the victim will be alone. Alternatively, where a caretaker or security guard has been left in sole charge.

The premises should also have an enclosed garden or back yard.

Another specific criteria should be the proximity to the nearest Fire Station. If the Fire Service arrives too early, they may extinguish the fire and rescue the victim.

Specific to the Proposition Victim, the Plough & Harrow Pub & Restaurant is the chosen location.

Select a victim. The above dictates the victim.

Select a time. Where possible the event should be timed to coincide with:

The morning or evening rush hour. This would hinder the fire service in attending.

The early hours of the morning. As there are less people awake to notice the flames, the fire would be well established before the Fire Service can be alerted

Therefore the most appropriate timing for the event would be b) above.

Method. Gain entry to the backyard and secrete the below items out of plain site.

The gate should be left unlocked and the bolt drawn such that the gate will impact on the frame and cause a distraction. Should this not prove successful, a bin may be upturned as an alternative.

When the victim investigates, administer the sedative and transport the victim to the lockable room.

Sedative: Sodium Thiopental 250 mg, slow induction by injection of 50 (2mL at a 2.5% solution) at intervals of 20 to 40 seconds. Induction of 250mg as a single dose can be used as a rapid sedative, although victims breathing should be monitored to avoid an apnoeatic episode and asphyxiation. Sedative effects last for two hours.

Remove the victim to the murder room and place duct tape over mouth.

The fire should be set using the following items:

An accelerant such as gasoline or paraffin in a plastic fuel container.

Two car tyres. The size of the car tyres is not important, however 195/50 R15 is a common tyres size, which can be readily obtained.

A cigarette lighter and a length of material (approx. 50 cm).

Site the tyres outside the lockable room, but allow access to the room. The suggestion is a nearby room. Douse the tyres with the accelerant leaving approximately half the accelerant in the container. Place the container approximately 1 metre from the tyres.

NOTE. Care should be taken when obtaining tyres as forensic examination of the remains of the tyre may lead the Police to the murderer.

NOTE SPECIFIC TO PLOUGH & HARROW: The site is equipped with a remote fire alarm and sprinkler system. The sprinklers are disabled using a stop tap above the door in the beer cellar. The Fire alarm can be disabled with the code 2835 and admin code 9999 entered into the panel beside the rear door.

Return to the victim and await consciousness.

When fully conscious ensure that the victim is aware. Lock the room and return to the set fire. Leave the key with the fire to prevent escape. Light the end of the material and ensure that the flame has taken hold. Retire to a safe distance (approximately 3 metres). Await combustion of the accelerant before leaving the building. Once at a safe location nearby await the combustion of the accelerant container. This indicates that the fire is sufficiently robust and will result in murder.

***

Carmichael yanked the cap lower, the coat tighter around his waist, suddenly feeling exposed. He furtively scoured the ranks of faceless houses for any glimmer of recognition, any signpost that would help him figure out where the hell Carol had brought him. All around, he felt the myriad curtains twitching as curious faces studied him. It was still early on Saturday but a few people were walking about. If he had had any sense he would have dragged Carol back upstairs, given her good seeing-to and be enjoying a deep, restorative post-coital nap. Instead he was risking arrest to confirm whether those vivid images of the boring pub were a fabrication of a mind under stress, or murky memories from a dissociated alter-ego. Scanning right and left, through a narrow corridor of trees and redbrick garden walls, there was nothing to choose between either direction.

To his right a door opened and a father and his two kids erupted from the house, chattering and howling. The commotion set his mind and he headed left at a sharp pace to keep ahead of the group, but they crammed into a car and sped off the opposite way. Eventually, the road spilled out onto another running perpendicular, a main road with ranks of shop forming an honour guard to the sparse early Saturday traffic. Scooting across he headed what he believed to be North, based on the sun struggling it's way over the horizon. He passed a row of shops and a couple of bus stops, none of which afforded much of a clue. Eventually, a vague rumble sounded ahead, a distant regular scraping and a whining of motors - the Tube.

By the time he reached Northfields, the platforms were filling with Saturday shoppers, hunter gatherers on their weekly commercial safari, wrapped up in their own worlds, gazing into middle distance, scanning a small phone screen or simply staring moodily down at their feet. London was a Capital where millions of people swarmed about each other every day, so close that they could breathe the other's body odour, run their hands across the fabric of their clothes, press tightly together on a crowded train, and yet barely notice the existence of one another. It was a complex living organism driven by individual components, each divorced from the next, separate, alone and always lonely. And today the unseeing eyes stared right through Carmichael as he hid in plain sight. *That man off the adverts, him from the telly, the mass murderer from the news.* The board above him indicated three minutes to the next train.

The images from his dream billowed through his mind like the clouds of acrid smoke that filled them. His nostrils stung

276

with half remembered smells of bitter choking woodsmoke and pungent melting plastic. Why were these so real? Of course he had experienced vivid dreams in the past, but with an element of surreality, an absurdity separating fantasy from fact. As the eyelids drew back, the dream would vaporise, often only the merest notion of the dream at all. But these dreams had lingered, and those from previous days. They refused to crumble under the harsh light of dawn but became sharper each time he recalled them. Or was his own paranoia filling in the blanks, elaborating hysterical memories, fabricating the material of unreal events? And how in the world could he be aware of them even before he had switched on the television? There had to be a rational answer. Maybe it was *déjà vu*? That unsettling notion that one had experienced an event before?

He fished out his phone and pressed the button and swore under his breath, remembering it had been turned off the night before. He quickly switched it on. He could hear the howling, grinding snarl of the train as it approached. The Tube was a notoriously poor reception area, but his trip would be mainly above ground, changing at Acton for Ealing Broadway, so apart from the train itself he should be OK. The first car had almost met the impatient gaggle of waiting passengers, each surging forward to that special crack in the platform or piece of flattened chewing gum, which marked the lucky spot where the doors would magically align. The phone finished its arduous start-up sequence. There were seven missed calls in the window - they would have to wait. He couldn't be dealing with Thornton, or that idiotic policeman. For God's sake, was not the balance of his mind disturbed?

The small crowd in front of him slowly crunched its way through the bottleneck of the carriage door. He located Marcus' number and dialled it. To his frustration, the voicemail picked up and he searched for something to say. What could he say? In hushed tones, to avoid being overheard, he decided on the straightforward approach.

"Hey, Marcus. Call me back as quickly as you can. Look, man, I need your help. I keep having these weird dreams. Look, you're a doctor...well, just call me." A sonorous insistent regular beeping sounded and the doors scraped past his face, and soon the deserted platform, distorted in the cheap, scratched glass, was sliding away from him. He knew that a thousand heads were touching a thousand disk drives and the simple message was being relayed across thousands of miles to be stored in a single incriminating recording. Saved by the beeps. Best to be brief. He hung up the call and dropped the phone into his pocket, keeping his fingers clasped firmly around it, so he would not miss Marcus' return call.

And unbeknown to him, radio waves hit seven mobile phone masts, and signals scurried down hundreds of feet of cable to computerised exchanges where they sent data to a number of data centres, which in turn sent information to a series of small white panels on Sergeant Dave Monaghan's desktop screen.

Chapter 30

With overwhelming apathy, Marcus stared at the phone. Such was the preternatural pull of Carmichael that he struggled not relent and listen to the voicemail. The TV was broadcasting looped images of the fire and the word *arson* was repeated every fifteen minutes. He wondered whether he should try *their* phones again, whether anything would have changed since 7:00am when he had first attempted to reassure himself that they were both fine. Even his contacts at the Hammersmith had been unforthcoming. The Police had made sure of that. So he had been left to piece together what had happened.

Someone was definitely exterminating the Monday Club.

There was no doubt now. This was too organised to be mere chance. He thought back to the conversation with Drew in the hospital storeroom, the panic that had driven him from the hospital. He neither looked back nor caught his breath until he was inside his own front door, closed and bolted. As the night drew in, darkness had shrouded the house, elongating shadows faded to the vague haze of street-lamps. He had resigned himself to Friday night in the still emptiness of the living room, cramped and foetal, beside the sofa, hoping that no-one knew he was there, the silence roaring in his ears.

The sound of the phone, juddering rhythmically on the table beside him, had made him start, his nerves launching a rainbow of fireworks across his retinas. It had been Alice, and her voice had instantly made him the traitor and she the betrayed, her words tremulous and filled with the same fear he felt. He pictured her alone and frightened, like him huddled in the corner of the room, hidden, undiscovered.

"Marcus, where are you?"

"At home, watching the telly," he lied. "You?"

"Can you come over?" There was a pleading in her voice, she wasn't asking, she was begging.

"Not tonight, I'm sorry. I got work to do." Another lie that caught in his throat and threatened to choke the air from his chest. "What's the matter? You sound upset. Is it something I have done?"

"No, Marcus, of course not. It's just, that I've been thinking...about Dawn and Guy...and Rachel. About what's happening."

"Yes, and me. I have thought of nothing else today."

"It's Carmichael, I know it is. It must be. I kept thinking that maybe their deaths aren't connected. That shit just happens, but I couldn't get it out of my head that there is a pattern to all this." Her tone was emphatic. No more wild suppositions, or comic scenarios. The time for humour was past.

"What do you mean, it *must be Carmichael?* There's no proof. It's all hearsay, circumstantial." Carmichael and he had been friends for too long for the thirty pieces of silver to be accepted so readily.

"No, Marcus, listen to me. It has to be him. He's the only person it can be. There is more to it that just the murders. Of all of us that were there, of all of the Monday Club, it can only be him. He is the one person with anything to gain and everything to lose."

He had told her she was being fanciful, letting her nerves get the better of her, and his betrayal had continued. *Lock the door. Get a good night's sleep, I'll see you tomorrow. Nothing is going to happen before then.* Trite homilies, meaningless against the tears he could hear in her voice. He had told her not to answer her phone until he called; he would call in the morning. Reluctantly, tearfully, she had agreed. Perhaps she was over-reacting, even a little hysterical. She had fallen silent, allowing the static on the line to fill the void.

Hysterical, maybe. But what if there was even a grain of truth to it? What if this was the reawakening of an event from their University days - the day everything changed? It was certainly true that Carmichael had a reason to keep each of them quiet. But kill them? Surely with his powers of persuasion, there were any number of less lethal weapons in his armoury. Now he came to think of it, since that night they had shown him an extraordinary level of loyalty. It was not the exposure of his financial scam that Carmichael feared, it was something far darker.

Marcus had stared up at the nebulous patterns on the wall, the phone hard and clammy against his ear, the hiss of the empty line, punctuated by Alice's breath. He shuffled a buttock, flattened by the hardness of the floor. So, if this was all connected to that April night in Coventry, why was he so afraid? Carmichael's retribution would only be aimed at those there on that night; those that now threatened to expose him in the present.

And that meant Marcus was not, and never would be, a target.

It had torn him in two as he had pressed the disconnect button but now the fear was all for her, that small, lone figure on the other end of the line.

The morning light had chased away the shadows from the walls. Shamed by the knowledge that he valued his own life over that of Alice's, he had called a taxi, travelled to her flat and spent the night beside her, cradling her in his arms, squatting beneath the bay window overlooking the street. It had been 8:00am before he had finally emerged from the cocoon of that corner, roused by a passing truck, a thunderous rattle of windowpanes, turning the beasts of the night into the harmless pets of the day.

Why had he been so stupid last night? Stretching his folded limbs, prickling as the blood flow returned to his forearms and calves, he wondered if she would have stayed all night in the corner of her room, or whether she would have seen sense, as he had failed to?

Finally, the pull of Carmichael, and an ever-building curiosity got the better of him and he played the voicemail.

***

When the train disgorged onto the platform at Ealing Broadway, Carmichael raised his eyes to the horizon just below the crenelated fringe of the canopy. What was he hoping to see? A pall of dense smoke carrying debris high into the air? But the sky was a blanket of ink-wash grey, plain, unexciting. Hastily skipping through the gates, he thought back to the previous evening, as Carol had more or less dragged him in the opposite direction. He dipped in between a small huddle of travellers, using them as cover. Within fifteen minutes, he had circuitously navigated his way to Cordon Street and was approaching the Plough & Harrow, it's fate still being aired on the morning news in the cafes along the way, a sombre veil of tragedy hanging over the scene in front of him.

281

The ever-present crowd had been corralled onto the opposite pavement, squinting in morbid curiosity through trees on the green to get a better view, voices whispering in fleeting concern. Cafe owners rubbed their hands at the unexpected windfall, carved from someone else's misfortune. Carmichael jostled his way through and was soon up against the green and blue tape and, pulling the cap lower over his face, he surveyed the scene. Most of the pumps had been discharged, a solitary engine alongside the building, and a couple of weary firefighters were winding hoses and collecting cones. At street level the building was almost untouched, but the first floor was a gutted, blackened carcass, skeletal rafters reaching skyward, as if burnt by the stark morning sunshine. A single police car sat behind the engine, the officers keeping warm inside chattering on radios and an unlucky beat copper stood uncomfortably in the taped doorway awaiting further instructions.

And then it was dark, there were flashes of light and crashes of windows and a stern voice was ordering him back, a hand on his chest, and the fisheye face with the helmet peering at him. He sensed the cold and the water splashing at his feet, and the dread, the shouted orders, the organised chaos and an overwhelming feeling of panic. He felt a strong urge to flee countered by the pressure on his arm pushing him forward, as the voice in his head scratched at his consciousness. *Now she has to die and he will go with her.* He squinted his eyes and the day returned, ominous and quiet. Reflexively, he reached up to his bicep and winced, the flesh tender and bruised.

How could the dreams be so lucid? This was not some distorted *deja vu* image replayed the instant it was created. He was replaying the scene from six or more hours ago. The day had become night and embers were alive with flame. He looked around for something tangible to cling to; something real, like a lamppost, cold and steely against his hand, but there was nothing. The crowd around him seemed to wash away leaving him utterly exposed, utterly bewildered.

He had been there as the fire raged.

***

One hundred yards away, Scott Daley carefully scanned the same panorama but his focus was more urgent. Within the perimeter, he backed away under the trees on the Green, to see but not be seen. He had lost sight of Corby, who was mingling on the opposite side of the road, perhaps the only person not gawping past Daley at the remains of the Plough.

Sitting at his desk, earlier, wallowing in his feelings of self-pity and self-accusation, he had heard the bark - more a sharp yelp, from Monaghan's desk. At first he had thought the cry was one of pain, from a paper cut or a stubbed toe, but that changed as the other miserable wretches who inhabited the office on a weekend had all risen and gathered around the desk. Wiping his eyes, Daley had followed them, muscling his way through to the front to see eight neat lines of text regularly scrolling, updating the location of the signal they had picked up.

"Sir, It's Carmichael. He just switched on his phone. It went dead for a while but now it's come back on line, like he went through a tunnel or something."

"Where is he now?"

Taylor's finger hovered over one line of text. "Give or take a hundred yards, Ealing Broadway Tube, Gov. Look how much stronger this signal is than..."

But Daley was already six paces away towards the doors, Corby in hot pursuit, before the sentence had trailed off. The two had more or less stolen a pool Insignia and raced across the Borough. There could be only one destination for Andrew Carmichael on that particular morning.

A harsh, acrid odour was drifting on the breeze and Daley rubbed the irritation from his nose, a ring tone played in his ear. Whetstone would be finding a quiet place to take the call without being overheard by the squalid pack of Journo-vultures that had descended on Ealing. Finally she picked up.

"Gov?"

"Any news yet, Deb?"

"No change, Sir. It's a waiting game. Byrne has woken up but he is out of it most of the time."

"What about the woman, Shelley? How's she doing?"

"Touch and go. They don't rate her chances at the moment. They are giving her a blood transfusion to try and scrub out the chemicals, but the doc says she could be brain damaged or worse."

"Carmichael's on the move. You need to keep an eye on Nugent and Byrne. He's tried it once. If he gets wind that they are still alive, he might try again."

"No sweat, Gov. Brian Wilmott is outside the door." A large uniformed policeman filled the door to ICU as he chatted up a petite nurse who was playing with her hair. "He's a bloody brick shed. There is no way that bastard is getting anywhere near them."

"I have a feeling he's coming back here. Taylor tracked his phone to Ealing Broadway Tube. Corby and I will find him if he's here."

He closed the phone and peered over the crowd for Corby, who had been stopped by a couple and was urgently looking around.

***

The taxi had dropped Alice and Marcus off in Miller Street, a few yards from the intersection with Cordon Street, but a short walk to the corner where the Plough & Harrow stood forlorn against the backdrop of suburban London. Marcus held Alice's hand as if they were welded together. If she were right about Carmichael, then he would not take any chances. He would not risk losing her now.

Looking north they could see the spines of the rafters, exposed and broken. About two thirds of the roof had come down, like some gargantuan monster had bent down and taken a series of tearing bites.

"Let's go over there. We will get a better view." Marcus pointed towards the throng on the opposite side of the road to the Green. "And we won't be quite so obvious doing it."

Alice was looking around anxiously. "Do you think he'll come back this soon?"

It was a good point. A few short hours before, Carmichael would have been fleeing the scene having set the fire. Would he be hunkering down, letting the dust settle, planning his next move, or be back at the scene savouring his last? Marcus had known Carmichael for a long time. He would need to be certain that everything had gone to plan. He also knew that Carmichael would be shrewd enough to wait for the cover of the morning crowds. Too early and they would not have awoken to the drama in their corner of the Capital; too late and they would have lost interest and dispersed.

Staying close, Alice followed Marcus north along the row of shops, pausing briefly to purchase take-out coffee, each aware that they had skipped breakfast, but only she aware that the bread in the fridge was green. If Carmichael really were looking for her, she would need to make it difficult for him to recognise her. She had grabbed an old woolly Aztec flapped hat and jammed it on her head. She had kicked Marcus really hard when he had laughed. But a similar reaction from the teenage *barista* inclined her to think she had been too hard on him. She envisioned how she thought she should look - foxy, with a hint of playfulness and a dash of indefinable allure. Instead, the hat made her look like an undercooked bun with multi-coloured icing and a furry grey cherry flopping about on top. It also looked like she had two furry testicles growing out of her throat. Not exactly a good look for a thirty-something embarking on a new relationship. But the hat was staying on.

Marcus nudged her, and pointed, coffee geysering from the tiny hole in the travel lid.

"There. That guy standing on the corner. I'm sure that's the copper who came and spoke to me the other day."

"Ok. So *they* think he's here too," replied Alice. On tiptoe, she scanned the cobbled layer of bobbing heads, wishing she had a massive fairground hammer to hit each in turn as it popped up. She had been blessed with her father's *short-arse* gene - shorter than normal, but too tall to shop in the children's department with no VAT. It was no use. All she could see was a line of backs, snotty bawling babies and small children, bored and squabbling. Pulling her collar up and her hat down, she set off up Cordon Street, around the crowd, dragging Marcus behind her, until she stood at the head of the throng with a view of the whole length of the crowd. If Carmichael were there he would surely barge his way to the front.

She sighed and folded her arms. "He's not coming Marcus. Why would he? It's just stupid! Come on. Let's go. I don't like being out in the open." She looped her arm in Marcus' and pulled him back towards Cordon Street.

Lazily, the police constable, whom Marcus had recognised,

turned and was heading off towards the Green. Marcus spun around and held Alice close to him, shielding both of their faces from his scouring gaze. But he was heading back to the group of officials who were huddling beneath the trees on the Green. Maybe the Police had given up searching too, at least for now. Then, someone caught Marcus' eye. He squinted harder at the tall figure, a navy blue beanie hat pulled forwards shielding his eyes, a large, ill-fitting Worsted overcoat, collar up around his head. The man was standing about a third of the way along the line of barriers, gazing up at the pub, motionless in a sea of random activity.

He nudged Alice. "Look. Over there - don't turn round! He's there. I am sure it's him."

Alice, rather enjoying the warmth of Marcus' chest, gently craned her head around until she could see the man. Beneath the hat were the brown laser eyes and hard defined chin of Drew Carmichael. She felt her heart leap. She squeezed the arm she was holding a little tighter. "What are we going to do now?"

"Shit! I don't know! I hadn't got this far with my planning."

"Well, I'm not hanging around out in the open. He could look towards us at any moment." She slowly tugged Marcus behind the line of the crowd.

"OK - OK" Marcus put a hand to his forehead and thought hard. "Right. Let's circle back behind him, the way we came. You go back in the coffee shop and chat up that lovely boy, whilst I will go and grab hold of him and shout like fuck at the policeman."

"Don't be stupid, Marcus. He'll beat you to a pulp. He's a murderer, for God's sake." Alice gave Marcus an exasperated look and shook her head in disbelief.

"What, in broad daylight? I think not! Drew plans which way his socks are arranged in a drawer. Anyway what would you rather have, Carmichael coming after you, or me with a slight bruise on my nose?"

"Well, if you put it like that - neither! Why don't we just shout and point."

"Because he will run away."

Just then a figure loomed over the pair and they turned to see the policeman regarding them suspiciously.

286

"It's Dr Balfour, isn't it? DC Mike Corby. We met yesterday. Can I ask you what you're doing here this morning?"

Just after Marcus' mouth had flapped open, but before he could insert his foot into it, Alice piped up.

"Mike, mate - over there. Blue hat, dark coat. That's Drew Carmichael. We are not the droids you are looking for."

"Nice Star Wars reference, love!" Marcus beamed warmly at her, as Corby turned on his heel and started to scan down the line of pedestrian's, alighting on the figure in question. Fishing his phone out, he hit the shortcut for Daley's number and stared across the Green to see the senior officer looking his way and putting the phone to his ear.

"Gov. He's here. About level with the shoe shop. Blue hat, Dark coat. I am going round the back. Give me a minute and then you come at him from the front...Who? Oh, Dr Balfour and...?"

"Alice Bown." She beamed him a smile.

For a short moment, Corby's expression turned quizzical. "And *Alice Bown*, apparently...yes. I will."

"Miss Bown. You wouldn't believe how hard we have been looking for you. Don't you ever fill in Change of Address forms? Anyway, you stay here. My Inspector wants a word with you later."

Clamping his phone to his ear, he headed off in the direction of the crowds.

***

Daley, his phone against his ear, edged out towards the line of barriers, keeping one eye on the tall man and the other on Corby, his breath panting in Daley's earpiece. Apathy triumphing over ghoulish curiosity, the crowd was thinning, but Carmichael was motionless, unaware, staring at the burnt out shell of the pub, transfixed, either by the terrible thing he had done or the knowledge that he had failed. Daley turned away until Carmichael, now less than ten yards away, was just visible out of the corner of his eye, the phone and his arm affording a small degree of cover. Beyond him the three or four people were murmuring to themselves, as Corby edged his way around them.

"When you are, Sir..." Daley nodded and the two men

pocketed their phones.

There is a strange and much ridiculed phenomenon, known as scopaesthesia. An idea coined at the start of the twentieth century, likened to the extra-sensory ability of some animals to sense a predator watching them, such an ability making the difference between fight or flight or even life or death. Corby himself was a true believer in scopaesthesia, not because he was a whack-job who believed in voodoo mind-shit, as his girlfriend called it, but because he had seen the phenomenon in action. Walking through a shopping centre, catching sight of a small child who then promptly tumbles to the floor, or watching the buttocks of a particularly well-upholstered woman, who then scratches the back of her neck before looking around. It had happened to him countless times, so he guessed that there must be something in it.

So it was with Carmichael. Utterly transfixed until the two men were in position, and then, dragged from his trance, his eyes fell on Daley and in a spark of recognition, a look of panic burst across his face. Daley vaulted the barrier and launched himself at Carmichael, who swung around to meet the challenging eyes of Mike Corby, arms raised. Carmichael lowered his head and ran directly at the Constable who grabbed at the flapping jacket, forcing the former into a comical slow-motion action as the coat dragged him back, and then as the sleeves slipped free of his arms Carmichael was once more at full pelt, with the two men following him. Heading up Cordon Street, he immediately veered right down an alleyway, dodging and weaving through the mobile chicane of surprised pedestrians. And then he was gone. Daley followed Corby, scarcely able to keep up with the younger man, under the car park ramp, until they reached a turning towards the rear behind the shops. Out of the corner of his eye he caught the glimpse of a shadow to the left and both men set off after their quarry, twisting right to follow the path down the side of the Mall building. Their footsteps resounding of the hard red brick of the walls, the two men came to a halt as a street of houses opened up to their right. Daley looked ahead. A group of shoppers filled the breadth of the path, deep in conversation, oblivious to the chase. Carmichael had not gone that way. His legs aching and his chest threatening to burst, Daley indicated down the street and Corby took off at an undaunted pace, dodging left and right, checking gateways and drives, while the senior officer crouched on his haunches and struggled to re-oxygenate his protesting muscles.

After five minutes, the spots had begun to clear from his vision, and Daley felt almost normal again. Corby was walking back dejectedly, raising his arms at his side in abject frustration. Carmichael was nowhere to be seen. Dispirited, the two men trudged back to the Green with Corby apologetic and Daley seething with anger at the seemingly endless good fortune Carmichael possessed when it came to Police. And to add insult to injury, the spot on which Corby had ordered Marcus Balfour and Alice Bown to remain was now empty.

Behind the dwarf hedges that bordered the barren walls of the Broadway Shopping Centre, Carmichael screwed up his eyes and contracted every muscle, assuming the smallest possible profile. It had been a spur of the moment decision to leap behind the hedge, hoping upon hope that he would fall through and be hidden. Luckily for him, the hedge was a foot clear of the wall. Unluckily, the space had been used as a litter bin and, he suspected, a cat's lavatory. Stifling the urge to retch, he peered through the lower limbs of the bushes as the two policemen slowed to a halt. For five agonising minutes, the legs of the one copper paced a few yards each way in front of him, and he fought to slow his breathing. Then the younger one returned, and they stood together for a brief moment. Carmichael shut his eyes and prayed that they would piss off. Which, in a hail of *shits* and *buggers*, they eventually did.

Chapter 31

Finn Byrne lay in the bed and stared at the electricity conduit on the ceiling, struggling to recall what day it was. The ceiling was a pale cream desert, devoid of any feature, except the conduit. For the umpteenth time, he traced it's track ferrying power across the vast unadorned voids to the oases that were the light fittings, like staging posts on a caravan trail of electricity across the magnolia desert. To the south of the caravan trail, a lonely fire sensor sat in it's own acreage of nothing, idly flashing a tiny beacon of red, waving a shirt in the hopes of a passing plane. But never would the beacon be seen from the caravan trail; it just continued it's solitary existence waving the red shirt every 42 seconds. Alexander Selkirk, the real-life Robinson Crusoe, over four years marooned on the Juan Fernandez Islands, just 300 or so kilometres from Chile, yet a million miles distant as he waved his shirt to the empty horizon. Just as in the next room, the sonorous beep from Shelley's heart monitor continued it's lonely existence, separated by a flimsy aluminium and Perspex wall that could have been a million miles thick.

He was having trouble concentrating. It was Friday, no Saturday. He had been out with the lads and when he came back... Once more the memory surfaced, his hands stung; once more he suppressed it before the tears welled. Had he been out for long? Wednesday, Thursday, June or November. Time was an illusion, in this desert. It could have been ten minutes or ten years. With no windows and no clock, just endless magnolia, how could he know? Maybe he should use the spoon that he struggled to hold through these damn plastic gloves and mark the bed-head, once for every check-up from the dumpy nurse, two an hour, forty-eight a day, three hundred and thirty-six a week, one thousand four hundred and seventy two a year. *How are we today?* We? He had no interest how she was and he certainly didn't care about himself. In two part harmony the beep from his own monitor counterpointed a quieter, more concerned beep from the next room. Through the panelling between them he could hear the faint murmuring of voices, a world beyond that in which he was marooned, a world with it's back to him as he waved his shirt. He could see hazy figures in pale blue and white drifting like spectres behind the frosted panel. As long as the beep continued there was hope.

Yet, in the backwater away from the trade routes, there was the occasional visitor. The tired policewoman with the kindly eyes. So young, her sympathetic smile was warm yet pained, the troubles of the world etched on her face. She had lain her hand on his shoulder and the sorrow in her eyes was genuine and heartfelt. She had sat beside the bed and spoken with him, her kindly eyes ignoring professional detachment, moistening. And she had snatched half an hour, eyes closed, the cares draining away leaving a beautiful woman that rarely had a chance to shine. And when she spoke, her voice, laden with concern, had brought back the memory of the bar, a plate of ham sandwiches and Shelley's hand in his.

She had asked him who might do such a thing, had he any enemies, anyone he had fallen out with? For a moment, his mind wandered along the trails and tracks on the ceiling above, lost in limbo, cloistered from the grief and pain that he would need to face in the real world, but then the sonorous beep had broken through and the pain had ripped at his hands, and he had told her everything. As she scribbled, he told of the scheme that Carmichael was running; some stock market scam with which they would all get rich quick. He told her reluctantly of the money that they had loaned to Carmichael and of the extra money that Shelley had raised. And he had told her of the previous morning, how he had burst into Carmichael's office full of bravado and demanded the return of what was rightfully his. How there and then he had probably signed Shelley's death warrant with his own anger.

But the one secret he did not tell.

The large amorphous mass of black, frosted and indistinct, like a whale beneath the water, moved and bobbed outside the door. The policewoman had given it a name, said it would always be there and he would be safe. But the room felt empty and distant from the reality. He regretted his foolishness. Did he believe that Carmichael would just swan into the Plough & Harrow with a brown bag full of readies? That he would roll over and play dead? Dead. The irony hanging in the air wrote itself large on the plain tundra above. Carmichael would be the last to die, whilst all around him, his friends paid the price for crossing him.

From somewhere a million miles away, the world outside the room grew ominous and dreadful, as he realised there was just one beep and from the next room, a solid insistent whine and the murmuring voices became more urgent.

Finn Byrne clasped the bagged hands across his eyes and wept like he had never wept before.

Chapter 32

"Do you think we are going to be in trouble now?"

Marcus paused his demolition of a boxful of Southern Fried Chicken. He looked obliquely over at Alice sitting cross-legged on the carpet, the Aztec hat still rammed down over her head, her woollen testicles bobbing frantically with each mouthful.

"Nah! Wouldn't have thought so. They might be a bit tetchy, but hey, we weren't under arrest or anything."

"Still, perhaps we should have hung around out of courtesy or something."

"Not bloody likely. I am much more scared of Drew Carmichael than I am of some plod. Anyway, they couldn't catch a cold. Did you see that older one's face? Like a frigging beetroot."

"Come on, Marcus. Be sensible. You know what I mean. If he's coming for me, surely it would have been better to speak to the Police, maybe get protection or something." She sucked noisily on a straw.

"No Alice. Being sensible is keeping our heads down. What did you expect the Police to do if we had stayed around? Give you a safe house? Mount an armed guard outside? No, we would have spent most of the weekend in an interview room and they would become fixated with why we were there in the first place. Then, they would have let us go and maybe put a car at the end of the road. You heard what that Constable said. Not even the Police know where you live. Right now the best place for both of us is somewhere no-one can find us."

"They just haven't looked in the right place. I pay my electricity on a card and I have a TV licence - oh, no, that's still at my old address - but I *do* get post every now and then, so someone knows where I live."

"What about work? Did you tell them you have moved?"

"'Course I did! I am not stupid. They have to know because I get my payslip posted here every month. So there's another one. See, I am not some sort of recluse. I just don't have any reason to shout it from the rooftops."

"And that story you told me, about the tramp in 1997. What proof have you got of that?"

Alice placed her cardboard drinks container precariously between her crossed legs and stretched out to fetch the laptop bag from under the television stand. Opening the lid, the screen flashed alive with the text she had been reading the evening before. Marcus patted the sofa beside him and together they scrolled through the notes from a lifetime ago, the Murder Book and the killing, the night the fantasies became real and a lifetime of secrecy and deceit had begun. The night that everything changed.

Alice closed the lid of the laptop and the room fell quiet, each lost in their own thoughts. Finally Marcus took up a chicken thigh and proffered it.

"How did you live with a secret like *that* all this time?"

She took the chicken thigh and shrugged. "Over time it sort of drifted away like a bad dream, like it had happened to someone else. Eventually, it just slipped from my mind. After all, it was their secret, not mine. I was just a bystander. Since I reread these notes yesterday, a whole load of bad memories have come back. I remember waking up the next morning. I'd not set my alarm and halls were quiet. Everyone had gone to lectures, or to the library, or even just into town. I was still in my clothes and they smelt of vomit. I let Chris down Marcus. I should have dragged him away, even forced Guy to drag him away. Instead we left him there to face it by himself. I never saw him again after that, not at the Monday Club anyway, and soon he was gone, dropped out or something."

"What about the rest of them, Dawn, Rachel, Shelley?" Marcus was rapt, transfixed by her eyes, round and vulnerable. He reached around her shoulders, and she fell into the crook of his arm, linking her hand with his.

"I could have dreamed the whole thing. It was as if it had never happened. The Monday Club was a subdued affair. I remember we all drank a little too much for a couple of months after that, but a set of shutters came down and no-one mentioned it again. I don't think Drew knew I was even there. He never mentioned it. It was only a week or so later that the girls found out, and by then the veil of silence had descended.

"But why me, Alice? Why, all of a sudden did you freeze me

out? I could have helped you to sort things out. Why did you drop me?"

She gazed up at him earnestly. "It was Drew Carmichael, Marcus. After that, the mild dislike turned to a deep abhorrence, and you and he came as a package. At first, I found it scary knowing he was on the same campus. Every time I saw those cold eyes, I wanted to scratch them out, throw acid in them, so that when I went to sleep at night I would not see that callous stare, and be dragged back into that hideous nightmare. Unfortunately, you were like his shadow. Where he went, you went, and whilst you two stayed friends, you and I were never going to be together."

Marcus recalled that morning, almost exactly fifteen years ago, how she had pushed past him on the library stair, tears streaming down both their faces, how he had feigned complacency yet cried into his pillow for a week, how like her, he had compartmentalised his life to avoid confronting those feelings again.

She laid her head on his shoulder and her arms held him tight. "Marcus, I know I have been stupid. I have missed you so much for so long. How can you ever forgive me?"

He encircled her in his arms and tenderly kissed her forehead. "There is absolutely nothing to forgive. Just, please, never do it again. I couldn't stand to lose you again. I promise, Carmichael is gone. I wont ever speak to him again. Just promise you won't leave me, ever?"

"I think that can be arranged!" She squeezed his hand and smiled."

"But first, we have to make sure that Carmichael never finds *you* and the only way to do that is to tell the Police everything about the Book. To put them on the right trail and divert the attention away from us. Then we are going leave here until the heat dies down. Just go somewhere far away, somewhere he will never find us, at least not before the Police have found him."

"Marcus! I can't just go away! What about work? I can't just take a holiday whenever I want."

"In theory, nor can I but you know what? Carmichael has a phrase for that - *Fuck 'em, Fuck 'em all!*"

It was almost 4:00pm before Carmichael finally returned to Carol's front door, such was the convoluted route he had used to get there. He had walked nearly five times the distance necessary. Despite attempts to remove the suspicious smear on his sleeve, it had persisted, so he had nipped into Boots to buy a cheap cologne which, liberally doused, had proved more offensive than the cat poo. The girl in *Next* had sniffed the air around her, discomfited by the aroma, and his purchase of a new hooded overcoat had taken place at arms length. But she was probably a dyke and like that with all the customers. Carmichael had noted the features, the small pointed rather angular nose, the prominent jawbone and tied back lank brown hair, and saggy breasts. Not even the most desperate flap-queen would go for such a scrawny specimen of womanhood.

Letting himself in, he loosed a sigh of relief. The house was still and quiet. Maybe Carol's R *and* R had lasted longer than she had anticipated? He was both relieved and jealous, thinking of her having a good time behind his back. A good time which he had yet to give her. If he didn't deliver on soon, she might abandon him to his fate. He hung the reeking jacket in the hall and chucked the key into the drawer from whence it came, and the overpowering odour of cat crap, which had fermented nicely in the controlled environment of body heat, assaulted his nostrils. So he trotted upstairs and was soon feeling the welcome needles of warm water washing away the malodorous stench. As the last guttural noises echoed from the draining bath, he felt through the shower curtain to the towel rail. Frustrated, he reached further, his foot slipping on the soapy water.

"It's not there, pet."

His heart almost leapt from his naked dripping chest and did a lap of the small bathroom. Her voice was flat, clipped, menacing, showing no compassion. He wondered if she knew he had been out, if she had smelt the treasonous cat crap?

"Carol! When did you get back? Thank goodness, I was starting to worry. I got stir crazy, thought I would take a shower, you know, freshen up."

"Don't lie to me Drew. I was back by one o'clock and you were gone. I've been sitting here ever since waiting for you, and when I saw the news, your face plastered all over it. I knew you had directly disobeyed me. What were you thinking?"

She drew back the curtain, the rings pinging against the chrome plated track and, like the lies he fed her, he was exposed. She was standing not two feet away, arms folded holding his towel, and as she looked at his manhood she let out a small chuckle and uttered two words guaranteed to cut any man to size.

"Ah, bless!" She cast him the towel and smirked. "Next time, might pay to have the water warmer, eh, little guy?" And with that she turned and the bathroom door slammed behind her.

In the living room, the TV had ceased its relentless regurgitation of the pub fire and was now concentrating on a myriad men who earned obscene amounts of money kicking a ball about. She was sitting in a chair. Her legs were crossed and her face was stern and solid.

"Sit down. We need to have a little chat." She nodded towards the sofa opposite. Not a request but a demand.

"Look, no harm done. I just needed some fresh air. By the way nice hair." He cursed himself for failing to offer the compliment earlier, especially given how pissed off she seemed to be. He shared the natural ambivalence of most men to the parallel universe of women, of hair and make-up and clothes, of Louis Vuitton and Chanel. The concrete stare she returned told him she didn't give a toss about the hair. Reaching down she took up a remote and clicked a button, the footballers were replaced by a jerky camera, which tracked along a smouldering shell before suddenly sweeping right and catching a brawl between three men in the thinning crowd of onlookers, and then cutting to a smiling well shaven face, whilst all the while, a red scroller repeated the phrase 'Pub fire suspect spotted in Ealing'.

"Last night, this was a fire. This morning, it was arson by person or persons unknown. Now, thanks to your *gallivanting*, it's a manhunt and you're the prime suspect in a murder investigation! What on Earth were you thinking, Drew?"

"Come off it, Carol, don't overreact. So I went to see what had happened, you know, my friends' misfortune, showing my face. Big deal! By the looks of it so had half of West London."

"But you did show your *actual* face! You were very nearly

caught." She replayed the recording on loop. "For goodness sake, But for my husband's coat they would have grabbed you for certain!"

Drew was affronted by her lack of faith in him. "No way! I saw them coming. That inspector guy - Dimly or Dumbly or whatever, he came sidling up, speaking into his phone, like I wouldn't notice. Mind you, had to do a double swerve to beat the younger one. He was a bit tasty. They have to get up a lot earlier to catch me." Drew marvelled at the athleticism he had shown.

"You arrogant bastard. You have absolutely no concern for anyone but yourself, have you?"

"Charity begins at home, love, and for me that's where it stays. You've got to look after number one in this life."

"Do you realise what is happening here?" Her voice was raised, high pitched and frantic, and immediately he regretted the callous remark. "Do you *really* understand? You are in the frame for three separate murders and now, after that stunt today, you are in line for a fourth, maybe even a fifth. Listen!" She pressed a key on the remote and the TV came off mute.

"...the front room of the living area above the popular local restaurant, where two people were known to be staying. There are as yet unconfirmed reports that this has resulted in one fatality. We'll bring you more as soon as we get it. Meanwhile Police are asking for help in tracing Andrew Carmichael, a Richmond man who works locally and who is wanted for questioning in connection with the fire, and with a string of murders in the area over the last few days. It is believed Carmichael is on the run following the discovery that he had been embezzling thousands of...the front room of the living area..." Drew sat and listened as the tape looped and a lump knotted in his stomach.

"Jesus Christ! How did they know about the money? I thought you said the accounts were tighter than a ducks bum? You said it would take them ages to find anything."

Carol testily clicked the mute button. "I did! There is no way they found out from me. Why would I tell them? Some of that money is mine. You owe me Drew." She pressed the button and the footballers reappeared on the TV, and then, with another press, they vanished into blackness. "Why on Earth did you go

298

back? You must have known they would be watching the place. How could you be so stupid? Isn't it enough that you torched it in the first place?"

Again his mind was consumed with swirling indistinct images and the pungent odour of burning rubber bit the back of his throat. He was looking down at the closed door of the bedroom. He could feel the heat on his face and the gloved hand turning the key, and the billowing black as he floated down the stairs and out through the gate. He looked at the flickering flames in the window, heard the exploding glass and saw the hazy black shapes against the gate. The fish-eyed man was peering and the lights were flashing, voices were shouting and blue and white tape fluttered in the breeze.

He sank back into the sofa. Bombarded by the vivid images, he struggled to understand their significance, how could they be so real? But then he saw Guy once more, the eyes staring through the visor, the head bent and twisted. Why was he seeing these crazy visions, events that he could not possibly have witnessed first hand? He stumbled over his words, as the evocations threw up mental roots for his brain to stumble over.

"I didn't torch the pub. How could I have done? I was here, surely?" But how else could the images be in his head if not from last night? He looked across at the sombre, slightly puzzled face, starkly illuminated by the orange glare of the table lamp. She commanded him to stay where he was, returning moments later with a bulging black polythene bag. Her mouth was turned down, her eyes round and questioning.

"These were in the dustbin out the back here. I fished them out this afternoon when I put the rubbish out." Tearing at the plastic, she disgorged the contents at his feet. Immediately, the stench of petrol and burnt rubber assailed his nostrils and, once more, images fluttered through his mind, the limp, lifeless form of Shelley Nugent, the key glinting gold as it was cast down the corridor. He stared up at the silhouetted figure towering over him, his breath catching in his throat and his skin growing cold beneath the meagre sweater he had thrown on after his shower.

"Before you say anything, think carefully. What are the odds of the arsonist travelling all the way over here and picking my bin to drop his clothes in?"

Shards of disconnected memories splintered his mind as he

struggled to piece them together, like pages torn from a book and cast into a billowing breeze, disordered and meaningless.

"I don't think there is any doubt that you torched that pub, Drew, do you?" She loosed the tattered plastic bag and it fluttered to the floor, as the last vestiges of resistance fell from his confused, tired mind. He leaned forward, his head in his hands, as if to shut out a world that continued its assault on him.

This must be some form of insanity. He had been harbouring these demons and just not known of their existence, orchestrating a double life of which he had no conscious knowledge. How could it be that the mind of Drew Carmichael could hold two such different individuals; the normal, chauvinistic, arrogant Drew, self assured and brash, and the darker more sinister monster that would stop at nothing to keep the secrets buried? How many other people had the Hyde within him killed? Utterly spent, he lay back on the sofa and closed his eyes, the newsreel playing in his head as he began to sob.

She sat back down on the chair opposite and leaned forwards resting her elbows on her knees.

"I don't know what's going on in that head of yours but it's scaring me and I have to stop it before it takes us both down. You can't leave this house again. The police can't trace you back here. And most of all, I have to sort the money out once and for all before they trace it back to me. I will not have you jeopardising everything I have worked for all this time."

As she left the living room, she reached into her bag, pulled out her mobile and dialled a number stored in the memory.

***

Marcus Balfour stared at the envelope and the five discrete lines of text scrawled on it, the numbers and letters, the précised lines of instruction, uneven and spidery but distinct enough for him to decipher. His hands were shaking, which hadn't helped. Scrunching the phone between his shoulder and ear as he wrote had been difficult, but he had asked the caller to repeat the lines and he was sure he had written them down correctly.

Pocketing the phone, he raced upstairs, to his small study, a rather grand description for an economy computer table, a director's chair and a creaking steam-driven laptop. Quickly, he transcribed the notes onto a separate piece of paper, checked and re-checked them. There could be no mistakes. The tremors in his hands had become much worse as he switched on the laptop. Knowing it would take it's time stretching and yawning before being capable of anything useful, he moved to the front bedroom and retrieved a bottle of scotch that had been nestling at the bottom of the wardrobe since Christmas. He was not a scotch drinker, so he had a choice and decided that the one with the Pheasant on it would do just as well as any. Returning to the computer, he unscrewed the top of the bottle and took an unwisely large slug, which tore at his throat and forced a death rattle the like of which not even his most infirm patients would issue. Through watering eyes, he saw that the bright blue screen had now appeared and the laptop was busily and laboriously drawing each icon on the screen. He also realised his hands had stopped shaking. Maybe he could get a taste for whisky.

The secret of concealment of information, Drew had once tediously told him over a lunchtime pint, comes in three basic principles.

Principle One is obfuscation. Concealment through confusion. If the telephone number does not appear to be a telephone number, then anyone viewing is less likely to consider it one. You could reverse the order of the letters, such that *a* becomes *z*, *b* becomes *y* and so on. The same with numerals. *0* becomes *9*, *1* becomes *8* and so forth. For example, *abc123* becomes *zyx987*. *drewcarmichael* is represented by *wlvdxzinrxszvo*. Of course, the government would use a more complex coding system, but they teach teenagers to crack codes these days. K.I.S.S. As Drew had said - *Keep It Simple and Stupid.*

The Second Principle is not to try too hard. Information hidden too deeply is more difficult to retrieve in a crisis. For example, Drew had droned, consider Samuel Pepys. To protect them from the Great Fire of London, Pepys had famously buried his cheeses in his garden. What would have happened if the fire had consumed a nearby building and the resultant tumbling debris had made the location of the cheeses unreachable, or even unrecognisable? A million squirrels looking for a million acorns buried last autumn.

And, of course, the Third Principle, and probably the most important. Tell no-one. This principle had caused Marcus the most grief over the last seventy-two hours. Since Carmichael had effectively gifted him the Fund, he had been troubled by the third principle. He could see the money, almost touch it but he had no idea how to get hold of it. Of course, his first approach had been to log on to the Cayman Bank's website, but the ubiquitous username and password prompt had stopped him dead. So he had resorted to the first principle but after an hour of thinking and a complete shift musing over potential credentials that Carmichael may have used, he had drawn a blank. It had seemed that the money would remain tantalisingly close yet out of reach, aside from Drew telling him the details, which was as unlikely as Marcus receiving an unexpected windfall from a hitherto unknown benefactor.

Which, in a strange way, was exactly what had happened.

The voice was not one he had recognised, although it had some slight familiarity to it, which the caller immediately crystallised.

"My name is Carol Hughes. I work with Andrew Carmichael. I think we met briefly last year when you called in the office?"

"Oh, yes." Marcus was bemused. It had been a brief encounter waiting for Drew to finish up at the end if the day. They had spoken for two minutes. Her face was lost in a morass of other faces that had flitted through his mind since. "What can I do for you?"

"Well, really, it's more what we can do for each other, Dr Balfour."

"Go on..."

"Mr Carmichael is in a bit of trouble at the moment. You may have seen the news?"

"No, er, I have been busy today," he lied.

"No problem. I suggest you check the BBC News tonight. Anyway, I am sure you know there is a large amount of money, which right now, he seems to have signed over to you? Well, some of that money is mine, so I have a little proposition for you. Are you open to that?"

"O-kay? Fire away." Marcus winced at the pun, bearing in mind he was supposedly oblivious to the day's events.

"To speak frankly, Dr Balfour, between you and me, I think it is a forgone conclusion that Drew Carmichael is going to spend the rest of his life in prison. If that happens, you will spend the rest of *your* life staring at a bank account full of money which you can't get hold of. As you know I work, or rather by now, *worked,* with Mr Carmichael and I can help you to access the money, to transfer it elsewhere, to spend it and enjoy the life you have always promised yourself."

Marcus' heart had leapt to his throat and it was at this moment that his hand had started to shake, the handset frapping against his ear. As his hand did the shimmy, he took a deep breath and kept his tone as level as possible.

"I'm listening."

"I have the account number of the bank account and the username to sign into the account on the web portal. I have these memorised. But what I don't have is the password to the web portal."

And again, the pile of cash, like the final scenes from *The Italian Job,* slid away as he reached out. Would anyone have a great idea this time? Stemming the disappointment, he resolved to hear her out.

"Nor do I, Mrs Hughes, or is it Miss?"

"Call me Carol. I haven't been Mrs anything for a long time, pet. Makes me sound ancient." Her tone was matter-of-fact. He'd heard it a million times from the senior nurse on his ward.

"Sorry, er, Carol. Nor do I. Drew gave me no details except the account number on a statement."

"But you do. You just don't know it yet. Has Mr Carmichael ever told you about his Principles of Concealment?"

"Oh, yes, frequently, incessantly amongst other favourite homilies of his."

"Hmm, yes, he does go on a little now and again. You remember Principle one. That of obfuscation."

"Yes. A simple substitution code based around changing the order of letters or numbers?"

"That's the one. Well, it's taken me some time but I believe I have found the string of letters and numbers and I am willing to share them with you. It was on a piece of paper in his wallet. Don't ask me how I got it."

"Pardon me for asking, but if you have the password details, surely you could just as easily cut me out and empty the account yourself?" He heard her quietly laugh to herself and wondered if he had gone too far. "Sorry for being rude but, well, it seems really generous?"

"Dr Balfour - Marcus. I have spent two years hearing how Drew speaks about you, how little regard he has for you. The continual put downs and derisive comments. And if he says those sorts of things behind your back, Heaven alone knows what he must say to your face. But you have always stood by him. The one thing that always amazes me about Drew is his overall capacity for disregard of people, even in the face of their absolute loyalty to him. I am the fortunate one because he still needs me. He has yet to descend to the levels of cruelty which he has meted out to you all these years."

"Oh, I wouldn't go that far..."

"There it is again! Absolute loyalty, even in the face of overwhelming evidence to the contrary. He has stolen vast amounts of money from people, from his friends, from you, and now worse, he is killing, time after time, just to protect this sordid Fund of his. Don't you think it's time he got his comeuppance?"

He could not disagree. It was all true, even the idea of killing was gaining more veracity by the second. Why was he running if he had nothing to hide? And yes, Carmichael had been a complete bastard all of these years and, yes, Marcus' eyes had been opened over the last few days. What would it serve now to roll over once more and play dead? Maybe this wiggle room was leeway enough for the worm to turn?

"OK, so you have sympathy for all us poor bastards that enjoy the company of Drew Carmichael but that doesn't fully answer the question. Carol, what is *your* angle? I can tell by your voice that you're a good person, but there is an obscene amount of cash here. Surely, if you have all of the required information, all of the passwords, you could just take the lot."

"You remember that whole audit thing that Drew spoke about a month or so back?"

"Yes, but didn't that all blow over?"

"Oh yes but only because I helped him hide the bodies, figuratively speaking. If it weren't for me, Drew Carmichael would have been in the Old Bailey by now. So I think I deserve my fair share of the money."

"Which is?"

"At the time, he promised me ten per cent, but I think as you are to benefit so highly, maybe you would be willing to pay for the information I have? Say fifteen per cent?"

Marcus recalled the figure off the statement and did some mental maths. "That's..."

"Two hundred and seventeen thousand five hundred pounds, ignoring any minor increase since I last looked."

"Yes, two hundred and seventeen thousand."

"Five hundred, yes."

"OK, so if I agree to your demand, I ask again why you haven't just taken it all? I would be none the wiser. I can't access the account, so I have no way of knowing the balance, or even if it is still there."

"And that is exactly why you deserve the break, Marcus. Because you, out of all of Drew's so-called friends, are the only one that really cares. You need it most. Also, the codes mean nothing without you. Drew has been particularly devious, always leaving part of the answer obfuscated. The code is a question to which I don't know the answer, but you do. Look. I am offering you the chance to get hold of one million, two hundred and thirty two thousand, five hundred pounds."

"Give or take..." It was late and the Hang Seng was just waking up.

"Yes, give or take. I will give you the code and you can transfer my fifteen per cent into accounts I have set up. Do you agree?"

"How do you know I won't just take all the money myself?"

"I don't, Marcus. I have to trust you. Again, of all of Drew's friends, probably including me, you are the only one I know I can trust."

"And why only fifteen percent? You could have asked for more, much more."

"Two hundred and seventeen thousand is more than enough. I don't get the feeling I will have the time to spend much more than that. You, on the other hand. Your life is just about to begin."

Marcus sensed a huge amount of sadness in Carol's voice, which no amount of money could make right. He sensed her need to make things right, a noble purpose behind the deal, taking only what was necessary, only what was needed. And he sensed a kindness.

Eighty-five per cent of the Fund was still an enormous amount. With it, he and Alice could disappear; make a new life for themselves. One hundred per cent of nothing was of absolutely no use to anyone.

So he acceded to her demands.

"Carol. I promise I will transfer fifteen per cent of the contents of the account to you, as soon as I can access it. You have my absolute word."

Carol Hughes had read out the codes and he had written them onto a discarded envelope. She also dictated the account number and sort code for three accounts into which he should transfer her share. He was to use the reference ANON. On no account, should they be able to trace the money back to either of them. And she told him to take care of the information because whilst Carmichael was about, no-one was safe.

As she rang off, Marcus had stood in the hall, staring at his tired face in the mirror. His hair was unkempt and there were signs of grey appearing at the temples. In that second or two, he had run a gamut of contradictory emotions. Should his loyalty to Carmichael prevent him acting upon this newfound information? Should he take the money and be continually looking over his shoulder for Carmichael? He recalled the fear in Alice's eyes as he had ordered her to bolt her door and answer it to no-one but him.

Now sitting at his computer, he took another, slightly smaller, slug of scotch and opened a new spreadsheet document on his computer. Carefully, he wrote the letters of the alphabet and number 0 - 9, along with their reversed counterparts:

a b c d e f g h i j k l m n o p q r s t u v w x y z

z y x w v u t s r q p o n m l k j i h g f e d c b a

0 1 2 3 4 5 6 7 8 9
9 8 7 6 5 4 3 2 1 0

Then, he transcribed the code which Carol Hughes had dictated, and underneath, methodically used the rudimentary mechanism to decode each letter from his chart:

n z i x f h y z o u l f i h f n n v i 1 4 z x x r w v m g
m a r c u s b a l f o u r s u m m e r 8 5 a c c i d e n t

Carol had asked him to change the details to save Carmichael from himself. So using the same system, he created a new code and access number, as instructed by Carol Hughes.

1 7 8 6 2 1 2 3 4 5
8 2 1 3 7 8 7 6 5 4

With an exclamation, he looked at his handiwork. In the summer of 1985, Marcus and his family were travelling to North Devon for their holiday, when they had come across an overturned car. First on the scene, Marcus' parents had tended to the occupants of the car and marshalled the traffic around the wreck until the emergency services had arrived. The accident had happened at a placed called Loxbeare. Quickly, he protected and saved the file to his desktop.

Next, he googled cloud storage and set up an account using fictitious but easily memorable details and this gave him enough online storage to access the document from anywhere in the world anonymously, another trick of Drew's which would now work against him. Principle two. Don't try too hard to conceal the information. Finally he deleted the local copy of the document and resolved that nobody, not even Alice would find it. Principle three, tell no-one.

Soon, he had accessed the Cayman's Bank site and entered the username and password, gasping as the screen accepted the code and progressed to another similar screen that requested the ten-digit access number. For a moment, he hovered over the enter key, his heart in his mouth, weighing up the enormous repercussions of a single keystroke. There would be no going back, the lure of the huge sum of money might be too great for him to handle. How much had the account grown in the last few days? Would it continue to grow, if Carmichael was arrested and sent to prison? This single key press could determine his whole future. For a moment, he thought about Alice, about the time they had spent together over the last few days and all at once he felt fearful that the simplicity of their relationship would be tainted by the money in the same way that this money had tainted the life of Carmichael, how it had robbed so many others of their life.

But he pressed the key.

CHAPTER 33

The phone in his hip pocket vibrated, breaking Daley's waning concentration on the diagram hovering on his computer screen. It was a Venn diagram he had been working on for want of a breakthrough, trying to crystallise their ideas and bring some focus.

There were two important dynamics - the Monday Club and the money, so he drew two interlocking circles. Central to both was Carmichael, the name circumscribed with a bold red ring, which had almost worn through the sheet. The other players orbited like satellites. First he placed Dawn Silverton. She was central to the case but also instrumental in the whole furore over the money, so she sat in the overlap the two circles. Close in death as in life. Similarly Guy Higson. He had helped hide Carmichael's scheme. Then there was Rachel Jones. She was a member of the Monday Club but did she know about the money? Daley surmised not so she fell in the Monday Club circle alone. Carol Hughes, Office Manager at Barraclough and Leavis. She was a conundrum. Had she too fallen for the charms of Carmichael the cad? It was entirely plausible considering the run-around she had given them this morning. She and Carmichael's boss, Gerald Thornton. Did they know about the money? Daley dropped them both firmly into the Money circle.

Of the rest - Marcus Balfour, Alice Bown and Shelley Nugent - there was no evidence that they were involved in the financial scam, so he placed them in the Monday Club. But what of Finn Byrne? There was a festering hostility towards Carmichael and he had admitted blackmailing Carmichael over the money. He too occupied the centre ground.

Carmichael surveyed a printout of the diagram. There was one more job he needed to do. Deliberately and finally he struck a red cross through the names of Rachel, Dawn, Guy and Shelley, each of the known victims. And Alice Bown? Corby had seen her earlier but she had buggered off. For now, he drew a question mark over her name.

The only other name was Christopher Betts. Entering left

field, Daley could not decide where he should be placed. Did he know about the scam? Was he a member of the Monday Club? Nobody had seen him recently and the team had been unable to trace him. Daley hovered over the name. Cross or question mark?

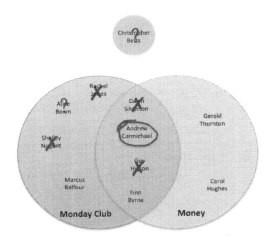

Surveying his handiwork, a pattern became evident. With all of the crosses in the Monday Club circle, it seemed likely that someone was exterminating the Monday Club. Was it to do with the money? If Rachel and Shelley, even Marcus and Alice were not involved in the scam, then clearly not! And all the while Christopher Betts hovered like a cloud over the whole group. Daley felt sure he was the focus of everything. Which camp would he eventually fall into when they caught up with him?

Fishing the phone out he grimaced at the unknown number. He shrugged and for a second considered the cancel button, as the phone vibrated once more. There was no voicemail set up as it was a Met phone and he was expected to answer day or night. Unless this person got bored, it would ring until the battery died. In for a penny...

"Hello."

"Is that Inspector Daley...on the Dawn Silverton case?" It was a female, Daley guessed young with a hint of Home Counties. The voice was faint and quiet, to avoid being overheard. In the background, he could hear the familiar noises of a pub. There was a football match on.

"Who is this?" There was a pause. She was thinking. "This is Daley. Who am I speaking to?"

"I need you to ring me back. This is a pay-as-you-go and I haven't got any credit."

"Fine, but tell me who you are."

"When you ring back. So you know I am genuine I know that Dawn probably had her head cut off and I am number four, or five if you count Rachel." She paused. Daley surveyed the diagram, the ring of satellites orbiting Carmichael. With his pen he inscribed a ring around the only other name that would fit.

"Do you have a pen?" The voice was urgent, business-like.

"No need. It's in my phone now. Look, You need to give me a minute or two." He needed to buy time, enough to mobilise Deb and for Dave and Steve to set up their magic mobile phone location software. And of course time for him to think.

Unless, of course, the name was not on the sheet.

"OK. You have about ten minutes. I don't want anyone to find us, so I am going to switch the phone off now. I'll switch it back on at 7:00pm." Daley glanced at the clock. It was 6:50pm. Hopefully that would be plenty of time.

The line died.

Fumbling through the menus, Daley located the recent calls list and wrote down the number, checking and rechecking each digit. It had to be her, surely?

Standing bolt upright, his chair launching backwards as his legs straightened, Daley peered across at the central pool of desks where Monaghan and Taylor were beavering away at Carmichael's hard drive. That would have to wait. Whetstone was looking up from her paperwork - she had caught the gist of the call. She grabbed a pad and pen and they both hurried over to Monaghan.

"Dave, Steve. Just had a call from Alice Bown. Do we know where she is at the moment?"

"No, Gov. Not since she slipped our net on Saturday." Monaghan paused the software he was running.

"She must pay Council Tax, or have a TV licence, even a

fucking parking ticket, surely?" Daley was irritated.

"The ones we've been allowed access to, all at her old address, Gov, I'm afraid, and she doesn't drive as far as we can tell."

"What about her new address? She must have registered it somewhere, forwarded her mail, something."

"Yes, but we have to find where she has registered it. You know, rental property, no landline. We've called her office but they're shut for the weekend."

"So if she is next on our killer's list, hopefully he won't find her either...?"

"He's had a lot longer to look than we have, Gov." Dave was sympathetic but helpless. The wheels were turning painfully slowly.

"Right. This number..." Daley proffered the yellow page. "...it's a mobile and I think Alice Bown just used it to call me. We need to ring her back on it in...," he checked the clock again, "...six minutes. Deb, you and Mike get in the car. Drive towards Ealing. We'll put a mobile on speaker phone."

Whetstone and Corby headed out, while Monaghan fired up the cell locator application. Once it was up and running, he typed in the cellphone number and clicked find, up came the IMSI and IMEI numbers for the phone, declaring it as a new number, less than three months old. The phone was off and the box below which should a show list of masts with which the phone was communicating remained empty. Taylor used the Met's secure log-on to Ofcom and entered the IMEI and IMSI numbers. The phone had been activated three hours earlier, probably bought that same afternoon from a supermarket. They could do nothing until the phone came on. Daley's mobile once more buzzed. He recognised Whetstone's number and put her speaker; he would use the landline to make the call back to Alice. The room lapsed into an expectant silence. 7:00pm passed and still they waited. Whetstone reported in. She was parked off the Broadway, awaiting directions. At 7:04, the screen in front of Monaghan changed to indicate an SMS baseband conversation; the phone had been reactivated and was looking for text messages, and then a flurry of masts linked to the phone and suddenly the screen was alive. Quickly, Taylor typed in the references to the three strongest base station signals and located

312

them on the map. The phone was less than a mile from the scene of Dawn Silverton's murder, on a housing estate to the north of Hanwell. Daley craned over his shoulder.

"What pubs or bars are there in that area?"

Taylor ran a finger like a cursor over the map.

"The Queen Mary, The Swan and The White Hart. But Gov, its football night, cup replays, they'll be packed!"

"Whetstone. Get over there. You and Corby split up."

"How are we going to recognise her, Sir? There must be hundreds of people on their mobile phone right now."

"Just get over there. We'll worry about that later." Daley sat down in front of the grey boxy Met landline and clicked the 'Speaker' button. A dial tone startled the whole office. Dialling the number he held his breath, hoping she would answer. The phone connected and rang once, twice and then on the third ring...

"Hello."

"It's Daley, who's that?"

"Erm, I'm Alice. Alice Bown."

"Where are you Alice? Can I come and talk to you face to face?" He needed to keep the dialogue slow and deliberate, extend the call.

"I am in a public place. I don't feel safe at the moment so I am staying amongst people where he can't get me."

Whetstone gunned the car along the Broadway, hooked a left through the traffic lights and up Church Road towards Hanwell station.

"We can send someone out, Alice. We can look after you." He knew he was playing for time. How long would she allow the small talk? "Why don't we send a car to your home. Where do you live, Alice?

"No, I think we need to look after ourselves from now on."

"Who's 'we' Alice? Who's there with you?"

"That's not important. Please can you just *listen*. Please." She sounded exasperated, stressed. Daley was concerned that she would drop the phone and bolt.

"Ok. Ok, Alice. I'm sorry. I'm listening."

"Look. Dawn Silverton. She was a friend of mine, from way back, Like Rachel. From Uni. We all used to hang out together. Well, *they* used to hang out. I was more a sort of hanger-on."

"You said you knew about their deaths? That you thought you were next. Tell me again."

"If I am right you are tracing this phone, so I don't want to stay on much longer. Dawn Silverton was killed with a machete, or a sword. If I *am* right, so was Rachel Jones. And Guy Higson hit a piano wire. Shelley died in that pub fire on Cordon Street. Tell me I'm wrong?"

"Alice, You know I can't go into details. We have to..." Daley was momentarily taken off-guard as this disconnected voice recounted key facts known only to the team. His mind replayed the images. The staring eyes, the pools of blood. Was Alice the murderer? How else could she know such precise details? Who was the 'he' she was so concerned would find her? "We have to catch this person before anyone else gets hurt. Alice, we can look after you, please..."

"Each one of them was numbered. They had a counter or a stamp, or something, a number. Rachel was one, Dawn was two and Guy was three and Shelley was four, or maybe he started again with Dawn as one, I don't know..."

"Who started again, Alice? Who was it?" The entire team had stopped breathing, turning an uncomfortable shade of blue.

"It's all to do with the Murder Book, from Coventry. It was a silly game that the Monday Club played, you know, inventing ways to murder someone without getting caught? We each had turns at it. And now someone is using it to kill us. Rachel and Dawn both suggested chopping heads off and Guy, who was always playing with his motorbike, suggested a trip wire because he had seen it on *Midsomer Murders*. You need to find him, find The Book. That will tell you everything."

"Find who?" Daley rifled through a mental list. "Marcus? Finn?"

"No, No!" The pitch of her voice was raised, angry at the interruptions, scared that they might be near to tracing the mobile, unaware that those days are long gone; the trace was almost instantaneous. "Look, Carmichael was the leader of the Club. This is about Carmichael and what happened in Coventry when we were at Uni. It's about revenge. If I am right he has already got to Rachel and Dawn and Guy and Shelley, and now he is coming after me, just like it says in The Book. It was all just a stupid game."

"Who is coming after you? Tell me more about the Book?"

"Look at the Monday Club. It's all to do with the Monday Club and what happened in 1997. The tramp that died. You need to find Chris. He is the only one that knows all about this."

Whetstone had practically thrown Corby out at the entrance to the White Hart and was herself pushing through the rear doors of The Swan. She dialled Daley's Mobile. Dave Monaghan picked up and transcribed her words on a piece of paper - '*I will be coughing a lot*'. Above the hubbub, Daley heard a cough, he motioned to Monaghan with his hand, rolling it vertically - *again, keep it going.*

"Chris? Is that Chris Betts? Is he there, now?" The cough was overly theatrical and had become louder in the background now. Daley gave Monaghan a thumbs up sign, and rolled his hand once more.

"Chris? No. I haven't seen him in ages, not for years."

Whetstone was handed a glass of water by the chap behind the bar. It was the first person who had bought her a drink since Daley at the Easter piss-up and, just like then, she didn't really need it. Monaghan's coolness was legendary, but right now she needed more information. She had to hand it to Alice Bown; she had picked the best pub to hide in. The commentator was telling her that Spurs were drawing with Crystal Palace and most of the punters were on their feet hurling encouragement and abuse in equal measures. A phrase about needles and haystacks sprung to mind.

"I'm at the bar, Dave. Louder or quieter?" She coughed so hard her lungs almost ruptured. After a brief pause, in which she imagined Dave miming 'louder' or 'quieter', and wondered how you would do that, Dave told her quieter. In frustration, she barged her way past some of the drinkers, throwing an uncaring 'whatever', when a small slop of something leapt from their glasses.

"Right, I'm going towards the back of room." Again the cough and a pause. Then Dave told her close, very close.

"So where do we find this Book, Alice? Please. People are dying. Help me here." Daley was willing Whetstone on. She must be close. The coughing was so loud he could almost feel phlegm hitting his ear. He gestured to Dave - *keep coming.*

"Find Chris Betts and you'll find the book. Look, I've got to go."

Whetstone pushed passed the last throng of drinkers. At the back of the room, an arc of upholstered benches lay forlorn and empty. From this position, the football was not visible. Neither was the door, just the saggy jeans and unpleasant rears of thirty men. She picked up the phone that was lying on the table. It was still warm to the touch and the screen showed Daley's mobile number. At the other end, Daley started as she put it to her ear.

"Gov. It's me. She's gone."

***

Daley threw the handset down in exasperation and thumped the desk as hard as he could, given the Met's Health and Safety Policy. DC Taylor, knowing his pay grade, carefully placed the receiver on its cradle. Monaghan was already searching various archives for any incident worthy enough to record that involved Chris Betts and a tramp in 1997. Billy Davies had mentioned a vagrant but the details had not yet come through.

They were almost within touching distance of the killer but their fingertips would not stretch to the leap of deduction that was necessary. Returning to his desk, Daley opened up the rough diagram of Carmichael's planetary system. He looked at the solitary bubble containing the name *Christopher Betts* and his mouse dithered. Certainly Alice thought he was the key, either to understanding that whole thing, or as part of the story. Daley circumscribed a new Venn circle, intersecting the others. And like mustard gas clearing from a battlefield, the whole landscape changed. This was never only about the Monday Club nor the money. This was about an event that happened to the Monday Club, probably in 1997.

Across the top circle he wrote the words '*What happened?*' Whatever it was had rippled through the fabric of these peoples lives, four years ago ripping at the seams of Rachel Jones' existence before renting apart the Monday Club less than a week ago. And within hours, days or months consuming the rest of

316

them, unless he could check the rupture before it spread further.

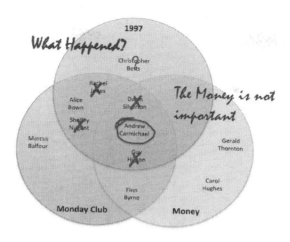

But what exactly connected these seven individuals, apart from the Monday Club and Coventry University around 1997? Maybe nothing else connected them. Daley moved across to the whiteboard, to the sheets of A4 that they had found on the victims. Were these pages of the Murder Book? It was clear that the same person had written each of the pages, but the first was subtly different to the rest, bearing a different typeface, different paper. Was this just an accident of timing, printed out at a different time? Or did this hint at different people - multiple killers working together, or separate ones working alone?

Deb finally returned from her trek out to Hanwell. Entering the double doors and into the team room she shrugged her shoulders - *sorry*. She joined him at the board and he explained his picture, the planets revolving around the sun that was Drew Carmichael's rectal helioluminescence.

And the seven names whose orbit was set on course for collision in the spring of 1997.

Was this the secret that Carmichael was hiding? Some terrible event that had happened in 1997, which had lain dormant until something or someone had disturbed the silt at the bottom of Carmichael's particularly murky pond? Was the death of Rachel Jones remedial action to keep the secret hidden to allow the waters to settle, only for Dawn Silverton and Guy Higson to stir them up once more?

For the first time, Daley could see disparate pieces of the puzzle beginning to knit to form a coherent image. Alice had named the players and the Book held the script, but what was the story? Whatever had happened in 1997, whilst they were all at university, that had effectively been the prologue to the grisly drama now playing out.

***

Returning to his desk, Monaghan caught sight of the *Post-it* note placed on his screen during Alice's call. The Irishman yanked off the note and scanned it quickly.

"Gov, Billy Davies has just called from Coventry."

"Phone him back, Dave, for Christ's sake." Daley paced across the floor in frustration, sure in his own mind that the delay had cost Shelley Nugent, and possibly Finn Byrne their lives.

Monaghan let out a wearisome sigh and dialled the number. When the call connected, Monaghan put it on speaker.

"Hi, Sergeant Davies. I'm DI Scott Daley and with me is DS Deb Whetstone. Literally just come off the phone to one of the ex-students - Alice Bown - she definitely said spring 1997, the death of a tramp, and she mentioned the Murder Book. So there has to be a vagrant in there somewhere."

"Yeah, Sir, but this city gets loads of deaths, far too many to report in the papers, or even for serious case files. Especially tramps or migrants. They live and die in a sort of parallel world. Often no-one sees them come and no one sees them go. It must be the same in London?"

Daley's heart sank. He felt sure that the death of the tramp would be the breakthrough they needed. "So no tramp then, Billy?"

"Now that's not actually what I said. The case files finally came back from the archives. I have had a chance to read up on what happened in 1997 with Chris Betts and Andrew Carmichael. Looks like a whole hoo-ha about nothing, loads of witness statements but not a lot else."

The three colleagues were willing Billy Davies to get to the point, feeling the life ebbing away from the murderer's next victim with every dropped aitch. It was obvious the West Mercia didn't let Sergeant Davies out much and he was taking every opportunity for a chinwag. Daley wanted to say 'Get on with it'. Instead he said, "So what did you find?"

"As we know, Christopher Betts, Andrew Carmichael, and the other names on your list were students at the same time. Betts was a bit of a loner, by all accounts. I remember he had these voices, special friends who he would talk to, rarely ever left his room except for lectures, but even then only if he could tag along with someone else. Apparently the monsters could only get to him if he were outside alone. Anyway 23rd April 1997 around 11:30pm, he was pulled in wandering the streets in Coventry. He was covered in blood and accosting strangers asking them to make it stop. Eventually one of our cars was called and he was hauled off to Central in Little Park Street. He himself was uninjured. We couldn't get any sense out of him so we sent him to Walsgrave Hospital, who in turn packed him off to their Psych unit at Clifford's Bridge. Eventually, about a week later, when he finally became lucid again, he was able to tell us a bit about what had happened, and this led us to connect him with the death of a vagrant behind the bus station - an old favourite in the custody suite at the time, a guy called Michael Sean Watkins..." Deb strode over to the Incident board and drew two bold circles around two of the names - the person Rachel had gone to visit whilst looking for lodgings and the name of the viewer who had arranged to meet Dawn - both according to their respective diaries - called Watkins. She looked at Daley and nodded purposefully. The links were starting to be made.

"So what do the witness statements say?"

"I have got this lot on a bike down to you already. Should arrive later today, but basically the story is this. It seems Betts came across the vagrant, just after he had been mugged. He had a fatal stab wound to his chest and was bleeding out. The poor kid just kept muttering that he couldn't make it stop, I suppose referring to the blood. He was questioned under caution with a solicitor present but was too far gone. The CPS wouldn't take it on."

"So what happened? How did it all end up?"

"For Betts, it only just started there. As I say, we sent him to

Central and they despatched him of for Psychiatric evaluation. However, he did mention some names during the interview and there are several witness statements, all of which say the same thing. Apparently they were all out for a stroll after going drinking with friends. They were walking up Cox Street, looking to go on to *The Kasbah,* which was a popular nightclub with the students. Anyway, they heard a noise and found young Betts crouched over Watkins and applying pressure to the wound. They all say it was clear that life was extinct, but that they were unable to get Betts to leave the body. They all apologised for not contacting the police and reporting the incident themselves. Basically, we could have photocopied the first statement and got the others to sign a copy, that's how similar they were.

"And did you ever find out what really happened?"

"Well, no. There was no weapon recovered and the only notable forensic evidence was from Betts, whom we knew had come into contact with the vagrant. The witnesses were re-interviewed but they all said exactly the same. Michael Watkins' murder remained unsolved. We put it down to some yobs, who wanted a good time and their idea of a good time was killing a tramp. I'm afraid a dead tramp doesn't rate very highly when you've got drug gangs and rapists coming in every night, so we had to let it go."

"Do you have the names of the witnesses who gave statements?"

"Yep, they were our Mr Carmichael, a Dawn Silverton, a Rachel Jones and a Shelley Nugent, all of whom are on your list."

"Is there any mention of Guy Higson or Alice Bown, or any other members of the Monday Club? Did anyone else give statements?"

"No, Sir. Nothing. As you'll see, the files are sparse. The only reason the others were interviewed is because Betts specifically gave us their names. Why'd you ask?

Daley scanned the diagram, the blue shaded area, *1997 - Coventry. What Happened??* He looked at the names within its perimeter. "Because Billy, it seems that someone has the Murder Book and is following its instructions. First Rachel Jones, then Dawn Silverton and Guy Higson, then Shelley Nugent, and Alice Bown seems to think she is next. I am thinking that they

320

were all present at some time during that evening and that Christopher Betts covered for them."

"Jesus Christ, Inspector. Seems like you have a messy one. I can only apologise that it's taken me so long to come back to you."

"It is what it is, Billy. Whoever is doing this has been one step ahead of us all week. What you have found out moves our enquiry on a huge amount. All we have to do is join the dots now, and see what picture emerges."

Deb leaned into the phone. "And Christopher Betts? What happened to him?"

"Poor bastard. Who the hell knows? He was picked up a couple of times after that but we never did anything. He was completely off his trolley. In the end his family had to collect him from University and took him back up North. There's an address in the file for the booby hatch they sent him to. Hopefully you should have got the main points, but I've scanned a few pages and sent them in an email. Not sure that's much help but there you go."

"Cheers, Billy. Actually that's been a great help."

CHAPTER 34

As impatience took hold of him once more, Scott Daley pushed through the glass doors and peered in both directions down the street outside Lambourne Road. It was still and quiet, as it had been for the past three quarters of an hour. Off the beaten track for late night revellers, it was always quiet. Muttering under his breath. He returned to the lobby.

"Where the fuck is he? How long does it take to bike down from Coventry, anyway?"

Deb Whetstone tutted and the duty officer smiled sympathetically before returning to his paperwork. "It will take as long as it takes, Sir." Sergeant Davies' call had been an hour ago and the minutes had dragged their heels like reluctant schoolchildren ever since. She took a slug of water from a bottle, now warm and no longer refreshing.

They both turned to face the glass-panelled doors as a beam of white light traversed the building opposite and the roar of an engine broke the stillness outside. Soon a motorcyclist in a fluorescent over-shirt was hopping up the steps carrying a large opaque plastic wallet. As he pushed through the doors, he raised his visor.

"Sergeant Monaghan?"

"No. His boss, DI Daley." Daley flashed the warrant card and the slit in the visor scanned it for a long moment.

"Thank you, Sir. Can you sign here, and warrant card number here?"

Even before the visor had come down and the doors had swung to a squeaking halt, Daley had bounded up the stairs with the package in hand, ready to rouse the dozing coppers above.

***

The hourglass is turned and the sand is draining, their lives are ebbing away. Soon it will be just you and I. We can go to our peace together. They all watched and they did nothing, and now they have paid, each responding to the roll call, submitting themselves to their fate, leaving only her. The kindly one, the caring one. The one who could have helped yet who abandoned us to the night and the terrors that consumed us whole. The one who ran.

And now, Alice, it is your turn to succumb to the night.

The bannister is cold on my face, and my breath grates hollow through the chasm of my mouth. The spindles of the stair cast shadowed fingers that stretch across the landing pointing upwards, leading me to her. The hands are moving so slowly around the face, the hours glowing white from beneath my cuff, and I realise I haven't breathed for a complete revolution of the tiny circulating dot which marked another minute. But soon, very soon, it will be after two in the morning and I can continue the plan that the Book dictates.

The Book is meticulous. A few sparse lines of an idea expanded into a full set of instructions. Becoming richer. Meticulous is right. All of the 'i's dotted and 't's crossed. A living breathing organism. An intricate series of operations, woven into each act, emphasising the years of preparation, analysis and observation. Mitigating the risks and reducing the chances of mistakes. That was *your* strength. I am merely the organ of its execution. The simple expedient of the empty house, of the outstretched wire across the deserted lane, of the regular girl's night in and the chloroformed rag. Ensuring that nothing was rushed and no evidence was left, except the number. That was set down in the Book. Each one would be numbered. Each one would have their turn in the order that they themselves dictated. There will be no doubt that these events are connected.

And the page of the Book left with each one. It would be obvious that they themselves had engineered their own ends.

There has been no movement in the room for some time. I had watched the amber glow from beneath the door, vague shadows moved left and right, but those had ceased at eleven-thirty and the light had been extinguished quarter of an hour later. But that was in the Book also. These people have been watched for a long time. Their inane habits were well known. Their obscene proclivities recorded. Their lives committed to the pages of the Book.

My hips and knees ached, turgid and cramped. I had to wait for the allotted time. Waiting was important, rules were important. And now her time has come. My legs are wide as I climb the stair. The building is old and the stair will creak, so each footfall is measured along the edge of the step, close to the skirting, slowly and deliberately rolling the sole of my shoes. Spreading the weight, pressing my gloves into the wall, feeling the embossed pattern on my palms. And then I am at the top and the dark shadow of her room is to my right. Immediately in front, a gaping door beckons, but not yet. Her door will be unlocked. The Book tells me so and I trust the Book. Caressing the round doorknob in my hand, feeling the creases in the latex glove, the almost imperceptible, seemingly endless twangs of the spring inside the latch a cacophony in the dead of night, as I am turning the knob oh-so slowly. And then the dullest clunk as the catch yields to emptiness and the door cedes to the merest of pressure from my hand.

The streetlights outside beam bands of dull orange across the silent living room. The room is small and cluttered, a sofa, a TV, a sideboard, tawdry ornaments to a tawdry life. Across the room, not ten paces away, I can see the bedroom. I hear a faint monotone hum of a refrigerator and to my left, eerie green digits seem to float and pulse to the beat of my heart and punctuate the black void of the kitchen. The microwave, reminding me of the time, urging me forwards. As she sleeps, there is the luxury of time. The microwave clock can beat to its own helpless rhythm.

I feel the ache in my biceps, and it makes me warm to recall the exactness of the swing, the suddenness with which *she* had ceased to be. To recall the wide, surprised eyes and the momentary, startled realisation before they dimmed. And the homosexual, the wild rag-doll flung into the glow of the streetlamp, kicking up the dust as the motorbike sidled slowly but surely to a halt in the bushes. I reach the other door, lit bright by the invading streetlight, slightly ajar. I stop and listen. Holding my own deep within my straining chest, I hear the slow ebb and flow of the other's breath. I smell the scent of creams and lotions, of nightly rituals, prayers to the elusive gods of immortality that would be in vain tonight, the aroma of body odour, the pungent personal scent of sweat. My eyes are fully adjusted to the near-blackness of the room with a shard of dim grey following me through the doorway, dancing shadows across the wall and bathing the bed. She is lying, her head above the duvet, her hair swept across the pillow. Her face is peaceful, her eyes are shut, like the corpse on the mortuary slab, shrouded in white. The syringe is already prepared and I pull it from my pocket. Just as in the Book. I scan the inky gloom and sense the dark smudge on the floor at my feet. Though the thin latex, I feel the satin or silk. A slip, an under garment. I can smell her on the fabric, as I press it to my face and inhale the air through it, deep and sensual, the taut nervous tension metamorphosing into a need for sensual gratification. I am the intruder, the stalker, the unseen predator of the night, privy to her space and her secrets, to her possessions, to her body and even to her soul.

I will use the slip. The handkerchief that I have brought will remain in my pocket. I will amend the Book when I return. Less evidence to be concerned with. I remove the plastic cover from the hypodermic needle and I shock as she sighs and turns onto her side, unprotected and defenceless in the treacherous depths of sleep. Beneath the sheet, her legs are brought up into a foetal twist.

And then she is struggling as I sit on her, her hips writhing between my thighs, almost sensual, sexual, the garment pressed to her face, stifling her screams, her eyes wide with terror, entombed by the bedclothes and her free arm trapped beneath my hand. She tries to shake her head violently from side to side but I bring my face down so close that in the faintness of the room, I can see her eyes. She knows that I am smiling, that I will have her and that she is living her last conscious moments in torment and panic. My muscles ache as she thrashes and contorts but I bring down the syringe and feel the resistance as it enters her forearm. Slowly, ever so slowly, her slender form, so powerful in it's instinct for self preservation, begins to yield, the arms fight against my grasping hand but the pressure weakens, the serpentine writhing abates, and the eyes cease to see. And then she is still once more, the gentle ebb and flow of breathing.

I draw back the bed sheets and unfold her contorted body as if laying her out for her funeral. That pleasure will fall to someone else. I glance at my watch and two-thirty is indicated. Accomplished in five minutes less than the anticipated schedule. She is wearing a chemise, slender and satin. I kneel across her once more, placing my hands on the shoulder straps; I drag the chemise down towards her feet, bright fireflies dancing as the static arcs and crackles. Soon, in the sacred haven of her

325

bedroom she is naked, laid bare to the darkest terror of the night. I brush her hair from her face and run my hands down her warm flesh, riding the rise of her breasts and the fall across her flat stomach, rimming the deep caldera of her navel and the coarseness of her unshaven pubis. Crouching close I smell the warm aroma of her neck, moist from perspiration, I smell the animal warmth of her groin and a thrill of sexual charge starts through me. She is defenceless, not to yield to a lover, nor to the defilement of a rapist, but to me, to the Book, and the ultimate surrender. I draw the small torch and a roll of duct tape from my outside pocket. I use it to bind her ankles and wrists, her mouth. Her nostrils flare as her breathing changes.

I wanted the water to be cold, icy and sharp, to bite at her flesh as she entered it. I wanted to see her tremble but the Book said no. Cold water would overcome the senses, make her less reactive, and she needed to meet her end in full awareness. So the water is warm and the boiler pops and bangs as it disgorges into the bath. I scoop her from the bed, her head flopping to one side as I carry her in my arms, her skin rough with goose pimples, minute hair filaments standing on end, the perfume from her naked skin filling my nostrils. I lower her into the water and watch it settle around her thighs, and her groin and rise up beneath her breasts, clinging to her flesh and stemming as it reaches her chin.

And I sit and I wait.

I wait as her breathing slowly raises her body with each inhalation and watch as it sinks again. The light is on, the door is locked, and there is no-one to see it limbo through the crack beneath. Gradually her eyelids flutter and open. As she awakes, her expression is one of peace and comfort. The warm water cossets her, perhaps lifting her from a pleasant dream. But soon her expression is one of confusion, as the dream evaporates and reality consumes its last echoes. She squints in the harsh unguarded light from the bulb and her eyes alight upon me seated as I watch. She tries vainly to expel the tape from her mouth, struggling to bring her bound arms to her face, and despite the warmth of the water, she begins to tremble and her eyes moisten. I check my watch. She has three minutes but there is no way she can know this. She is as Ophelia fell into the weeping brook waiting for the elements to pull her under. Her eyes, frantic and fearful follow me as I crouch at her head. I explain why I am here, and why she is here, how she deserved to suffer as we have suffered, as I am still suffering, and she shakes her head and her muffled pleadings denounce us even now. I reach into the water and run my hands down her flesh, rippled with goose pimples, shuddering with terror. I find her calves, smooth and shaven, bound tight with the tape, bucking and shaking in the warm water. I run my hands around her knees and up to her thighs, so soft in the warmth of the water. She recoils and she clamps her knees together and I smile. It is not her virtue I seek to take tonight. My hands turn and make their way down to the sinuous slimness of her ankles to the tautness of the tape and link my fingers around it. Slowly, deliberately, I draw her bound feet up from the water, watching it envelope her shoulders, hearing her muffled screams subside as her flailing head sinks beneath the surface. Despite the bonds, she is thrashing her torso from side to side, her animal instinct for survival once more an exercise in futility. Her hair spreads like a halo around her head and her eyes bulge wide, distorted by the foment. The tape comes free from her mouth and muted cries gurgle to the surface as the last true breath is expelled from her lungs. My arms are tiring from holding the legs aloft, a writhing eel hanging in the bath, but after a minute, maybe two, the writhing ceases and the kicking stops and the water settles smooth and unruffled across her expressionless face as once more I watch the life drain away. My breath is harsh and rasping from the exertion, water drips from my elbow and the dampness of sexual climax clings to my body beneath my clothes.

And then she lies in the bath as if asleep during a soak, enjoying the warmth of the water as it percolates through her tired frame, her eyes now closed, her arms and legs untied, her hair fashioned down onto her left shoulder and a neat circle bearing a numeral '5' in the centre of her forehead.

In that bathroom, unremarkable and shabby, I watched the light disappear from Alice Bown's eyes and I knew that I had warmed to my task.

CHAPTER 35

The fumes filled the bedroom and clawed at Carmichael's throat, wisps of grey, teeming like elvers poured from a bucket, writhing and wriggling up the edge of the counterpane and wrapping themselves around his legs and torso. Fingernails scratched on the door outside and the muffled sounds of voices called his name. Parchment covered arms reached through the fabric of the door, stretching until the claw-like nails were and inch from his face. And the wailing banshees were abroad, filling the room with their high, melancholic howls. Terrified and quaking, Carmichael sat up and scrabbled back towards the headboard but the arms stretched further and the elvers slithered up and entwined his throat, choking the air from his lungs and the banshee wails turned to malevolent moaning, their eyes wide and glowing green as they repeated *Your time is coming, Drew Carmichael. It will soon be your time to die.*

And at once the sound collapsed into silence and he was awake in the blackness of the room, a faint greyness leaking around the curtain. He was propped up against the headboard, blankets pulled around him like a barricade against the demons. He was shaking, drenched in cooling sweat that turned his skin to beads. A solitary car droned past outside and the room once more descended into stillness. He looked across at the door, the gap below now black and solid, untroubled by smoke or things that creep. Grabbing his watch, he put it to his eye, to discern the faded luminosity of the fingers. It was 3:45am. He strapped on the watch and made to reach down for his clothes, momentarily flinching from the eels. He snickered to himself at his own timidity. Frightened of dreams and shadows. What was he like?

Outside the room, the rest of the house was also black, except for the faint glow of street lamps, coming in through the front door panes and ascending the stair. He was relieved he hadn't woken Carol for a second night running with his silly nightmare. Sheepishly, he strolled towards the bathroom and turned on the light, the glare instantly banishing any remaining demons. The water was refreshing and cold against his parched dry throat. It was as if he had been eating razors!

Again he had woken in the spare room. He trawled his mind back to the previous evening, to the argument with Carol over him leaving the house, to the comfort of the sofa but then nothing. He must have watched some television, or even read a book maybe, but the memories were not there. All he had were the terrifying beasts of his dreams and a chasmic void. He rubbed his hands across his face, smoothed down his hair. The face that looked back from the mirror was haggard and troubled. It was as if he was staring at someone else, someone lesser. He, Drew Carmichael, had a swagger, an insouciance that would always see him through, but the face that stared back at him was confused and afraid.

His arm ached as he raised it. He pulled the skin around and stared at the back of his biceps in the mirror. It was bruised and purple. Maybe that fall into the bushes was harder than he had imagined? But had not his arm hurt yesterday morning too? Why could he not fix these things in his memory? Night after night, strange dreams, weird hallucinations, premonitions of the future, uncannily accurate visions of the past. He thought of Carol, asleep, warm, and defenceless in the next room. Stealthily he pulled down the handle of her door and eased it open, a thrill of anticipation coursing through him, as he saw the mound of her form under the bedclothes. She was still, seemingly undisturbed by his terrified screams. Allowing his trousers to fall to the floor, he slipped between the sheets contemplating the convected warmth of her body, as he wrapped his arm around...

At once he was upright, reaching for the light switch, then staring down at the pillows arranged in the bed, struggling to make sense of a situation that was both nonsensical and illogical. Why would she arrange pillows in her own bed? Unless it was in anticipation of his unwanted advances.

And it occurred to him that apart from a kiss or two, they had shared very little intimacy. Perhaps he was hoping for too much from her? Perhaps, he had misread the signs, she had led him on? Maybe she was simply a cock-tease, like all the rest? He grabbed his trousers, his nakedness making him foolish, and returned to his room to dress before trotting down the stairs. Every room was in deathly night silence, broken only by the whine of a refrigerator, or the settling plop of a floorboard, but he poked his head around each door to make certain.

Nothing.

Switching on the kitchen light, he tested the kettle and resolved that a warm drink would get him back to sleep which, as opposed to a hectic, invigorating shag, was what he needed most right now. Then, out of the blue, as if clutched from the back of a deep dusty drawer, he recalled her words from earlier - *And most of all I have to sort the money out once and for all.* Uttering expletives under his breath, he raced into the living room and fished out the laptop from behind the sofa, squinting in the harsh light as the screen lit up. Soon he was typing the address of the Cayman's Bank website and facing the log on screen. Frantically he typed the logon details. Bouncing of several keys at once, he cursed his clumsiness and deleted the characters, calmed himself, to have another go. The blue progress bar raced across and a red message announced *Username or password error. Please retype and try again.* He held his breath and once more typed the details, once more to be derided by the mocking message. He hammered his fist on his forehead. How could he have forgotten? He had used that password every day for the last six years. He cast his eyes over the laptop and found the *caps lock* light. Was this the reason? Were the lower case letters being transformed to upper case and vice versa? It was a different computer to the one he normally used - but no, the light was black. He tried again, slowly, deliberately, one character at a time. He was certain the information was correct. But the message appeared once more, the realisation now dawning upon him that no matter how many times he tried the computer would always say *No*.

Rising to his feet he held the laptop above his head and released all of his pent up frustration in one single movement, sending it crashing and splintering against the plain beige wall, the laptop dying in a shower of plastic and metal shards. He strode over and kicked the twisted machine hard against the wall. Now he knew that all this time, from the very moment he had selected her to help him with the Fund, to cover his back, even to sleep in his bed, she had been biding her time and waiting for this moment of ultimate betrayal. Was there ever any hope with her? Was he just deluding himself that, in her subtle, mature and ever so erotic way, she held any sort of feelings for him? Was it all his imagination? Surely not! She had made the moves on him in this very room.

But now was not the time. Quickly, he switched on the light and cleared the shattered laptop from the floor, piling it back into its bag and shoving it behind the sofa. The gouge in the wall was deep. He would just hope that she didn't notice until he had had this out with her. He ran upstairs and packed his things into a travel bag from the bottom of the wardrobe, and fished around in the drawers until he found some warm clothes left by the husband. His house would be off-limits but he wouldn't be staying here any longer than he had to. In the kitchen he made himself the strongest coffee he could find as he waited for her to return. He would need to stay awake, keep his wits about him. Soon, he was sitting in the darkened kitchen. Beside the chair the bag heaved with as many carbs as he could find, biscuits and chocolate, anything that would help if he had to sleep rough for a night or two. It was 4:00am on a Sunday morning. Where was she?

Unless there was another man. Perhaps that was her plan? Perhaps right now she was astride another man riding those hips over him like an animal while they both toasted their good fortune in champagne bought with his money. Perhaps that was what this whole charade was about all along. As soon as she had sniffed the money, she was in it for the long haul. *Softly, softly, catchy monkey*, everyday biding her time until his back was turned. Carmichael seethed as he thought of the two of them laughing at his stupidity, sharing a joke at his considerable expense. If it was the last thing he did on this Earth he would find them both and force twenty pound notes down their throats until they choked to death and then he would gladly swing for them. No-one gets the better of Drew Carmichael.

The front door clicked and he was instantly alert, focussed on the doorway. He heard her remove her coat, the clink of the keys into the drawer, the dull thud as the drawer was pushed back against the stops. An arm came around the frame, fumbling for the light switch. Then she was in the doorway, recoiling as he stood.

"Bloody Hell, pet. You nearly gave me a heart attack!" She raised her eyes to the ceiling and wafted a swoon from her face.

"Where have you been?" His delivery was cold, measured, but there was a fire burning inside.

"I - I couldn't sleep. Thought I would go out for a walk,

that's all. Get some fresh air." She hugged herself and rubbed her arms. "It's right nippy out there."

"Don't talk bollocks. It's four in the morning. No-one goes out walking at four in the morning!"

"Well, I do. Anyway, it's my house, my life. If I want to go out at four in the morning I will! If I want to do the hoovering naked with the windows open, I will. I have had enough of men telling me what I can and can't do. Now, get off your high horse and put the kettle on. I need a brew." Emotionless, unswayed by her response, he kept his eyes firmly on her, checking her expression, weighing up her mood.

"Where's my money?"

"What do you mean?" She looked puzzled, but Carmichael was not taken in. He would never be taken in by her again.

"Look, let's stop the small talk, shall we? When you said you were going to sort out the money once and for all, just exactly what did you do with it?" His voice was now raised, sharp but his eyes remained fixed.

She smiled, looking down at her feet, coquettish, lightly shaking her head. Then her expression changed, cold and hard, the eyes round and challenging. "The money hasn't gone anywhere," she growled, "but you will *never* get your hands on it. I've made sure of that." She sat down in the chair, there was no fear, just a brooding malevolence. The face he once thought breathtakingly attractive now hard and hostile. He knew that, all this time, that she had been playing him until she could take the money from him. And for that there was no forgiveness. No-one takes Drew Carmichael for a ride. He had put Guy Higson right on that score. Come to think of it both Rachel Jones and Dawn Silverton too. No-one crosses Drew Carmichael with impunity.

"I thought we had a deal, an understanding. When this is all over you are going to very rich. You can't go back on that now."

"Shut the fuck up about the money!" she barked, almost screaming, and briefly he was taken aback. "This has never been about the money. This has always been about you. You think you are so clever, so much better than everyone else. You don't care what happens to the people around you as long as you are OK. As long as you get *your* way. And everyone else is cast aside in your wake. You have absolutely no idea what this is all about, do you?"

Her eyes were wide and the tears of anger were coursing down her face. She reached into her handbag.

"Bloody Hell, Carol. What the fuck has got into you? OK. So I am a bit of a bastard. Just give me the passwords. I'll make sure you get your cut and, well, that's it. We never have to see each other again."

"I don't want your filthy, stinking money. I never wanted the money. I just want you to pay for everything you have done."

She leapt from the chair and was instantly upon him. Instinctively, he was on his feet, grabbing both of her wrists, fending her off as she dived towards him. She was strong and, try as he might, he could not resist as she pushed him back against the cupboards. The edge of the work surface cut into the small of his back and his right arm ached as he held her off. Out of the corner of his eye, the light sparked off the object in her right hand, the plastic vial and thin shard of metal inching closer to his head. In one desperate push, he thrust himself forwards, tried to straighten his arms, a knee was raised and an excruciating pain exploded in his groin sending bullets of pain up through his chest and into his brain. Gasping for breath, he fell to his knees and stars danced before his eyes. He felt a sharp scratch and a cold inrush of liquid into his arm and then the world rippled away.

CHAPTER 36

It had been tipping it down for most of the night and as dawn broke timidly from behind the seething grey clouds, the pavements shimmered in the rain. 5:00am was an ungodly hour but one that Marcus was accustomed to, especially with the hospital rota unfairly skewed against bachelors. He now regretted buying the cheaper waterproof. Above him, garish in the street lamps, the red and grey panelling of the lift column seemed to holler to the world that he was there. The Westfield Shopping Centre, even Ariel Way below, was a hive of activity even at this time on a Sunday morning, delivery vehicles taking the opportunity to make their drops before the morning rush started. The bank of lifts encased in their opaque green glass columns were still and dead and would be for another hour yet. When she arrived, they would use the steps to reach the car below. Despite the ever-present hum of generators and air conditioners, and the ubiquitous background rumble of London, the upper level was empty. He felt like king of the hill. Life was finally starting to turn his way. *One and three quarter million pounds!* And that was without Carol Hughes cut. He really should have bought the thicker coat. Only a fool would be standing outside the Westfield five hours before it opened. But given what they now knew, they had surmised that a public place at an ungodly hour was perfect for their getaway.

The previous evening they had decided to phone the Police from a public place; the Swan in Hanwell was probably the most public of places she could have found. Despite the recent refurbishment, there was still an air of latent enmity, hanging like a pall through the saloon bar. A favoured haunt of villains and ne'er do wells, the new landlord had sought to change the atmosphere of the establishment with an external coat of white render and an internal wash of *bon homie*, but to little effect. Paradoxically, in a place was full of villains, Alice knew she would be safe.

The saloon bar was around half full, but Marcus had immediately spotted Alice, waiting on a high stool by the bar, nursemaiding a glass of white wine, and another of Fullers. His relief had been enormous. He had left her so he could do some chores in preparation for their imminent departure, to steal some number plates for the BMW, to buy a mobile from the supermarket. Together they had moved to a table furthest away from the cacophonous televisions broadcasting Spurs vs. Crystal Palace to a small but rapt crowd. He could sense she was deeply troubled. The make-up she had hurriedly applied was caked and thick but still unable to mask her beauty, or hide her recent tears. He couldn't imagine how she was coping. The deaths of Dawn, Guy and Shelley had come in quick succession. He thought back to the previous afternoon, to the warmth of her friendship, the warmth of her body, to the desperate love-making that had waited fifteen years, to the soft rise and fall of her chest as she slept.

"You ready?"

She looked at him her eyes round, her mouth turned down. He dug the mobile from his pocket and he turned it on. From another pocket he pulled Inspector Daley's business card.

"Right, It hasn't got much charge. I plugged it into the car so it should be OK for an hour or so. And I didn't waste money on credit either, so make it quick. Get him to phone you. That way we can get out of here before they find us." He smiled reassuringly at her.

She puffed hard and took a swig of her drink, and then she placed it on the mat in front of her and grabbed his arm squeezing it tight.

"Are you sure that this is the right thing to do? I mean what if I am wrong. Won't that just make things worse?"

"Alice. This is no time for cold feet. Do you love me?"

"Yes, Marcus. Of course I do."

"Do you trust me? You need to trust me completely and you need to know you can trust me forever. Come what may."

A tear was forming in her eye. He watched it grow and wiped it away with his thumb. "All those years ago, I trusted you. I saw the rest of my life with you. And then I let Drew Carmichael stand in our way. Of course, I trust you. You were the only one I could ever trust. Keeping all this quiet, it was stupid. If only I had told you then, everything would be different."

He looked earnestly into her eyes, aware of the enormity of what her was asking of her. "If you trust me now, there will be

335

no going back. Just like then, everything will change."

"I have a shitty flat on a shitty street and I work for a shitty company doing a shitty job. If everything *did* change, how much worse could it be, Marcus?"

"Well, flippin' get on with it. My pints getting warm.

And so they had finalised their plans, she had spoken to DI Scott Daley and had both taken a taxi home. As he left her to sleep he had busied himself with preparations for their new life together, screwing on false number plates and topping up with fuel, and he had felt beyond the law, cruising in the early dawn and parking under road bridges awaiting secret assignations. If this was change, he welcomed it!

Nine agonising hours later the sky was filling with fierce, grey clouds and a stiff breeze had kicked up. For the fifth time he heard footfalls on the steps to the top level of the lift column, and for the fifth time, it was not her. He checked his watch again. He had been here an hour and she was forty-five minutes late. A knot formed in his stomach and under his breath he anxiously called for Alice to come.

CHAPTER 37

Five miles away, as Marcus rubbed his hands against the damp cold air, a hazy red glow was slowly hauling itself up over the silhouetted roofs above Lambourne Road. The large Sixties glass windows oozed an insidious cold that descended the walls and seeped around the ankles. Dave Monaghan had kept his coat when he arrived half an hour ago, and the red dawn took him slightly unawares, such was his concentration on the screens in front of him. Through the window, a light flickered across the road as the newsagent wearily hauled in the bundles of papers stacked outside the door. Monaghan craned his neck to look at the clock, which had crawled it's way to 8:00am and swore under his breath, *Rach-air-muin* - a Gaelic phrase that none of his colleagues would understand, even if they had been there to witness it. Even Scott Daley had pissed off the previous evening, murmuring something about needing more alcohol to think.

He was too old for this sort of thing. Margaret was going to kill him, which is probably why he hadn't told her. The one thing that brought her pleasure these days was the thought that, come what may, her dear, sweet, ever-loving husband would bring her tea and toast in bed on a Sunday morning. He pictured her sitting up against the studded velour headboard, face like thunder, and he felt deeply ashamed. Not even chocolates from the garage would put this one right.

He and Taylor had pored over the files that had been despatched from Coventry. Billy Davies had been right. The evidence was scant to say the least. Christopher Betts' interview notes brought no further enlightenment. The poor boy had been so distressed that the interview had consisted of a few lines acknowledging that had had been unfit to interview. The final one showed the doctors *affa davit* that Betts was under Psychiatric distress and should be sent of to a specialist unit for his own well-being. Monaghan had rung the specialist unit but apart from the night staff at the desk, they were all in bed waiting for their significant others to bring tea and toast.

The double doors opened and Scott Daley waved an idle greeting at the Sergeant. It was clear that the Inspector had pulled an all-nighter. Now, at stupid o'clock on a Sunday morning, stifling a yawn, Daley plonked down the coffees noisily. Dave Monaghan glowered disapprovingly and centred the paper cups on the coasters, turning the coasters perpendicular to the edges of the desk. There was an order to the universe. Leaning back in his chair, Daley crossed his ankles, folded his arms and gazed at the Incident board. He felt his eyelids grow heavy.

Dave Monaghan nudged him. "Don't you nod off to sleep now, you bastard. If I have to be here then so do you."

"Piss off, Dave. I am the senior officer and I was undergoing a case review." Daley cast an insouciant glance at the Sergeant. "One phone call from me and you'll be on the beat come Monday."

"You promise? At least it will be regular hours and I won't have to look at your ugly mug every day. Just think, I could have a lie-in on a Sunday."

"You should be so fucking lucky, Dave!" Deb Whetstone had hung her coat on the hooks behind the door and was standing behind the both of them, arms folded. "Took me out last night, wined and dined me, drove me home. Not so much as a grope. Mind you, looking at the state of him, could've been a lucky escape."

"No, I don't think I would grope him either Deb. Take far more than an Indian for me to go that far. Bloody loser."

"If it weren't for the fact that you're good coppers, you'd all be picking up drunks outside Sainsbury's. Deb, you're the youngest and also the last one in. Make us all another brew. Some of us have been here since early!"

At 9:30am on the dot, Daley felt a buzz in his jacket pocket and the screen showed it was Patrick Gascoigne. Another sad git who never went home.

"Scott, Preliminary results of the DNA tests have come through. Now these are not confirmed. That takes a whole lot longer, but they may give you a direction."

Daley switched the phone to speaker before Gascoigne launched into the headlines.

"OK, so a brief recap. We have hair and skin fibres from the overalls found at Chapel Row, and these were sent for DNA analysis earlier in the week. We also have hair fibres retrieved

338

from the headrests of Carmichael's Mercedes. There were two specific samples of hair from the house and twelve samples from the car. Interestingly, Simon was able to isolate some matches between the two sites. So..." there was the sound of papers shuffling "...so there were two sets of hair fibres on the overalls, one male and one female. DNA confirms this. One sample was fairly degraded but they can work marvels these days."

"Of the two, which were the oldest, Patrick?"

"They were from a male. There are other markers which may give us more information but, as I said, this is a preliminary analysis." Daley scanned the Incident board. A male suspect with light or blond hair cast a wide net over Byrne, Carmichael and possibly even the mysterious Chris Betts, his face on the board supplanted by a question mark.

"The other sample, the one we thought was female indicated that yes, indeed, they were from a female." A female suspect who could be linked to a male suspect. The only candidates were Byrne and Nugent... or Betts and Bown. Daley imagined a line from Alice Bown to Chris Betts.

"In the car, of the twelve samples obtained, ten are anomalous. Based on a scant examination, they all appear to be female, so probably relics of some of Mr Carmichael's more interesting liaisons. If necessary, we can send these off for further analysis; however, the other two probably interest us more at this stage. One set of fibres was an exact match for Mr Carmichael's own hair. Simon stole a fibre from Carmichael's office chair, so we will have to seek to obtain a formal sample, if you need to use this."

"So we know he drove his own car. What of it?" Interesting though this was, she couldn't see where it was leading.

"Ah, but Deborah. He was also a passenger in his own car. His hair was found on both the driver and passenger headrests."

She was puzzled. "I can't see him letting anyone else drive his company car. I wonder what that's all about?"

"Me, Forensics, you detective, I'm afraid!"

"Now, more excitingly, the other sample is a match for one of the ones we found in the overalls. I say the same. A visual examination shows they are the same. We would need to do more tests..."

339

"The same but not Drew Carmichael? Is that what you are saying?"

"Subject to more thorough tests, yes. Found on both headrests. So the female sample from Chapel Rise matches one of the female samples in Carmichael's car. Whoever our mystery female was, she wore those overalls *and* she sat in both front seats of Carmichael's car."

The room fell silent, as the three tried to process the data hurled at them. It was Daley who broke the silence.

"OK. So two people wore the overalls. A male who may have killed Rachel Jones and later a female who wore them to kill Dawn Silverton. Then at some time, either before or since, the same female was a guest in Drew Carmichael's Mercedes, where she drove and was driven."

"Subject to a lot of *maybes* and *perhaps'*, yes. That sounds plausible."

"Could it be one of Carmichael's old girlfriends? Someone we don't know about? I mean, if he had a string of them on the go, maybe there's a *bunny boiler* out there who has an on-off relationship with Carmichael, and during the off periods, he is busy with Rachel and Dawn respectively, she takes the hump and *off with their heads!*"

"And Guy Higson? Was he another one of Carmichael's conquests? Nobody has reported that he was that way inclined..."

"There is one other important piece of information I need to share before you start to soar to the dizzy heights of fantasy. Now I stress that the DNA results are still preliminary, there are checks and reviews to happen yet, so you must proceed with caution!" Gascoigne paused for effect. "The skin samples found on the overalls came from the same two individuals as the hair fibres. The DNA traces look identical. And...roll on the drums, please...they are a familial, probably a filial match for one another."

"What, related?"

"Most certainly related, but also more than likely brother and sister."

Chapter 38

1997 - Tuesday 8th April, *Browns* Bar, Coventry

The outsiders are braying like asses, their withered faces pressed to the windows, but their scratching fingers can't break through and they never will as long as he is vigilant. Their place is on the outside. They are waiting for him to fail as the coursework becomes harder, the deadlines closer, the loneliness greater. But he will not so much as stumble. Gossamer thin, the bubble dints and contorts but his will is stronger than theirs, his concentration greater. He will keep them out just as he keeps the rest of them out.

The swing door to *Browns* bar yields, wheezing and scraping over the threshold strip. Chris Betts holds it as she passes through - *always give way to ladies, it's how a gentleman behaves.* He has been unable to look at Rachel's face the whole of the way. The bubble constricts and the air burns as her body presses it against him. He panics as her fragrance permeates the membrane. She has protected him from the outsiders and now they are trapped outside beyond the glass, a force field they cannot penetrate, even their technology is not that powerful. Still they guffaw at his discomfort.

And then he is hit by the cacophony. A hundred conversations and chairs that screech on floors and doors that scrape on thresholds and glasses that tap on tables and laughs that come from mouths and music and coughing and whispers and jeers. Each makes sense in isolation and the threads intertwine and the spaghetti is tangled and inseparable as his brain leaps in directions to follow every conversation all at once. The thud of his heart fills his ears. He balls his hands into a fist and the bubble expands and filters out the noise. And he looks at his feet, and he hates his brain for wanting to recognise the faces and catalogue the words and identify the noises. The polished shoes are scuffed and he must clean them as soon as he can.

Coventry University is a city campus. A higgledy-piggledy mess of unordered buildings as if someone had thrown them in the air over the city and let them lie where they fell. He missed home, his rituals and the edges he could touch but they said University would be good for someone as intelligent as he. He chose York, Lancaster, even Aberystwyth; enclosed separate campuses, places where he could hide, immerse himself in his rituals and where he could contain the outsiders. But they made him come here, to stay in halls - *don't be silly, do as you're told, we know what's best.* Sharing lavatories and showers, stray hairs in the plughole, shit on the bowls, assaulted by the odour and filth, smelling their breath, polluted by the noise which throbs through the walls. The strands of their sordid lives autonomically recorded, swilling about amongst the flotsam and the jetsam of his mind, corrupting the purity. The outsiders have seen it all before. *Run back and hide with Mommy.* But life needed validation, which could only come through experience. The alternative is *Browns*, a sad amalgam of Swedish sauna and East European departure lounge. The walls and ceiling overwhelmed by wood panelling and sometime, a very long time ago, they had been stained a shade resembling old teak, the floors are a charcoal grey tile interspersed with islands of carpet. Whether the colour is maroon or brown or shit, he cannot tell, but there is no way to cross the cigarette smogged void without pressing a foot against the sticky surface, the crack-smack as the sole peels away with every footfall. Around him, in ancient leather sofas that smell of stale weed, stale piss and fresh mould, students are lolling, downing the hair of a dog that is still gnawing at their souls from the previous night. It is like a town centre a minute after the bomb and before the wailing starts.

Chris' eyes are on his shoes, on the fine mud around the edge. *Rain for thirty-six minutes, south-easterly breeze, fine until morning.* The clock above the bar says 7:00pm. He is exactly on time. They are round a table, an unordered profusion of glasses and crisp packets. Tall by short, full by empty, a discordance grating in his head, colours of the noises popping like fireworks, he has to turn away. They are always at this table, always in the large faux-leather chesterfields. Clockwise, his brain calls them off. *Marcus Balfour on the single chair, then Alice Bown on the sofa at the back with a gap where Rachel Jones will be soon, then Dawn Silverton - she will be looking towards the end of the table and the other single chair, where Drew is and then Guy Higson, he's the homo, next to Finn Byre and Shelley Nugent - they have sex.* He clicks his eyes up towards Drew Carmichael at the head of the table in the tired winged chair with

342

the missing studs. The outsiders have warned Chris about Andrew Carmichael. *Best not to mix with his sort - lie down with dogs, get up with fleas.* He wants the outsiders to punish Drew like they punish him. He wants the outsiders to stop them all from staring and grinning. He wants them to see him, hidden down the deepest hole and calling to the tiny speck of light above for someone to peer in and pull him out.

Then his hand is free, clammy sweat prickling cold. Rachel bounces onto the sofa between Alice and Dawn, and the bubble expands and the noise is an orchestra playing different tunes. This is a trap. His pulse pounds, his chest tightens, the air in the bubble thins and chokes him. He must not be here but the outsiders block his path.

A voice in his head, quiet at first, raises it's volume, but still cannot compete with the howling outsiders, mouths pressed against the stained windows, vibrating them, amplifying their mockery until he is overwhelmed by it. A million miles away, he hears Rachel and Dawn giggling. The others are saying rude things. *Jeez, Drew! Do we have to? For fuck sake! Shit, Twat alert!* Then the bubble collapses in and all he hears is Carmichael.

"Ah, Christopher. Where have you been? We'd almost given up on you. How's it going?" He filters the words from the avalanche in the bar, sets them on a board in his head and moves them around, to understand the sentences. *But which question first? Where had he been or how was it going? How was what going? If you can't say something sensible, then don't say anything.* Carmichael has his hand extended. He won't look at Carmichael, in case Carmichael's eyes see his terror - *eyes are the windows to the soul.*

His mother said be careful with people. There are clues. Look at their expression, at their body language, for clues. Are their eyes laughing? Are their arms apart, open and inviting? Are there arms folded? But all he sees are flat people, their expressions smudged on their cardboard faces like a barcode, filled with information he cannot read.

"Sit down and take the weight of your intellect." He sees Carmichael's hand outstretched pointing to the seats. There is no space. Marcus and Alice and Rachel and Dawn and Drew and Guy and Finn and Shelley all have their spaces. He panics as two arms grasp his wrists and pull him down onto the chesterfield behind him. He is between Rachel and Dawn, their legs pressing through his trousers. The bubble is squeezed to bursting point and the sounds of the room meld into a miasma of noise, like fairground music and the noise of the generators and the screams of the crowd. He wants to shout a long bellowing cry and stop time, bore a hole in the fabric of the world and climb through it. And then his name is heard and he snaps back to the room, like the teacher at Brookfield, when the outsiders drew him away from the class.

"Chris. Got a job for you. Means a place in the Monday Club. You up for it?"

The eyes are all turned and their drills press against his face, turning it red hot. The words writhe and contort. The outsiders makes his head nod.

"Well, do you or don't you, fuckwit? Look, there's a queue a mile long out there for your seat. Do you want in or not?" Carmichael's cardboard face confuses Chris. Has he done something wrong? Chris' head makes a bigger nod and he drags out a 'yes', as if pushing a golf ball from his oesophagus. And for once the outsiders are quiet, rapt, even their breathing has slowed, not wanting to miss a single moment. Rachel squeezes his arm and her legs are long and naked and the voices of the others swim around the air, a meaningless, incomprehensible tongue, as the bubble envelopes Carmichael and his is the only one tuned in.

"Good man! Now, look, the Monday Club isn't for everyone. It's like..."

"A rite of passage!"

"Nice one Rachel. Yes, like a rite of passage. In fact it *is* a right of passage. If you haven't been part of the Monday Club, well, you aren't part of anything. And right now Chris, you are *not* part of anything. You get my drift?"

The words are cast about the railway yard of his mind, gradually being shunted into a sentence, but loaded and shipped before he can process them. The girls have each grabbed and arm and their fingers gouge through his shirt, holding him down, forcing him deeper into the smells of leather and ash and patchouli.

"Yes, I do. I get your drift. I do get it." He hopes the answer

344

fits a question.

"OK. So here's the thing. We need you to help us out here. We sit around this table and have some fantastic ideas but in the morning, they are all gone, forgotten. Now I know you have a photographic memory..."

"Eidetic."

"...and can remember...come again?"

"Eidetic memory." *If it's right, it's not wrong and if it's wrong, it is definitely not right.* The words pour out like the man who reads the teleprinter on Grandstand and whose name is Tim Gudgin. "Photographic memory allows people to recall visual information such as pages from books, magazines, and car registration numbers. Eidetic memory involves senses other than vision. For example, eidetic memory might include sounds, touch, taste, and smell."

"You fuckin' pervert. Jeez, Dawn. He'll be touching and tasting and smelling us next." Rachel theatrically looses his arm.

"Maybe he's got a really long tongue, you never know!" And then Dawn has turned to him and her moist lips part and a foul pink slug worms from between them to within an inch of his face, and the girls collapsed across him, their caterwauling drowning out the thoughts in his head, bewildering his mind.

"OK. So it's eidetic. Look, you can remember shit, right?"

And his voice is silent and the outsiders scream *admit nothing! It's a trap.*

"We need you to write up our ideas, right? Finn, have none of you bog-trotters got any manners? Piss off and get the man a fucking lager will you?"

"You are a fuckin' British cunt, Carmichael. A decade ago, I'd have stuck a fucking bomb under your car, you prick." He is angry and Chris does not know whether he has done something wrong. Finn Byrne gets up; Shelley Nugent's arm outstretched until finally he releases her fingers and the arm lingers like the vapour trails of a jet plane in the sky. Finn's voice is hard and angry but his face is bent and smiling and the dichotomy fogs Chris' mind. But he hears the sound as Carmichael starts to talk, reaches out for the sound, tuning, focussing.

"We've got this game, OK? We call it the Murder Game. Marcus thinks that one day it's going to make him rich. Mind you he thinks one day he will be a doctor, so you can't believe a fucking thing he says. Anyway, we all think of ways to murder someone without getting caught and we then promptly forget it all the next day. So we need someone to write it down..."

"Rules." Willed on by the foolhardy outsiders, the word slides treacherously from his mind and finds it's way through his clenched teeth.

"...so basically..."

"A game has rules and rules are the game, like football with a referee and two linesmen. The teams toss a coin and decide which end they will play from and the one who wins will kick off the ball and they cannot use their hands, only feet, except for the goalkeeper in the penalty area and in a throw-in which is where the ball crosses the side-lines..."

"Look, dude. You really have to stop interrupting. I think this is the bit where I talk, OK?" He stops and the bubble is silent except for the vibrations of the jeering outsiders.

"Alright, Betts. It has to have rules, so tell us the rules." A dry roasted peanut impacts the bubble over his arm. He tracks the trajectory back to Guy Higson who slouches, *bad for posture, Mother says never slouch, back straight knees bent, keep the spine in it's natural curve.*

"Bloody hell Guy. It's a bit of fun, OK? What is it about you Accountancy wallahs, that you always need rules? What's wrong with a bit of anarchy? Well, here's a rule for you. Next one to interrupt will...have...to...drink....this. A dirty pint for the dirty foul-mouth who speaks over me. Don't say you haven't been warned." Carmichael has picked up a glass and has decanted the dregs from the other glasses and now everything is tidy. All the glasses are empty except one that is full, and then he pours ash into the full glass and now it is dirty. A dirty pint.

Higson draws on a thin reefer and coughs asthmatically and the smoke shoots out in blasts like the poppet valves on a locomotive, short and loud. "Sounds fair enough. We all know Balfour will end up drinking it. He'll drink bloody anything. No, the boy's right. It's his gig. Let him set the rules. Chris?"

And they all turn to face him and a prickling starts in his forehead. A glass appears in front of his eyes and a trail of bubbles snakes its way up the side of the glass, tiny strings of bubbles that dance and weave like the snake charmed by the music from the jukebox. Slow and rhythmic, entrancing him. But he can see through the liquid. It isn't dirty.

"So?" He snaps away and looks at the sound and it is Carmichael. He sees them all and he counts them all and he wishes that Marcus would sit where Shelley is because Marcus is taller than Shelley. The machine that is his body takes the glass and sips the liquid. *One of the gang. In with his mates. Part of the crew.* And the liquid tastes sour. And the words form a chain and the chain is pulled across his brain. "Uh?"

"The rules, man. We have to commit the perfect murder without getting caught, OK? What are the rules? Come on. Rule 1..."

But they are confusing him. The only perfect murder is one that doesn't happen. "Murder is wrong. The law is there for a purpose. You can't break the law."

"Look, Drew. This is fucking pointless. The kid is a retard." Finn falls into the spot beside Shelley, but Shelley should have moved left and Finn sat to her right. The order is wrong.

"Finn!" Shelley is telling Finn off, and that is right because retard is a word that hurts peoples' feelings and makes them sad.

Carmichael's cigarette smoke tastes of mud and stings his eyes. "Look, Chris. It's pretend. Nobody gets murdered. It's a game, and every game needs rules, OK?" Carmichael's voice is different and his eyes look cross.

A game without rules cannot be a game, as by definition there must be a framework to determine the winners and the losers. He looks at Drew and a small locomotive shunts the letters into words and the words into sentences. "Tell me about the game? How many players? Who are the players? Where is it played? How can we tell who wins?"

"Whoa! Alright. Erm, we are the players. Everyone around this table. The idea? Well, each one of us has to come up with the perfect murder. You know, like Poirot or Columbo..."

"Nah. Columbo is shit, because you know who did it straightaway." Carmichael looks at Guy who winks. He is a homo and it is probably for sex with Carmichael.

"OK. Like Poirot. Anyway, no-one gets killed. Just pretend, eh, Chris? When we have all thought up our idea, we all vote on

347

whose idea is best and the one with the most votes wins."

"What?" Chris is stone and the bubble contains just him and Carmichael.

"What do you mean 'What'?"

"What does the one with the most votes win?"

Carmichael throws his hands in the air. "I don't know! A teddy bear, a goldfish, a night of passion with me..."

"I'll go for that." It was Guy the homo. He has sex with men.

"You should be so lucky, you queer. Look Chris, the prize isn't important. It's just a game. Anyway, so, you want rules. What rules would you have?"

So, the murder game is alright as no-one is murdered. Chris reads the pages of his mind and finds the words to make the rules.

"Rule 1. The murder has to be motiveless. You don't need a reason. The people Poirot catches always have a reason for killing someone and that's how he catches them. He works out the motive and then works out who has that motive."

"OK. I like it!" Drew scratches his chin and is nodding. "So there must be no motive, like a cat killing a bird, this exercise is for fun."

"Rule 2. The person you pretend to murder can be anyone. It does not have to be someone you don't like because that breaks rule 1. It can be anyone."

"OK. So the murder has to be anonymous. Apart from the research required to select a victim, there must be no connection between the murderer and the victim. Rule 2."

Now the words are tumbling from his mouth and the outsiders are howling but the people are smiling and Chris is happy because they are friendly.

"Rule 3 - It is only murder if the one person kills another. The victim cannot fall off a cliff, or jump in front of a train. The death must be clearly murder and not suicide or an accident."

"Sounds fair. Any more?"

"Rule 4 - The murder must be directly inflicted by the murderer. Murdering by poison or other indirect means is not allowed, because then it would not be possible to say that the murderer actually committed the murder."

"Drew. This guy's scary. Are you sure he hasn't done this before? He's not on day release from Broadmoor is he?" The voice comes from Finn Byrne, and Chris considers the words and shapes the intonation. Is he joking? Does he know about Brookfield? But Carmichael makes an answer. "I reckon he's just a clever lad. You're not a raving psycho, are you, Chris?"

Psycho starring Anthony Perkins, late at night, the house on the hill and the lady in the shower, it was a pretend murder too because the blood was chocolate sauce and Janet Leigh married Tony Curtis which cannot happen if she is dead. "No, I am not a raving psycho. I have Asperger syndrome and that is different."

"So, shut the fuck up Finn and give the man a break. He's disabled for Christ's sake. Do you *Micks* have no compassion? Next Rule?"

Chris is happy because Carmichael is his friend.

"Rule 5 - You cannot kill a person in their sleep or whilst unconscious because they would not know they had been murdered. And that is the last rule."

Chris looks around the table and all of the sixteen eyes are looking at him, and he can feel the pinpoint indentations on the bubble, and he waits for the eyes to turn away. The noise of the bar warms the air in the bubble and presses the heat against his face.

"Fucking brilliant. The man is a legend!" Chris feels a slap on his shoulder, the meniscus twisting, the bubble stretched to bursting, and the hand is attached to an arm and the arm is Carmichael's and Carmichael is falling back into his seat.

"If I may Chris? One last rule, because I know these people. Give 'em an inch and they will take a mile. If we are going to do this let's do it properly. No ray-guns, aliens, dinosaurs or similar shit. It has to be real stuff. No Doctor Who or Star Wars, OK?"

The glass has chilled his fingers and condensation is leaving blacks spots on his jeans. The panel in his head was wiped clean and his mind clicked *File/ New* and a blank sheet appeared onto which the words of the rules drifted and were formatted in *Times New Roman* and his mind clicked *File/ Save As* and typed *Murder Book Rules*. But the Book was incomplete. *Neatness is completeness.*

"What are the murders?" He looks around but no-one is

looking at him.

"All in good time, Chris. Drink your pint. Relax."

The pressure of their bodies against him squeezes the bubble and he can sense that it will burst and the torrent of effluent will pour in and he will drown in the noise and the smells. He rises from the sofa and then he has retraced the twelve paces to the creaking door, as the spiny fingers of the outsiders beckon him towards them, surrounding the threshold awaiting their time to scratch and claw at the fabric of the bubble.

Drew says he can be a member of the Monday Club if he writes the Book but, for now, it must remain incomplete. He must obey the rules and write the Book. Mother had warned to be mindful of people taking advantage but he has not listened to her and now he has to write the book for them and they will take advantage.

So he will write the Book and he will be a member of the Monday Club and he *will* show them.

Chapter 39

"Come on, Dave. You're the computer here." Daley had pounced on the sergeant's desk and flicked through the folders looking for details of the suspects, their families and more particularly their siblings.

"I've told you, Gov. Carmichael has one sister but she's in Canada. The rest of them, who knows? We never even checked. There was no need."

Daley threw his arms in the air and searched around for inspiration. He strode over to the whiteboard, grabbed a marker pen and wrote down their names - a checklist. "Guys. We're looking for a brother and sister. Come on! Throw some names out!"

"Andrew Carmichael and his sister Sarah?" Steve Taylor ventured the obvious. "I'll call and see what I can find out." Straightaway, he set about locating details of Carmichael's sister without having a clue how he would go about it.

"Ok, Good." Daley drew a line adjacent to Carmichael's and added the sister.

"Dawn Silverton, Rachel Jones, Guy Higson, Shelley Nugent?" It was Deb. "Can we really be suggesting that they collaborated with a sibling to kill each other?"

"Dawn Silverton's an only child. I went to see her parents." Daley struck through Dawn Silverton's name.

"So is Rachel Jones," chipped in Dave. "I remember from the files." Another name, another struck through. "...and Higson has no sister but two older brothers, so unless one of them started out as a woman..." A stroke of blue was sent through Higson's name.

"So from our victims, that leaves Shelley Nugent." Daley tapped the name with the marker. "Anyone know about her family?"

"I'll get onto that as well", piped up Taylor. His finger was on a line in a folder and his other hand held the phone.

"So from the Monday Club, that leaves Finn Byrne, Marcus Balfour and Alice Bown. What about Finn Byrne? Does he have a sister?"

"No idea, Sir." huffed Taylor. "I'll ring Mike Corby at the hospital. He can ask. Just give me a few minutes."

"Sorry, Steve. Just do your best, eh?" The senior officer acknowledged the junior's efforts. Taylor and Corby were the grunts of the team, dealing with the heavy lifting. Often overworked, often overlooked. "So, Marcus Balfour, the doctor? Anybody know about him?"

Deb shuffled through her notebook. "Yes, Gov. Him we do know about. He has a biography on the Hospitals website. He has a brother and a sister. The sister is in Australia and the brother has a newsagents in Hemel Hempstead. Alice Bown, we know absolutely nothing about."

"So do we know if Balfour's sister is visiting the UK?" He was met by a bank of shrugs. "Deb, get onto it as soon as. Steve's got enough on his plate." Whetstone nodded.

"Sir?" It was Steve. "Mike says Byrne has a brother in Ballymena and Shelley Nugent is an only child." More names were struck from the list.

"OK. So assuming everyone is telling us the truth about their respective families, who does that leave?" Daley scanned the list on the whiteboard. "We have Carmichael and his sister, Marcus Balfour and *his* sister and Alice Bown and God knows how many siblings.

OK, guys, outside the box!" Daley scanned them all, imploring them to see a connection he had yet to make. Let's look at it from the other end. Let's concentrate on 1997. There were a group of them involved in the death of the vagrant. This all centres on that group. Whatever is happening now stems back to that group and whatever happened on that evening. Who was there that evening?

As the names were reeled off, Daley drew an asterisk next to the names on the list.

"If we're discounting the ones we have already crossed off, and Marcus Balfour is out because Alice didn't mention him as part of the group, that just leaves Alice Bown, Chris Betts and Carmichael himself."

"And out of that lot", Monaghan remarked, "it is Carmichael who stands to lose out financially, Carmichael who has gone

AWOL. He still has to be out hot favourite."

"I know Dave, but I just keep getting drawn back to Chris Betts and here he is again. What do we know about his family?"

"Nothing. Nothing at all." Dave scratched his thinning scalp. "We know from the notes that he was collected from the booby hatch by his family but apart from that..." When Monaghan had reviewed them earlier, the reference to St. Nicholas' - the *booby hatch* - had frustratingly turned out to be almost a dead end.

Almost.

Christopher Betts had been admitted at various times in the Nineties, but that was all they were prepared to divulge, apart from stating that his file was empty because his notes had been sent to Park Royal Hospital in Brent four years ago. Daley hoped that line of enquiry would prove more fruitful. As yet, the mysterious Christopher Betts had been able to sneak around under the radar unfettered.

"My money's still on Carmichael." Deb had been listening intently. There were several scenarios that all seemed plausible but, in her mind, led to the same conclusion. "Somehow he murders the tramp and along with the girls and Guy, they run off, leaving Betts holding the baby. Maybe when they left the tramp wasn't dead. Maybe he died in Betts' arms? The report did say he was covered in blood and wandering the streets. Perhaps the incident was so traumatic he was unable to handle it and flipped his trolley?"

"And the shame won't go away. He has to set things straight tidy up after himself. So now he is systematically giving them a taste of their own medicine. Maybe when they're all gone, he will have atoned."

"But why such a long gap? Why did it take him ten years to suddenly start feeling so ashamed he had to atone?"

"Perhaps when he was admitted they put on psychotropics and he enjoyed playing with building bricks for some time. Then he stops taking the meds and relapses. Then after he has moved down to *The Smoke* his medication wears off and he has a recurrence of the screaming abdabs, goes off his trolley and kills Rachel, and now Dawn Silverton? Maybe?"

"But what about Alice Bown? She mentioned this Murder Book that Betts is supposed to have. She specifically said to find

Betts and to find that book."

"Those pages have to be pages from the Murder Book. If whoever is doing the killing is leaving us this breadcrumb trail, then they must have the Book. Each page in the Book is another Murder, narrated by the person who then goes on to be murdered. These people foretold the manner of their own death, a decade and a half before it happened."

"Alice seemed adamant that it was Betts who has the Book, so she seems to think he was the murderer."

"And we have still not located Betts?

"No, Gov."

"We have to locate Christopher Betts before he has a chance to turn another page of that book. Come on Deb, we're off to Park Royal."

Chapter 40

1997 - Thursday 17th April, Subway Cafeteria, *Fifty-four*, Coventry

What the hell does he want now?

Carmichael skulked deeper into the blue fabric armchair as the omnipresent form of Chris Betts rounded the doorway. At 11:30am, *FiftyFour* was milling with a scattering of students, as the early birds got their lunch and the slackers thought about breakfast. Vainly, he hoped there were enough of each to cover him, but still he scratched his ear, hid behind his forearm and slouched lower over his coffee, the smallest target possible. Maybe the retard will give up, walk past, or get the message and just piss off. But it was a forlorn hope, given Chris Betts' almost autistic single-mindedness. The wanker had been after him for days now and however much Carmichael had dodged and weaved, Betts sixth sense had always located him. And there would be only one reason he would be in the Union at 11:30 in the morning and that was his *bloody Murder Book*. Carmichael's patience was wearing thinner than the sinuous roll-up he had carefully manufactured.

And that was gossamer thin.

In his experience, there were several kinds of people who attended University. There were those stellar students who hit the ground running and seemed to breeze through, always attending lectures, assignments in on time. *Perfect*. There were those out to have a good time. They delivered but assignments went to the wire, lecturers were exasperated, other students astounded. Then there were the normal ones - if such a word could be used in this place, combining the most desirable - or undesirable, elements of the two. Reading Law at Coventry had been a well-considered choice. He had done his homework. He knew he could breeze through with minimum effort for maximum results, but also have enough spare time for a little fun.

All work and no play...which just about described Chris Betts. There was no doubt that the guy had a screw or two loose, mumbling away to his imaginary friends. And the work ethic? Well, his was extreme to the point of exclusion. Like a terrier with a rabbit, no sooner was the assignment issued than he had latched on to it, locked himself away and handed it in. Even the rising stars were in awe of him. It was unbelievable, given that these were supposed to be the best three years of ones life, how much time he spent on work.

And that was the point of the exercise in the first place.

It was supposed to be a bit of fun. Out of his depth, Chris was hanging around *Browns* and the SU like a spare dick at an orgy, listening to conversations and staring at people. In his capacity of leader of the Monday Club, it had befallen Carmichael, to sort it. But apart from locking Betts in a cupboard, he hadn't a clue what to do. Then Dawn had suggested the *Murder Book*. She was always the brains of the outfit, the enterprising one. She said Carmichael himself spent too much time thinking with his cock. Looking at her, as she sat across the low table from him, he could see why. She was the most beautiful girl he had ever met.

Anyway, the solution was simple. Like throwing a sock to a Jack Russell and watching it spend hours tearing it apart. Take any idea, the more outlandish the better and set Chris about producing an assignment. Like the idea of perpetual motion, or nuclear fission, or what existed before the Big Bang. Something that would melt other people's minds, but for Chris would set him off at full tilt and keep him away from all the serious stuff, like sex, and drink, and well, more sex. Unfortunately, he had taken them more seriously than even the very serious Shelley Nugent could have imagined. He had only gone and delivered.

They had settled on an extension of the *Motive, Method, Opportunity* game that they played when they were pissed - the Murder Game. An idle Sunday afternoon muse played off and on for a month or so. It was amazing how expansive their minds could get after a few tokes, and before long they had ray guns and transporters and giant wombats with razor teeth bred in remote parts of Hampshire. It had become puerile.

Then Dawn had had her bright idea.

"Why don't we get Chris Betts to write all of these ideas down? Refine them, make them sensible. See what he comes up with. Knowing him, he'll research the great murders, get into the minds of the famous criminologists, develop motives and

356

methods and all that shit. You never know, we could have a best seller, and buy a plantation in Jamaica and write novels forever, whilst listening to the humming birds buzz."

Of course it would never happen. It was just a Sunday afternoon muse. Even Chris would understand his leg was being tugged from its sockets by a bunch of sadistic bastards. But he hadn't. Even when they told him point blank. And here he was now, carrying that blue folder, chasing after Carmichael with yet more amendments for him to approve.

When is he going to get the message that I don't care anymore!

Scooching lower, he leant his head on his hand but Chris Betts' homing beacon had been activated and nothing could stop his inward trajectory now.

"Drew. All the changes are done. I have left a space for your story."

"Great work, Chris I'll read it tomorrow." Drew waved his hand dismissively and purposefully stared into middle distance the other way, where an apple-perfect arse in tight jeans sidled past.

"You have to check and you have to make sure and I need your story." Chris stood still, a waxwork, arms outstretched the blue folder proffered, as a waiter offering a wine list to a particularly belligerent customer.

"*Chris!*" The word left Drew, sharp and terse, heavy with exasperation. Composing himself, he added "In the morning, dude. Look, we're a little busy right now. All work and no play?" He thrust the smouldering roll-up in Chris Betts face, smirking callously as the eyes blinked and the head shied away. "Now, come on. Kindly fuck off and come back during working hours." But Chris just stood, rooted to the brown carpet tiles, looking between Dawn and Drew, confused. *He is here. Drew is here. The Book is here. Drew must take it.* Drew rolled his eyes dramatically. Chris had no understanding of social cues. Through the irritation, Drew kept his composure but it bled through into the words he spoke. "Just run along and find somebody else to annoy, will you?"

Across from him Dawn, leaning on her elbow on the arm of the uncomfortably modern sofa, still half asleep, lifted her head lazily. Rachel was out for the count at the other end.

"Oh, come on, Drew. Just take a look and have done with it?" Chris' eyes flicked between Dawn and Drew, the eyes of a puppy standing over a pool of urine, uncertain of the best ally. Drew looked squarely at Dawn, briefly betrayed. He allowed his eyes to drift downward. She was wearing a long ribbed jumper, so long it doubled as a dress, softening the curves of her breasts and undulating hips, stopping abruptly halfway up her thighs. That dress always made his so damn horny. If Dawn took umbrage now, he could be robbed of her for many nights to come - or more appropriately, not to *come*. He decided discretion was the better part of valour in order to keep Dawn Silverton moist and available.

"Alright, alright, whatever! Chris - sit." He pointed to the vacant squab beside him. Chris scooted around the sofa and sat himself obediently beside Drew like the puppy, having received his admonishment, now back in favour with it's master.

***

As the last cold flush from the syringe had entered his biceps, Carmichael felt the breath leave his body and his vision faded to green. A weird shade of mouldy green, somewhere between verdigris and the phlegm of an infected throat and it sparkled with black dots. And then it was gone and he was awake. His parched tongue had stuck to the roof of his mouth. He tried to raise a hand but his arms were leaden. Was he still dreaming or had the dream bled over into consciousness? He opened his eyes to blackness. So black that there was nothing to confirm his eyes were open at all, but the pressure of his lids removed from his eyeballs. Flipping his head from side to side yielded no clues. He was surrounded by a writhing, consuming darkness. Deep in the pit of his stomach, a foreboding grew. He began to feel nauseous, whether from the effects of the drugs, or from the sense of disorientation, or simply from the unease breeding inside him.

"Hello?" He spoke tentatively, fearing someone or something in the blackness with him, but the blackness held it's ground. "Hello?" This time a bark and a resonating echo, ringing from the walls, dying almost as soon as it had started. Once more he raised his arm but a thin band gouged at his wrist. In turn each of his arms and legs met the same solid resistance, the confinement turned to unease and then to panic, a need to escape, to break free of the chair, to break free of the blackness. Wildly he rocked from side to side but the chair creaked and groaned and did not yield an inch. With all the strength he could muster, he straightened his frame against the tethers feeling them bite into his flesh, red and white sparks of electricity lighting his eyes against the void. Defeated, he settled back into the chair and the room, his staccato breath roaring in the confines and a clammy sweat forming on his brow, pulsing blood throbbing past his eardrums, the cold, silent black closing in once more.

Calm. He must remain calm at all costs. Drawing deep breaths, Drew steadied his nerves and his heart slowed, the pounding in his ears ebbing away into the white noise of the space.

"Is there anyone here?" The room responded with silence.

Slowly, like the dawn of a new day after a night of storms, recollections returned of the moments before he had faded to unconsciousness. The struggle in the kitchen, her wild eyes, the pin prick pain in his arm. How long had he been out? It had seemed like a few meagre seconds but it had been the same during a minor operation a few years ago. General anaesthetic squanders time.

Resistance against his restraints was futile. Settling back in the chair, relaxing his wrists, trying to ease the pain, Carmichael knew he could be there for some time. He decided to learn as much about the place as he could, using each of his senses in turn. He scraped his shoe on the floor beneath the chair; it was smooth and free from debris, and clicked like concrete beneath his feet. He uttered a constrained yell.

"Ah...Ah..." The echoes rang briefly and vanished into the black. The room was small, probably as big as the kitchen, maybe smaller but not vast, but the walls were hard.

He sniffed the air. It smelt of cold and decay, of old cardboard and must. He could smell burnt dust. Behind him a sharp metallic sound broke the silence. A key in a lock? He tried to twist his neck but the back of the chair prevented him seeing. He screwed his eyes against an excruciatingly painful white light. His eyelids quivering, he strained to ease them open, to resist the shards of white, hearing footfalls on stone steps behind him.

"What the fuck are you playing at?" he barked, bravado overcoming wisdom, his eyes gradually becoming accustomed to the glare, blinking as his surrounding began to take shape. "Get me out of these bloody things, you bitch!" The slap across his head sent a jar through his neck.

"I don't think you're in any position to tell me what to do, pet, do you?" She spat the words out. There was no pretence anymore, just hate. Her face had turned to stone, expressionless and cold, drawing every last degree of heat from the chill air. The lips, so fulsome they had once begged for his kiss, were now a thin malevolent sneer. Her eyes were dead black studs. "We have waited so long for this moment. So long to see you suffering the way we have suffered." The last sentence was plaintive, as her eyes turned to imagine a happier past. A past when he, whoever he was, was with her. "The way he suffered."

The room was in sharp relief now. He squinted down at his bonds, commercial plastic cable ties. The wields on his wrists were already red and angry, struggling would be counter-productive. He would need her cooperation to break free, and that seemed in short supply right now. Looking out at the wall opposite he could make out the pattern of brickwork underneath a thick coat of whitewash, here and there pockmarked with cracks. Up against it, sat an old leather easy chair, faded and pale, here and there mottled with mildew, an old sideboard, Fifties or Sixties chic, it had seen better days. A tablecloth covered the surface and on it sat a vase with what appeared to be plastic carnations, and an old wireless set, cream faded beige through age, ovoid and bulbous, a relic far older than the sideboard. In the centre there was a blue lever arch folder, containing about one hundred pages, it was open midway through. And behind that there was a small plain photo frame, maybe six inches by four. A smiling face beamed out from it, familiar but Carmichael could not pin it down to a name. He turned his head sideways as Carol passed to the left of him, unhurried, arms folded. Her hair was tied back with an elasticated band. She was smiling at the photo on the sideboard.

Drew twisted his head right and a primeval terror gripped his chest as he stared into the dead black eyes. The blood drained from his head causing it to shimmy sideways, in overload as he tried to process what he was seeing. As the panic took hold, his breathing, fast and shallow, pulsated around the confines of the cellar and his feet scrabbled in vain to escape, held fast by the bolts that affixed the chair solidly to the ground. The vile decaying body sat, as he was, slumped in a chair, but it was dressed in a mouldering white shirt and blue tie along with a dusty black suit. A folded white handkerchief poked forlornly from the breast pocket and the head lolled towards him, a sightless stare fixing him in its gaze. The face was brown and dried parchment, cheeks sunken like a fallen soufflé, the jaw wide and gaping in a lifeless yawn. Strands of dry, white hair hung from the skull, combed and neatened, flakes of rotten skin fallen like dandruff upon the shoulders. Behind the obscene form, the wall was plastered from floor to ceiling with snapshots, of Drew, of Dawn, of Rachel, of all of them, laughing and joking, kissing and petting, driving and walking, dismembered heads and spreading pools of crimson, bent motorcyclists and raging infernos. The wall was an almanac, a pictorial diary for the Monday Club, detailed, comprehensive and grotesque.

She grabbed his chin and yanked his face forwards, her fingernails gouging at his jaw.

"Look at me. Look at *me*!" She was shouting, her eyes wide and deranged. "What gives you the right to look at him?"

Frantically, he recalled the previous days, their building rapport, the warmth of her body against his. He recalled that one kiss and finally he realised. The pain in his biceps, the wild dreams, her pleas for him to comfort her. She had never wanted him; she just needed him there. She had needed to keep him away from the police, not to protect him but so she could have him for herself, for whatever twisted game she was playing. His diaphragm convulsed, acid stung his throat and it was all he could do to steady it.

"Are you out of your fucking mind? The police are already looking for me. It will only be a matter of time before the work out where I have been hiding out."

Her hand loosed his chin, casting it aside, wrenching his neck. "Oh, Shut up whining. Why is it you men always end up whining? We don't want to hear it, do we?" Her eyes momentarily flicked towards the thing seated next to him. And then they were back, shining, crazed. "By the time the Police find you, it'll be too late for anything."

And it occurred to Carmichael, that the house, Carol's house could be anywhere, that the cellar below it, for that's where he must be, could be anywhere. Abandoned in this lightproof, soundproof hellhole, how long would it be before madness and starvation and death took over? Would he linger for days, smothered by the blackness as it slowly consumed him? How long would he languish, a desiccated brown parchment, a fixed black stare and hideous death grin, entombed below the London suburbs?

"For God's sake, Carol what's this all about? Whatever it is, let's just talk about it, please?" He had to keep her talking. Give him time to think, to persuade her to cut these ties, a chance to get his hands round her neck. She would regret the day she took on Drew Carmichael. "Just tell me, what have I done?"

Once more she grabbed at his chin and stared angrily into his eyes. "What have you done? What have *you* done? You did everything. Everything! It was always you! *Always.*"

He shook his face free of her grasp. Suddenly her demeanour changed and, as if a great weight had descended onto her shoulders, she was somewhere else gazing into an unseen distance. She backed away and placed herself in the musty chair, crossing her knees and leaning back. He felt the physical presence of the corpse drawing his gaze but he resisted, his eyes firmly set on her face, now distant, calm, reflective.

"He used to come down here a lot, my Kitt. He was very troubled, and they couldn't get to him here - his demons - he used to say they lived in the outside and would never come indoors because they needed the damp to survive. It was the peace and quiet he liked. Listen..." The room fell silent, deathly silent, except for the faint ubiquitous London rumble and the noise of the crisp air moving. "I love it down here too, just me and him. I come down here to listen to the radio, or maybe to read. Sometimes, I read out loud. Pretend he can still hear. I ask him questions and sometimes I can still hear him answer. He always knew the answer, my Kitt. He was so clever. Cleverer than I could ever be, that's for sure."

"For God's sake, Carol, untie my hands. Let's sort this out."

But she was lost to Carmichael, away in a world of

362

reminiscence where the pain was yet to come and the gnarled corpse lived and breathed.

"Do you know I used to pretend he was my son, sometimes? In those down days, when the world became too much for him, he would curl up in bed beside me and it would all go away. Of course, I never had any bairns. It just never happened, so I didn't mind taking care of him. I never wanted him to leave home. It was Mam and Dad. They pushed him away, pushed him out of the house and he just couldn't cope."

"Look, you can take the money, go away somewhere. Somewhere nobody will find you. Start a new life. We can do it together." Drew had to drag her back to the present, away from the past. He had to try and keep her here with him, to find some way to persuade her to release him.

She jumped to her feet and grabbed his arms, as he backed his face away from her round, demonic eyes, but he was held fast by the unyielding chair. "Money!" she screamed, "Money! You think this is all about money? He thinks this is about his money, my sweet!" Her eyes once again flicked to the corpse, then back to his face angry and challenging. "I never wanted any of your filthy money!" She let go and fell back in the easy chair, her voice again growing pained and tortured. "It was never about the money. It was always Kitt. I did it all for Kitt." Abruptly she turned her head towards the corpse. He saw her eyes soften, tired and careworn, a rim of moisture welling in the corners. "You know he looked up to you? Spoke about you in his letters? He would have given anything to be like you, to be accepted like you were accepted - just for a day. But all he got was your ridicule and derision, all of you laughing behind his back, mocking his condition. You never tried to understand, to accept him for who he was. To you he was just an injured animal, to be played with and poked at. You were always too busy with those - girls, with the Monday Club."

He let out a sigh. His head ached from the anaesthetic and his mouth was dry. "Carol. Please! Let me go and we can sort this out. Believe me, I don't know what your talking about". His tone was pleading, undisguised, for once genuine. The ties were digging into the raw flesh of his arms and the pain was becoming insistent. How long had the body been there? Was it the husband, Phil or Pete or whoever? He was struggling to remember the name. Or was this Kitt? The brother, Kitt. Perhaps she had told no-one of his death, brought him down here in a final act of charity, to keep him safe from the world. He could have been here for months, years. "Look, I don't know any Kitt. I never knew you had a brother until the other night. I've never met him before, honestly!"

She leapt to her feet and shouted so loudly he could feel his eardrums. "Don't you ever, *ever* mention his name again!"

"But I don't know who you are talking about, really. This must all be some mistake. I am telling you, I don't know who you are talking about."

"Shut up. *Shut up!*" An open hand hit him full across the face and he winced as the chair back impacted his skull, the ties gnawed at his wrists. She turned and took the picture from the sideboard, held it away from her, admired it, a warm distant smile crossing on her face. "He was so beautiful." She turned the photo to Carmichael. "Don't you think?"

He stared at the image for a long moment, trying to process the glimmer of recognition. A young man, sallow and frail, an awkward, uncomfortable smile, strands of unkempt blond hair blown by the wind, frozen by the shutter and the eyes, wide and lost. From years ago, submerged in a deeply repressed memory, he recalled seeing those eyes, shining bright in the orange glow of the lamps, full of desperation, appealing to him to make the blood stop. Her voice, lost in her own memories was chanting:

To die, to sleep -

To sleep, perchance to dream - ay, there's the rub,

For in this sleep of death what dreams may come...

In that instant of recognition, he knew that he had met the corpse before.

Chapter 41

1997 - Friday 18th April - Bar 54, Coventry

As soon as he spotted him rounding the corner, peering into the cafeteria, Carmichael knew it was going to be another evening of hide and seek. He grabbed Dawn's hand and with a squeal he pulled her down the corridor and out through the fire doors into the refreshing night air. Closing the door to a tiny crack, Carmichael squinted back down the corridor, recoiling as Betts rounded the dogleg by the bogs and pushed open the door to the gents, briefly disappearing inside. Then he was back out and staring straight at the fire door. Carmichael's breathing snagged. He snatched his head away from the gap in the door and waited in silence for the inevitable. Dawn was draping herself over the back of his neck, her soft lips toying with his skin, usually a pleasurable experience, especially when, as now she was slightly drunk and slightly stoned and her inhibitions had melted away. But Betts was once more on the prowl and his irritation with the retard was becoming explosive.

"Not right now, Dawn! That bloody spak is in there again."

Dawn pulled away, sighing deeply, the mood built and now shattered. "Something has to be done, Drew." She too had become weary of the constant stalking. "He is really freaking me out now. Everywhere we go he just follows us. It just too creepy."

Drew puffed his cheeks and peered at Dawn, exasperated. She was coiling a thin braided plait around her index finger. Her eyes were wide and deep and her lips were full and moist and he needed to have her. He pressed his lips to hers and wrapped an arm around her waist, his hand delving down the back of her jeans, sliding down the small of her back to the soft crease beyond. Then she broke away. Annoyed he threw his hands into the air.

"Oh, come on! You were up for it just now."

"Not here, not now. Not with that pervert skulking about."

It was true that there wasn't a single square millimetre of this damn campus where Betts wouldn't find them. Returning his eye to the gap in the door, Drew scrutinised the corridor. *FiftyFour* was getting busier as the evening wore on and the toilet doors were creaking as people went in and out, but Chris was still there, passing students eying him curiously, his brow furrowed, perplexed, processing his next move. Under his arm, he had that damn blue folder. As Drew watched, he turned and headed back down the corridor and left into the smaller of the two bars.

"Look, Dawn. It's nearly the end of the semester. He'll get fed up over Easter, find some new *cause célèbre*, and anyway, even he's got exams coming up. Just give it until the end of the week and we'll be away from here." But Drew didn't know if even he had the patience to wait that long.

Clutching Dawn's arm, they re-entered the building and discreetly trotted down the corridor, round the corner and into the larger of the bars. Beyond the swing door, the vast room plunged into silence. The larger bar would not be used for another hour, when every student in Coventry would descend upon it for a cheap night out. Aside from a few background bulbs over the bar and the cicada hum of the refrigerators, the cavernous room was theirs.

"What if he comes in here?" Dawn was on tiptoe looking through the windows in the swing doors.

"He's gone the other way now. It'll take him hours to check everyone in the other bar. If he does come in here it's so dark he won't be able to see anything. There must be somewhere we can find to hide." He took Dawn's hand and she let out a playful girlish giggle as he led her over to the far side of the darkened room. Spinning around he pinned her against the stage. As she found his lips with hers, he hitched his hands behind her thighs. Soon she was lying, he had loosened her blouse and he was taking her to places where not even Chris Betts could find her.

Chapter 42

Daley folded the warrant card back into his jacket pocket. Dr Helen Wainwright sat behind the desk, a picture of concern. Leaning forwards, she held eye contact with Daley throughout as he related what they had managed to piece together. Now she lent back and rested her chin on the points of her fingers, weighing patient confidentiality against the growing inevitability of another murder. The wall behind her was a mosaic of certificates and a ragged spider plant abseiled down from the window ledge. Dressed in a sweat-laden white T-shirt and running shorts, it was clear that she must live close, as it had taken Daley longer to drive there than it had for her to jog. She had already pulled Betts notes, which were tantalisingly close on the desk.

"What will happen to Mr Betts when you find him?" She looked from Daley to Whetstone. Did she expect more sympathy from another woman?

"Honestly, Dr Wainwright. I can't say. If you can demonstrate a history of mental illness, we will take that into account. Whilst potentially he is a killer, they are planned rather than spontaneous, so whilst he might run, might struggle, he is unlikely to resist arrest. Apart from a little rough stuff at the initial arrest... Hopefully he won't resist. Our guys are used to this sort of thing."

"And you say the original murder happened in 1997? And then a further one in 2008 and the rest more recently?" Daley nodded and Dr Wainwright reached forward for the folder, a waft of body odour and cheap deodorant drifting across the desk. She perched her spectacles on to the end of her nose and flicked through the file in silence, occasionally looking up to the two of them, as if for some kind of validation.

"Looking at the history, it does seem to tally. Mr Betts was originally admitted to a Psychiatric hospital in Coventry in July '97. He was released into the care of his family in 1998 returning to Newcastle where St. Nicholas' took over his care. In 2000 he was discharged and the next record we have is 2008, again in July, when he admitted himself voluntarily."

"Is that usual?" Deb was taking the notes. "I mean, to admit oneself?"

"Yes, quite usual. For some people, the world is a daunting place. They need to escape periodically."

"How long did he stay that time?"

"Until Christmas 2008 when he went to stay with his family."

"And after that?"

"He has been reassessed twice since, but the last time we saw him was..." She licked a finger and turned the pages of the file. "January 2010."

"Do you have the details of the family members he stayed with?"

"Oh. Yes." Once more she riffled through the notes. "St. Nicholas' released him to his parents, in Washington, Tyne-and Wear, not far from Newcastle. Park Royal has a forwarding address in Ealing - 58 Wescott Road. It says he was released in the care of his sister, Carol."

***

Carmichael's eyes were now wide against the bright white of the walls, against the hideous deaths head and against her manic scowl. He longed to close them, squeeze the lids so tight he could pretend it was all just part of an elaborate dream. But an innate sense of self-preservation willed him to keep them open. A fundamental need to remain connected, to confront her, to react and perhaps to survive.

"What do you want from me?"

"That's just it. Can't you see? We don't want anything from you. Either of us. Not now. Too little too late."

"I don't know what you mean." He knew exactly what she meant. That April night, centuries ago, the acrid smell of the tramp, unwashed and stinking, and the stench of terror that hung about the place, the fragrance of Dawn as she pulled him away, the faint odour of his own sweat as the fear gripped his throat.

And he saw the wide terrified eyes of Chris Betts.

"Look, Whatever has happened, it's all in the past. History. We can't change that now. None of this is going to do any good.

I know people. They can help you. I can make sure you get help. I can support you financially. We can lay Chris to rest. Give him a proper burial. We can make this right."

She rose and again was filling his field of vision, her eyes contemptuous and angry. "His name is Kitt, *Kitt!* He was never Chris or Christopher, Chrissie, or spak or simple or retard, or any of the names you gave him. Not to those that really knew him, who actually cared about him." Once more he felt the sharp impact of a hand across his face. This time a cry of pain escaped his lips, his mouth filled with the metallic taste of blood. "He is not *yours* to sort out, *yours* to lay to rest. I don't even want you to touch him. You were all there. *All of you!* You all had your fun, kidded him he belonged, he was part of the gang, part of the Monday Club, but all along, it was never him, it was always you having fun at his expense. He never fitted. In his heart he always knew that but he tried so hard to be like you, and you all just led him away, away from us, away from his family. You took him away from - *me*."

"I am sorry, Carol. What else can I say? It was a lifetime ago. We were all young."

"And now you are all dead. All of you! Rachel, Dawn and Shelley. They all looked on as you goaded him, as you made him do it. Even Guy Higson and Alice Bown, who turned their backs on him when he needed them most. You left him there while you all ran and hid. You killed him that day, just as much as you killed that man. And now you are going to die."

She opened a drawer on the sideboard and brought out a syringe and a vial of colourless liquid. Suddenly it made sense, the weird hallucinations, the mixture of fact and fiction, the wild swirling miasma of reality and dreams.

"Jesus, Carol. What the fuck! Is that what you have been doing?" A spasm tightened his left arm and the bruising stung. Surely that was the answer. She had been filling him with who knows what. Filling his head with visions of death.

"You stood there that night. You stood over him as the knife slid in and you did nothing!" Then she stopped and the cellar fell quiet. She eased the needle through the seal and drew a measure of the liquid into the metered chamber, depressing the plunger slightly, a well of liquid returning through the point. She looked at him, her face now devoid of expression.

"Rohypnol. They call it the date rape drug. Makes one supplicant, willing. A man can do anything he wants with a girl who has had some of this. Surprised you haven't used it yourself?"

"You're fucking crazy..." Drew sneered. All he had was contempt.

"But the trouble is, the girl forgets. She wakes up, her knickers torn, her cunt still dripping and sore but she has no memory. I wanted you to have a memory. I needed you to remember, so I mix it with a little of this..." She placed the vial in the drawer and pulled out a different, slimmer ampule "...lysergic acid diethyl-amide, or LSD. Of course, you have to get the dosage right, otherwise it's fatal, but you probably know that. Let's hope I get it right now, eh?" She drew a small amount into the syringe and shook it slightly ensuring the liquids blended. "In truth, I have no idea how much is too much, so let's both hope that the famous Carmichael luck that has served you so well all of your privileged pathetic life holds out for you now, eh?"

"So all those dreams that freaked me out. They were LSD? I was tripping?"

"Oh, no! No, you weren't tripping. You were there. You were in your car in Treddle Lane when that piano wire garrotted Guy Higson. You were there, sitting on the end of Shelley's bed as the smoke started to drift in. And you would have been there in Alice's bathroom too, if I hadn't got your dose of Sodium Thiopental wrong. Silly me! It was meant to put you to sleep for a few hours, but hey, can't win em all, eh pet?"

"And Dawn and Rachel?"

"No, I'm afraid not. I had to do Dawnie all on my own. I watched the light go out of her eyes and I am sure she asked me why as her head lay on the floor. I saw your car, up by the church. I was willing you to come down to the house. To witness Dawn, your beautiful Dawn, getting her comeuppance. But you turned back. Deserting her in her hour of need. I told her all about it as her mouth flapped and her eyes blinked. How the *Great* Drew Carmichael failed her once more. I told her about Kitt but I think she was already gone."

Drew's head filled with images of Dawn's decapitated corpse, of her head discrete from her body. He recalled his hands

370

brushing her slim white neck and his diaphragm spasmed once more.

"Rachel. No, that wasn't me. That was all you! You and this stupid book." She gestured to the lever arch file on the sideboard. "This *Murder Book*. He was so happy to be part of the Club, for once to feel he had been accepted. He worked so hard putting the Book together. All he wanted was for you to take a look and appreciate the time and effort he had put into it for *you*. All he needed was your approval, just for one of you to even read it."

"It was just a game, Carol. Nobody meant him to take it that seriously. We were just having fun."

"Yes, you were having fun - at his expense. He hated you, all of you, for that. For leading him on and then abandoning him. When he killed Rachel, it was you that wielded the blade. And when he could no longer take the shame of what he had done, I knew I would have to finish where he had left off. You all have to die for what you have done."

"Don't be so bloody stupid. You're as mad as he is."

He saw the point of the syringe, a flash of silver in the light from the overhead bulb. His feet scrabbled on the concrete as he backed away. He backed away but the chair held him firm, shards of pain attacking his wrists. He felt the skin depress on his arm and a scratch. A howl of terror rebounded from the whitewash and the face before him turned inside out as the eyes became a circle of stars and the sound roared like the wind through the trees in the wood.

Chapter 43

Tired of hammering on the door, Daley signalled to the uniform to break a shoulder on it. On the second attempt the door gave way and in a hail of shouts they tumbled into a darkened hallway and absolute silence. Daley placed a finger to his lips. The uniforms and Deb fell quiet.

"Check the back. I'll look upstairs." Daley took the steps two at a time and peered round the dogleg towards the landing. The upstairs of the house seemed subdued and dark, all the curtains and doors closed tight. His heart was hammering and a familiar foreboding gripped him. Starting nearest the stairs, he edged open each door with his foot. The first room, a small box room was crammed with boxes and suitcases. Flexing the latex gloves between his fingers, Daley drew back the closed curtain and the grey forms took on a colourful ordinariness. Smelling old dust in the air, he resolved that he was probably the first person to open the door for some weeks. Moving to the front master bedroom, he started as he faced the double bed and saw the mound beneath the bedclothes.

"Police!" He screamed. "Get up. Get up now!" In his pocket his hand was firmly gripping his torch, metallic and substantial but there was no response. One of the uniforms had scaled the stairs when Daley had shouted and raced through the door. Together, they stealthily approached the sleeper, one either side of the bed. The uniform looked across at Daley and shrugged. Daley understood. No rise and fall of sheets. No breathing. Daley's heart thumped harder as his hands grasped the sheets, afraid of what lay beneath.

"What the..." The pillows had been arranged to mimic a sleeping form. Arranged too well, in Daley's view. "Who does this in their own house?"

"Dunno, sir, but I nearly cacked myself then." The uniform cast his eyes about the room as once more Daley drew back a curtain. "A few bottles, a dressing table, not much else. I wish our bedroom was this tidy." But Daley understood that this was not an issue of tidiness, it was an issue of loneliness; one he knew only two well. Function over form. Daley had a room just

372

like it back at his flat. He signalled to the door and the two moved past the airing cupboard with nothing but a glance inside. In the last room, the spare room, the bed was unmade and the air hung with perspiration. On the floor lay a crumpled sweatshirt. Daley was sure it was the one he had seen Carmichael wearing the other day as the overcoat was dragged from his arms by Corby.

"Sir, you need to come and take a look at this." It was a shout from Deb. Nodding at the uniform to check out the bathroom, Daley trotted back down, doubling back towards the rear of the house. Deb was waiting by an open door that led under the stairs. She had the back of her hand across her mouth and he could smell the menthol. She held out the small tin and Daley smeared some across his upper lip. He followed her down the short flight of stone steps, wrinkling his nose against the must and decay. A bare filament bulb cast a pale glow across a sparse one roomed cellar. On the opposite wall there was a sideboard, maybe a shrine, with a framed photograph and some other articles that had some significance to someone. Along the back, mounted on it's dark wood plinth sat an empty curved leather scabbard. On the right-hand wall was a montage of tens of photographs, heads and shoulders, people walking, smiling, hailing cabs. Daley recognised the Monday Club. He recognised Andrew Carmichael, Dawn Silverton, Rachel Jones, they were all there. He studied a photo of a small slim girl. Perhaps that was Alice Bown? He recognised the bodies and was perplexed. These were crime scene photos but unlike any that SOCO had taken. They were trophies. Two hard chairs stood in the middle of the floor. There was something, someone in one of them. Then he stifled a gasp, as his eyes fell on the occupant. It was Deb who broke the eerie silence.

"I think we have found Chris Betts, Sir."

CHAPTER 44

1997 - Monday 21st April - *FiftyFour*, Coventry

"Oh, oh! Call the pound. Here comes your poodle, Drew. Hey, Chris, you wanna drink?" Finn exchanged an amused smile with Marcus and Guy, as Carmichael closed his eyes and pleaded for salvation. Having spent half the previous evening and all morning dodging and weaving, looking over his shoulder, now he had to contend with Guy and Finn ripping the shit out of him. It was just one huge joke to them, but Dawn was starting to become pre-occupied with it, and Rachel too. It had become the only topic of conversation. *Just one night of peace and quiet without Betts!* Even in the crowded *Bar 54*, Chris stood in his own exclusion zone, so separate and out of place, motionless, as he had been each day that week and for virtually every day since they had started that stupid book. He just waited for the cue to approach the *Great Drew Carmichael*. A cue that hadn't come the previous day, or the day before that, and still he stood.

Drew felt Dawn tug at his sleeve and she leaned close to his ear. "I just don't like it. It's not normal. You've got to make him understand...and anyway, have you seen the way he looks at Rachel and me? It's as if he's never seen a girl before, like he is examining us." She grabbed her cardigan from the back of her chair and pulled it around her bare shoulders, clasping it tightly across her bosom. "He just stares. Doesn't even try to look away when we catch him looking. The other day, Rachel thought he was going grab her, you know, feel her up."

Drew smacked a flat hand on his forehead, exasperated. He was sick of going over this same old problem. "Look, he's got Asperger's Syndrome, you know that. I read up about it the other day. He's like a radio tuned to all the stations at the same time. He has to filter out the crap. Then when he does latch onto something, he can't understand. Like the only radio station he can tune into is in French or Spanish, so he has to continually translate everything. Cut him some slack, eh, Dawn. Can you imagine how difficult it must be coming here?"

"I know, Drew, but he's everywhere. He hangs about the

kitchens in Priory, in Browns, in *FiftyFour*. Even in town, Pizza Hut, he's there. And he always just stands, or sits, absolutely still like some kind of stalker. It's just really creepy."

Drew huffed and slammed his cigarettes onto the table. "What would you have me do?" he grated." I've told him to piss off. I have manhandled him out of the door. For Christ sakes, I have even had a word with Student Welfare."

"Just deal with it. Tell him it's finished." Her eyes were imploring and round. He could never resist her when she looked at him that way. He stood and faced Chris, took a deep breath, fixed a smile on his face and summoned up what little enthusiasm he had left.

"Hey Chris. What can I do for you?" Behind him he heard wheezing and cackling as the other collapsed in fits of hysterics at his misfortune. Dawn alone was not laughing. Her stern face hinted at privileges denied if this was not sorted.

Betts squinted his eyes as if shutting out the light, as his brain processed Carmichael's greeting. Then, as if summoned before a court martial, he approached the table and stood beside Dawn looking directly at Drew. "I have done the amendments and I need you to check them."

"O-kay." Drew looked down at the blue folder in Chris' hands. It was rammed with paper. The main chapters, the actual Murder Book, was less than a dozen pages but Chris being Chris, had researched to the *nth* degree, providing expansive appendices containing exemplars and citations, references and studies. Drew had been fool enough to take it from him before and spent a whole weekend trying to persuade the retard he had read it in enough detail to satisfy Chris' exacting standards. And still he kept making amendments and asking for Drew's approval. How many more amendments could there have been since last Thursday at *Browns* when *The Book* had consumed the entire evening? It had only been a month since Chris had uncomfortably sat amongst them clasping a pint of Heineken, like it was a vial of nitro-glycerine and they had outlined the game. The whole thing had started to become a huge ball-ache. Drew had unleashed a monster.

That first evening it had been Rachel who had led, her prowess in *Motive, Method, Opportunity* was legendary within then group. Like an actress preparing for an audition, she pulled herself upright and uncrossed her legs, laying her outstretched hands on her knees and squirming her backside into the sofa to straighten her back for perfect posture. She cast a withering scowl at Marcus, who averted his eyes from her endless legs and smiled rather sheepishly at Alice.

"Ok. My Da used to watch a lot of those old American gangster films where the guy gets shot and he falls down stone dead without even a bullet hole. Bang Bang, you're dead and it was all over. Occasionally they dragged themselves along for a while moaning and groaning but essentially it was boring." She paused briefly as Drew and Guy, collapsed in fits, putting their interpretation on *moaning and groaning*. "Death is a big event, especially in the life of the victim. If you are going to kill someone, make it an event! It has to be spectacular, violent and gory, at least interesting. Otherwise why bother? I reckon they had it right in the olden days. A fiery poker up the arse, hanging drawing and quartering. Some of the mediaeval methods of torture and execution, which inflicted grotesque amounts of damage to the victim, keeping them alive for as long as they could, forcing them to endure their seemingly endless agony."

"Jesus, Rachel. You've given this some thought, I can see. Gonna have watch you in future." Drew had smirked as Rachel's withering scowl again came his way. Dawn had held on tighter to her property.

"Then there is execution. A whole performance. Think of the French Revolution. An execution was an event. Crowds of peasants converging on the *Place de la Révolution*, baying for the blade to fall. Blood spurting from the severed neck and the head held up to the crowd. They say the eyes would still be looking around. Cool!"

Dawn Silverton raised her hand to interrupt Rachel, who was in full flow. "Hang on. The rules say that the murder must be committed in such a way that the murderer isn't caught. Isn't that right Chris? How could you do that without anyone noticing? Setting up a guillotine at Hyde Park Corner would be a dead giveaway. Far better to lure the unsuspecting victim to a secluded place and catch them unaware."

"Come on, Rachel," added Finn, "None of that is really practical is it? How can you execute someone without them being aware of what is about to happen? You can't wait until they are sleeping and you can't persuade them to put their heads on a block. And after all, there is a reasonable argument to say that execution is not considered murder."

"Depends on your viewpoint, love! Tell you what, if someone wanted to chop my head off, I would certainly consider it murder."

"OK, OK," interjected Drew." So we have decapitation. Can't use a guillotine, and they ain't going let us do it voluntarily, so how would you go about it?"

Dawn placed her hand on his knee and as she advanced it ever closer to the top of his thigh, she said: "You lure them into a private place, like a back garden or a warehouse, or a building site, where you have secreted an axe, and you grab it, swirl it around your head. *Schrrupp!* Or you could use a sword like King Arthurs Knights, although those were heavy bastards so you would probably have to be a bloke!"

"Or a scimitar. Anyway, whose murder is this?" Rachel leaned back and folded her arms.

"Now, now, girls don't bitch! You can share it. Anyway, who's coming into town? Chris, write it up. Same time, same place next Monday. Guy, your turn next."

And so it had started. Every Monday night a new murder was described and most of the next day was spent dodging in and out of doorways to avoid the ever-increasing pressure from Betts to check his work and bring the project to a conclusion. Such was the insistence of Chris Betts, that he could not be shaken off.

And now he was here again.

Drew proffered a hand, took the familiar blue folder and opened it across the table, turning each page carefully. The book was presented immaculately, each page a succinct and accurate transcription of every Monday since the beginning, followed by an expansive explanation of how each method could be realised, and then a burgeoning Appendix providing references and citations, diagrams and photographs, physical and empirical detail: which type of sword would be best for Rachel or Dawn to wield, what gauge of piano wire would garrotte most effectively, examples of house fires where accelerants had been used and, as usual, except for a couple of amendment markers in the left hand column, absolutely complete.

"Chris, what do you want me to say, man? It's finished, complete. Great job!" He closed the covers and without turning his head away from the table, resignedly raised the folder towards the still standing figure beside him.

"It's not finished."

The back of Drew's neck prickled and a spurt of adrenalin hit his brain. Still seated, he swivelled his head and raised his eyes slowly, deliberately towards Betts. "Shit Chris. If I say it's finished then it is finished. Now, please, *fuck off*." Drew turned back to the group and looked around the table. Marcus was sniggering, always behind the curve, but the rest had stopped and were staring uncomfortably at Drew and Chris; the latter standing his ground, a frown across his brow. There was joke but he didn't understand. Confused, Drew looked from his friends to Betts. Was the *spak* taking the piss? Drew didn't mind a little fun at his expense. Hey, it made for good team dynamics, but this retard was humiliating him. Shit, even Dawn was smirking now. Drew began to boil. "Just take the fucking book away. I never want to see it again."

Chris, like an automaton, made to leave but turned back, repeating the action several times, utterly conflicted. "It's not finished. It can't be not finished. You have to finish it."

"So fucking finish it, you moron. Just piss off and leave us alone!"

"Drew, steady on. Can't you see he's confused?" Guy had leant across and laid a hand on Drew's arm. Drew shrugged it off.

"I can't finish it. I am not in the Monday Club. You have to finish it. You have to add your page. I can't leave it incomplete. Can't you hear them? The outsiders? They are in the words, they're angry with us from between the lines. We have to finish the book."

By now an uncomfortable hush had descended on the bar. All eyes had turned to see what the fuss was about. The jukebox played but no-one was listening. Drew ran his hands through his hair and looked around at the rest of the group, at

378

the discomfort rippling through the bar. Rachel was avoiding his glance, as was Dawn. Chris was making him look really stupid. Drastic action was called for, otherwise his chances of a screw later would vaporise, as would his hard-earned respect within the rest of the fraternity. It was time for him to reassert his authority on the group, to take charge of the situation and regain the upper station.

Quietly, forceful and deliberately he said: "Make up the pint, Marcus. Chris has broken the rules." There was a murmur of disquiet around the room. The tramlines of misunderstanding undulated on Chris Betts forehead.

"Oh, come on Drew!" Marcus craned his head round and looked Chris Betts in the eyes. "Chris. Go home. You really don't want this. Just go. We will talk about this in the morning. I promise." But Chris stood his ground, unhearing, almost catatonic, not knowing whether to wait for Drew or follow the voices or to obey Marcus.

"Make the pint, Marcus!"

"No, Drew. This isn't fair. Look at him."

Drew's fist resounded off the table sending glasses rattling and a start through everyone in the bar.

"Make the fucking pint, Marcus!"

Marcus, defiance in his eyes, nodded curtly, almost imperceptibly and began to assemble the dirty pint. Soon a glass was half full of a murky, scummy mixture of dregs from the table. Hesitantly, he grabbed the ashtray, heaving and putrid. Alice took hold of his forearm and shook her head, concerned and frightened. Marcus glanced at Betts. There were tears in his eyes and Marcus felt ashamed. He lowered the ashtray.

"The *whole* pint, Marcus. Come on..." spat Drew, his eyes still firmly on Betts, burning with rage. Conflicted, Marcus turned to Alice and sighed, out of his depth, torn between his almost servile friendship with Carmichael and his deep seated belief in what was right. Once more Alice shook her head, this time more definitely, squeezing his arm until her nails dented his skin.

"You're a fucking pussy, Balfour". Drew snatched the ashtray from Marcus and soon the litter of ash and butts swirled in the rank cloudy liquid. Marcus gagged as Drew held the pint in front of Betts. By now the jukebox had stopped and no-one was feeding it. The assembled crowd prickled with a mixture of sadistic intrigue and outraged disapproval, but no-one could look away. Carmichael knew better than to back down now. Respect is earned through fear not favour. To back down now would be to concede defeat.

"Drink it Betts."

Chris stared into the dirty pint, tears running rivulets down his cheeks. He was shaking uncontrollably, rooted to the spot, unable to run or stand his ground, unable to take any action at all. The outsiders were hanging him out to dry. Drew's hand and the dirty pint approached ever nearer. The weakening meniscus of the bubble distorted as the glass and the crowd and the wailing taunts of the outsiders pressed in on it. Quietly, he began to rationalise, repeating over and over "I didn't break the rules. I didn't break the rules. I didn't break the rules..."

"That's enough now, Drew. I think he's got the idea now. This isn't fair." Alice was leaning over the table. She was imploring Dawn to intervene, but Dawn just gestured helplessly. *What could she do?* Drew raised his free hand to silence her.

And still Chris repeated, his voice becoming louder by degrees "I didn't break the rules. I didn't break the rules. I didn't break the rules..."

"Rule 8. Chris. 'If the submission is deemed unacceptable to the judging committee...'. You've just told me the Book is not finished. That is unacceptable. You have broken the rules. Now take the punishment." He pushed the glass at Chris. A streak of grimy fluid slopped out down his shirt, matting cold and uncomfortable against his chest. Drew stood and pressed his face close to Betts.

"Drink the pint, Betts."

Chris' voice rose to a crescendo "I didn't break the rules. I didn't break the rules. *I didn't break the rules...*"

The rage in Carmichael increased until it also reached a crescendo and he shouted:

"Drink - the - fucking - pint!"

Around Chris, the noise of the room pounds through the

thin stretched veneer of the bubble, but the conversations have stopped and the eyes of the people are drilling holes through him. He can feel the outsiders' hot breath on the doors and windows. He can hear the roar of his own breath in his head.

A loud bang echoes through Chris' mind as he realises that the bubble has burst and the smells and sounds and dirt and the sweat are cascading in around him. He can feel the words mocking him from the Book, he can hear the outsiders jeering in triumph and the pint ebbs and flows in his hands.

And he starts to drink.

In a sudden explosion, his mouth erupted and a spray of vomit drenched the floor, spattering Drew and Dawn. Rachel screamed and her foot kicked the table, sending glasses and drinks tumbling and spilling. A cry of disgust echoed around the bar. Chris fell to the floor in the repulsive mess and began rocking on his knees and whimpering.

"Jesus fucking Christ!" Drew attempted to wipe the remains from his shirt feeling his own gorge rise. The air around him reeked of vomit, beer and ash. He pushed the Book back into Chris' arms and Chris raised his head, wretched and defeated, his eyes red and moist.

"Look, Chris. You want to finish it? You want to add my page? Well, here's my fucking page. Why don't you give us all a break and go and play on the railway lines. Come on Dawn, Rachel. I am sick of this fucking place."

Drew grabbed Dawn's wrist and yanked to her feet, scratching chair legs across the floor. She was still busily picking pieces of ejecta from her hair. Defiantly she stood her ground, resisting Drew's pull.

"Drew, this thing, between you and Chris, has got to stop." She stood her ground, jerking at his arm until he turned back to her, clouded by a red mist. A dark stain matted his shirt to his torso. "Listen to me Drew. He needs to be taught where the boundaries are. He has got to be taught to leave us alone. I can't stand this for another two years. I am telling you, either you sort him out or we're finished."

Drew exhaled deeply but the anger and frustration were boiling ever stronger. Looking around the Bar, all eyes were still firmly on him, though now they held nothing but

381

contempt and ridicule. Dawn had laid down her challenge and everyone had heard. As Marcus and Alice helped Chris to his feet and led him from the bar, Drew pulled Dawn close and with more than a hint of menace he whispered under his breath. "Don't worry Dawn. I'll think of something. Something to put the frighteners on him, to end this whole bloody Murder Book thing forever."

***

Daley screwed up his eyes and the room was awash with light as Corby recorded the scene onto an SD card.

On the way over to Wescott Road, he had called Monaghan. Carol Hughes had lived there since 2008, and her driver file on PNC had confirmed that her maiden name was indeed Betts. The strands were drawing ever closer.

"The house is empty now, Sir." Deb was running her eyes over the photo gallery on the wall.

"Well, Carmichael was definitely here. The clothes he had on yesterday are in the spare room."

"The kettle is still warm, so we have only just missed them. There's been an argument or a disturbance recently. The laptop in the front room has been trashed and there is broken china and cutlery all over the kitchen floor."

Daley crouched down by the chair. "We don't need Gascoigne to tell us this poor sod has been dead for more than a week. Probably more like years. It looks mummified to me."

Deb picked up the framed photo. Short of a DNA test there could be no doubt that the self-conscious smiling boy in the photo now lay ignominiously slumped in the chair.

"Well, that kind of rules out Chris Betts for the murder of Dawn, Guy and Shelley. Poor bastard. I wonder how long he's been down here?"

"Dry air. It just draws the moisture out. Could be months or even years."

"Take a look at this, Sir." Deb was crouching by the other chair, her finger extended to a small dark patch on one of the arms. "That's blood, and it looks fresh. Someone slightly more

382

alive has been in this chair."

"And the wood on the arms has been rubbed away. Whoever it was has been restrained." Daley turned his head and peered under the chair, grasping at the severed cable tie. "There's a fair bit of blood, so he or she must have really struggled."

"Carmichael?"

"Or maybe Carol Hughes? If Carmichael has discovered who she is, that she is related to Betts, then perhaps he has been hiding out here, using her, befriending her, trying to discover where Betts is."

"And all the time he was here, right beneath his feet."

Deb's eye was caught by something small that had rolled under the chair, hidden behind one of the legs. Her latex hand reached under and fished it out. "Not just restrained, Sir. Drugged as well." She held up the plastic cap off a hypodermic syringe.

Daley turned around to the sideboard. "What do you make of this lot, Deb?"

"It's a shrine to him. I am assuming that's his watch, those are his specs... this radio is still warm."

"She's been keeping his memory alive down here."

Daley eased open the drawer in the sideboard. It was full of syringes and fresh doses of drugs, neatly arranged in a shallow tray. Behind them spent bottles rattled and clinked.

"Thiopental, Flunitrazepam, er Rohypnol, and some bottles that haven't got labels, Looks like whoever was strapped in that chair has been going on trips in more ways that one."

"So maybe he's stayed over and played house with Carol, then discovered her little secret down in the crypt. He must know that this is Betts. So, the only one left who knows about what really happened in 1997 is Carmichael himself. He's in the clear."

"Apart from Carol. Do you really think she could have lived with Chris since 2008 without him telling her?"

"So Carmichael befriends her, discovers that she is also in on his little secret?"

"But there's no way he could prepare all of this in her house in such a short space of time." Daley's hand pointed towards the chair bolted to the floor, to the array of photos, to the chemical cache. "If he needed to silence Carol, why the drugs, the restraints? Surely he could have strangled her, brought her body down here, locked up the house and left. Nobody would be any the wiser, at least until the rental payments stopped."

Daley took a long look at the blue folder laid out on the desk, and beckoned Mike Corby to take more shots, before bringing it over to the light. It was a simple A4 ring binder. Inside the transparent front slip was a single sheet:

The Murder Game

April 1997

Author: Christopher Betts

Devised by: Andrew Carmichael

Each page had been filed in it's own transparent punched sleeve. The frontispiece was a short description of the book along with the rules:

The Murder Game

How to commit the perfect murder and not get caught.

Purpose

The Murder game is a parlour game. The purpose of the game is to murder someone. The victim may be anyone, and the act may happen at any time and in any place. There is no requirement to carry out the murder; this is an academic exercise.

The premise is that a murder is only any good if the perpetrator gets away with it, therefore to qualify as an acceptable submission, the candidate must devise a method and perpetration whereby they do not get caught.

It should only be played when there are copious quantities of alcohol, cigarettes, or any class of illegal drugs.

Rules

1. The murder has to be motiveless. There must be no reason for the death, like a cat killing a bird. This exercise is for fun.

2. The murder has to be anonymous. Apart from the research required to select a victim, there must be no connection between the murderer and the victim.

3. The death must be clearly murder, i.e. it must be self-evident that the death is a crime and not suicide or an accident.

4. The death must be directly inflicted by the murderer. Murdering by poison or other indirect means is not allowed.

5. It is not permissible to kill a person in their sleep.

6. Extra points will be awarded to the person who comes up with the most spectacular murder.

7. Be sensible. No ray-guns, aliens, dinosaurs or similar shit.

8. If the submission is deemed unacceptable to the judging committee, the candidate will be required to collect together the dregs of every finished drink on the table into a single glass and empty into it every ash tray and then to consume to contents.

Failure to finish the glass will result in immediate exclusion from the Monday Club.

Puking, retching or skipping lectures the next day will result in expulsion from the Monday Club.

Narrative

This game has been devised by the Monday Club at Coventry University, purely for entertainment purposes. All characters appearing in this work are fictitious. Any resemblance to real persons, living or dead, is purely coincidental - except for the below, who by definition are named, and the victims, who by definition are not.

Contributors

MB - Marcus Balfour (Human Biosciences)

AB - Alice Bown (Art and Design)

FB - Findlay Byrne (Business Management and Administration)

AC - Andrew Carmichael (Law)

GH - Guy Higson (Accountancy)

RJ - Rachel Jones (Art & Design)

SN - Shelley Nugent (Geography)

DS - Dawn Silverton (Geography)

"So this is Alice's *Murder Book*. She said find Chris and we would find the book." Daley noted with some degree of poignancy, that Chris himself was not amongst the contributors. He had some degree of sympathy for Betts, working so hard to ingratiate himself with the group, joining in their antics, devoting his time to writing the murder book, all in the hopes they would accept him, but his conspicuous absence from the list spoke volumes.

Turning to the next page, he saw the now familiar text from Rachel Jones diary.

Flicking the page over, Daley reread the same text, the proposition now number 2, and the victim Dawn Silverton. Gruesome prophesies of their own demise over a decade earlier.

"There's something I don't get here, Sir." Daley turned to Whetstone. Her eyes were detached and thoughtful, her mouth turned up in the corner in puzzlement. "Chris flips his lid after the incident in Coventry, is sectioned and eventually released into the care of Carol and they set up house here where she looks after him, so grief-stricken that she can't even bear to be parted from his corpse. Why would she kill him in the first place?"

"I'm not sure she did. The lab will tell us for sure, but I think either he killed himself or he died of natural causes. See, she's dressed him in a shirt, a tie and his suit. This place is intensely personal to Carol. She came to London to take care of him, and even after death she has remained true to her obligation."

He turned to the next page - Guy Higson, and the next Shelley Nugent, and the next - Alice Bown, and he let out a sharp plaintive expletive. Whetstone, who had been examining the photographs, swivelled round. "So Alice *is* on the list." He skim-read the text, skipping to the last few paragraphs:

Proposition Victim - Alice Bown

My Proposition Development - The Proposition calls for drowning. The victim fully aware as there head enters the water, barely a ripple on the surface of the pool. The suggestion of a weighted body cast from a boat or bridge suggests a number of problems:

- an exposed location increases the risk of discovery, thus violating the rule of anonymity.

- The use of weights would require considerable strength to ensure that they were heavy enough to adequately submerge the victim. This might therefore suggest two murderers and is therefore inadmissible.

- The rules state that the victim must be conscious at the time of death. Unlike previous submissions, death by drowning is a lower, less instant process. Transporting the victim to the murder site could be a noisy, cumbersome affair.

My Proposition Method - It is a known fact that a person can be drowned in a relatively small amount of water. The suggestion is that a bathtub is used.

The selection of the victim should bear in kind that a bathtub is a requirement. NOTE: many properties are fitted with wet rooms and showers rather than bathtubs, so care should be taken in the research.

In order to minimise the risk of a disturbance and this discovery, the murder should be committed in the early hours of the morning. Suggest 03:00hrs when most potential witnesses will be deep in their second cycle of Stage Four sleep and thus unlikely to awaken.

The water used to drown the victim should be warm water. Cold water risks the victim suffering a cryogenic effect and thus being less able to fully comprehend the nature of their demise.

The victim should be subdued with a sedative.

Sedative: Sodium Thiopental 250 mg, slow induction by injection of 50 (2mL at a 2.5% solution) at intervals of 20 to 40 seconds. Induction of 250mg as a single dose can be used as a rapid sedative, although victims breathing should be monitored to avoid an apnoeatic episode and asphyxiation. Sedative effects last for two hours.

The victim should be securely bound, gagged with tape and transported to the bathroom. The victim should then be placed in the water but allowed to become fully conscious before death in order to obey Rule 5.

When the victim is drowned, they will inevitably struggle in order to avoid death. Suggest they are bound hand and feet and that a cord is tied between hands and feet to render the victim unable to move. The victim's feet should be raised to around one metre above the level of the water. The victim's head will naturally slide below the surface of the water and drowning will be complete within two minutes. Under no circumstances should the victim be drowned by pressure to the head, as this leaves the full torso and lower limbs free and the victim may break free of any handhold.

When the murder is complete, the murderer should retrieve all bonds and ties and any evidence of sedation, as these could compromise anonymity. Proof of murder will be evidenced by the bruising to the wrists and feet and by damage to the mouth from the tape used.

"Shit! I hope we're not too late."

Daley raised his head and scanned the photos; the small self-conscious smiling girl, the lifeless corpse in the bath, and he swore out loud. Deb reached into her bag and dialled Monaghan. "Dave, Get someone round to Alice Bown, as soon as possible...I don't know where she lives. Improvise. Try her last known address. Oh, and try Doctor Balfour's house. They were pretty matey when Mike saw them yesterday morning. Oh, and I'll email a photo." She cancelled the call and turned to the photo wall. With the camera on her phone she sent a snap across to Monaghan. She turned back to Daley who was crouching, his head in his hands, distraught. Another death on his hands.

"Look, Sir. Alice was already a dead woman when she called us last night. These are planned events and she was going to die come what may. After all, it was she that spoke in riddles about the book, about Chris Betts, and you offered to bring her in. It was she that refused our protection."

"But maybe, if we had looked harder for her on the first place, if Corby had held on to her..."

"What, and if I had got to that pub quicker? Don't go there, Sir."

"That's not what I meant, you know it."

But she knew what he meant. The killer had always been tantalisingly close yet one step ahead. She cursed Carmichael and the rings they had run round trying to catch him whilst the killer mocked them with impunity.

"We have to keep going, Sir. You know that. Turn over the page. We need to see who's next."

Daley bit back the anger and the frustration and turned to the next page but they both knew what they were going to see.

Chapter 45

As the car came to an abrupt halt, a sharp jolt jarred Carmichael into consciousness. Immediately he gasped for breath, unable to swallow and his hands reached for his throat, grabbing at the tape that bound him to the headrest.

"I can't breathe. Please."

"Oh, stop whining! It's true. All you men ever do is whine. Stop struggling and you'll be fine. Anyhow, soon we'll take a little walk, stretch our legs. Just wait a few moments longer."

Steadying his breathing, Carmichael eased his head to the left and looked out at the cluttered yard, a jumble of rusting freight containers muscling for space like forwards in a line-out, a couple of skips and a burnt out Mondeo. Fragments of litter fluttered and flapped from the rusting razor wire, while spindly weeds clung to the compacted surface. He didn't recognise the car; it wasn't his Mercedes but that would most likely be in a police compound somewhere. A blue Ford logo was embossed into the centre of the steering wheel. Did Carol own a car? He realised just how little he knew about her even after all this time.

"Where are we?" He couldn't see her. She had left the car and was arranging things on the back seat through an open rear door. There was a smell of diesel oil and rust on the dirty air.

"Soon enough pet, soon enough. Take it easy for now. There'll be time enough for questions later."

Free of the cellar, free from an eternity entombed in the cold, dark mausoleum, he allowed his bravado to return. "Look, Carol. This has gone far enough. Get this bloody thing from around my neck!"

"I said *not now!*" The heavy impact threw the seat forwards and his head with it. The ligature cut into his Adam's apple and once more he was coughing and choking. "You just take it easy. I said there'll be time enough for questions later, I promise. It won't be long now and you'll know everything you need to know. In fact, you have to know. It's a rule." In front of him on the dash, the electric clock chirruped. 11:30. Mesmerised he watched the red second hand beat out the degrees of the dial. It was his time that was being consumed second by second. He was shivering and his throat was dry.

"Look, I'm cold and I need a drink. At least give me some water." If he could persuade her to open the door, maybe he could overpower her, perhaps throw her to the ground.

"That's the Sodium Thiopental. You've had quiet a lot over the past few days. Gives you the shakes. It's a lovely day. I daresay the afternoon will be quite bright. Not that the weather will be your top priority."

Behind the car, out of his vision a loud rumble shook the earth and a massive throbbing diesel locomotive sidled its way past, screeching wheels on tracks and the rhythmic clack of freight wagons over joints. Then he knew where he was and all at once, dredged from the back of his mind, the answers to all of his questions boiled to the surface. In his mind flashed the pictures from the cellar wall, the two bodies decapitated, sodden with gore, the crumpled motorcyclist and the growling motorcycle, the prostrate woman and the smoke filled room. He counted them off one...two...three...four... "Alice? What about Alice?" Behind him, Carol stopped and quietly she quoted:

"When down her weedy trophies and herself

Fell in the weeping brook. Her clothes spread wide;

And, mermaid-like, awhile they bore her up:

Which time she chanted snatches of old tunes;

As one incapable of her own distress,

Or like a creature native and indued

Unto that element: but long it could not be

Till that her garments, heavy with their drink,

Pull'd the poor wretch from her melodious lay

To muddy death

It was how she wanted to go, she decided that herself. You are all the architects of your own end. I thought you knew that by now. Kitt always looked up to you, Drew, but I don't think you're as bright as you make out."

As the sodium lamp burned and Chris' hand held the thin blade, Drew's mind scanned the faces. One by one the faces, filled with contempt, disappeared from the scene until it was he

391

and the frightened, lonely boy. Each foretold their own murder, each had witnessed the act and now all but he were dead. The red hand danced staccato steps around the dial and soon the final page of the blue folder would be turned. As the finality struck him, all pretence slipped and he began to whimper. A hand reached over from the rear of the car, a sharp pain scratched his arm and as the wasteland before him washed away like a sea of sand, he heard her say:

"I must be cruel only to be kind;

Thus bad begins, and worse remains behind."

***

Proposition 6 - Death on a Railway

Date - 1st May 1997

Proponents - Andrew Carmichael

DC - Go play on the railway lines

Proposition Victim - Andrew Carmichael

My Proposition Development - Railway lines are protected from trespass, so the space must be chosen where there are no gates and guards. Presence of railway personnel will alert the network administrators and the train, which will be the weapon, will be stopped or diverted.

No adult will knowingly play on railway lines when there is a train coming as the power for self-preservation will make them move before the train hits. The victim must not be made to kill themselves. Rule 3 forbids suicide. Therefore the victim must be taken to the railway lines and persuaded to stay of their own volition or forced to remain.

The location of the murder must be chosen such that it is not visible to the oncoming train. This indicates either a tunnel, a sharp curve or an area of a train yard protected from onlookers.

My Proposition Method - Locate the site of the murder. Suggest Cement Works (derelict), Western end of Sealey Road W13. Left of the entrance to the cement works, the fence to the freight container storage depot is broken, providing access to the site of the cement works. Once inside the compound, there is a level crossing one hundred yards North East. This is the site of the murder. If a vehicle is used, this should be left in the freight container yard to be collected later.

Timing of the murder. Freight traffic operates the line between the North East and Channel ports, so this is a busy stretch on weekday with trains passing every forty minutes. Thus the most convenient time for the murder is weekends (Saturday - frequency of trains every hour, Sunday - frequency 9:00hrs, 12:00hrs, 15:00hrs, 18:00hrs). One hour thirty minutes should be allowed from arrival on site to the arrival of the train to ensure preparations can be carried out.

Selection of the victim. The victim is pre-selected. The outsiders have dictated that it must be him.

Preparation of the victim. The use of amnesiacs, sedatives and hallucinogenics is recommended to make transportation and placement of the victim more successful.

- Amnesic: Flunitrazepam (Rohypnol) 2mg in a solution of distilled water. This will produce pseudo narcotic effects for a period of up to 5 hours. Half-life of around 150 hours could cause cumulative effects if dosed regularly, which will increase the narcotic/ sedative effect. NOTE: should not be used with Sodium Thiopental - allow 24hr for either drug to leave the system.

- Sedative: Sodium Thiopental 250 mg, slow induction by injection of 50mg (2ml at a 2.5% solution) at intervals of 20 to 40 seconds. Induction of 250mg as a single dose can be used as a rapid sedative, although victims breathing should be monitored to avoid an apnoeatic episode and asphyxiation. Sedative effects last for two hours.

- Hallucinogenic: Lysergic acid diethylamide (LSD), 270µg in a solution of distilled water. NOTE: chlorine in tap water will destroy LSD compound. Hallucinogenic effect will commence within ten seconds of injection. The half-life of the effect is approximately three hours with the average trip length around five hours. Towards the end of the period, the victim will become lucid.

A combined minimum prepared dose of Flunitrazepam and LSD can be made up in order to make the victim more supplicant but retain the amnesiac effects of the LSD. This will allow the victim to stay lucid and open to compliance with reduced risk of truculence. The dosage should be flunitrazepam @ 1mg plus LSD @ 270µg in a solution of distilled water rapid induction.

Recommended method. Use an injected preparation of Sodium Thiopental to sedate the victim. Use the slow induction method to ensure that the victim is partly lucid.

Move the victim to the transport and complete the induction. The victim is sedated.

Transport the victim to the scene of the murder. The vehicle should be left in the freight yard, preferably between or near to other vehicles or containers.

Allow the victim to regain consciousness. Restraints may be required.

Await the arrival of the locomotive prior to the murder weapon. Note the track that the train uses; the site has multiple parallel tracks. The down line freight is the first track in from the north side of the level crossing.

Thirty minutes before the allotted time, inject combined minimum dose of Flunitrazepam and LSD.

Relocate the victim to the railway line and restrain hands and feet. Attach the victim to the track using large cable ties. The victim should be seated on a sleeper with ankles attached to rails on one side. NOTE: The victim must be facing North West. He must see the train coming.

Relocate to the roadway outside the level crossing and await the arrival of the train.

Following the murder, remove all evidence, return to the car and ensure the gate to the freight depot is closed. NOTE: Do not remove the cable ties from the rails as these will provide proof of murder.

***

Leaving the uniforms at the house, Daley dug out his mobile and called SOCO, following it with a quick call to Gascoigne. The Prof would not want to miss this one, weekend or not. He flicked the switch on the dash and the Insignia's front grille erupted in blinding blue staccato flashes. Flooring the throttle, leaving overly dramatic black lines down Westcott Road, he headed back up towards the Broadway.

Corby and Whetstone were following in Deb's less well equipped Golf, struggling to keep up. Peeling off, they took a different route. Now they had the Murder Book they had all the information they needed. He just hoped they wouldn't be too late. For once it would be good to be leading rather than following.

Snarling in the traffic on the Broadway, Daley pressed the Bluetooth button and called Monaghan's number.

"Dave, you know the old cement works, Sealey Road."

"I thought that closed down years ago, Sir. Wasn't there something in the paper about redevelopment?"

"Yeah, maybe. Look I need to get in there. I have just sent Deb and Mike to the front entrance in Sealey Road. I need to find a back way onto the tracks. If I am right, Carmichael's got an appointment with a train.

"What, really? Like Mabel Normand? Pearl White, Perils of Pauline? Jesus Christ, I love this job, sometimes, so I do."

"Uh?"

"Silent movies, Gov. Tied to the railway tracks, swooning while the loco comes down the tracks."

"You've got some imagination Dave. Now, about the cement works..."

"Sorry Gov. Where are you?"

"Northfields Avenue. Junction with Mattock Lane."

"Just head straight across the Bridge towards Argent Road, take Keppel Street and double back down Bessemer Drive. Part of the cement works has been redeveloped for housing. That should bring you in on the North side."

"Life Saver, Dave."

"Oh Gov. Uniform have just broken into Alice Bown's flat. They have found a body in the bath. Seems she drowned. Signs of foul play. We've call Professor Gascoigne."

***

And the black suddenly became a million light bulbs that stabbed pins at his eyes and the world swam in the bright soup. A black shadow hovered above him and he tried to shield his eyes. A stiff breeze was blowing grit at his face and he wanted to shield his eyes from that but the arms would not budge. Bloody cable ties. Then Drew remembered the yard and the car and the almighty shit heap he was in.

"This has gone far enough now, Carol. For fuck's sake get these cable ties off." Carol Hughes was sitting cross-legged in front of Carmichael, curling her hair around a forefinger. She was humming under her breath. He himself was sitting, his arms and legs pulled to one side. The cable ties had been threaded through the W shaped tension clamps that secured the track to the fishplates. Cramp was already setting into his hips and the shit she kept pumping into him was making him nauseous. "Carol, listen to me. What happened all those years ago. It was an accident. I was leaning over him, I stumbled. I am really sorry."

In a flash of black against the sky, her hand landed across his face, almost pulling his arms from their sockets. She brought her face close to his and growled under her breath: "Conscience is but a word that cowards use, devised at first to keep the strong in awe."

"You're bloody mad. It must run in your family, you Northerners are all a bunch of inbreds."

"Of course I am bloody mad. If you prick us, do we not bleed? If you tickle us, do we not laugh? If you poison us, do we not die? And if you wrong us, shall we not revenge? Do you think any sane person would do this? But you know? It doesn't matter, does it, pet? You, me, sane, mad, we'll just be dog meat when that train comes in a few minutes."

Carmichael frantically tugged at the ties, feeling the ligaments at his elbows and wrists tearing as shouted for help at the top of his voice, the sound carried off into the featureless ecru wastes of the rail yard, to be answered by the soft howls of the unforgiving wind.

Carol grabbed his chin and squeezed so hard he thought his teeth would explode through the side of his face. "Just be quiet now, Drew. Resign yourself to it. Accept that this is the end and that at last you will have paid your dues like the rest of them."

Was this how he would end this life? After all he had lived through, with all the promise which life had to offer? Another corpse strewn around a railway yard? One more statistic, just like the tramp. Just like Chris Betts. Nameless, featureless, anonymous. Hanging his head between his knees he succumbed to the abject hopelessness and was consumed in tears, which dripped and pooled on the dusty sleeper. Then he felt another sharp scratch assail his arms and the railway track roared and looped an aerobatic display though the million lights above.

***

Deb abandoned her Golf in Sealey Road as it meandered disappointingly to a dead end and a set of galvanised gates with an industrial sized padlock. Peering through, there was no sign of Carmichael or the woman. Telling Mike to ring the site office, Deb locked the Golf and retraced her steps along the high fence, reaching a point where the fence was down, patched with a rickety barrier cobbled together from signs, old metal fence panels and wooden pallets, and beyond it a gate into a yard, ringing as it tapped loose against the latch.

Easing her way through into the yard beyond, she pulled up sharply. *Steady girl. This is a multiple murderer we're looking for here!* More cautiously, she advanced along the rough path between two rusting mustard coloured freight containers, her tongue dry in her mouth, a frantic tempo beating in her ears. There were few signs of life in the yard. On the far side, beside a brown corrugated building, windows smashed and grubby, Carol Hughes silver Ford Fusion nestled alongside a rubbish filled skip. The doors were open and the interior light shone. Carefully scouting her route, she edged around the yard until she could place her hand on the bonnet. Hot to the touch.

Her phone buzzed in her pocket. She looked at the display and pressed it to her ear, speaking quietly.

"Mike? Yes. I found the car. They have to be around here somewhere."

"Site owner is in Brentford. Won't be here for an hour. I am going to see if I can shimmy over the fence."

"Be careful, Mike. She's a bloody nutter, remember."

"Same goes for you, Sarge. If you find them, wait for Daley and the others."

She rang off. There would be no others. Not just yet.

Bringing in the cavalry was not Daley's style. He preferred the cosy, casual approach, much to Deb's chagrin.

Beyond to her right, the yard opened into a wider expanse of scrub and gravel leading straight onto the rail tracks. Rough and barren the outer yard was bordered on one side by the railway perimeter fence, the ubiquitous galvanised palings, and on the other by the worn, pitted site access road. Picking her way carefully along the fence, using the line of palings as a natural barrier she scanned the scattered piles of sleepers and track, brick rubble and old mattresses that had taken up residence. A warm breeze had struck up and grit dust stung her face. About half way along, as the signal lights on the crossing stood tall in front, she espied a movement to her right amongst the derelict plant buildings. It was Mike. He was limping. He threw his hands up, an apologetic gesture. A sprained ankle. *If you want a job done properly, leave it to a woman.* He was pointing toward the level crossing, but the same fence that was affording her cover hampered her view. Clambering a few yards further, she crouched behind a pile of rubble, in clear sight of the level crossing.

Part of the industrial site, the level crossing was unrated and open, in normal circumstances an accident waiting to happen. At either side of the track stood a rectangular lollipop sign with amber lights to warn of the approach of a train. Catching sight of something on the tracks, Deb had the feeling she wouldn't have to wait long for that accident. She edged closer, looking around the fencing, trying to make out what it was.

The man and the woman were sitting in the middle of the level crossing. The man had his back to her, but she could tell it was Carmichael, even at this distance. It had to be. The woman was facing Deb, her hair wild in the stiff breeze. Cross-legged, she appeared to be speaking to Carmichael, her voice on the breeze just too quiet to discern. Mike Corby had limped around the plant building and was hunkered down a hundred yards to Deb's right.

Now she was thirty feet from the level crossing and her pulse was pounding in her ears. Her phone buzzed and she reached into her pocket. Just then, Deb started as the amber lights on the lollipop signs began to flash alternately and an inane two-tone alarm sounded. Behind her, a low rumble became an ear-splitting, animal roar. She saw the woman look up and thought a faint smile crossed her face as the enormous locomotive thundered across the level crossing.

Chapter 46

Everything Changed

Cradling the glass of flat cider, Alice Bown stared down at the distorted shape of her knees in the bottom of the glass, alternately pulling them apart and closing them together. She was bored. Wednesday was already the most boring day of the week, thanks to the laundrette, a tedious *History of Art* lecture and two hours of *Post Modernist Art in Berlin*. And now here she was at Brown's, the conversation going round and round. On her left, his arm weakly linked through hers, Marcus was huffing and his eyes were darting impatiently around the bar. Drew and the girls had just left without him and he was having a crisis of loyalty, honour bound to forego whatever excitement had been planned and stay and keep Alice company. Marcus was such a prat sometimes.

"Why don't you just go?" she huffed irritably.

"Uh?"

"Look, if you are that desperate to play with Drew, why don't you just go?"

"No....no, I'm here with you. You're having a good time aren't you?"

Alice turned the corners of her mouth downward and glowered. As if he needed to ask! It's true, she had never imagined meeting someone like Marcus so soon after starting University and she loved every minute with him, but he really needed to dump Drew Carmichael. It had been three months now, and although the sex was good, she needed to persuade him to cut the social foreplay and get on with it. Drew and Dawn were always in each others rooms, Shelley and Finn were positively joined at the crotch and even bed-hopping Rachel was getting serious with the tall handsome guy behind the bar. Obviously Guy didn't count. There weren't any other poufs in the Monday Club, so if he was seeing someone, he was keeping it quiet.

Like every other evening, she had been forced to endure the teachings of the *Great* Drew Carmichael and the sycophantic chattering of his pitiful group of friends, to drink half a pint of cheap sweet cider and be bored witless. And her pleas of *can we go now* or *let's go back to mine* had fallen on selectively deaf ears. Why did she do it? Of course, it was Marcus. Since they had first met and that bolt of electricity had coursed through her, she had known it had to be Marcus. But it was all wearing a little thin now. When on earth was he going to realise?

"Look, seriously, can we go now?" She fidgeted in a way she hoped would annoy him sufficiently.

"If you want. Mine or yours?"

"Mine I think. I have some work I need to get done for tomorrow." It was a ruse of course. There was always work. She was horny and she knew she had a better chance of chivvying Marcus along if he came to her room. Fewer distractions aside from herself. She downed the dank liquid and shuddered at the taste. Dragging Marcus to his feet, they headed off into the chilly air.

Outside Browns, a steady stream of students headed for the brighter, more raucous lights of the city, whilst Alice and Marcus moved in the opposite direction towards Priory Hall, a monstrous grey-green block of flats which squatted over Priory Street as if it was going to defecate on passing motorists. Raised on stilts, it housed five floors of demoralising, depressing, 1960s student cells where 500 students, including Marcus, debated the relative merits of life and death and getting up before noon, probably explaining the popularity of Browns, ten minute's away or indeed Singer Hall where she stayed.

"I just don't know what you see in that Drew Carmichael. He's the biggest dickhead I know."

"Oh, don't start again! We've been friends forever. You just don't know him like I do. Sometimes you just have to let that *dickheadedness* pass you by. It's all a front."

"A front for what? Being a dickhead? Well, he's got that one sussed. Next you'll be telling me he's a shy sensitive soul, struggling to come out of his shell."

"Come on, Alice, Let's not go through all this again."

They lapsed into an uncomfortable silence as they reached the top of Bayley Lane and the massive skeletal windows of the derelict cathedral loomed admonishingly overhead. Before them the University Square thronged with students on their way to or from somewhere, footsteps echoing off the solid brick and glass facade of the new building, water gurgling from the ludicrous fountains, cardboard drinks cups teetering precariously on the spherical, shin-splintering sculptures.

"I know. It's just that when he's around, you're not with me, you're with him and I am just some kind of ornament. I mean all evening he has been strutting around, centre of attention, making a right fool of you and of Guy.

"I, I don't know. I try to keep out of it."

"No you don't! You and the others just seem to go along with it. I mean, OK, Dawn has a vested interest, but Shelley and Finn. Surely, they can see through him. *Surely!*"

"I don't know. It's just how he is."

Marcus was becoming perplexed, but baiting him was the most fun Alice had had this evening. "You'll get splinters in your arse, sitting on that fence!"

"Look, he's an old friend. That doesn't mean I condone half the things he does but sometimes it's who you know, not what you know. Drew seems to know a lot of folks here already. One day that might be quite useful to me. I can't even make friends with a Jehovah's Witness! So it pays to keep on the right side of people like Drew...just in case."

"On the right side of, yes, not up their arse." Whenever the subject of Drew *Bloody* Carmichael surfaced, Marcus always turned the tide in his favour, regardless of the number of put-downs and let-downs he had endured.

"Come on, Alice, enough already. Please."

"No, Marcus. It's just the beginning. What about poor Chris Betts? It's unforgivable what he did to him the other night. Like pulling the wings off a fly."

"OK, so perhaps that went a little too far, but Chris was being a pain in the neck."

"No, Chris was being Chris. We all know he's kinda special and we make allowances but Drew! That was just brutal. And it doesn't help when you join in the *tame poodle* stuff. That just antagonises Drew more and who does he take it out on? Chris."

"Oh, come on now! Fair's fair. Who was it who took Chris home, made sure he was OK?"

"Only because you felt guilt about giving in to Drew and making up that pint!"

They had reached the foot of the huge tower block that stood at the eastern end of Priory Hall, rising head and shoulders above the new cathedral, one monstrous carbuncle cocking a snook at another. They had bickered their way to an uncomfortable standoff and the atmosphere was tense. Alice stopped and turned to face Marcus.

"Look, I think I'll go home on my own tonight. I can't deal with you when you're in one of these moods. I'll see you tomorrow at lunch in 54. One o'clock?"

"What mood? I'm not in a mood. You bloody started it!" Marcus donned that hard-done-by expression he did so well, but she wasn't fooled anymore. She smiled and took his hands in hers. Even when she was thoroughly pissed off with him, she loved him. He was kind and generous and he had a smile that took her heart and held it in a warm embrace. He was just a fool when it came to Drew Carmichael.

"Bollocks. You're sulking because Drew decided to go into town, and I didn't want to so you had to stay here with me. Tell me that's not true. Go on!"

"That's not true! I asked *you* out tonight and we've had a great evening together - you and me. I never wanted to go into town with Drew, honest."

"Only because you didn't know he was going! I saw the look in your eyes when he said 'Who's up for a bit of fun' and you had to say no! Sorry to cramp your style and all that."

"You don't *cramp my style*. You are the best thing that has happened to me in years. I love being around you."

"So why have you hardly said two words to me all evening since Drew left? You are so transparent, Marcus!"

"Sorry."

"And don't keep apologising. It makes you look stupid."

"Sorr...Oh,"

And she kissed him. A long, deep, warm kiss and they held each other for a long time.

"Go home Marcus. Have sweet dreams about me and I'll have some about you...and maybe tomorrow you will tell Drew Carmichael to fuck off and screw the arse off me instead!"

"I could...?" Marcus raised his eyes towards an imaginary love-den on floor three. She could tell it was more out of duty than desire. She smiled and pecked his cheek once more.

"Go home, get some sleep. I'll see you tomorrow."

They kissed again and Marcus reluctantly disappeared through the double doors, his eyes fixed on Alice until he was lost in the gloom beyond. She sighed again and began her walk up Priory Street and across the barren, dark car park towards Ford Street and Singer Hall beyond.

As she reached the corner of Cox Street, the old Theatre One to her left, recently closed and boarded up, she heard the voices. She recognised them instantly as Drew and Dawn, and she wondered what they were doing over this side of town. Further along the Street, where the old cinema met the back of the bus garage, there was a void, a vee-shape, a popular stopping-off point for tarts and their tricks or for courting couples who were after a quick knee-trembler before going their separate ways. The council had conveniently planted plenty of trees, which obscured the street lamps, and one that stood at the entrance to the void and afforded a modicum of privacy and decency. She cast her mind back to the entrance to Priory Hall, to her rather abrupt dismissal of Marcus, and the thought of Dawn and Drew having it off, made her as horny as hell. She seriously needed to go hammer on Marcus' door.

Drawing level with the void, she was about to wave, to shout 'Get a room!', but something stopped her, something dark and ominous, the hairs on her neck stood erect and she was filled with foreboding. Quietly she edged back, peering around the corner staying close to the wall of the cinema. A bitter stench of weed and piss hit her nostrils.

"Come on, Chris, You're so full of it, full of ideas, full of imagination. Here's your chance. Show us what you're made of. Come on!"

Alice stared harder into the gloom and, as her eyes adjusted to the dimness, she could make out Drew and Dawn, Rachel and Shelley, and Chris Betts standing over a pile of rags, a look of abject terror across his face. He was mumbling to himself, his head swaying from right to left, like the polar bears at the zoo. Dawn and Rachel were chanting, goading, a malevolence in their voice that Alice had never heard before, animal and cruel, taunting him, enticing him further into the dark.

Drew nudged Chris hard on the arm. "Come on, you fucking ponce. Isn't this what you wanted all along? To be part of the team? Part of the Murder Game? Well, this is your initiation. Here's your chance." He nudged him again, this time with more force and Chris stumbled to his knees. It was then that Alice caught her breath. The rags started to move and swear, a deep rasping, Irish voice. Two eyes appeared from the pile and a filthy hand in tattered fingerless gloves waved them away.

"Fuck off, you bastards. Piss off and leave me be."

Drew kicked Chris once more and again he stumbled at the vagrant, crying out.

"What's the matter? Game too hard for you all of a sudden?"

And the girls were braying and laughing, egging Drew on, and Chris lay across the old man, turning his head away from the smell, or from the eyes, or from the sheer helplessness.

"Come on, Drew. That's far enough." It was Shelley. She was backing away. 'This is getting scary, now."

"Get on with it, Chris. If you want to be in the Monday Club, you've got to pay your dues. Now - get on with it." Drew crouched over Chris Betts; there was a flash of silver and a rattling, gasping moan.

And then there was silence. Like the end of the world.

Alice closed her eyes and pressed herself flat against the wall, the rough shingle biting into the back of her head, her teeth chattering, an acid taste rising in her gorge. The trees rustled overhead and the traffic hummed on the ring road but nothing could break the silence.

Slowly she began to hear sobbing. It was Shelley.

"Drew. What have you done? For God's sake." And then they were all sobbing, Dawn and Rachel and Shelley and from beyond them the sound of a low plaintive mumble.

"I can't make it stop, I can't make it stop. Help me. I can't make it stop."

"Fucking hell, Chris. I didn't mean you should really do it. I just wanted you to show that you could, if you wanted. I didn't mean he should really do it, honest. It was just a laugh, that's all. Surely you know that?" There was a sound of panic in Drew's voice. It was a strange alien sound, an emotion she had never heard him express before. She wasn't sure whom he was trying to convince, Chris, the girls or himself.

But Shelley wasn't listening. "You've gone too far. I can't be here. I can't be party to this." And she turned and fled, a black shadow crossing Alice's eyelids as she screwed her eyes up and clung hard to the wall.

"You fucking twat, Chris. What d'you have to go and do that for? Jesus!" It was Rachel. "You're supposed to be the clever one! Look what you done now!" She was moving towards Drew, transfixed by the eyes of the tramp, the life ebbing from them, wide and accusatory, but she could not look away.

"What are we going to do, Drew?" Dawn was in tears also. There was a tremor in her voice.

Chris twisted his head and looked from one to the next, silver streaks lining his cheeks, his hand still clutching the knife, his face pleading with each of them as their eyes met. Pleading for help, for guidance. Just for once, pleading for Drew to come down on his side and make the horror go away. But when he looked at Drew, the eyes he saw were cold and hard, devoid of any hope of salvation.

"Nothing. He's a fucking retard." Once more, the voice was measured and steely, detached and icy. Alice sensed the arrogance, the self-righteousness, and the superiority return to Drew's voice. "He got himself in this mess. He can fucking get himself out. We're going - now!"

"But what if the tramp dies?" Dawn looked down at Chris hunched over the convulsing shape. She heard the low rasping voice muttering and gasping and Chris begging for help.

"Look, Dawn," begged Rachel, "Drew's right. Why should we all go down because of this tosser? Nobody asked him to actually stab the guy. Why should we get done for his stupidity?" She was clinging to Drew's arm, hiding behind his shoulder, striving to purge the image from her mind. She was dragging Drew towards the street, but Drew was reaching out to Dawn.

"It's a tramp, Dawn - a hobo, a bum, a nobody. Who cares if a tramp dies?" It was Drew. There was desperation in his voice. "Tramps die everyday. Nobody will give a fuck, but I am buggered if I am going to have my life ruined by this *spak*." He gestured wildly at Chris who was still crouched, rocking on his heels, audibly sobbing, a pained animal noise.

"Drew." Dawn was pleading, torn between the plight of Chris Betts and the power that Drew Carmichael wielded over her, between what was right and what was easy.

"Dawn. Leave it. Let's go! Come on." Rachel was starting to panic.

"I don't know."

"Look, this is no time for a mother's meeting, you two. We have to get out of here." And Drew turned with Rachel towards the amber light, and still Chris was mumbling, "I can't make it stop, I can't make it stop." Drew shook free from Rachel and crossed the void to where Chris was crouched. He grabbed at Chris' shoulder and shook.

"For fuck's sake, Chris. Come on. Leave him. We have to get out of here." Business-like, focussed on self-interest. Soon they would be noticed.

"Leave him, Drew," implored Rachel, her words filled with tears. "He's a fucking nutter, anyway."

"Chris! Get up! Come one!" Allowing himself the briefest cold spark of sympathy for Chris' predicament, Drew pleaded with him to stand, to turn and flee, but Chris was overcome by the magnitude of the event and his senses were completely overwhelmed, crowded by the demons whose palms held his grasp firmly on the knife and whose weight thrust it deeper with every breath. Their baying and jeering flooded his mind and robbed him of his sanity.

"We got to get out of here before someone comes. Come on, Drew, Rachel's right. Leave him. He'll sort himself out. Come on!" Dawn grabbed Drew's wrist and dragged him away towards where Rachel was covering her face and biting at her knuckles.

As quietly as possibly, Alice made her way back up Cox Street. Her legs were shaking and her mind was reeling as she climbed the steps to the old boarded up doors, where she crouched in the shadows. How long she waited she wasn't sure but it seemed like hours before Drew strode past back towards town dragging Dawn and Rachel on each arm. She watched them cross the car park towards the bus station and, holding her breath, she quietly crept back to the rear of the abandoned building. Chris was still crouching over the old man. In the dimness of the streetlamp she could see his hand rise and fall, clamped to the hilt of the knife, reacting to the spasmodic jerking of the tramps breathing, now slower and more laboured. Oily streams of blood pulsed around his fingers and seeped onto the pavement in an increasing black pool. The eyes of the vagrant were wide and pleading, the thick beard moving as he mouthed his final string of foul expletives. And then the eyes were wide and still, the chest dropped in a rattling sigh and the blood flow abated.

And still Chris was mumbling, "I can't make it stop, I can't make it stop."

Alice turned and on faltering legs teetered across the road, venting her stomach over the wall beyond. In her mind flashed the silver, ran the blood, stared the eyes. She looked back to the tree, the void black beyond, protective of the secret within and she looked left towards the lights of the pub and the Ford Street, still and quiet, and the world became an ominous alien place.

She stood there conflicted, her conscience wrestling with the strong draw of self-preservation, the desire to flee, to wake up tomorrow morning cradled in the arms of Marcus rubbing the nightmare from her eyes. But there was Chris; disparate, separate, striving to be accepted yet always set apart, always the foil for Drew's pitiless cold-heartedness, the butt of all of their sadistic contempt. And now, in the void that they had created for him, he was lost and she was his only hope of redemption.

Turning, she made her way back towards the shadows. Chris was still crouching over the man. His head was turned towards her, his expression one of incomprehension. She anxiously looked around. The lights in the Elastic Inn were still shining brightly, snug and warm in contrast to the consuming chill of the space around her. The streets were empty. Students, drinkers and revellers yet to leave their bars and make their way home. The entire scene had been played out to an audience of none. None except Alice.

"What's up, Alice?" She started and it felt like her heart had leapt through ribcage, Chris turned to look over her shoulder and his head was shaking.

Guy Higson had appeared from the north end of Cox Street. It was all she could do to will her arm to point in the direction of Chris. Guy followed the lead and strode into the gloom, and suddenly his lighter clicked bright, a searing red flame casting chiaroscuro fingers across the void. She saw the tramp, eyes wide and lifeless, and Chris hunched over the obscene mass of rags, mumbling and shaking, a deep burgundy pool spreading and tracking along the seam in the block pavement, soaking and matting the detritus and rubbish, a gothic tableau of death. And then as the lighter extinguished, the scene went blank, etched in a negative image on her retinas.

"Shit!" exclaimed Guy. "What the fuck is going on?" His voice had risen an octave, broken and panicky. He backed out of the gloom and grabbed hold of Alice's arm and he shook her, and she started out of her stupor. "Alice, tell me. What's happened here?"

"Chris stabbed him. Drew was here. And Rachel and Dawn. And Shelley. It was a dare or something. They never meant it to happen." Alice instantly loathed herself for the implications in her words, the implication that Chris had exercised any free will in the action, that Drew, Dawn and Rachel could absolve themselves of blame through her words.

"Look, fuck it. I don't want to know. Shit, shit, shit!" Momentarily he was lost, pacing this way and that, unable to make a decision, to determine the best course of action. He looked at his watch. "They're going to start coming out of the pub soon, Alice. We've got to go. There's no sense us all going down because of this wanker."

She looked back at Chris, her eyes wide and urgent, but invisible to him in the deep black beyond the tree.

"Chris. You've got to go. Come on. There's nothing you can do here now. Leave him. It's not your fault." She stepped towards him and grabbed at his shoulder, pleading earnestly for

409

him to leave. But he just stared, and she knew that she could not make him leave.

"Alice, come on...please!" Guy's voice was rasping and frantic.

And so she ran.

CHAPTER 47

Rounding the corner, Daley jogged across the car park and hefted himself up the six-foot perimeter wall. With the sinews in his arms complaining, and feet scrabbling for purchase, he peered over and scanned the fly-tipped yard beyond. At the other side was the railway perimeter fence. With a sigh, he fell back onto his feet. Finding a back way in had proved difficult, as London's suburban streets became ad hoc car parks on a Sunday. He prayed he could get over there before Whetstone and Corby did anything stupid. Hauling himself up again and dropping into the yard, he picked his way through shopping trolleys, and black sacks until he was against the galvanised fence. Between the palings, he could just make out the two figures sitting on the railway track, and just beyond them Deb crouching unseen. He drew his phone from his pocket and scrolled to Deb's number. He typed a few words and sent the text. He saw her head drop and her hand reach into her pocket, as the warning lights flashed and the speeding locomotive raced towards the level crossing. A sonorous howl echoed across the yard, the driver moving too fast to stop, the machine raced across the level crossing, passing within inches of Carmichael and Carol. Daley could see the pair rock on their haunches and their clothes billowed in the wash from the huge mechanical beast and Deb had buried her face in her hands.

But they just sat watching the endless train of aggregate wagons as they roared past clacking and rocking across the joints. Daley raced to a corner on the fence where the junkyard petered out to a point and scrabbled his way up the wall. The sharp barbs from the fence dug into his palms as he launched himself over, landing noisily on the gravel, unheard against the thunderous roar of the empty wagons. Quickly he crouched down by a fence. He watched as Deb anxiously looked up and almost felt her relief as she spotted the pair unharmed, still sitting, still talking as the last of the wagons sidled it's way northwards. Glancing at her phone she looked across and raised her hand slightly as she saw Daley. He held out his hand, a time-honoured gesture. *Stay there!* Then he rose to his feet.

Tentatively, he inched towards the level crossing. Deb had

kept station behind her cover. They had exchanged texts.

'deb. sty there. Want to talk her out scott'

'mike fking crap hurt ankle'

'u and me no sweat'

'drew tied to tracks'

'wait for signal then you take drew i take woman'

"Carol, Carol! It's me, Inspector Daley, Scott. We met on Thursday, at Barraclough and Leavis?"

The woman peered around her, confused, her eyes alighting on Daley as he stood beside an open freight container. She swivelled her body to face him, Deb now further on to her rear.

"Mr Daley. Nice to see you again. Come to join the party?"

"How's Mr Carmichael? Is he alright?"

"Call him Drew, pet. He prefers Drew, less formal. He's enjoying playing with his trains." Carmichael was staring down into his lap. Hearing his name, he raised his head and looked about and then lowered it again. He was clearly out of it, probably tripping on the drugs they had found.

"Makes a change for you to let me actually see him, Carol. Usually he's skipping out the back as I arrive. Not this time though, eh?"

Carol smiled. "Well, you know how it is. If you had gotten to him first there would be no fun for the rest of us. Still, he's here now."

"We found Christopher, Carol. He looked very peaceful. You really looked after him."

"*Kitt, His name is Kitt*, Why must I keep telling everyone!" Her voice strained with an intense sadness.

"Sorry, Carol. I never met him. That's my loss. I am told he was very clever. You must have been proud."

"Proud doesn't cover it, Scott. He was a genius. You know he had an eidetic memory? He heard and saw everything and remembered it all. I have trouble remembering my own name sometimes." She smiled, lost once more to her remembrances.

"Tell me about it! Look, I want to make sure he gets looked after, a proper burial. Somewhere where you can sit and talk to him."

She laughed, a slight laugh. "That's not important anymore, love. I do appreciate the thought, I really do, but soon I'll be gone too and what happens with our earthly remains is not important." Carol raised her head and studied Daley earnestly. "Tell me, Scott, do you think there is a heaven?"

Daley, his arm leant up against the container, surreptitiously twisted his arm and peeked at his watch. The up train was due in about twenty minutes. The small talk had to end. "In my job, Carol, I see so much of hell on earth, I have to hope that there is something better. Look, I've got the car outside. Lets get out of this wind and we can talk more."

"There is nothing to talk about. The *Murder Game* is nearly complete. I can finish what Kitt started and we can close the Book forever. What, pet?" She looked down at Carmichael. He muttered something incomprehensible. "No, I'm afraid not. You'll have to just piss yourself there." Daley saw a dark patch spread between Carmichael's splayed legs, a final ignominy for the *Great Drew Carmichael.*

"I never wanted him to go to university. He was far too sensitive, far too easily led. He would just end up in trouble."

"And is that what happened in Coventry, that night when the police picked him up? Did they get him into trouble?"

"It was this bastard here." She turned and lashed out at Carmichael, a loud smack ricocheting across the empty space. "Him and his high and mighty ideas. My Kitt thought they were being friendly but that's Asperger's. He wouldn't know what friendly looked like. He never had any real friends, he just found it too difficult."

Behind her, Carmichael was looking around and pointing, incomprehensible, high as the proverbial. Daley raised his hand to scratch his forehead. Deb got the message and began to inch nearer. Far in the distance, behind the gates, blue lights were flashing. To his left he heard gravel crunching under carefully placed feet. Sneaking a look he saw Corby wincing with each footfall about thirty yards away. He gestured for him to stay.

"So what happened that night, Carol. What did they do to him?"

"The Book was finished. Did you see it? In the cellar? He

413

put so much work into that Book. Of course they all thought it was a lark, just one big joke at his expense, but Kitt never saw the funny side. He researched it, typed it all up, made their stupid ideas real and do you know what? They weren't interested in what he had done. Not one of them even cared. And Drew. Drew was the worst. You see with his condition, everything had to be just right. Everything had to follow a pattern, an order. He needed rules to live by, to shut out the chaos of the real world. He used to say *'Carol, if it's right, it's not wrong and if it's wrong, it's definitely not right.'* And the Book wasn't right. Yes, they had all made their contributions, but Drew just couldn't be bothered. His was the only entry that was needed to finish the Book. The Book was right, the table of contents was right. It listed Drew's entry, but the contents were missing.

"They made him drink the dirty pint you know. That last night when he took the Book to them. Drew forced him to drink the dirty pint, forced him to foul himself in front of everyone. That's when he had to leave the University." She scowled at Carmichael, sodden in his own urine. "We know what that's like now don't we, pet." She grabbed Carmichael's collar and forced his face down towards the spreading puddle. "How do you like it, now?" She released his head and Carmichael jolted from whatever daydream had taken him and shouted "Make up the pint, Marcus. Chris has broken the rules," and then he laughed at his own in-joke, throwing his head back hysterically, his torso bobbing and shaking as he guffawed into the air. "Make the fucking Pint, Marcus. Make the fucking pint." She threw another crashing hand at his face. Tears began to etch streaks down his dust-caked cheeks.

Daley sneaked another peek, ten more minutes and this whole conversation would be over for good. "So what happened that night? Why did he go out with Drew and the girls? Where was he going?"

"I don't know, Scott. Honestly I don't. Kitt said they just turned up at his room and invited him out. He said he showed Drew the Book, with the new pages for Drew, and Drew had finally given his approval. He was so proud of himself! They took him off campus up towards the old cinema. Then he said they had taken him into an alcove and he had a knife in his hand."

414

Carmichael's eyes narrowed to slits. "You want to be part of the Monday Club, retard, go ahead. The Murder Game requires a victim. Get on with it, Chris, do him. You really think Rachel's going to blow you if you can't even do this for her?" And he stopped and looked directly at Daley, his tone now contrite. "It was an accident. I leaned on him and the knife went into the tramp. I never meant for him to really do it."

"So is that what all this is about? Surely you know that with his condition, he would never be charged with murder, probably never even serve time. Why did all of these others have to die?"

Carol swung her arm and pointed directly at Carmichael. "They had to die because of *him!*"

She fell to her knees and began sobbing quietly. Deb shifted her weight, poised. Now behind him out of sight, Mike Corby whispered, "Just say the word boss." Through the corner of his mouth, Daley rasped "Just stay here and get her if she makes a run for it...and don't twist the other ankle."

Carol once more raised her head. The tears had stopped, her face blank, devoid of emotion as she went on.

"It was just another accident. Kitt had moved down to London and was in the Westfield when he saw Rachel Jones again for the first time. She was with Drew. He must have just snapped. In a fit of rage he smashed up half the centre. They sectioned him and, you know how those places mess with your head. All he could think about was that night. Rachel and Dawn and Shelley, laughing at him as that tramp died and all the time bottling up the shame. It was inevitable that one day it would explode. When he came out he tracked down Rachel Jones and he killed her just like in the Book. *Live by the sword, die by the sword.* But rather than help him, it just made him worse. Then one day, he just took all his pills and fell asleep."

"And Dawn and Shelley and Guy? What about them? Did you kill them?" Forty yards away, Deb was tapping her watch, one hand splayed out in the air. *Five minutes!*

"Of course, I didn't have the *bottle* at first. It took me a long time to summon up the courage, but it's amazing what you can do if you put your mind to it. All I had to do was to follow the Book. One by one, I looked into their eyes as they died and I let them know - *this one's for Kitt.*"

415

To his right Daley heard a bizarre flexing, crackling noise, and the echoes of the train down the track. He nodded abruptly and saw Deb start across the last few yards and he ran himself colliding with Carol and dragging her to the ground.

"She's used fucking cable ties, Sir." Carmichael was sobbing quietly as he looked down the track towards the distant rumble. Daley gasped as, for the first time, he could clearly see the number '6' on his forehead.

"Get rid of her, quick!" Daley yanked out his key ring, all fingers and thumbs as he dithered over the penknife. Then he pounced on Carmichael.

Dragging his leg, Corby hobbled over to the level crossing. Deb had leapt onto Carol who was moaning and growling; pinned to the road under Deb's full weight and together they dragged her kicking from the tracks. Overhead, the amber lights began to flash and the sirens wailed.

"Leave him, Sir. It's too late!" but as she spoke, Carol Hughes let loose a stunning fist and Deb tumbled to the floor, clutching her face as stars burst in her eyes. And then Carol had torn herself free from Corby and was launching herself at Daley.

"He has to pay for what he has done. He must see the train!" She grabbed Daley's shoulder and leant all her weight against him, dragging him away from Carmichael.

Fruitlessly sawing at the cable ties with the puny blunt penknife, they defied his every effort. After an age he had broken through the first one and turned to the second. Carol Hughes flung her arms around his neck and gouged at his throat with her nails and pulled at his head but still he sawed at the unyielding plastic. Below him the ground began to vibrate and the thunder grew. Carmichael's eyes were wide as pennies as reflected in their pupils, Daley could almost see the mammoth beast drawing nearer. He cast a desperate glance over his shoulder, as the huge square of black loomed large.

"Scott. Get out of there!" Deb spat blood from her mouth. Then the thunder struck once more and she fell to the floor shielding here eyes.

EPILOGUE

Detective Sergeant Deborah Whetstone stood beside the open grave as the thin group of mourners melted away. She ran her fingers over the chalked lettering on the temporary marker. *Died 2012.* Another wasted life. As the priest had read the committal service, it seemed that no-one around the grave had managed a dry eye and she was no exception. Her black gloves were drenched in tears and the salt stung her cheeks. Fittingly, a fine drizzle began to fall and clouds bustled in on the wind.

"Sergeant Whetstone, isn't it?" Deb swung round surprised that anyone here would know her. Following the death at the railway yard, Allenby had suggested she take a few days off and she had decided to travel to Nottingham for Dawn's funeral. She was greeted by the pained yet warm smiles of Mr and Mrs Silverton and she took the hand that was extended. She nodded, imbuing the simple gesture with as much compassion as she could muster, and that still wasn't enough.

"You were there at the formal identification. When we came down to London."

Again Deb nodded weakly, embarrassed for intruding, recalling the discomfort of escorting the Silverton's along the austere corridors to the glass panel beyond which Dawn lay stitched together and swaddled to her chin in a purple shroud.

"We wondered if you would like to come back to the house. For a bite to eat before you head back."

"Oh, no. I am sorry. I have to get a train soon....but thanks for the offer." She was ashamed at the white lie, but past experience had told her that sympathy only had a short shelf life. She watched as they smiled and turned towards a large black Daimler that burbled respectfully on the tarmac nearby. Their hands were linked with a unity that time had annealed. Not even the tragic death of their only daughter or the evil of Carol Hughes could break that bond.

And the tears welled in her eyes once more. Whether it was the sombreness of the occasion, or the immense feeling of loss that she had sensed from the Silvertons, she couldn't be sure. Maybe it was the gaping chasm where Scott Daley should have

417

been, or just the horrors she had witnessed were all over. She let the tears flow unabated as she turned towards the gates.

PC Parrish, 'Keith the Uniform', paradoxically in *civvies,* smiled as she met him at the car. He extended a hand to her and she took it, drawing herself close to his side. Together they travelled down the motorway towards Coventry. There were a few places she needed to see for herself.

Browns bar was as they had all described it, a wood and stone growth on the remnants of ancient walls, now called *Drapers*, however *FiftyFour*, the old Students Union had been razed to the ground and a small park now occupied the land, peaceful yet resounding to a million raucous student nights out. An all-new glass and steel building replaced it, several hundred yards away in the midst of the campus.

Carmichael had recounted the route he had taken on that April night so, hand in hand with Keith, she strolled up Bayley Lane, looking up at the austere shell of the old cathedral, standing defiant against the evils of the world. They crossed University Square. It was early autumn and devoid of life, aside from a few commuters wending their way home in the late afternoon. The students were still away on summer vacation but she could imagine the space thronging as early evening fell and academia gave way to fun. They passed under the imposing dullness of Priory Hall, across the road and over a car park towards Cox Street. The corner where the Theatre One had stood was boarded up and empty. Shortly after the events of 1997, though in no way connected, the Theatre One became a nightclub but, after a few run-ins with authority, even that had closed. Now the hoardings outside the site promised high rent accommodation. Even the Elastic Inn opposite was now forlorn and empty.

"It should be just up here." Keith pointed along Cox Street. After a hundred yards or so, the hoardings turned a sharp left towards the back of the bus garage, forming a deep brick-lined alcove around three metres deep, bedecked with all manner of graffiti. A spiteful breeze whipped up the fallen leaves sending eddies scurrying around the place and a chill down Deb's spine as she stepped into the void. A silence descended as, cut off from the road, shielded by a sentinel tree standing guard, she replayed Carmichael's account of that night. She imagined Sean

Watkins slumped in the corner and Chris Betts pleading for it to stop. She imagined three girls sobbing in terror, and one arrogant, self-assured man brought down to size and wracked with indecision. In this deep alcove, everything had changed, not just for an elderly tramp, but for six students, whose lives were irrevocably transformed.

***

It would take nearly a year for the insurance to pay out, for the rebuilding work to be completed and for the Plough & Harrow to re-open. The police investigation was ongoing and the insurers were waiting on that. Finn Byrne knew he would be unable to re-enter the building and after three months he had lost interest. A consortium of Chinese businessmen had offered a fair price, costs were covered and soon *Greta's Bar and Restaurant* would herald a new chapter in the establishment's chequered and sometimes precarious history.

Often, as he languished in the hotel room provided by the insurers, and the pain in his hands defied any amount of painkillers, he would recall the day the regular beep down the corridor had turned twice to a solid plaintive whine. For him, that was the day everything changed. He wondered whether she knew that he was willing her to live, sending urgent telepathic signals along the caravan trail of conduits on the ceiling and through into her room. Or whether that tiny seed he had unknowingly planted inside her was struggling to survive despite overwhelming odds. But survive it had. When she had finally been released from intensive care, Finn had learned that Shelley's heart had stopped twice and, but for the dedication of the team battling to keep her alive, she would have succumbed.

They had decided that London was toxic. They would start a new life. She and the bump would soon be out of hospital but the damage to Shelley's lungs would take years to heal. Still, she had acquired a new found determination which pulled her through and, apart from an insistent cough, which the doctors assured him would fade with time, she was back to her old exuberant and often irrepressible self, her demons long since banished.

He scanned the internet pages and nodded to himself. The pub was in a small village outside Northampton where the beer was a lot less gassy and the clientele less exciting. He could run it on his own and Shelley would thrive in the clean air. Hitting the print button, he watched the pages land in the out tray. Perhaps on the weekend, when she was released from hospital, they could take a road trip. Gathering up the papers and slipping on his coat, he smiled and headed out for Ealing General. The world was still turning and the future at last was looking bright.

***

The red kite hovered at around one hundred feet from the tough scrubland grass. There was a stiff wind strafing the barren countryside from the east, sending fibrillations through the hemp-like grass, bringing with it a bitter chill. Despite the wind, it appeared suspended from an invisible thread, surfing on the currents, it's tail twitching periodically to hold it's geostationary position, laser eyes fixed on a single point on the field below. Brad Martin and his partner Rebecca, held each other against the chill as they stood in the rear garden of the Gwyn Bedr hotel, twenty miles inland from Barmouth. Below them, the insistent racket of the thunderous waterfall faded into the background as they watched the bird still against the sky. Beyond the gorge and into the fields, Brad strained his eyes but he could not see what the kite was tracking. Invisible in the grass, maybe it had escaped the watch of its pursuer, as they had theirs.

When Alice had finally puffed and panted her way up the steps to the upper level of the Westfield, Marcus was fit to explode from the crescendo of anxiety that had consumed him. And no wonder she was late! In common with the majority of the fairer sex, she had managed to overpack her meagre belongings and the two holdalls dragged along the pavement at her side. They had embraced for what seemed like a lifetime before choosing a direction and heading off in it.

Three months, twenty thousand pounds and umpteen favours called in, Brad and Rebecca Martin hoped that their watchers would now find the trails cold and give up. Both had changed their hair colour, even though Marcus missed Alice's fiery red, he was going to make sure that blondes had more fun. Following the fire in the Plough & Harrow they had both abandoned their nicotine habit for good and Brad had joined a gym in Aberystwyth, losing four stones, an almost impossible feat that changed his appearance completely.

"Marcu...er Brad." Rebecca squeezed his arm and smiled.

"Yes, Becs?" He loved the way she winced at the diminutive.

She held up a copy of the Daily Mail from the previous day and pointed to a small article above an ad for hair gel. "This is really strange. I am sure that's a picture of my old house before I moved to Waterloo Street."

"I dunno. I only ever went to Waterloo Street. Why, what's it about?"

"Really odd. Seems like the person that moved in after me was murdered in the bath. Police found her the day we left."

"You know that *Murder Game* thing. How did your murder go again?

Alice closed her eyes and thanked every known god and a sizeable proportion of the universe that Marcus had entered her life again when he did, that fortune had smiled on them both and they were rid of the Monday Club, Andrew Carmichael and all of the worthlessness of their previous existences.

About two weeks after they had hunkered down in a desolate part of the Pembroke coast, Marcus had finally summoned the courage to spill the beans about the money and in an Internet cafe near the docks she had discovered that, not only need they never work again, but Carmichael's precious fund had grown unfettered and unchallenged to over two and a quarter million pounds despite the expenses they had endured in their disappearance. Not only that but the automatic scheme that Guy and Drew had established was still working its minor overnight miracles, at least for now. Sooner or later, someone was going to find out, though, so Marcus and Alice cut their losses and moved the money into a separate account at Butterfields where it would be safe and, more importantly, theirs.

Above them the kite hung, it's head bobbing left and right; it's prey away in the undergrowth. Then it conceded defeat and headed off in search of a new target, as they both hoped the Met had also done. After a month in South Wales, they had moved across to Aberystwyth where they changed the car, rented a house and resolved to make their plans for the future.

"So, then *Brad*. What shall we do today?"

Brad smiled down to Rebecca. "Well, really, we can do

anything we flipping well like, but first I thought we would get out of this cold air, have some breakfast and then take a walk into town. If we are supposed to be married, I need to make an honest woman of you. Will you marry me, Becs?"

"Thought you'd never ask Brad. Just don't call me *Becs* ever again."

And once more they both cast themselves off on the wind and trusted to serendipity.

***

Detective Superintendent Bob Allenby strode purposefully up the corridor following the line of blue tape, as the pretty receptionist had again instructed him to. Why did they make these places so damn big? Like a rabbit warren! He had spent the morning speaking to the remand board regarding Andrew Carmichael. As a result of Scott Daley's heroic efforts that day, Carmichael had been thrown clear of the scything wheels of the locomotive and, apart from a few cuts and bruises and a severe case of the DTs from all of the drugs he had been given, had come out of it unscathed. Except for his reputation. The Financial Conduct Authority misconduct hearing was still a considerable way off but there was every likelihood he would be struck off and Barraclough & Leavis would receive a severe reprimand and substantial fine. The word on the street was that Gerald Thornton had thrown in the towel and was liquidating the business.

In the final analysis, the CPS had been satisfied that Carol Hughes had acted alone to extinguish the Monday Club for their part in the murder of the vagrant, Watkins in that lonely alcove on Cox Street. Once Shelley Nugent had recovered she was able to tell them the whole story of that damp night, of them baiting Christopher Betts and of the scuffle that led to the fatal wound. However, Michael Sean Watkins had been forgotten and there was insufficient evidence to proceed against Carmichael, so Allenby had put that down to experience.

Patrick Gascoigne, however, had constructed a compelling array of evidence to put Rachel's Jones' murder at Christopher Betts door, although it could not be proved definitely. The samples in the overalls, rust from the sword found on her body, were enough for the case to be finally closed.

In a strange twist, the body that they had assumed was Alice Bown turned out to be one Eleanor Hewson, who had just moved into the wrong flat at the wrong time. A dirty shoe print dried onto the bathroom floor was later matched to shoes at Wescott Road, and skin cells on a chemise cast aside in the bedroom attested to the presence of Carol Hughes. So Eleanor's unfortunate death had also been chalked up to her. As for Chris Betts, Patrick Gascoigne had examined his mummified remains and resolved that he had died from a massive opiate overdose. An open verdict had been returned. Carol Hughes was laid to rest alongside her brother in St Nicholas cemetery in their home town of Newcastle.

In Daley's absence, Allenby and the rest of the team had formally told Edgar Sampson to fuck off and then thrown everything they could, and a few they really couldn't, at Andrew Carmichael. They had torn Barraclough and Leavis apart and DC Taylor had traced the account postings in audit logs back to a closed account in the Caymans, where the trail had gone cold. IP Address logs led to a computer in Carmichael's house, which had vanished. In the end the best they could pin on him was railway trespass but, as he was high on LSD at the time, not even that raised eyebrows from the CPS. So Carmichael was duly released, jobless, penniless and friendless, except for a dwindling group of paparazzi that had not yet taken the hint. Allenby was sure that, like a bad penny, he would turn up sometime, probably smelling once more of roses and a faint odour of cad.

As had happened many times over the past three months, Allenby spotted Finn Byrne coming the opposite way and exchanged pleasantries, handing over a bunch of supermarket flowers he would otherwise have delivered himself. Mr Byrne had shown him the printout and Bob Allenby had voiced his enviousness and wished him well.

Finally, he came across the door he sought and peered through the wired glass window. Inside was sombre and dark, the haze of a single lamp in the frosted glass. Gently, he eased down the handle and the door popped open enough for him to crane his head around. The machine was gone and the patient lay still in the bed. Allenby made his way to the uncomfortable PVC covered chair and sat down, resting his head on the points of his fingers as he had done after work twice a week for the past three months.

"So we finally had to let him go today. Not a single scrap of real evidence, you see. His sort always comes out on top." Allenby glanced across at the prostrate form, the bedclothes gently rising and falling. "It was Dawn's Silverton's funeral today. Sergeant Whetstone and PC Parrish paid your respect in your absence. She's a good girl that one. You need to look after her. Oh, and I heard from Rachel Jones family today. Of course we had already told them about Carol Hughes and Christopher Betts but they needed to hear it from the horses mouth, so to speak."

"You do know that I am awake, Sir. Have been for a week now."

"Of course I do, Scott. I just enjoy being able to speak to you without you answering back." Allenby smirked. "Got make the most of it while I can. If a flaming great diesel locomotive can't knock any sense into that skull of yours, what chance do I have?"

"Precious little, Sir. Precious little."

As the freight train had borne down on him, Daley had been down to the last cable tie securing Carmichael to the tracks. The financial advisor, high as a kite on LSD, had done everything he could to escape the monster which was turning the sky before him dark and had leapt clear of the track. Just a trailing arm remained affixed, ragged and bloodied by the biting plastic. Standing on the sleepers, Daley had frantically pulled at Carmichael's forearm as he pressed the feeble knife against the stretching tie. Breaking free of Whetstone and Corby, Carol Hughes had leapt across at Daley in an attempt to prevent him saving Carmichael from his pre-ordained fate. Suddenly, the tie had yielded. Daley pushed Carmichael clear as the sonorous horn on the locomotive sounded. Carol had been grasping at Daley's legs as the two men fell from the lines, the buffer beam striking Daley a glancing blow that fractured his shoulder and skull. For Carol, the end was quick and poetically gruesome.

Allenby leaned forwards in the chair. "You do know you're up for a gong, don't you? QPM no less."

'Makes a change to be noticed. I wonder who put me forward for that?"

"Oh, I don't know. Some senior officer without the sense to tell his argumentative Inspector he was bloody fool risking his life like that."

Just then, the door latch clicked. Lynne Daley poked her head into the room and smiled awkwardly. "Good Evening Mr Allenby. Did you know Scott's coming out tomorrow? He's going to spend some time with me until he gets back on his feet."

Allenby, suddenly feeling like a spare part, rose from the chair and placed a hand on Daley's arm. "I don't want to see you in Lambourne Road until the quack says so. Is that clear? And give Deborah Whetstone a call. She needs to hear you voice. Oh, and don't play on the railway!"

That night, as Daley slept, the eyes of Rachel Jones came to him again in his dreams but this time they were smiling and filled with peace.

ABOUT THE AUTHOR

Austen Gower has a long and arguably distinguished career in Business Analysis and Consultancy. Throughout that time, he has been commissioned to write technical works on topics as diverse as network communications, project management methodology and anger management, for which he has a number of published articles.

After a hankering to write a novel, which stretches back around twenty years, finally Austen has taken creative writing seriously, with a view to quitting the rat race and using some of the left side of his brain so repressed by his day job.

Writing as Ryan Stark, *Killing by the Book* is Austen's first work of fiction.

Married, with a wife and two grown-up children, Austen lives in Redditch, Worcestershire and has never attended Coventry University, except to see his daughter graduate.

Made in the USA
San Bernardino, CA
26 April 2019